Revenge

SHARON OSBOURNE

Revenge

sphere

SPHERE

First published in Great Britain in 2010 by Sphere

Cover design: LBBG – Jennifer Richards; Cover illustration © Kate Forrester;
Hand lettering © Ruth Rowland

A CIP catalogue record for this book
is available from the British Library.

Hardback ISBN 978-1-84744-283-3
C format ISBN 978-1-84744-284-0

Typeset in Bembo by M Rules
Printed and bound in Great Britain by
Clays Ltd, St Ives plc

Papers used by Sphere are natural, renewable and
recyclable products sourced from well-managed forests and certified
in accordance with the rules of the Forest Stewardship Council.

Mixed Sources
Product group from well-managed
forests and other controlled sources
www.fsc.org Cert no. SGS-COC-004081
© 1996 Forest Stewardship Council
FSC

Sphere
An imprint of
Little, Brown Book Group
100 Victoria Embankment
London EC4Y 0DY

An Hachette UK Company
www.hachette.co.uk

www.littlebrown.co.uk

Revenge

Prologue

Just before Amber slapped her sister, she closed her eyes, knowing she was going to enjoy it far more than she should.

'So, come on, Amber,' Chelsea said, walking towards her. 'Say what you've got to say to me, and let's get it over with.'

They faced each other, the Stone sisters, two of the most famous women on the planet, adored for their talent and their beauty, and yet so different.

Chelsea: stunning, voluptuous, with her thick, wavy black hair, creamy skin and those eyes, an extraordinary dark blue, framed with thick black lashes. She was a classic beauty, like an old-school Hollywood film star, possibly the most talented actress of her day. But that talent hadn't come without its problems . . . At the age of twenty-nine, Chelsea had seen more things in her young life than most people experience in a lifetime.

And her little sister Amber, commonly known as America's Sweetheart even though she was from Weybridge, Surrey. A pretty heart-shaped face, green eyes like her mother's and amber-coloured hair – it was one of the many pieces of luck she'd had in her life, that her name matched her hair colour. Amber had been the biggest pop star of her day. Now she was one of the most popular movie stars on the planet. With three platinum albums under her belt, a string of massive hit films followed: boys loved her, girls wanted to be her. She had a voice like velvet. Soft, innocent, pure, vulnerable, yet with an underlying, breathy sexuality.

But, as the saying goes, you have to be careful what you wish for.

All their lives, the Stone sisters had pursued their dream. And it turned out there was room for only one of them at the top . . .

'Do you even know who you *are*, Amber?' Chelsea said, curiously. 'I mean, do you have any fucking *idea*? You're not even a real person. You're' – she waved her fingers dismissively at her little sister – 'you're manufactured. Fake. You smile and nod in interviews, and it's like you've got a "For Sale" sign up next to you, you're so vacant.'

'You don't know me,' Amber said. Tears were welling up in her eyes. 'Get out of my life.'

'I don't *know* you?' Chelsea was mimicking her. 'What's your favourite film? Your favourite food? Song? Colour? You don't have any fucking idea who you are! The sweeter than sweet bullshit front that you put on. You might fool everyone else, but not me. Ever since we were kids Mum's told you what to do and say, and you've got no backbone, with your cutesy fake personality that Mum's created for you!'

'That's not true.' Amber gritted her teeth. No one knew the real her, least of all Chelsea.

'It's true, Amber. You're just Mum's puppet. She designs your clothes, hair, make-up, tells you who to go out with – she even picks your films for you. What does Amber want? Who the hell are you?'

By this time Amber was erupting. She couldn't take it any more. She slapped her sister so hard that Chelsea's neck clicked as her head flew to one side.

'Now you know who I am,' she said, smiling slowly and opening her eyes. *God, it felt good to wipe the satisfied, sarcastic smirk off that bitch's face.*

Chelsea clutched her reddening cheek. 'Fuck you!'

'No,' Amber said. 'Fuck you, you jealous bitch. You're trying to destroy my life.'

It was just the two of them, in the vast marbled hall of the Beverly Hills mansion. Outside, the sun was just beginning to set. The sky was streaked crimson and the palm trees were swaying in the warm Santa Ana winds.

'I'm not trying to destroy you,' Chelsea said softly. 'We're sisters. You know I'd never do that. I love you, Amber.'

For a fleeting second, Amber remembered the old days. Hard to believe that they were once as close as sisters could be. She remembered them as little girls back in the perfect house in Weybridge, how they'd wait till their mum and dad had gone to bed and take it in turns to creep into each other's rooms so they could spend the night together, talking and giggling, singing songs softly, dreaming of what it'd be like when they were grown-up, famous film stars living in Hollywood.

Well, it had happened. Here they were, both of them. But what had happened in between? When everything should have been right, how had it come to this? Was there no way back for the Stone sisters?

Amber drew a deep breath and looked at her sister, thought about all the terrible and wonderful things they'd been through together and where they were today.

'Screw you,' Amber said, and walked towards the driveway.

PART ONE

Killer Queen

Chapter One

London, 1976

She'd made it. She was finally here.

'I'm going to be a star,' Margaret Michaels whispered to herself, staring up at the lights of Piccadilly Circus. 'I am. And nothing's going to stop me.'

As she shivered in the chilly September evening, she heard the flatness of her northern vowels creeping through, and winced. Though she was only sixteen, Margaret had been having elocution lessons for over a year, hoping to sound like her idol, Julie Christie. And here she was, in London, by herself, ready to make that dream come true.

Because ever since she was born, that was all she'd wanted to be. A star.

When she was twelve, Margaret had informed her mam and dad that she would only answer to Maggie from now on. When she was thirteen, she'd started saving her pocket money. When she was fourteen, she'd got herself a job at Toni's, the upmarket hairdresser's near her parents' small, terraced house on a drab backstreet in Sheffield. The salon was a ten-minute walk away, but it was like entering another world. A magical world, far away from rusting steelworks, tired women and men, strikes and depression. It was a glittering world of skinny, edgy girls who looked like Glenda

Jackson, delicious smells, hairspray and perfume and the promise of glamour, of escape.

Maggie swept the floor, made tea and coffee, shampooed the ladies' hair, watched as dowdy, shy housewives came in with flat greasy hair and left, faces shining, eyes aglow, smelling of Elnett and looking a little bit more like the person they dreamed of being. And Maggie watched, listened and learned, entranced. She would have done it for nothing, for the chance simply to be in this exotic world. But the pound a week wage was very welcome. And that was how she afforded the elocution lessons, the fancy handbag she'd bought from Castle House, the posh department store in town, the eyeshadow and the perfume.

'You're getting ideas above yourself, my girl,' Ron Michaels had told her any number of times. 'You ashamed of your father, Margaret? Is that it? Sheffield not good enough for you any more?'

''Course not, Dad,' Maggie had answered dutifully. But she was lying. It *wasn't* good enough for her. She was something special. She didn't know why, she just knew she had to make the most of it. Her dad was a steelworker, her mam was – well, there was summat wrong with her mam and no one knew what it was. She stayed in bed most days, terrified of her husband, afraid of her own reflection and increasingly afraid of her headstrong, beautiful only child, who seemed, to Maureen Michaels anyway, to be from another planet. Like someone had left her on the doorstep and she had blossomed over the years into this exotic creature living in their house, a beautiful, ethereal thing with long legs, a mane of strawberry blonde hair, flawless skin and huge green eyes that would alternately flash fire or glitter with pleasure.

No, Sheffield was not big enough for Maggie, and by the time she reached puberty, she knew she didn't belong there; she was going to London to fulfil her dreams. The girls at school hated her: they thought she came across like she was too good for them, with her posh voice and her hoity-toity airs and graces. And they didn't interest her: acne-ridden, greasy-haired girls who would hang around at the back of the toilets, smoking and listening to their cassette players, content to moon over saps like the Bay City Rollers, or Showaddywaddy – pathetic!

She liked the grown-up stuff. Old stuff, too. The Stones – Dusty – Jimi – she loved the clever catchiness of Queen, the coolness of Bad Company, the dirtiness and the raw energy of Led Zep. *That* was music. Music that pulsated through you. Listening to 'Can't Get Enough', 'Jumpin' Jack Flash', or 'Killer Queen' – how could you not feel like a woman, a grown-up? Who the hell wanted to listen to a group of drips singing 'Bye Bye Baby'?

They were boys. Maggie wanted a man.

As for the local boys, she ignored them too. They could drool all they wanted at her, at her smooth skin, budding, pert little breasts, and her full ruby-red lips that she would unconsciously lick, coupled with those coltish limbs and that provocative stare. But she felt nothing but contempt for them: their spots, their awkward gestures, throbbing Adam's apples and pathetic stares, like rabbits caught in headlights.

Was Maggie lonely, growing up in the terraced brick house in the backstreets of Sheffield, walking home on her own from school, ignoring the gaggles of girls skipping on ahead of her, the loitering boys who kicked empty cans around the streets, gazing at her distractedly when she glided past, tossing her hair? No, she wasn't. Maggie moved to her own soundtrack. In her head when she was going home through the park she was really Julie Christie, on her way to meet Terence Stamp; Faye Dunaway, about to drive off with Warren Beatty; Anita Pallenberg, a cigarette hanging off her lip. It was the soundtrack in her head, the soundtrack to the life she knew she was going to have . . .

By September 1976, two months after she'd turned sixteen, Maggie knew there was nothing left for her in Sheffield. She told the girls at Toni's she was moving to London. 'To become famous', she told them, and they were so impressed, so intrigued by quiet little Maggie Michaels, that on her last day at the salon Janine, the head stylist, gave her a free set of highlights. 'It's a going-away present, love,' she said, as she deftly pulled the rubber cap on to

Maggie's hair and proceeded to hook strands of hair through the colander-like holes in the cap. 'Summat to help you on your way.' Maggie had smiled at her in the mirror, anxiously. 'Not that you'll need it,' Janine said. 'Promise.'

They had waved her off as she left that evening, her strawberry blonde hair flecked with golden caramel streaks, silky and heavy, rushing in the evening wind. They had pressed a bottle of Quiktan into her hands. 'It smells disgusting,' Danielle, the owner of the salon, had told her. 'And it streaks if you don't put it on proper. But it'll be worth it. Give you a California tan. Set you apart from the others, little Maggie. Good luck, love. Let us know how you go on. Remember us when you're a big star!'

Maggie remembered them fondly now as she hugged herself, staring up at the lights of the big city. She was tired, and a bit hungry, but she wasn't looking forward to going back to the hostel she'd booked herself into, round the corner from Victoria coach station. Funny – it sounded so glamorous round there, just off Buckingham Palace Road, but it wasn't. It was dirty, there were rings in the sink, damp on the walls and she was sure it had mice. Maggie liked things tidy. For a brief second she wished she was at home, in the warm, comforting familiarity of the kitchen, with her dad reading the paper in his vest, covered in grime, and her mam making the tea. She got up to make tea in the evening, that was all she ever did, it seemed to Maggie. What would they say when they found her note, and realised she wasn't coming back?

Dear Mam and Dad

I've gone to London. You know I don't fit in here. I never have. I want more from my life. I want to be famous. Don't worry about me. I'll be fine. I'll call soon.

Your loving daughter,

Maggie

Would they be devastated, upset, angry? She shrank at the thought of her dad's anger, at the magnitude of what she'd done . . . But no. She had come here for a reason, and she knew she could never go back to Sheffield, not now.

It was almost dark in Piccadilly Circus. The lights seemed brighter than ever. Maggie wrapped her thin fawn-coloured coat around her body and headed for the tube station, wondering if she would get lost on the trains back to Victoria like she had on the way there. She cast one last look up as she navigated the narrow steps down to the station. Through the railings of the balustrade, her eyes darted from one neon sign to the other, the bright red of the huge Coca-Cola sign to the glowing yellow of the SKOL lager banner and then to the Max Factor make-up logo. The lights of Piccadilly were hypnotising, the atmosphere intoxicating. She knew she was here to stay. Nothing was going to stop her.

Chapter Two

'Camilla?'

Nothing. Maggie sighed, and put her hands on her hips.

'Camilla? Are you there?'

She hadn't heard her come in last night, so perhaps she wasn't there, but Maggie had been caught out like this before. Two girls in a tiny, dirty, one-bedroom flat was bad enough, but when the girl who slept in the sitting room lay in till lunchtime, naked, you needed to check. She was bewildered by upper-class people, Maggie realised.

She knocked cautiously and then looked at her watch. She was going to be late for the audition. She opened the door.

It was worse than she'd expected.

'Camilla!' Maggie yelled. 'What have you –'

She had been so tired the night before that she'd crawled into bed, and had not heard Camilla come in, nor the long-haired, bearded man who slept beside her in the pull-out bed, also naked. Two condoms lay on the ethnic-print bedspread, one wrinkled up, the other fully extended, and she could see the creamy grey cum still at the top of it.

Two months ago, Maggie had never seen another person naked, much less a condom, but living with Camilla had soon changed that. She wouldn't have dreamed of going to sleep with the dishes still to do, either, or drinking the amount Camilla drank, but down here she was terrified of being thought of as square, and so she bit her lip more than she would have thought possible.

Camilla Sherbourne was fond of saying to Maggie that they were the same – two girls who'd run away from home to the bright lights of London.

'We're here to experience *life*, my darling,' Camilla would say, licking her tiny rosebud mouth and squeezing Maggie round the shoulders.

But the reality was very different, something Maggie couldn't ever get her to see. Camilla was the daughter of a wealthy businessman from Hertfordshire. Her parents thought she was living in Chelsea, doing a secretarial course she had signed up for herself. They sent her money every week, proud of her for having taken the initiative to pay the rent on the pretty Onslow Square flat they thought she was living in and to cover the cost of Camilla eating out with friends, going to a couple of concerts . . . If only they knew. Camilla had never even been to the flat. She was spending the money on pot, LPs and on going out to gigs, and God knows what else. And she was paying half the rent to live on Hopkin Road, the grottiest part of Shepherd's Bush, a narrow sidestreet full of tall, spindly houses that never seemed to get any light. It was bedsit-land, crammed with sad lives and young hopefuls. Maggie was there because she couldn't afford anywhere else.

An enterprising landlord had divided one of the larger bedsits into two, so that Maggie slept in a tiny place like a corridor that you could barely fit a single bed in, with just enough room for a chest of drawers and a pole above it where she could hang the few clothes she owned. A tiny slit of a window looked onto a brick wall that never got any light. Camilla slept in the 'sitting room', which was larger and had a window, and a little counter dividing it from the kitchen. And that was it. At first – maybe for one whole night – Maggie had found it exotic. She soon came to hate it.

'Sorry, babe.' Camilla looked up at her, her lank blonde hair hanging around her face, her huge eyes with pupils dilated, like she

9

was still high, or drunk, or both. 'This is . . .' She paused for a moment, then giggled. She raised her arms above her head languorously, displaying tufts of wispy underarm hair that she took pride in never shaving. 'Shit, Keith. Maggie babe, say hi to Keith.'

'Hey,' said the bearded man, twisting his head and looking intently up at Maggie. 'Hey Maggie, it's good to meet you.'

Maggie stepped smartly over an empty wine bottle, its base covered in raffia. 'Hi. I'm going to be late. I can't stop.' She cast a look of disdain at the sitting room.

'I'm gonna clear up, babe. Promise. Sorry, it's a real tip.' Camilla ran her hands through her hair. 'See you later?'

She reached over to a full ashtray and relit a cigarette butt, then sat up and stretched, apparently unconcerned about her nudity, her large pendulous breasts wobbling slightly as she moved her neck from side to side. Keith watched her appreciatively.

Maggie said nothing. One day she would have her own place, and it would be immaculate, she told herself, as she did almost every day. It would be clean, perfect, a palace, the opposite of Hopkin Road. She climbed past the two of them, over the moth-eaten mattress, the armchairs covered with rancid orange and brown textured fabric, past the old, peeling, damp kitchen, where the washing-up from the dinner party Camilla had had four days ago still lay in the sink, and shut the door behind her, blinking hard. She could never bring anyone back there. Not that she had many friends in London anyway, but she'd be too ashamed to let other people see how she lived.

Camilla seemed to think it was fun to live in a hovel, never shaving her armpits, never doing the dishes, lounging around all day smoking and allegedly 'experiencing life'. But Maggie had to go out and find work and, two months into her London life, she was starting to wonder if it would ever happen.

The truth was, London was nothing like she'd expected it to be. She had been for every bloody audition going, and she laughed now to think how naive she'd been when she'd first arrived. It was either that she wasn't posh enough, she thought, or that she was too prudish. (If she'd been Camilla, she'd thought bitterly more than once, she'd have been fine.)

Endless auditions. Auditions at the Royal Court or in tiny pub theatres, where they said they were casting for plays about 'real life', but where everyone spoke about university, Shakespeare and politics. Maggie knew she could act, she knew there was nothing to it. And she could sing. She loved to sing – in fact, she had to stop herself singing, as she walked along the streets with that soundtrack in her head. But the feedback was always the same. 'Nice-looking girl, but she just doesn't have "it"', she'd heard a casting director say dismissively to the director, as Maggie crept out through the silent stalls.

She wondered, if she had known then what she knew now, would she still have come down here? She would think with horror of her first week in London, when she'd gone for an audition for a new run of *Hair*, and had stood there rooted to the spot in the crowded rehearsal room when she realised she'd have to take off her clothes. She was becoming wearily used to that, now. At least *Hair* was honest: mostly it was just seedy, the stuff she was asked to do. There were the auditions for 'musicals' that turned out to be nothing more than strip shows, where the director casually said, 'Oh, just – just pull down your top a little bit, dearie.' Or the audition for the commercial advertising corn plasters: 'Just lick your lips, love, like that. Open your mouth, like you're . . . Pout a little bit for me. Great.'

She'd had some work. If you could call it that. More like bit parts – displaying the new Rover car at a motor show, smiling politely while some fat, sweaty businessman casually draped his hand over her bottom. Greeting the guests – the male guests – at a dinner function for the pharmaceuticals industry at the Grosvenor House Hotel, one of a row of girls in red silk dresses, smiling and showing them to their table. That was the best of it.

Her dreams were being cut down to size day by day. Two months ago, she'd have assumed she would walk straight into a leading role in a film opposite Robert Redford – she just needed to be discovered. She could laugh at that now. She was going for a bit part today, in *The Sweeney* – a seventeen-year-old runaway from the North who'd ended up on the London streets. If she couldn't nail this, what hope did she have?

Walking along the cracked pavements towards the tube in the thin November sunshine, Maggie drew herself up. She was heading into Soho for the audition, a place she loved, she didn't know why, for all its chaos and seediness. Perhaps this was the day, the day when things would turn around for her. Yes, it was. She breathed in, ignoring the faint stench of dog shit and petrol fumes. She saw only sunlight, looked down at her faintly streaky but – she hoped – fairly evenly tanned hands. She had spent all the previous night applying her Quiktan, so that her sheets were now patchily stained a peculiar biscuit colour, and she would have to wash them again tonight.

It would all be worth it, she was sure. It had to be: she was down to her last twenty pounds. Maggie shook her hair, summoning up the Maggie she knew she was inside and carried on towards the tube, her long hair blowing in the wind, head held high.

'You're a pretty kid, that's not it.' Davey Carlton, the producer, stared at her as if she were a piece of meat, saliva slapping around his mouth as he chewed a piece of gum.

'So what is it?' said Maggie, trying to keep the desperation out of her voice. She slid her hands, in an effort to be casual, into the pockets of the denim hotpants they'd asked her to wear, and shifted her weight from one long leg in a platform mule to the other, as she stood on the tiny stage of the small theatre where the auditions were being held. In the background, other girls waited for their chance to shine.

'Look, you're a nice girl,' said Davey. He sighed, as if reluctant to reveal a universal truth. 'But you don't have it.'

'"It"?' Maggie was tired of hearing this. 'What is "it"?'

Davey waved his arms, vaguely. 'Star quality. I don't know. It's hard to define. You're not bad, honestly. But – you're like all the others, darlin'. Something's not quite there.' He looked at her, not unkindly. 'You know?'

12

You know? Maggie wanted to stamp her feet. Of course she didn't know. She didn't agree, either. How could he walk all over her dreams, just like that?

'Please give me another—' she began, pleading into the darkness, but the voice in front of her simply said, 'Next.'

And a ginger-haired girl in tight green linen shorts and an equally tight striped T-shirt that strained over her breasts ran onto the stage, her heels clacking, her smile bright. 'Hi!' she called. 'I'm Charlotte. It's great to be here!'

'Number eleven? Please leave the stage,' came a bored voice from the darkness. 'Hi Charlotte!' it said, with enthusiasm.

And so Maggie slid off into the wings, pent-up tears running down her cheeks.

Five minutes later, she was standing on a Soho sidestreet, her eyes still bleary with tears, the despised hotpants neatly folded in her bag. It was not yet eleven o'clock. The day stretched ahead of her, hunger already gnawing at her stomach. She was running out of money and, too proud to ask Camilla for anything, Maggie had started to skip meals. She was running on empty, she knew it, but this – this was the final straw. She looked up at the grey sky and a gentle rain started to fall. It was too much – Maggie started to cry again, hating herself, hating the aching pain of hunger, the loneliness, the grime and dirt . . . Something caught her eye, a sodden flyer glued to the rainy pavement. *See England by coach*, the advert offered politely.

It was a sign. She should go home . . . sobs shook Maggie's body. Home – where was that? Not Sheffield, that was for sure. She'd spoken to her parents a couple of times, wrote them dutiful letters, which they didn't answer, too mortified by their runaway daughter to show any interest. Sheffield wasn't home. But Hopkin Road was even less so . . . She sniffed loudly, feeling as low as she'd felt since she'd got to London, and looked around her.

She had walked through Berwick Street market a couple of times, and she thought perhaps she'd go back there now; it cheered her up, the fruit and veg all colourfully piled up, the bright bolts

13

of fabric stacked in the windows of the shops, the cheery stall-holders, the theatricality of it all. She started walking that way, humming 'Killer Queen' to try and cheer herself up, get her back into her stride, but it didn't work. She walked faster. Damn them all, all of them, the snobbish, stupid, sexist idiots. She would show them all! She'd be a star one day, yes she would! She just needed a break. One little break, and then –

'Hey!'

Just past the last fruit stall, she collided with something. Someone. A tall, lanky man with a languorous air, smoking a small cigar on the pavement, looking at his watch.

'Eh up,' Maggie said, catching hold of him to steady herself on her platform mules and momentarily forgetting her vowels in her confusion. 'I'm ever so sorry.'

She was clutching onto him; he patted her arm and released her. 'Don't apologise, love. It's been decades since a young woman clasped me to her bosom.' He smiled, steadying her on her feet. 'Those shoes are the trouble, I'd say, wouldn't you? Why does a lovely tall thing like you want to strap those things on her feet?'

Maggie looked down at her mules, which stood two inches off the ground. She smiled. 'Don't know,' she said, sniffing.

'You been crying?' The man nudged her and threw his cigarillo stub to the pavement, looking at his watch again. Maggie gulped.

'Just a bit.'

'Oh, dear me. I hate crying women. Don't cry,' said the older man, completely unfazed. He put his arm round her. 'Cheer up, sweetheart. I'm Nigel.'

He had faintly purple hair; Maggie'd never seen anything like it. She knew enough by now to suspect he was probably a homosexual: back in Sheffield no one was homo, or at least if they were they weren't talking about it. It was one of the things she liked about Soho, amid the theatricality and the tawdry glamour of it; the different people she saw on the streets every day.

'Hello, Nigel,' she said.

'What's wrong?' said Nigel. 'Tell Uncle Nigel.'

'Everything,' said Maggie. 'I'm a failure.' Her stomach grumbled

14

again, reminding her that she had fifty pence for lunch and dinner that night.

'Listen,' Nigel said, casting a glance down the street. 'How old are you?'

'Eighteen,' said Maggie automatically. She had got used to lying about her age.

'That's nice. You're not looking for a job, are you?'

'Oh,' said Maggie, wary of being co-opted into another audition for underwear, or sitting on a director's knee. 'Where?'

Nigel jerked a thumb at the pub behind him. 'Here. The Black Horse. Stupid Sandra, my barmaid. She's done a runner. With last night's takings, the little bitch. I need a new barmaid, just three nights a week.' He trailed one finger leisurely over a perfectly shaped eyebrow and drawled, 'Who won't steal from me, if that ain't too much to ask.'

Maggie looked up at the black peeling window frames, through the distorted glass into a cosy little bar, lined with old black and white photos, hundreds of bottles, it seemed, and a row of silver tankards dangling from hooks. 'Oh,' she said again. 'Well, no. I'm an—'

She stopped. *I'm an actress,* she was going to say, but she realised that sounded so snooty. *I'm hungry. I need to pay the rent tomorrow. And I don't want to take my clothes off . . .*

Necessity won over, and she smiled at Nigel. 'Can I come in and have a look?'

'Of course, sweetheart,' said Nigel, pushing open the rackety wooden swing door. 'Welcome to The Black Horse. The best pub in Soho.'

Chapter Three

Though she would never admit it, Maggie found after a couple of weeks that she actually liked being a barmaid. Working at The Black Horse was interfering with her dream, obviously, but at least it paid the bills and still left her time for some auditions. She would never have thought she'd enjoy being behind a bar, and part of her was horrified at herself – had she moved to London for *this*? Serving drinks to people?

But it got her out of the hovel that was the bedsit with Camilla, it earned her money and, to her surprise, it was interesting. They were a strange bunch of people, the regulars at The Black Horse. Some of them reminded her of the alcoholic old men she'd have seen in the Duke of York, her dad's local back in Sheffield – red noses, white bristling hair sticking out of their ears, stale and meaty-smelling. But the others were fascinating to her: struggling actors, all black polo necks and long sideburns, who came in after auditions to drown their sorrows, or before a show, to rev themselves up. She met struggling artists, fresh from the Slade or Chelsea, raving on about how much they hated everyone else's work, how they despised the chocolate-box watercolourists who hung their work on the railings at Hyde Park every Sunday. (Maggie had been to Hyde Park one Sunday afternoon and seen the paintings – pastel colours, pictures of trees and lakes and white stucco houses. She thought they were ever so pretty, but she knew better than to say so.)

There were strippers, waiting to go into the seedy 'theatres' that littered Soho, their make-up garish and stagey, their smiles painted on as much as anything else, but they were always friendly to Maggie, who looked down her nose at them. There were shop-keepers – the man who ran the Italian food shop round the corner, where huge salamis hung in the window, and inside it smelled of basil and garlic; the owner of the Jewish deli that sold delicious salt-beef sandwiches. There were market traders from all over Soho, on a break from selling herbs and spices, dodgy knock-off LPs, fabrics. And there was always the odd gangster, hair slicked back, in his pristine suit with huge collars and over-the-top cuff-links, flashing his cash around.

It was a far cry from Sheffield, but Maggie was growing to love Soho, and to her The Black Horse was right at the centre of it all. It felt like home, a home she'd never had before. Nigel was kind, and the regulars were too, asking after her auditions, sympathising with her when she failed, which she continued to do. They teased her, flirted with her, moaned when she forgot their drinks orders, praised her as slowly she grew more confident, enjoying her little empire behind that bar: polishing the wood, rearranging the glasses, dusting down the bottles, keeping things shiny and clean in a way she couldn't at the flat.

Maybe, one day soon, she told herself, someone would spot her serving behind that bar and recognise her talent, maybe give her a break. She consoled herself with that thought: *this* was how it was going to happen, of course! She'd be spotted, like Lana Turner in the 1930s, at Schwab's on Sunset Boulevard in Hollywood.

So far, the only job offers she'd had were to join the ranks of strippers and prostitutes who crowded the Soho bars like The Black Horse. But Maggie refused to use her gorgeous body that way. She would rather starve on the street.

In fact, she was something of a prude. The regulars called her 'Princess Margaret'. They tried – increasingly half-heartedly – to chat her up, with the low-level banter that was a constant at The

Black Horse, but soon realised they'd be getting nowhere with her, and stopped.

'Maggie May,' Nigel said, one night, to roars of approval from the bar, 'but Margaret Certainly Won't.'

All that changed the night Derek Stone came into the pub.

The first thing she noticed was his eyes.

The second thing Maggie noticed about Derek Stone, when he burst into The Black Horse one cold February evening, was that he was hiding something. Always running away from something or someone, that was Derek. She should have known, that first time.

He tried to pretend otherwise, but the way the door flew open that freezing evening, bringing in a shaft of sleeting rain and dirty, cold London air, and the way he flung himself into the warmth with such a clatter that Maggie looked up from her barstool, gave him away. She was trying to learn some lines for an audition for a bad *Carry On*-type film the next day, where she'd been told to turn up with a 'skimpy' bikini.

The door slammed shut again, and the regulars raised their eyes and went back to their drinks while Derek straightened himself out. The panic that had been on his face vanished, and those dark blue eyes twinkled at her.

'Hello! You're new here, ain't you?' he said, shaking his shoulders just a little so that the smooth wool cloth of his suit fell back into place. He cast a brief look at the door, checking for whom or what, she didn't know. Then he walked towards her, smiling that smile, fiddling with his cufflinks.

'I've worked here for three months, thank you.' Sometimes Maggie's elocution lessons were a blessing; sometimes they just made her sound like that Sybil Fawlty, from the sitcom. She heard her own voice, prim and high.

'I haven't seen you before,' said Derek. He stroked the metal pole running along the bar with his hand and looked frankly at her. 'I'd remember you, you see.'

'I'm sure,' said Maggie. She tossed her hair a little uncertainly, because she didn't want to tear her eyes away from him. Derek Stone was like no one she'd ever seen before. Smartly dressed, too smart, like so many of the guys around here. A pale blue handkerchief poked out of his breast pocket, and a heavy gold chain with a disc on it nestled in the hair on his chest. She wanted to laugh, scoff, like she did at all the others. But there was something about him. The sweat on his brow, like he'd been running. His easy smile, his close-cropped, thick black hair. And his beautiful blue eyes. Eyes which were roving over her, waist up, as she stood behind the bar.

'Have you been running?' said Maggie, haughtily.

Derek tore his eyes away from Maggie's breasts, snugly encased in a tight denim shirt with pockets which served only to emphasise them. 'Need to hide out here for a while,' he said. 'There's a bloke round the corner who's got the wrong end of the stick.'

'Why?'

Derek was vague. 'Well . . . He thinks I did him out of a deal.'

'What kind of deal?'

'Misunderstanding about some Oriental rugs.' He raised his eyebrows. Down the other end of the bar, Nigel snorted. Derek said, frankly, 'Ran halfway through Soho to get here.' He smiled back at Maggie. 'I'd have run faster if I'd known what I was going to see when I stepped through the door. Where have you come from, then?'

'Sheffield,' said Maggie.

He laughed, not unkindly. 'What brought you to London?'

'I'm going to be a star,' Maggie said. She pouted. 'You can laugh, but it's true.'

'I'm not going to laugh,' Derek told her. 'What – actress? Dancer? Singer?'

'Anything, really,' said Maggie. 'Don't mind. I just want to make it. Make it big.' She was nervous telling him this, she didn't know why. But Derek looked at her sympathetically, and like she was a person, Maggie Michaels, not just a girl with nice tits and long legs, which was how she had become used to being looked at.

'I think you'd be bleeding great on the stage,' Derek said. 'I can tell who's got it. You got it, babe.'

'How do you know?' said Maggie, unbending, and unable to stop herself.

'Oh,' Derek said casually. 'I run a theatre. Round the corner from here.'

'*Theatre?*' Nigel laughed loudly from his position a few feet away. 'Pull the other one, darling. It's got nipple tassels on.'

Maggie, looking from one man to the other, saw Derek shoot Nigel a look of – what? – amused outrage, it was. Derek winked at him. 'All right, Nigel?'

'Not too bad, duckie,' Nigel said, smiling at him. 'Nice to see your beautiful face in here again. Leave my staff alone. As it were.'

'Any time,' Derek said. He turned back to Maggie. 'What's your name?'

'It's Maggie,' she said.

'I'm Derek,' he replied, and he took her hand, holding it in both of his. 'And you are the most gorgeous girl I've seen in a long time.'

'Stop messing about,' Maggie said pertly, doing her best Kenneth Williams impression, and he laughed, delighted almost.

'And she's funny, too.' His eyes rested on the swell of her breasts. 'Maggie, eh?'

'You really own a theatre, then?' Maggie tried not to sound too impressed.

'Yeah, yeah,' Derek said casually.

'What's it called?'

'*Amours du Derek*,' Derek said, nodding seriously.

Maggie didn't know what that meant. It sounded to her like Amorzzdoo Derek, but she didn't want to sound unsophisticated and show she didn't understand. 'How nice,' she said, politely.

'It's French,' Derek said. 'You know. Little bit classy. I'm opening up another place next year, just round the corner. Don't believe what you read in the papers. Business is booming.'

'Yeah,' said Maggie, nodding to show she understood. 'That's – impressive.' She caught Nigel's eye. 'Can – can I get you a drink, then?' she said, trying to sound businesslike.

''Course you can, darling,' Derek said. 'That'll do for starters, anyways.' And he winked at her, and smiled.

For the first time since she'd arrived in London, for the first time in her life, really, Maggie Michaels blushed, a flush of desire rising up her breastbone, staining her cheeks red. Derek saw it, and laughed, softly.

Nigel turned the page of the London *Evening News* and snorted. 'Another one bites the dust,' he said to Graham, one of the actor regulars who was gazing gloomily into his pint.

'Hm, love?' Graham said.

'That,' said Nigel. He nodded ominously at Maggie, who was handing Derek his drink, leaning over the bar so her hand touched his, her eyes sparkling. 'He's trouble, that one.' He smiled. 'But dammit, I can't help but like him.'

That night, alone in her half of the bedsit, with a pillow over her ears to block out the sound of Camilla and two of her Hooray Henry mates laughing with increasing hysteria over a bong, Maggie smiled into the darkness. The flat was even more disgusting than ever – someone had been sick in the toilet, there was a mulch of burnt toast, cigarette butts and rancid avocados, Camilla's favourite food, in the sink – and it was freezing cold as usual. She had another depressing round of auditions tomorrow, and she knew she wouldn't get the parts. Knew it. But she didn't mind, somehow.

She thought of Derek, grinning stupidly to herself. She knew he was a shyster, as Nigel called them. Dodgy as you like, unsavoury, but immensely likeable. Nigel had even warned her to steer clear of him. 'Derek's charming, and he's a nice chap underneath it all, but don't trust him,' he'd told her in the doorway after they'd closed up and Maggie was swinging her satchel over her shoulder. 'Little Maggie May Well Regret It, you know, dear.' He had looked at her so seriously.

'I'm not a little girl, Nigel,' she'd told him.

'Yes, you are,' Nigel had replied, sombrely. 'I sometimes wonder if I did the right thing, hiring you.' He saw her stricken face.

21

'You're an innocent, Maggie, my love. You're not cut out for this.' He waved his hand round the bar. 'The conmen, the wankers who talk rubbish all day, the rubbish itself, the Big Smoke. You should be in a nice little cottage somewhere, you know, with a thatched roof, roses round the door.'

'I don't like thatched roofs,' Maggie said promptly. 'Mice get in there. I'd rather live somewhere big and modern with proper radiators. With a built-in garage for my sports car.'

Nigel had laughed and put his arm round her and hugged her. 'You ain't going to get that from Derek, ducks. Trust me.'

She wasn't remembering that now, though. She was remembering the touch of Derek's hand on hers, his eyes on her body, the expression on his face, the curiously kind way he looked at her, laughed at her. He had charisma, that was it. He was going places, he shared her dream for a better life. But no, Maggie told herself firmly. Derek Stone was trouble, she was sure of it. And then she smiled again, snuggling under the scratchy sheets and ignoring the screeching noises from the next room.

Chapter Four

'Come on, Maggie.' Derek's hands were roving around, tracing the neckline of her lacy top. He kissed her neck, and she closed her eyes briefly, wanting to give into him, knowing she mustn't, couldn't. Good girls didn't do this. But what if they really, really wanted to?

'Not here,' Maggie said, squirming on her barstool. Nigel had left early – 'nocturnal business', he'd said mysteriously – and she was locking up. Derek had stayed behind to help her, he said, but instead he'd spent the last ten minutes kissing her and trying to put his hands down her top.

It was spring, and in the few weeks since Derek Stone had run into The Black Horse, ducking out of trouble, he had pursued Maggie almost relentlessly. He was unpredictable, and that was what annoyed sensible, organised Maggie, but also excited her, about him. She never knew when she'd see him next, when he'd appear in the bar with a bunch of wilting yellow freesias (a couple of days past their best; 'nick them from the ladies' bog at Kettners, did you?' Nigel had enquired cattily) or a little cupcake from the old-fashioned baker's round the corner, or a ladies' magazine he thought she'd like to read on the tube back to Shepherd's Bush. 'To take your mind off me for a bit,' he'd said, staring sorrowfully at her, and then he'd smile and those deep blue eyes would blink lazily at her and Maggie's heart would take a leap. He was like a dark-haired Alfie – beautiful, but all man.

She kept saying no to him, though.

The truth was, she was scared.

Maggie was still a virgin. She'd kissed a couple of boys before. But the idea of the rest of it repulsed her. She'd been on a date with David Crouch, three years older than her at school, up at the cinema back in Sheffield. They'd seen *Tommy*, his hands roving all over her upper half while she was trying to get into the music. And then he'd tried to do something vile to her in an alley on the way back home while they kissed. Maggie was chewing gum, getting increasingly bored of David's limp tongue in her mouth. But then he'd suddenly stiffened, started grinding his body against her. A few seconds later, he'd collapsed suddenly in what seemed to be agony, before she pushed him away in total disgust, running back home as fast as she could, a strange wet patch on the front of her patchwork jeans. In the cinema, he'd taken her hand and put it in his lap, and she'd felt this hard thing bulging out of his jeans that he'd run her hand up and down, shuddering slightly before she pulled away, bewildered.

Since then, there'd been the tiring groping from the sleazy directors, the oh-so-casual brushing of the breast, clutching her bum, and she'd just got used to men staring at her. She was sick of it, and confused. How could they tell her she didn't have 'it', that star quality, and then try and squeeze her tits, or get her to 'go for a drink' with them? It bewildered her.

At least with Derek she knew where she was. She knew he wanted her. He was quite clear about that.

'Let's go for a drink somewhere else, then,' Derek said, running his hand lightly over Maggie's right breast. She shivered, and pushed his hand away.

'No,' she said, tossing her hair. 'I've got to get back. I'll miss my tube if I don't go soon.'

'Come and stay with me,' Derek said. 'I've got a lovely little place round the corner.'

Maggie said, 'Above a knocking shop? What do you take me for?'

Derek looked wounded. 'It's above a gentlemen's cinema. And it's bleeding nice, I'll have you know.'

'So it *is* above a knocking shop, then,' Maggie said. 'No thanks, Derek.' She looked at her watch. 'You'd better go.'

Derek shoved his hands in his pockets. 'Sweetheart, you're killing me.'

'Tough,' she said. 'Good night.'

In the last few weeks she had come to see that what Nigel had said was partly true – Derek was dodgy. But after she'd watched him saunter out of the bar, after days of Derek's expansive descriptions of the wonders of *Amours du Derek*, Maggie decided to take a detour. On her way home she walked down Brewer Street, looking curiously in and around the alleyways, till she found what she was looking for.

The neon sign outside hummed loudly. There was a neon palm tree and a picture of a girl in a Hawaiian skirt – she never found out why. Above them, in purple neon, the legend *Amours du Derek*. The doors were bolted shut and she couldn't get in. Still, she'd been impressed. It was a theatre, then. He was telling the truth.

Maggie was still a naive little girl, though. She didn't see what went on inside. She only saw the outside, and that was enough for her. Perhaps she should have looked a bit further.

Derek knew how to play her, too. The next night, Maggie was behind the bar, trying not to wonder when he'd next come in, when the door swung open and there was Derek, in a flashy checked coat, velvet collar, the gold medallion glinting in the low light from the pub. He had his arm round a curly-haired blonde girl, and as they ambled casually to the bar he moved his hand to her ribcage, casually caressing the side of her breast.

'Daisy, Daisy,' he said, nuzzling her neck. He turned to Maggie and said, as if she was an old friend, 'Hello darling. Bottle of your best champagne, please.'

'Sure,' said Maggie automatically, trying not to show she was bothered.

'Thanks, doll.' He squeezed Daisy's bum and said casually, 'Daisy and I, we're going to the Hippodrome in a bit, catch a show, then onto Sheekey's, nice fish supper.' He blew nonchalantly onto his nails as Daisy snuggled up next to him. 'So we won't be staying long.'

'Right,' said Maggie, tossing her hair as she turned to the bar to fetch the glasses. 'That sounds great. Hope you have a wonderful evening.'

'Oh, we will, we will,' Derek said airily.

Watching Maggie from his usual vantage point, Nigel said nothing, but he saw the bright glistening in her eyes, the colour in her cheeks, and he shook his head. Poor, silly Maggie. Why Derek? Why did she have to fall for him?

She didn't see him in the pub for two weeks.

And when Derek Stone finally reappeared, and asked her if she'd like to have a late dinner with him, at the Italian round the corner, she only hesitated for a second before saying yes.

Chapter Five

It took two dinners and three glasses of wine for Derek to lure Maggie back to his studio apartment, high above Beak Street. It was a warm spring night as they arrived back from Andrew Edmunds, the restaurant and artists' hang-out, to Derek's bachelor pad. It was painted white and was almost completely bare, apart from a record player, a pile of LPs, a bed that came down from the wall, a safe and four cardboard boxes overflowing with papers and wads of cash. In the corner were three TVs.

'They're colour,' Derek said casually, throwing his keys on the floor. 'Know anyone who wants a colour TV? I can do them a good price, tell them.'

'Er – no,' said Maggie, standing in the doorway, twisting the fringe of her shoulder bag around in her fingers. She felt a bit drunk. She didn't know what she was getting herself into. She'd shaved her legs that morning – much to Camilla's amusement. 'Got a date, dahhling?' she'd drawled, watching her from her bed, smoking a cigarette and winding a lock of thin blonde hair round her fingers. 'Who's the guy? Must be special if you're shaving your legs for him.'

Since Camilla had never shaved any part of her body, Maggie wanted to tell her she didn't know what she was talking about, but she'd got quite used to ignoring Camilla, the squalor of the flat and the slightly hopeless state she found herself in, these days.

'Come here,' said Derek, walking towards her. He flicked a switch in the wall, and the bed fell out to the floor with a loud thump. 'All mod cons,' he said, taking her hand and kissing it.

A few minutes later, somehow, she was sitting on the bed with a glass of whisky in her hand, Derek was stroking her hair, loosening his tie and her shirt dress was off, and she was just in her white nylon and lace bra and frilly knickers.

'I – I can't,' she said, biting her lip nervously.

He kissed her neck. 'I love you, don't I? Don't I, Maggie May?' He blew cool air onto her neck, her breasts, in her ear, stroking her trembling body with a calm, certain hand. 'Just – do something for me, will you? You love me, don't you?'

'I don't know,' she said, hesitantly.

'Just lie down on the bed,' he said, patting the nylon cover with his hand, and taking off his shirt. 'Lie down next to me. Don't be scared, Maggie.'

'I can't help it. I am scared.'

It felt good to say it, to be honest. His blue eyes were smiling at her, and all of a sudden she felt at ease with him. It was Derek, after all. He was trouble . . . she knew that – it was part of the attraction.

She felt nervous, her heart pounding, but excited at the same time.

'Trust me. I won't hurt you.'

She didn't trust him, that was the problem. But she knew he wouldn't hurt her. She cupped the side of his face with her hand. No more needed to be said.

He breathed out. 'OK.'

He touched her and stroked her, and slowly undressed her; there was no tugging at her underwear, no clumsy groping. He gently removed her bra and knickers until she was completely naked.

'Oh, Maggie May, look at you,' he said, and he bent forward, licking her breasts, teasing her nipples with his tongue, his teeth. He moved his hands slowly over her body, so gently she wanted more, and then he pushed her back. She was lying on the bed, suddenly, and he had one hand on her stomach, and the other between her legs. His hand moved gently from her knee to the inside of her thigh. It seemed to take an eternity before he reached her lips, which guarded her virginity.

'I'm going to put my fingers inside you,' he said, pushing one, then two, slowly inside her, leaning over her again to kiss her firm breasts. Then he knelt between her legs, looking down at her, as she stared up at him, her beautiful eyes glazed over with desire, her mouth open, moaning as she bit her lip, trying not to cry out that she wanted him, wanted him to fuck her more than she'd ever wanted anything in her life. Her – prim, well-behaved, hard-working Maggie Michaels, and Derek Stone had reduced her to a writhing form beneath him, begging him to devour her.

He stood up in front of her and slowly proceeded to undress himself, while never breaking eye contact with her. She was hypnotised by his magnificent body. It was as if he was carved from marble. He lowered himself on to her. She closed her eyes and used her fingertips to trace his body. How firm, how soft he felt: his shoulders, his biceps, his chest, his ribs, his firm buttocks, his strong thighs. His smell was intoxicating.

She had never seen or felt a naked man before. She bit her lip, but then Derek smiled at her again, looking down at her, and she knew it was right, it was time.

He was breathing heavily, holding his now rigid cock in his hand, and then he took her hand and wrapped it around him. He gasped, closing his eyes.

'Is it too tight?' she said, releasing her grasp, terrified she'd hurt him.

'N-no, no,' he choked. 'No, that's great, my angel. Don't stop, carry on just like that.' She felt his warm breath as he exhaled and leaned over her and kissed her neck, still kneeling between her legs, as his fingers stroked her clitoris and she started moaning again. After a minute or so Derek took his cock back into his hand.

And then he placed the head of his penis inside her for the first time, starting to touch her again with one hand. Then he took his fingers away and smiled down at her. He thrust his cock deep into her body. He put a finger in her mouth; she wrapped her tongue around it and moved it with the same rhythm as his cock inside her. For the first time in her life she knew how she tasted – sweet, sensual, alive. He took his fingers away from her mouth. He pinned her arms above her head, leaning down to lick her nipples, touch her body, and he smelt delicious, like honey.

And then he thrust harder, touching something deep inside her. All the time he was watching her, a curious expression on his face, and when Maggie came she started sobbing, crying out for him to give her more, her breath ragged, her voice broken. Then Derek pushed hard, once, twice, three times, groaning deep, exploding into her, because he knew then he'd conquered her, he'd got her, she was his now.

He loomed over her, sweat glistening on his forehead, breathing deeply, and he could hear her heart hammering on his tongue as he licked the sweat beneath her breasts.

She gazed up at him, helpless, completely unable to move, her chest rising and falling.

'You know what, Angel,' Derek said, kissing her. He flexed inside her one more time and she jumped beneath him, powerless, a fresh wave of pleasure sweeping over her. He smiled down at her. 'I think you might just be good at this.'

Maggie knew it then, knew with a total certainty as she gazed up at him, still panting in his arms, that she wanted more. She felt safe. Because she had fallen completely and helplessly in love with Derek Stone.

Chapter Six

'But when will you be back?' Maggie asked, trying to keep the whining note out of her voice.

'Don't know, Angel,' Derek said. He kissed her on the lips. 'It's an investor, darling. I got to meet him. He likes *Amours du Derek*, been there a few times. I want to move it to another venue. Hire some new girls. Make it a bit classier.' He winked. 'Gotta have my eye on the future, babe.'

In the weeks since she had started seeing Derek, Maggie had learned a few things, the most alarming of which was that *Amours du Derek* was not the chic Broadway Follies show she'd wanted to believe it was, but something more sinister – just like Derek's various businesses, the TVs in the bedroom, the knocking on the door of the studio at night, the strange people who turned up in the pub asking for him.

Maggie leaned over the bar, trying not to sound desperate. 'Shall I come over later?'

'Best not, babe. We'll probably go on late. I'll catch you tomorrow, yeah?'

'But – Derek – I want to talk to you about something –'

'You off, Derek?' Nigel said, as Derek tucked his wallet smartly inside his perfectly cut suit. 'How's tricks?'

'Not too bad,' said Derek, smiling at him. 'All right, Pete?' he said, winking at another regular. 'Good to see you, mate.'

'Saw George the other day,' Pete said. 'He looked well.'

'Old Georgy Porgy,' said Derek. 'I haven't seen him for a while.'

'Who's George?' Maggie said, desperate to detain him for a little while longer.

'My brother, darling,' Derek told her, tucking his handkerchief back neatly into its pocket.

'Oh,' said Maggie.

It was this kind of thing that left her feeling miserable. She was absolutely in love with Derek, and the pain was enormous. She'd thought being in love would be a wonderful thing, and it wasn't. She wanted him with her the whole time. She was realising how little she knew him – five weeks after they'd first had sex, and she hadn't known he had a brother, for Christ's sake. She didn't trust him. That was the trouble.

Being with Derek was like being on a roller coaster – fun and flowers and amazing sex – he would wake her up by stroking her very gently between the legs, growing more and more insistent, till she woke up, gasping with pleasure, her eyes flying open. He knew exactly how to play her, she was helpless in his hands. But that only made her more miserable, as she told him.

'I've not had anyone and you – you've been with all these women!' she'd say, shyly.

'It doesn't matter, does it?' he'd say cheerfully, poised between her legs, just before he entered her. 'You're a natural, Maggie. Born to have sex, darling. Now come here . . .'

They'd picnic in Green Park before walking into Soho, or sit in dark cinemas in the afternoons, watching the latest films, or wander along the South Bank, by the river, hand in hand. Maggie would catch sight of their reflection in a window and think what a nice couple they made, him so dark, her blonde, the two of them so happy. Because he was happy when he was with her, she was sure of that.

Wasn't she?

And then she wouldn't hear from him for two, three, four days, and she'd call his flat from the pub, and there'd be no answer, go round to *Amours du Derek*, no sign of him, and she'd start to think he'd dumped her and then – is he dead? Perhaps he's dead, that's it, that's why . . .

And then he'd turn up, full of apologies – *I had to go to Rotterdam, urgent business. I had a meeting up North, Angel. I'm sorry. I had a tummy upset, terrible it was, sweetheart.*

She knew he was lying, knew it. But she couldn't prove it, and there was something about him that meant she didn't push it.

But it was worth it, she told herself, for those moments when they were alone. When he would stroke her cheek and kiss her tenderly, play with her body, stroking and touching her, teasing her slowly until she was screaming out for him to come inside her, to fuck her, till he left her panting, crying, exhausted, and he would draw her into his arms and hold her tight till she fell asleep. And she *knew* he was a player, but there was something about him, something about the way they laughed together, she could cut him down to size, how he would agree with her, smiling ruefully, how wonderful it felt to walk down the street with him, hand in hand, knowing he was hers . . .

Until the game-playing got worse, and the absences, the non-committal behaviour. It had started after a week or so, and now she was miserable.

She couldn't have him back to her flat, she was too ashamed of the filth left by Camilla, and the fact that most likely they'd have to step over her the next morning and whoever she'd spent the night with, naked, snoring, stinking of sex and stale sweat. So she had to go to Derek's – or wait for him to ask her round. And it was driving Maggie mad.

In fact, this particular May night, she was close to breaking point: tired (she didn't sleep, worrying and thinking about him), hungry (she wasn't eating enough; too sick with love), and increasingly disillusioned with her life in London, sick of Camilla and the flat and even sick of her own dreams of becoming a star. They seemed further away than ever, now, and somewhere along the line she wondered if she'd given up, in the back of her mind.

As if she'd conjured her up, just then the pub door swung open and Maggie was bewildered to see Camilla come in, her thong sandals slapping on the floor, her floaty dress wafting around her as if it had a life of its own. Maggie had forgotten that Camilla was actually rather beautiful, in a feral, lazy way. She stared at her.

'Wow. Camilla! What are you doing here?'

Camilla smiled round at the room, as if expecting an audience.

'I'm going to the Roundhouse. To see some new band with Debs and Jamie. So I thought I'd make a stop in Soho before I did, and then I thought, gosh, why the fuck don't I just pop in and see where Maggie toils all day – ha, ha!'

Her posh, clipped tones grated on Maggie, they always had. She thought Camilla was a big fake. But she smiled at this and said, 'What can I get you?'

'Ohhh,' Camilla said, flicking her sheet of blonde hair over her shoulder. She turned to the man next to her at the bar, who happened to be Derek, who was watching in amazement like she was an alien creature he'd never seen before. 'What's that drink? It looks awfully jolly.'

'London Pride,' Derek said, looking her up and down.

Camilla nodded at Maggie, who collected herself. 'Coming right up. Camilla, this is Derek. My boyfriend.'

'Oh my *God*!' Camilla said loudly, turning to Derek and taking his hand. 'You're the famous *boyfriend*! She doesn't stop talking about you.'

Derek looked at her. 'She never mentioned how lovely you was,' he said seriously, squeezing her hand. Camilla preened herself and Maggie felt her heart contract with pain. She knew then that Camilla was curious about Derek, that was why she'd ventured into Soho, an area she rarely visited. For all her alleged bohemian nature, Camilla was like those people who bored Maggie about their travels through Europe and then frowned when someone 'foreign'-looking came into the pub.

Then Derek looked up. 'I'm a lucky man, aren't I, though?' he said to Camilla. 'Oh yes.'

'You are,' said Camilla, putting both her elbows on the bar and pressing her slender body against the wooden panels. 'Very, very lucky.'

She smiled at him. Derek smiled awkwardly back, and Maggie breathed again, glad the moment was over. She handed Camilla her pint.

'So you live in Shepherd's Bush?' Derek asked politely.

'Actually, just outside Hertford,' Camilla said. 'That's where Ma and Daddy live, anyway.' She turned to Maggie. 'Didn't tell you, did I? They've raised my allowance. Hilarious. Daddy's just done some deal with the Arabs, really massive.'

'He's a camel salesman, is he?' Derek was only half listening.

'Sort of,' Camilla gulped with laughter. 'It's boring. He runs Sherbourne's.'

'Sherbourne's – the petrol stations?'

'Yes,' said Camilla simply.

Derek stared at her incredulously. 'You're having a laugh, ain't you?'

'Her surname's Sherbourne,' Maggie told him.

There was a silence at the bar, as Derek digested this. 'I've got a beautiful job lot of Persian rugs he can have. Give him a good price if he wants them,' he said eventually, and Maggie knew he was only half joking.

Camilla gazed at him. 'Right,' she said, uncertainly. 'You're funny, aren't you?'

He's a bleeding riot, Maggie wanted to scream. *I haven't seen or heard from him for days and now he's pretending I'm not even here.* 'Don't you have to be going, Derek, darling?' she asked him.

'Give it a minute,' Derek said. 'Get us another pint, will you, babe?'

'Can we talk afterwards?'

He ignored her; he was asking about Camilla's dad, how he'd got started, made it work. Camilla left an hour later, and when Maggie went to the cellar to get some more gin, Derek had gone by the time she returned. She slammed the bottle down on the bar, tears in her eyes, sweat rolling down her back. She had to talk to him. It was something very important.

★

The next morning she was up early, after another sleepless night, feeling sick, her heart aching. She raced to the toilet again to throw up, and when she had finished retching, she stood up miserably to find Camilla standing in the doorway of the damp-streaked bathroom. She was smoking a cigarette. Maggie wanted to tell her to put it out; it made her feel even more sick. Her stomach rumbled.

'Bloody great gig last night,' Camilla said. She looked Maggie over coolly, with an appraising stare.

'Right. That's good.' Maggie was trying not to retch.

'Derek's an interesting chap, isn't he?' Camilla said.

'Yes,' Maggie mumbled, a towel clasped to her mouth. 'Oh God.'

She turned around, wretchedly, and was sick into the toilet bowl again.

'You're pregnant, aren't you?' Camilla said, neither accusing nor excited; it was simply a question.

'Don't know.' Maggie stood up and nodded unhappily. It was easier just to tell the truth, a relief, in fact. 'Yeah. Yeah . . . I think so. I'm three weeks late and I feel awful.' She shuddered as another wave of nausea overtook her. 'What am I going to do?'

'Use protection next time,' Camilla said.

Maggie tried not to sound defensive. 'I did. The first time, we didn't. But I thought you couldn't – it was the first time, I thought it wouldn't happen.'

'Little Maggie,' Camilla's honeyed tones were almost kind. 'Wow, you really are an innocent abroad, aren't you? Can't get pregnant the first time you have sex? Well, you know that's a load of crap now, don't you? Have you told Derek?'

'N-no,' said Maggie, wiping her eyes, trying not to breathe in, the stench from the damp, rancid bathroom and Camilla's cigarette threatening to overwhelm her. 'I don't know how to.'

For a supposed hippy, Camilla was nothing if not pragmatic. 'Get rid of it,' she said, turning back to her bed in the middle of the sitting-room floor. 'And don't tell him, that's my advice, darling.'

'But I want us to be a f-family,' Maggie said.

'If you don't want to see him again, that's the way to go about it,' Camilla said. ''Cos I'm telling you, darling, once Derek Stone finds out you're pregnant, that's the last you'll hear from him.' She smiled almost sympathetically at Maggie and stubbed her cigarette out. 'I'm going out now, got to meet someone. I'll clear up later. Sorry, darling.'

She was right, of course.

In fact Maggie never got to tell him.

Because the next day, when she went looking for Derek in Beak Street, the landlord let her in. She found the place as it was, but all his stuff had gone, and he owed the landlord – who lived below him – three months' rent.

Derek had done a runner.

Chapter Seven

A week later, when there was still no sign of Derek, Maggie had passed from being frantic into a kind of numb limbo. What the hell was she supposed to do now? There was no point going to Beak Street any more – he clearly wasn't going to show up there. He wasn't going to come into The Black Horse, either, if his creditors knew where to find him. There was only one other place she could try. One wet May evening, she plucked up her courage and went round to *Amours du Derek*, to see if anyone could tell her anything that might be of use. She was desperate.

The curtain through which she'd had a glimpse of stockings a couple of months ago was open, and she walked in, glad she was relatively invisible in her oatmeal smock and jeans. She paused for a moment, her eyes adjusting to the light. She was used to Soho being seedy – she didn't mind that, it was part of the glamour, the bright lights, she knew it. But this – as her eyes searched out more and more, her mouth dropped open in horror, and she stood there, unnoticed by anyone, as a tear rolled down her cheek.

Some 1960s cabaret music was playing half-heartedly in the background, and up on the tiny stage an emaciated, tired-looking girl with ropelike bleached-blonde hair danced listlessly, holding her sagging breasts in her hands, waggling each one in time to the music. In front of her sat three men. The one nearest to Maggie was in a shiny grey suit, and he had his flies open and was frantically rubbing a stubby penis, which lay flaccidly on the zip. His eyes were glazed, his mouth slack. Next to him, another man rubbed himself, more leisurely.

Maggie shifted her feet, which were stuck to the grimy floor with God knows what. *This* was Derek's dream, the sophisticated cabaret paradise they'd talked about? No wonder he wanted to make it classier.

A movement in the corner caught her eye; a girl in a loose gold sequinned sheath, holding a tray of drinks was talking to an elderly punter whose clawlike hand gripped her smooth thigh as she put the champagne down on the table and bent over him, the promise of something in her eyes. He looked at her breasts, which were fully visible at that angle, and signed the bill. She ran her fingers over his balding pate. Maggie suddenly knew what this was – a clip joint. That bottle would cost the old man a hundred quid, at least, and who cares if he got to have sex with the girl or not? It was part of the job. At the table next to him, another man – greasy face, slicked-back hair – was lying back, his head on the banquette, as another girl slipped her hand into his trousers with a furtive, urgent motion, a fixed smile on her face as she tucked pound notes into her dress with the other hand.

The music stopped, and Maggie moved her feet again. Her shoes made a squelching sound, and the girl on stage looked up, squinting into the darkness. It was time to go; she felt sick, suddenly. She turned and walked out. The sign outside was sputtering slightly, and the girl in the hula skirt was only partly lit up. Maggie walked away from *Amours du Derek*. It wasn't funny any more. It was tawdry, pathetic, disgusting. She felt that this was her relationship with Derek, shown up for everything it was. How could she have got him so wrong? Without knowing it was happening, she leaned over the gutter and was sick, liquid dripping from her mouth and splashing the pavement around her.

She had never felt so wretched as she did at that moment. She was ashamed, but also dog-tired, confused and ill with morning sickness that seemed to go on all day. Maggie turned towards the tube station, longing to be back in the relative comfort of Hopkin Road and in bed, this awful day over.

But there was worse still to come.

When she let herself in, Maggie immediately knew something was up. It was dark – nothing unusual about that, Camilla was always out – but there was something different about the flat, she couldn't work out what. Maggie came into the centre of the room, putting her keys on the table and pulling her long hair out from under her satchel strap. She opened the window, looking for the milk on the sill.

And then she saw the note propped up by the dusty wooden bowl that held Camilla's fruit.

Dear Maggie

This is really hard to do in a note but I have to say it. Derek and I have gone away together. We have fallen for each other, in a major way. I told him about the baby – you didn't seem to have done so and I felt he ought to know. He isn't ready to settle down yet, Maggie, you must know that. He has a lot of potential. I think Daddy will absolutely love him.

I have left £10 for the bills. Hope that's enough!

Thanks for the good times. Lots of love and luck with the baby, no hard feelings I hope,

Camilla
Xxx ooo xxx ooo

Maggie didn't cry, not then. She must have stood facing the window, the note in her hand, for a good few minutes. But she didn't move. When she did, it was slowly, like a robot, through the tiny flat. At least everything made sense now, she told herself.

Camilla's bed was unmade in the middle of the room, the sheets tangled and creased. In the centre, two plates filled with toast crumbs and a used condom.

Maggie didn't cry then, either.

The rest of the flat was even messier than ever. Camilla's clothes littered the floor, the threadbare carpet was wet with damp, overflowing ashtrays stood on every surface.

The 'bathroom' was a sink and a tiny bath only four feet long, opening up like a cupboard. Maggie peered into it, dully, half expecting them to jump out at her. Something in the sink caught her eye. Long, dark blonde curly hairs sticking to the grimy surface, Maggie's razor clogged with them – Camilla had finally shaved her armpits.

Maggie cried then. She crouched down on the floor by the sink and wept, roaring with anger and misery, hugging herself, rocking backwards and forwards, feeling as if something inside her had cracked.

Her stupid hippy dream, where had it led her? She was totally alone here. She couldn't phone her parents – she hadn't seen or spoken to them since she'd left, bar her only phone call to them and the odd card to let them know she was alive. They were still horrified by what she'd done: to be honest, she didn't really care what they thought, anyway.

She was friendless, pregnant, with no money in a stinking, miserable glorified bedsit. She thought of the girl she had been back home in Sheffield, delusional with dreams of fame and stardom, floaty clothes, romance, a rock 'n' roll soundtrack thumping through her head. What a fucking idiot.

She climbed into her bed eventually and lay there, sobbing her heart out through the night.

The next morning, she woke up and the sun was shining through her greying net curtains. The window was open and she could hear a song playing from the flat below; something silly, it was 'Tiger Feet' by Mud, and despite herself she lay there listening, looking up at the blue sky. And it was then that Maggie made a decision.

She wasn't going to cry any more.

She wasn't going to be a victim any more.

She hauled herself out of bed, pulled on a long, shapeless kaftan and padded round to the corner shop down the road, the early-morning sun shining kindly on the back of her neck. And she bought bleach, rubber gloves, a mop, brushes, cloths . . . she carried everything back to the flat and turned her own radio on, made herself a cup of tea, tied her hair back and got to work.

Maggie scrubbed the flat clean that morning. She got down on her knees and cleaned and tidied from top to bottom, till every surface sparkled and there was no trace at all of Derek and Camilla. She didn't feel sick, in fact, she hadn't felt this good for weeks and weeks. She bagged up all her old flatmate's clothes and she chucked every trace of Derek away, not that there were many. She carried the bags downstairs and threw them into a skip that stood outside; then she knocked on the door downstairs and asked Rita, her neighbour, for a hand.

'You're chucking that mattress away?' said Rita. 'Don't you want it no more?'

'No, I bloody don't,' said Maggie grimly, and she could hear her Sheffield accent properly in her voice for the first time in months. 'I don't want it anywhere near me.'

They carried Camilla's mattress down the dark, grotty staircase together and threw it onto the skip, then Maggie thanked Rita, went back into the flat and, slamming the door shut, went to the bathroom and cut off her beautiful long hair. She cut it carefully into a bob, and as she looked at herself in the gleaming mirror, she nodded with satisfaction, pleased with her handiwork, the lessons she'd learned at Toni's, back in Sheffield. Not once did she question it, cry over what she'd done, what had happened. She picked up her coat and her cheque book, thanking her lucky stars she'd been saving a bit of money. She was going shopping.

When Maggie turned up to work that evening, Nigel did a double-take. The dreamy, long-haired, bohemian girl in her floaty smocks and high-waisted flares was gone.

In her place was a neat, confident young woman in a grey pleated skirt and belted jacket.

'There you are,' Nigel said, because he'd been worried about her. 'Look at you! Where've you been, darling?'

'Pitman's, Oxford Street,' Maggie said in a flat voice. 'I enrolled on a typing course.'

'A what?'

'It's time to get real,' Maggie said, slapping her purse down on the bar. 'I'm not an actress. I'm nothing, neither. I'm no one,' she corrected herself. 'I've got a baby on the way, and I need a proper job to tide me over before it comes.'

Nigel took this news calmly. He nodded. 'What about Derek?' he said. 'Still not heard from him?'

'Derek's gone, Nigel,' said Maggie. 'He's not coming back, we all know that. Like I say, it's time to get real. I'm making some big changes.' She stared at him like he was a stranger.

'What've you done with my little Maggie?' Nigel asked.

'It's Margaret now,' she said firmly.

'*Margaret?*'

'Maggie's gone. For ever.'

There was a silence. She looked at him impassively. Nigel sighed, and raised his eyes to heaven.

'Well, *Margaret*,' he said. 'There's a man over there who's been asking for you. He's been waiting over an hour. Not bad-looking. Bit square for my taste. Looks like an accountant.'

Looks like a closet case, too, he added under his breath, but Margaret didn't hear him.

She walked over to the table, aware of her heels clicking on the floor, holding her stomach in. 'Hello?' she said, tentatively. 'I'm Maggie – Margaret. How can I help you?'

He was a nice-looking fella, clean-shaven, neatly dressed in a grey suit with a pale blue shirt and dark tie. Nothing showy, but well put together. He was losing his light hair a touch, but it was close-cropped, nicely done. He had a handsome face, like a mat-inée star. He smelled of aftershave – nothing overpowering, just linen and something a little bit spicy. He was classy.

'Margaret Michaels?' The man at the table stood up politely and shook her hand. 'I'm George Stone, Derek's brother. Can we talk, please?'

Chapter Eight

George Stone was used to clearing up his brother's messes. As he waited for the latest mess to appear for her shift at work, he was making a note of what needed to be done afterwards, writing neatly in a black leather diary with a silver ballpoint Parker pen the company had given him on completion of five years' service. Nigel had been right: George *was* an accountant, at Davidson and Davidson, with offices just off Regent Street. He was doing well. He didn't brag about it, wasn't flashy, had no airs and graces like his brother. And he didn't have a string of failed businesses behind him, angry ex-partners, rejected ex-girlfriends.

In fact, George had no ex-girlfriends to speak of. No private life of his own at all, it would appear. Instead, he sorted out Derek's, when it came to crisis point; and to the outside world George was the boring one, the permanent bachelor accountant, on his own at the work functions, solo at the company dinner dance each Christmas, though there were plenty of secretaries who would have loved to have gone as his date. George was quiet, well-mannered, considerate. A nice man, and there were so many bastards around.

Lately it had started to bother him, though. He had seen Geoff Simkins, who'd started a year after him, rise further because he had a nice house in Crouch End and a wife who wore Laura

Ashley full-length frocks and threw elegant little dinner parties for the company chairman and his wife, and other members of the board. They'd had salmon mousse last time he'd been there; even George had been impressed. And he went back to his tidy, anonymous bedsit in Marylebone with his new shirt pressed and ready for the next day, and he wondered what he could do about it. Wondered why it was *him* who was made this way, how unfair it was. Perhaps it would pass, this way he felt; perhaps what he needed was to get married, find the right woman. That was all it was.

George didn't want to be like Derek, that was for sure. The chaos surrounding his little brother alarmed him; he was the one who had to sort out the angry employees, the gangsters, the girlfriends and the pregnancies. Waiting for the latest little slapper he'd knocked up that night, he was trying not to get irritated. He loved his brother, he supposed, and he couldn't afford the scandal, which was why he always agreed to help him out, when Derek rang him in a panic; this time from a service station on the motorway somewhere. He didn't know why they fell for it, every single time, these girls; couldn't they see what he was like? Were they that stupid?

And then Margaret Michaels had arrived, come over to his table and shaken his hand.

'Of course we can talk,' she said, answering his question. 'But I have to work, so it can't take long.'

He noted the neat skirt, the neat hair, the way she folded her hands quietly in her lap and looked at him with those cool, intelligent eyes; there was something interesting about her. She was no fool, this one. George Stone found himself liking her. He had brought the money he gave out in these situations to get the problem 'fixed'; it was in an envelope, in his breast pocket. He patted it now, and fastened his jacket.

'I won't take up too much of your time,' he said. 'But I wanted to meet you. I've spoken to Derek. He's told me everything.'

'He's told you everything, has he?' she said, looking down at the floor, not betraying a flicker of interest. 'Well, I expect I'm not the first problem of his you've had to sort out. Must be interesting, having him as a brother.'

'It can be,' George agreed, grimly. 'Look, Margaret. Do you mind if I call you Margaret?'

Margaret watched him, the fluttering in her stomach quietening down a little, the nausea she constantly felt subsiding for the first time in days. 'Of course not,' she said, amused and touched at the same time; it had been a long time since anyone had treated her with this kind of old-fashioned courtesy. She relaxed a little.

'My brother is – well, he's a bloody idiot, if you'll excuse me.' George cleared his throat. There was something very – pristine about him, Margaret thought.

'Yes, he is,' she agreed. She smoothed down her hair, still trying to get used to its dramatically short length. 'I hear he's left the club owing a lot of money, and he's not paid his rent. I hope you're not liable for all of that.'

The truth, which Margaret didn't know yet, was that George had had a difficult meeting with the landlord of *Amours du Derek* before coming on to meet Margaret. He was angry with his brother, who had skipped off to somewhere in the Home Counties because, as he told his brother airily on the phone, 'I hooked up with this posh bint and her dad's gonna give me a packet.'

'What about this girl you've got into trouble, what about her?' George had said, trying not to shout at his desk.

'Maggie?' Derek sounded gleeful. 'Maggie's lovely, Georgy-boy. In fact, if you weren't bent as a nine-bob note, I'd get you to have a go on her. She's a great girl, trust me. Goes like a—'

George had put the phone down, disgusted.

Now he looked at Margaret, as she signalled for a glass of lime cordial.

'When's it due?' he said.

'It's still early,' she told him. 'I'm not even two months in.' She looked at him. 'It's strange, you look so like your brother, and yet you're very different, aren't you?'

He could feel himself breaking into a cold sweat. 'What do you mean?'

She smiled. 'Oh, just that you're so well mannered – you stood up when I came over, and you haven't once stared at my cleavage.' She took a sip of her drink, as Nigel stood behind her. 'It's nice. Makes quite a change. I'm done with rough and ready, you see. It's time to act like a grown-up.'

'Sounds like a sensible plan,' said George, who loved a sensible plan. He reached for the envelope in his pocket. Time to make the pay-off. But then something stopped him. As he watched her drinking from the glass, sitting there so elegantly upright, George knew he couldn't just offer her money, pay her off like she was just another one of those girls, the strippers, the models, the girls Derek chewed up and spat out.

No, he told himself as he looked at her. Margaret Michaels was a cut above the rest. And an idea formed in his head; a tiny seed, but one that, over the weeks and months would grow, take shape, put down roots.

'Look, Margaret,' he said. 'I know you have to work and I'm taking up your time. I wonder if perhaps I might take you out for dinner tomorrow instead? I'd like to – to see if there's anything I can do to help you.'

Margaret looked at him appraisingly. 'I don't need any help,' she said, taking a deep breath.

'Fair enough,' George said, keeping his voice even. 'Perhaps you need a friend, though.'

And, much to her surprise and his, he found himself covering her hand with his own, and squeezing it.

Margaret looked up at him, into his eyes, and for one brief second felt her heart contract as she saw how like Derek's they were, a beautiful deep blue, and then she looked at him again, his neat, precise movements, kind face and the calm, safe feeling she got from him, after weeks of feeling like she was sailing in the choppiest of seas. 'Thank you,' she said, evenly. 'I'd like that.'

47

Chapter Nine

George shared more than his brother's eyes. He was driven and ambitious, but he strove for success within a company, not by breaking the rules and flying by the seat of his pants. George wanted stability and acceptance for himself, because he was by nature a cautious, careful man. And there was another reason too; one that he wouldn't admit even to himself. Nigel had seen it at first glance, and his brother had always known it, but this was 1977, and George was a shy, introspective man, and to him being homosexual was something you hid, a sickness that you cured by pushing it out of sight. There may have been people marching for gay rights, and in London and New York there was a growing acceptance of homosexuality, its normality even, but none of this meant anything to George. In a world in which people still didn't want to believe that Elton John and Freddie Mercury were gay, how could quiet, nondescript George admit he was?

It didn't occur to George that he might one day be open about it. He didn't want to be. His fulfilling of his own needs was shameful and furtive, best kept to himself. And in the meantime, he focused on work, on pulling himself up to the next level, finding that new stream of clients who would make him rich and successful, creating a world for himself that hid what he really was from everybody.

That was where Margaret came in.

He knew the money he should have given her would have helped her, but then that would have taken her away from him. And she wouldn't need him any more.

Over the next few weeks, Margaret and George spent a fair amount of time together. She really was alone in the big city: Margaret had never had many friends, even at school. He admired her spirit, her independence – the typing course was hard work but she never complained, and the long, smoky hours at The Black Horse were what paid the rent on the flat – and he found himself wanting to look after her. She was vulnerable, with little money and a baby on the way, but she never moaned, just simply got on with it, and George liked that. They went to the theatre together; he liked that too. Liked the way he could casually mention 'Margaret' to the fellows at work, and when George saw that fleeting glimpse of relief in his boss Tom's eyes, he knew this was all going to be worth it. He took her to smart restaurants, enjoying being seen with this classy, well-turned-out girl who listened politely to what he said and smiled at his jokes, even if there was an expression on her face sometimes when she looked into his eyes that unsettled him.

As the summer turned into autumn, they were spending more and more time together, and it was pleasant. Especially pleasant for him was the gradual swell of Margaret's stomach. George loved children, had always wanted them. The first time the baby kicked, they were at dinner, at an Italian they both liked in Soho, and Margaret impulsively put his hand on her stomach.

'Feel it,' she said, her eyes alight.

George flinched at the intimacy of what she was asking, but then his hand settled onto her warm, rounded tummy, and he felt it, felt a fluttering movement like a thumping heartbeat, and he laughed aloud and said, with joy in his voice, 'Margaret, that's wonderful. Aren't you a clever girl?'

Her eyes had filled with tears. 'Bless you, George,' she'd said, and even more than ever he'd wanted to hold her in his arms, to protect her and this unborn baby – who, now he'd accepted she was going to have it, he was determined to love – from the rough, cruel world out there.

George gradually started to feel like he and Margaret were together seeking shelter from a storm. He could help himself to the future he'd always wanted. And look after her at the same time.

The night it happened, they were coming back from the cinema. They both loved the film version of *Cabaret*, and it was showing at a small cinema off Leicester Square. They sang about 'Elsie back in Chelsea' all the way back to Margaret's flat. That was another thing George admired about Margaret. It was a horrible house she lived in, one bedsit on top of another, but her little space was really quite charming. He'd been invited back for coffee – just coffee, nothing more than that, of course – a couple of times, and he noted how spotless she kept it, how little there was, no clutter, no mess. A couple of geranium plants on the window sills gave a little colour; a battered old radio and some china storage jars were arranged on the kitchen surface, and basil and rosemary plants in the window. It was all very clean, and there was something restful about that to him. Nothing out of place, everything tidied away. She liked it too, she said. Made her feel calm.

George, accepting a cup of instant coffee from her, looked up at her face, her strong cheekbones, her pretty strawberry blonde hair, and he saw how tired she was.

'You all right?' he said, standing up. 'You look tired, shall I go?'

'No,' Margaret said, patting his shoulder. 'I like it when you're here, George. Don't go.'

He sat down next to her on the sofa, humming another tune from *Cabaret*.

'It was a good night, wasn't it?' he said.

'It's always a good night with you,' Margaret said, sleepily, and she put her head on his shoulder.

George sat there, gazing into space, holding his cooling mug of coffee, until he realised she was fast asleep. And then, without knowing why, only that it was right, he set his mug down carefully, scooped her up into his arms and carried her into the bedroom area. She stirred as he laid her down on the bed, but only a little, her eyelids fluttering gently. He lay down next to her, his breathing steady, and put his hand on her stomach, cupping it from behind, and in this innocent position George and Margaret spent their first night together.

Two months later, he proposed. They were married in December 1977.

Chapter Ten

It was so easy to convince people that you were happy, when inside you were crying.

Margaret found this out the day she accepted George's proposal. When Nigel said, his brow furrowed with worry, 'Maggie May – are you sure about George, love?' she had stared at him with her big green eyes.

''Course I am, Nigel. I've never been happier.'

'I don't mean that,' Nigel had said. 'It's just – George is – well, I wonder how well you know him, Maggie. That's all.'

'It's Margaret. And I know him well enough to know he's a good man.' Margaret had snapped the clasp on her patent bag and put it over her shoulder, heaving herself up into a standing position. 'If you don't agree, say your piece now, Nigel Walters, or else—'

'Now, now,' Nigel had said, soothingly. 'Don't go getting upset. I know he's a good man, too.' He sighed. He'd come to see, over the months, just how much he'd underestimated his Maggie May. When he'd first come across her, crying in the street, she'd seemed such a defenceless little thing.

Looking at this girl – woman, really – with the neat bob, the swollen stomach, the set expression, twisting her gold and diamond engagement ring round her finger, he realised just how

52

tough she really was. Still, something inside her had died when Derek ran away. The dream of being a star, was it? The spark that made her young, open to life, curious? He didn't know, but he knew she'd changed.

He patted her on the shoulder. 'I just want you to be happy, that's all.'

'I am happy.' She'd smiled at him brightly. 'You don't understand. Nigel, I was stupid to think I could make it as an actress. This is everything I've ever wanted. I can see that now.'

They had their wedding reception at The Black Horse. It was a small affair, a few regulars, a couple of Margaret's friends from the typing course, George's colleagues from the office. George got a little drunk and kept slapping people heartily on the back, accepting their congratulations enthusiastically while Margaret, stone-cold sober, watched him with what she hoped was affection. She wanted to make him happy. Sure, she had some nagging doubts, but she'd decided to make the best of it, and once she made her mind up, it was hard to change it. George Stone had come and saved her, that was how she saw it.

Nigel, flushed with his best brandy and with the recent tax windfall that George had negotiated for him, having casually offered to look over his books as a thank you for all his kindnesses to Margaret, was fully reconciled to the happy couple. Everyone was. Even Ron and Maureen Michaels, though they didn't attend the wedding, sent a biscuit barrel, perhaps relieved beyond all measure that their wayward daughter had seen the light and was, after only a year in London, settling down to domestic life – with an *accountant*, of all people! It was almost too good to be true, for everyone involved.

They rented a small house in Acton and spent their first Christmas there, and then Margaret settled down to wait.

In January 1978, one bitterly cold evening, Margaret was in the kitchen, cleaning, listening to Radio One, tapping her feet in time to the rhythm. Though she was heavily pregnant by this stage, she still loved music. She couldn't help it – her feet could be aching, ankles swollen, back sore, her head throbbing with tiredness – when she heard Jimi Hendrix or the Stones she wanted to dance, to scream and sing, to jump up and down, go into a frenzy. She told herself she should have blocked all this out by now, she was a housewife with a baby on the way, not a pleasure-seeking teenager, but it was impossible to resist.

She was making hotpot for George, for when he came back from work. George was never late. He didn't stay out and get drunk with 'clients'; she always knew where he was. It was one of the things she liked most about him. He called every evening before he left work.

'Just leaving now, Margaret,' he'd said that night, cheerfully. 'You all right, dear?'

'Yes,' she'd answered.

'Had a good day?'

'Yes thanks, George. Supper'll be ready for you when you get back.'

'Don't tell me what it is . . . I like a surprise,' George said. He sounded very buoyant.

When Margaret was absorbed in her cleaning and singing along to the radio, she didn't hear anything else. She loved cleaning. Loved the order of her neat little kitchen, the gingham curtains, the oatmeal-coloured Formica table, the spotless surfaces with jars for tea, sugar, biscuits. Everything had a place, and it was kept in its place. That was one of the other things she liked about George: he was as neat and tidy as she was.

Hopkin Road seemed a million miles away to her now: had she really had that life? Ever been that girl? Sometimes late at night, when she couldn't sleep because of the baby, Margaret lay awake and stared at the ceiling, as George breathed quietly beside her (he didn't snore, unlike his brother; he was a neat sleeper, hands folded on his chest), wondering how she had got here, seventeen years old, in a quiet semi in west London, married and pregnant. This time last year her dreams had been very different, but they were just that: dreams.

Now she was a grown woman, she felt. Sure, she'd had doubts about George. She had still been in love with his brother, she'd been desperately unhappy, but she told herself that was all in the past, now. *This*, here, this was what she wanted. What she needed.

She wondered about Derek, in those dark nights. He had completely disappeared. George hadn't heard from him for a while; they hadn't even been able to tell him about their marriage. Where was he? How was he? She would never talk to George about him now, but she couldn't help wondering. Where he was, who he was with . . . and she would sigh, and shift herself so her large, swollen stomach was more comfortable, while George slept on next to her.

George didn't pester her for sex. In fact, he had been very kind about it. He'd said he didn't want to bother her while she was pregnant. There had been no question of it before they were married; they kissed and cuddled, and he rested his head on her swollen breasts, stroked her hair, rubbed her back, but never disturbed her. Now she was pregnant, the thought of sex was repugnant to her. Nothing to do with George, it was her body, nothing more. With Derek, it had been non-stop. She'd wake in the middle of the night to find his erection pushing against her bum, his lips nuzzling the back of her neck, his hands gripping onto her from behind, clutching her breasts, softly teasing her nipples, running over her body till she gave in to the pleasure and he would sink into her, rocking against her gently, then harder, stroking her; he instinctively knew where to find her G-spot, and then he would push himself further and further inside her until she cried out, still half asleep, almost mad with wanting him . . .

But that was in the past, now. And every morning, when she woke up, sometimes dozing in fitful sleep because she was uncomfortable – the baby was big – she would open her eyes, suddenly, turn to see him lying there, smiling at her.

Because George had exactly the same eyes as his brother, dark blue and sparkling.

Yes, every morning, for one split second she would stare into his eyes, and then reality would take over, and he would kiss her on the cheek.

'Good morning, Mrs Stone. Cup of tea?' he'd say, perkily, and jump out of bed, humming to himself. She'd smile and watch him go downstairs, turn on the radio, move about the kitchen, happy as anything that all was right in his world, and another day would begin again. A day of waiting for the baby, of settling into her new home, of cleaning and scrubbing and polishing.

And Margaret told herself it suited her very well.

'Good evening, Mrs Stone!'

A face loomed in at her through the kitchen window and Margaret jumped, lost in thought. She caught a flash of brown hair, blue eyes and her heart raced, then she realised it was only George.

'Hello, dear,' she said, smiling as he came in through the back door. 'Did you have a nice day?'

It was a cliché, she knew, but it was what you did.

'Not bad,' said George, kissing her on the cheek. He put his briefcase down on the chair, and carefully unwound his check wool scarf from his neck, took his coat off, shook it out and went into the hallway to hang them both up. 'Good meeting today. You know Mr Davidson wants to expand our celebrity clients division.'

'Yes, you told me.' Margaret sat down, heavily. She was interested in George's work. 'What's happened?'

'They asked me who I could think of that we might approach. And I remembered you saying Micki Martin was probably looking for someone.'

Micki Martin was a girl singer in the Joan Baez mould, the kind of long-haired, ethereal, hopeful hippy Margaret had tried to be a year ago. Micki had reinvented herself as a purer-than-pure angel after a stint working at *Amours du Derek*, where she'd been one of the more popular girls, especially skilled at putting out a series of candles with her pussy. But everyone knew she'd always wanted to sing. She was a nice girl; she'd often come into The Black Horse before or after her shift for a glass of port, like her old mum used to have back in Bury, she'd say. She'd even come to their wedding reception, and that was when she'd told everyone she had a record deal.

Margaret loved music; she loved reading about the actresses and singers in magazines, and she knew a star when she saw one – she'd had enough experience of rejection to know it. Micki Martin was the girl she ought to have been, but wasn't. She liked her, too, so when George had mentioned this new initiative at work, Margaret had said he ought to find Micki, see if she had an accountant or a manager.

'She's got no one,' George told Margaret, with satisfaction. 'And the record's coming out next month. She signed with us this afternoon.'

He was beaming at her, and she couldn't help but smile back; his happiness was infectious. 'That's great, George,' she said.

George kissed his wife on the cheek again. 'It's all thanks to you, my dear. You really know your stuff, don't you?'

'Me?' Margaret looked embarrassed. 'I'm just a boring housewife these days, George. I don't know anything!'

'What a lot of rubbish.' George said jovially, as he went to the fridge. 'Couldn't do without you, my love. We're a team, aren't we? Oh, yes. It takes two, doesn't it!' She smiled, a little embarrassed – George never talked like that, really – and he looked up awkwardly and said, 'Yes. Well, have I got time for a drink before supper?'

'Of course,' Margaret said, setting the table.

George loved gin with Schweppes bitter lemon; he got through bottles of the stuff. A thick slice of lemon, lots of ice, gin up to the first knuckle of the finger, bitter lemon in afterwards. He was particular about it. As he was fiddling around making the drink, his back to her, he suddenly said, 'Oh, by the way, there's something I need to tell you.'

'What's that?' Margaret was only half listening.

'It's about Derek. He's in prison.'

Margaret dropped the knives she was holding onto the floor. They clattered loudly. 'What?' she said.

George didn't turn round. 'Yep, I'm afraid so. He's been arrested. Embezzlement.'

'Embezzling who?' Margaret said. 'What? This is – when did you find out?'

'His solicitor rang me at work,' said George. She couldn't bear how matter-of-fact he was being. 'He's just been charged. He could go down for a couple of years.'

'Prison?' Margaret felt dizzy. She gripped the kitchen surface for support. 'But – George, what did he do?'

George's expression was grim. He said, gently, 'He was given some money to expand his various businesses. By Camilla's father, Roger Sherbourne. I'm sorry, Margaret. And he ran off with it. Or at least, the businesses came to nothing, and he didn't pay the money back. They've just found him.'

The room was spinning. Margaret blinked rapidly. George turned around then. 'I'm sorry, Margaret.' He looked contrite. 'I didn't know how else to tell you.'

'It's OK,' Margaret said, trying to smile at him.

'Really?'

'Yes,' Margaret said, swallowing hard, as a rush of pain swept through her. 'It's all in the past now.' He gripped her hand. 'We took a decision, to cut him out of our lives,' she said. 'Didn't we? Turns out it was for the best.'

George nodded firmly. 'I love you, Mrs Stone,' he said softly.

'Right,' said Margaret. She took a deep breath. 'Well, if you really love me, you'd better call an ambulance.'

George leaped back, almost in horror. 'What's wrong?'

'Nothing's wrong.' She smiled at him. 'George, I think the baby's coming.'

Chapter Eleven

Chelsea Mary Stone was a big, bouncing baby, with a mass of thick, almost black hair and piercing blue eyes. Everyone said she was an exceptionally beautiful child. The neighbours said how extraordinary it was, she looked just like her father! And her proud parents nodded and said yes, it was true. Her name came from *Cabaret*, Elsie and Chelsea, and George said proudly, looking into her lavish wicker Moses basket, that she was going to be a real showstopper, just like the song.

1978 was a good year for Mr and Mrs George Stone.

Chelsea was delivered safely, and Margaret got on with being a mum, keeping organisation at the heart of everything she did, of course. She couldn't tell people what she really thought when she looked at her daughter: that often she'd stare into her huge blue eyes and think about how much this tiny baby had screwed things up. Now, when she thought of Derek, she realised how tawdry their affair had been. Derek had knocked her up in a Soho bedsit and run off with her slag of a flatmate. It was so . . . *vulgar*. She knew it was awful: she was a bad mother, blaming her daughter for messing things up, but how different it would have been if she hadn't got pregnant! She might have had her big break . . . she might be a star by now, instead of a mother, living in the suburbs. Margaret conveniently chose to forget that her shot at the big time hadn't worked out long before her pregnancy. She could only see how Derek, and his daughter, had ruined her life.

She was bewildered by her daughter's implacable will, how she would scream and refuse to be helped, and didn't do what Margaret wanted: it had been a while, now, since she'd had to cope with that, and she was used to being in control. Chelsea's big blue eyes, waving fists, chubby little arms and legs were adorable, everyone said: but to her mother, when she screamed she looked just like Derek, and Margaret had to grit her teeth sometimes. It wasn't Chelsea's fault that her father was a lying, cheating bastard who'd ruined her life. It wasn't Chelsea's fault she'd spoiled her mother's life, that every time Margaret looked at her she wanted to pour the anger she felt towards Derek onto his tiny daughter. It was just the way it was, she told herself.

And so Margaret kept her thoughts to herself and got on with it, never thinking how those feelings might affect her daughter.

Micki Martin's first single went to Number One, and that was the beginning of some golden times for George Stone. He was young, handsome and discreet. With Margaret's help, briefing him on up-and-coming stars, and their joint knowledge of the music and acting scenes from their time in Soho, he became eerily good at securing clients just before they hit the big time. Micki was the first of many, and for the company it was an extremely lucrative business strand. Within six months George had a strong list of names, and by the time autumn came around, he was bringing in more money than anyone else at the firm.

Sometimes he laughed when he thought of it, that a year before he had been living in a soulless bedsit, terrified of what he might become, the secret he tried to hide overwhelming him. That little prick Geoff Simkins, for example, where was he now? Still on the fourth floor, toiling away in Company Accounts, while his pudgy wife was by now bursting out of her cheap dresses from C&A – he noticed these things.

While he, George Stone, was on the sixth floor, given his own suite of offices and a team beneath him. Mr Davidson had invited him and Margaret to dinner in Weybridge, the sumptuous leafy suburb where they lived, surrounded by millionaires and rock stars.

He was so proud of Margaret, he could burst. She kept the house beautiful, she looked after Chelsea so patiently, even though she was a handful sometimes, he knew, and she had a head for business and an eye for spotting talent that most employees at Davidson's would never acquire. She looked good too, he supposed: almost regained her figure after the birth, and she kept herself neat and tidy, which was what he liked. Yes, all was well in his world.

But not for Margaret.

When Chelsea was several months old, Margaret realised she was missing something.

It took her a while to recognise it, and she was ashamed when she did – nice girls didn't want things like this, it was for the husband to demand it, she'd always thought. But she wanted it. She wanted sex. She was nearly eighteen, she was young, and she and George had still never really done it properly. They'd had a few failed attempts, and he'd not really bothered her after that. She thought it was because he understood what she was going through, first with the pregnancy, then with childbirth and recovery. But she was ready now: she loved George, in her own way, and she wanted that physical comfort, wanted to be closer to him, to feel that he wanted her: that was all any woman wanted, wasn't it? She didn't understand.

'I'm too tired, babe,' George would whisper, as she reached for him at night, sometimes daringly running her hand down to his crotch to feel his flaccid penis, hoping to breath some life into it.

'Not tonight, dear,' he'd say, when he turned his back on her in bed and she'd stroke his back, tracing her way gently between his legs towards his balls: Derek had loved that.

'I can hear the baby crying,' he'd said once, when she'd felt his hardness against her one morning and, tentatively, she'd started to stroke him. He'd got out of bed and strode towards the nursery, wrapping his dressing gown carefully around him, while Margaret flopped back down on the bed and watched him go.

61

Her eyes filled with sharp tears. She felt ridiculous, rejected, unattractive. Chelsea was nearly a year old now. She had proved she could do everything that was required of her: keep the house tidy, look after a baby, keep all her emotions in check, all these things that had seemed impossible. But she couldn't get her husband to touch her, hold her . . . fuck her.

And day by day, month by month, she grew more frustrated.

'Come here.' Margaret was lying on the silk coverlet over their bed, in her dressing gown. She held her arms out to her husband as he entered the bedroom.

He tiptoed towards her. 'She's fast asleep. Sleeping like a baby.' He smiled at his unintended pun, and crept into Margaret's arms.

'That's good.' She held him so his head was on her breasts, while she ran her fingers over his shoulders.

'Mm,' he said softly, as she stroked his back. 'Mm, that's good.' He sighed. 'Oh, Margaret. What a day, eh?'

'You've had a big day,' she said, continuing her rhythmic stroking. George had signed two new client presentations that day. He should be in the mood to celebrate, she thought. She had been planning for this.

Carefully, she eased herself away from him, so that she was kneeling on the bed in front of him and he was lying on his back, watching her. She put her hands to the knot of her dressing gown, her heart in her mouth. She couldn't believe how nervous she was.

'I've got a surprise for you,' she told him.

'Oh?' said George. He ran his tongue ruminatively around his teeth, like he was searching out a stray bit of food.

Her hands were shaking as she untied the sash of her gown. 'Yes,' she said, looking directly at him. George was watching her fondly, but his expression changed as the rayon silk slithered off her body to reveal what was underneath – a cream lace baby-doll nightdress that barely skimmed her pussy, with demi-cups exposing her breasts, fuller now after Chelsea's birth but still pert.

'My word,' he said, swallowing, but he made no move towards her.

'Do you like it?' said Margaret, leaning forward a little so he could see her tits. *My word?* Again, unwillingly came the thought of how Derek would have reacted; how he would have laughed with delight, his eyes sparkling, and then ripped this silly thing off her in his eagerness to have her.

But George simply stared, a strange expression crossing his face.

Margaret felt like a prostitute, having to display herself to him in this way. She hated it, but it was the last resort. Thinking about it for months, stewing on this, letting it fester – she'd realised it wasn't doing any good, and she needed to take action.

She'd bought the nightdress specially a few weeks before, and she'd been saving it for this day, in case he got the clients he wanted. Surely he'd be in the mood then?

'Do you like it?' she repeated.

That's when it happened. Her husband swallowed.

'It's lovely, dear,' he said, kindly. 'But I'm very tired.'

Ever since she'd found the note from Camilla, Margaret had worked hard to keep her emotions under control. She was terrified of the rage that lurked within her and its power. But now, kneeling in front of George in this stupid tart's nightdress, she felt something sweep over her.

'I'm eighteen,' she said, suddenly. 'George, you're twenty-eight. What . . . is this it?'

'What do you mean?' George couldn't even look at her. He was staring at the ceiling, hands folded in front of him. Rage took hold of her.

'We should be at it all the bloody time,' Margaret said. Her breasts heaved in front of him. 'Why don't you want me? Eh?' She could feel her Sheffield accent, which she worked so hard to control, coming through.

George said nothing. He just stared at her, embarrassed.

And then Margaret lost it. She slapped him. He did nothing, so she slapped him again, and suddenly she was beating him with both hands, screaming herself into a frenzy, bent over him, kicking him with her feet, and he curled up into a ball to defend himself, crying 'Margaret! What the hell . . . ? Margaret!' But he wouldn't fight back.

'You stupid fucking bastard!' she was shouting. 'Why won't you fuck me? *Why won't you just . . . FUCK ME?*'

Her hands were hitting him, scratching him, squeezing his arms, and then suddenly something inside George snapped.

He pushed her off him as she carried on waving her arms around, yelling obscenities at him. He knelt up, grabbed her by the neck, his normally calm expression replaced with one she'd never seen before, steely, determined, in the grip of something else. His eyes were blazing as he held her at arm's length by the neck as she flailed, still trying to hit him, and then he pushed her down on the bed, fumbling with his dressing gown, his sensible striped pyjamas, staring at her with his teeth gritted, nostrils flared.

She lay there, sobbing, kicking him, till he was naked, surprised at the size of her husband's erect cock flaring up between his legs, bobbing angrily in front of her. She reached to touch it, panting, but he brought her up by the neck again.

'No,' he grunted, staring at her intently. 'You have to be on all fours.'

Maggie didn't know what he meant. She'd never done it like that before, and so when George flipped her over roughly and fumbled between her legs she didn't realise what was happening until he thrust into her with a loud, strangled groan. He pulled her towards him, his hands clutching her hips, and she could feel him deep inside her, groaning, rocking against her.

He thrust harder and harder, moving one hand so it was on the back of her neck, controlling her again.

'You like that? You like that?' he was muttering, as Margaret panted beneath him, not sure what to do, how she could help him. She decided to say nothing, to let him get on with it, to enjoy the feeling of him inside her.

George's breathing grew more rapid, his muttering, the force of his hands on her body, and he carried on pushing into her, faster and faster, till she could barely support the weight of him on her, and then he exploded inside her with a bellowing cry that sounded like he was in pain.

There was a brief pause, and then he pulled out of her almost immediately.

Margaret, still on all fours, turned slowly around, then she lay down on her back next to her husband so they were side by side.

'I'm sorry,' he said. He was blinking up at the ceiling. 'I shouldn't have done that.'

'Don't be,' said Margaret. She didn't quite know what to say. 'I'm the one who should be sorry.'

'No,' said George. 'I've – it's been a long day.' Like that was an explanation.

He patted her hand, and reached for the bedside light.

'Good night, dear,' he said into the darkness.

Tears oozed down Margaret's face as she lay beside him. She'd got what she wanted, but there was something about it that unnerved her; she didn't understand what had just happened. She could still feel him inside her; she was pulsing. Soon his seed would be sliding out of her. Margaret raised her pelvis, just a little bit, and clenched her muscles. Stayed there like that till sleep eventually stole over her.

And that was how Mr and Mrs George Stone consummated their marriage.

Chapter Twelve

'Say Weybridge.'

'Wayyyy-brij.'

'What a girl! Well done!' George clapped his hands with delight at his beloved daughter. He thought Chelsea was a genius, and told her so regularly. From the pavement, Margaret watched them indulgently.

George picked Chelsea up. 'See that house there?' He pointed in front of them to a large red-brick detached house. It sat in its own grounds, with a small drive at the front and a garage. It had a gable roof and pretty lead-light windows.

'Yes.' Chelsea nodded seriously, her dark curls bobbing around her pretty, chubby face.

'Do you like it?'

'Yes!' Chelsea screamed excitedly, and her voice echoed down the quiet street. Next to her, Margaret patted her shoulder, gently. Chelsea was so exuberant sometimes.

'Well,' George told her, squatting down and looking at her seriously. 'We're going to live here, Chelsea.'

'Us,' Chelsea said solemnly, looking from George to Margaret. George took his wife's hand.

'Yes,' he said. 'You, me and' – he patted Margaret's swollen stomach – 'your brother or sister, whichever it is. Your mum is going to have another baby. We're going to be a family.'

'How?' Chelsea said.

How indeed, Margaret thought coldly. Standing next to her husband, she smiled faintly and looked up at the huge house again.

'We're going to be happy here,' George said. His hand crept towards hers; he took it and squeezed it, softly.

At first, he was right. For Margaret and George, the next few years were their happiest as a family. They moved into Bay Tree House, as their imposing home on Princess Drive was called, and a few months later Margaret gave birth to a quiet, well-behaved baby girl they named Amber.

From the start, she loved Amber, with a passion that took her by surprise. Chelsea was afraid of nothing; she walked as soon as she could, roared the house down when she felt like it. She was like her father; she looked after number one, she was fine.

Not Amber, Margaret could see that. She was small, with golden blonde hair and sweet green eyes; she smiled a lot but was quiet, as if she didn't want to cause any trouble. As she grew older, Margaret watched anxiously as little Amber let Chelsea walk all over her. She got so angry with Chelsea, pulling her off her little sister as Chelsea was often over-enthusiastic and sat on her, or tried to get her to eat worms or brush her teeth with toilet water.

Poor little Amber. Chelsea – she was fine! Derek was bloody fine, wasn't he? But Amber, even from an early age, needed someone to look out for her. A cheerleader to help her through life, and Margaret made up her mind that she would never let her down.

George's career was soaring: while the rest of the country was suffering mass unemployment, crippled by strikes, George and Margaret were doing better than ever before. It seemed that everything George touched – on his wife's advice – turned to gold. He had a whole floor to himself in the offices on Regent Street now, a subsidiary company of Davidson and Davidson that managed bands and gave them business advice, as well as handling their money. And he had never been happier at home, either. He doted on both his daughters equally, and he was a kind, considerate husband. Her fellow housewives in Weybridge told Margaret she was the luckiest woman they knew: George was the ideal husband.

I know, she wanted to tell them. *He is gentle and loving and thoughtful. We get on like a house on fire. We love our daughters. He's intelligent, he keeps himself fit and trim. He's neat, precise and tidy, like me. It's perfect. Just a couple of things though – Chelsea's his brother's child, and we've only fucked once, and that was after I attacked him. Yes, ladies. He can't get it up. Perhaps he can – just not for me.*

It was bound to happen one day, then. Just when everything was perfect. It was early April, 1983, and Margaret was indulging in some spring cleaning: housework was, increasingly, a source of great solace to her. She was the only wife on the street who didn't have a cleaner: as she told George, she wasn't too proud to do the work herself.

They had been in Bay Tree House for four years now, and it was still a place she took pride in keeping clean, presenting to the world as a sign of how far she and George had come in the world: a long way from The Black Horse and Hopkin Road, Shepherd's Bush. Outside, on the vast smooth lawn, Chelsea and Amber were playing; she could hear her eldest daughter yelling out instructions to her youngest. She was in the airy kitchen, and she turned away from the sink to watch them, their heads – one dark, one golden blonde – bent together to look at something in the grass.

And then there was a knock on the window above the sink. Margaret jumped, and looked up.

Found herself looking straight into a pair of blue, blue eyes.

'Hello, Angel,' said Derek Stone. His voice was muffled through the glass.

She stared at him. He looked exactly the same. Her heart was in her throat: she didn't know what to say. Margaret Stone, so cool, collected, in control: completely speechless.

'You forgotten me?' Derek said, smiling at her. *Oh, that smile.*

She forced herself to get it together; she cleared her throat and said, brightly, 'My goodness, this is a surprise! Come in!'

She went round the side and let him in. He came into that kitchen like he owned it, the same old swagger, the same impish grin, and he leaned forward to kiss her, but she ducked back.

'I thought you were still inside,' she said, lowering her voice, knowing she had to take charge, or else she'd lose it. He looked the same, though there were dark shadows under his eyes and his hair was even shorter than it used to be. And the smell of him: aftershave mixed with a fresh sweat, like hay – those arms, the hands, the touch of his skin on hers, the way he had made her laugh, made her cry out in ecstasy . . .

Total loss of control, that's what he represented for her.

It wasn't going to happen again.

'Time off for good behaviour.' He nodded. 'Honest. I'm a reformed man, Maggie.'

'Yeah, right,' she said, neutrally.

He ignored this. 'Got out last week. Didn't know where you was, had to do a bit of research before I found you both. I thought I'd come to see you,' Derek said, smiling at her. Then he ducked his head. 'Well, both of you. You and your *husband* – they told me it was George, is that his name?' He grinned at his own joke, but she didn't smile. 'Where is your lord and master, then?'

'George is at work, Derek,' she said firmly. 'It's three in the afternoon, where else would he be? I'll call him and let him know you're here. He'll want to see you, I'm sure.'

'Bet he will,' Derek said, trying to sound jovial. 'Yeah . . . I think I know your old man, Maggie. Strange how things turn out, innit?'

'Yes,' she said quietly, looking at him, 'it is.'

'You look exactly the same, Maggie.' He put his hand on her arm. 'Still as beautiful as ever.'

She pulled his hand away. 'Get off me.'

'I'm sorry,' Derek said. 'I just wanted to say . . . that, really. That's all. I'm sorry. I was a dick, wasn't I? I can understand if you hate me, Maggie. I've learned my lesson, that's all.'

'It's Margaret now,' she told him. 'Margaret, thank you.' She turned towards the sink, closing her eyes briefly. 'That was a long, long time ago, Derek. A lot's changed. OK?'

'I know,' he said, honestly. He put his hands in his pockets and said in a low voice, 'I'm glad. I just wondered – when I did a runner, Camilla told me you was pregnant. I presume you –'

There was a commotion at the back door, a rattling sound as someone pulled at the handle, and the clatter of small feet on the lino. Chelsea burst into the kitchen, her thick dark hair tangled into a halo round her pink face, grass stains on her knees, a smudge of dirt on her nose. She saw the grown-ups and stopped.

'Mum, *Mum!*' she yelled, her blue eyes blazing with fury. 'Amber broke my First Love doll, she pulled her arm off! Hello,' she said to Derek, curiously.

'Hello,' Derek said, watching her. 'What's your name?'

'Chelsea,' said Chelsea, wiping her nose with her hand. Margaret winced, but she couldn't move, she was transfixed.

'And how old are you, Chelsea?' said Derek, softly.

'I'm five,' said Chelsea. She added proudly, 'And three months.'

Derek stared at the little girl. He swallowed. 'Right,' he said.

Margaret slid off her rubber gloves and smoothed down an invisible crease in her pinny. She took a deep breath, looked round her perfect, spotless kitchen and down at her daughter and said, calmly, 'Chelsea, this is your uncle Derek.'

PART TWO

The Winner Takes It All

Chapter Thirteen

1992

'Come here, Roxy, give us a snog.' Chelsea's voice was deep. She cleared her throat and swaggered along the corridor like a young boy. Next to her, Amber giggled, clutching her script lightly in her hand.

'I wouldn't snog you if you were the last boy on earth, Robbie,' she said tentatively, in her clear voice.

'Oh yeah?' Chelsea growled, lunging towards her sister, who shrieked with laughter.

'Stop it, Chelsea!' she said, panting with hilarity. 'My tummy's swirling. I'm all nervous. Don't!'

'Aw. Don't be nervous, Amber!' Fourteen-year-old Chelsea Stone dropped the other script onto the floor and bounced on the hard plastic seats of the BBC rehearsal room. She stroked her younger sister's tight golden plait. 'You're definitely the best, I'm telling you. And it's a brilliant part, Roxy's ace. All them other girls, they're stupid!'

Down the corridor, a couple of other girls waiting with their mothers looked up, warily.

'Chelsea, stop getting Amber excited before her audition. Just sit still and be quiet!' Margaret Stone always seemed to be scolding her eldest daughter. 'Don't be rude. "Those other girls", not "them". Your father and I didn't raise you to talk like a guttersnipe.' She

73

paused. 'And you're not to say they're stupid, either. Amber dear, they'll be calling you in a minute. Come over here and sit next to me.'

Only a little chastened, Chelsea stopped bouncing on the chair and chewed her hair. Amber obediently got up and sat next to her mother, folding her hands neatly in her lap like Margaret had told her. They waited.

'Amber Stone?'

An amiable-looking man in his mid-thirties, in a shirt and jeans, came out of the audition room holding a clipboard.

'I'm Simon Moore,' he said. Amber, prompted by her mother, stood up smartly as he appeared, and Margaret looked with pride at her youngest daughter, in her blue and pink kilt and brushed cotton shirt with pearl buttons, dark blue tights and her beloved penny loafers, her golden-red hair in its smooth plait.

Margaret knew Simon Moore, he was definitely up and coming. He'd done some work on *Grange Hill* and other teen soaps, and he'd produced a couple of dramas, too. He was putting together a new teenage soap, *Roxy's Nine Lives*, about a girl who moves to a new town and a new school. It was to be edgy, like *Grange Hill*, dramatic, but with a bit more glamour. Everyone was excited about it; Simon had an excellent reputation for spotting new talent, and Margaret was determined Amber shouldn't miss out. She stood up too, leaving only Chelsea lounging on the hard seats, chewing on her hair and looking out of the window.

'I'm Margaret Stone,' Margaret said, briefly shaking Simon's hand. She handed him a portfolio of glossy pictures she'd paid to have taken, and a sheaf of cuttings from the local paper. *'Amber's a gem in nativity play'*, read the first.

'These are great photos, Mrs Stone,' said Simon, leafing through the studio shots of Amber. 'Wow. Very professional.'

'My husband got them done,' said Margaret. Carefully she added, 'George has a lot of celebrity clients, so he knows how important it is.'

'George?' Simon looked only half interested, and then he said slowly, 'Ah. George Stone – he's your . . . husband?'

'Yes,' said Margaret, trying not to look smug – she knew his name opened doors. Fourteen years of marriage to George, and his reputation had never been better. 'You know him?'

Simon Moore nodded. 'Right,' he said. 'Yes. I know of him, certainly. And – yes, I met him at a party once.'

He smiled, and gave Margaret a rather searching look.

Margaret didn't know what to do, so she pushed her daughter forward, momentarily flustered. 'So, this is Amber.'

'Ready to go and do your stuff, Amber?' Simon said, smiling at her.

'Of course.' She shook Simon's hand – very professional and grown-up – and they walked into the audition together.

Behind her, Chelsea suddenly stirred. 'Hey!' she called. 'Go for it, Amber!' Grinning, she stuck her thumbs up. Margaret, embarrassed, shushed her, but Amber gratefully turned round and smiled at her sister, giving her a little wave back.

Simon Moore smiled too, and looked at the girl on the hard seats as if he were seeing her for the first time, and Margaret inwardly winced.

'This is my other daughter, Chelsea. Sorry.'

Amber always looked neat, fresh as a daisy. Chelsea, on the other hand . . . Chelsea was a mess; hair everywhere, ripped jeans, awful magenta lipstick that made her look like a Goth. She was smiling now, that great big catlike smile, and Margaret was again reminded of how beautiful she was. No doubt about it. If only she'd behave like a young lady, comb her hair, keep her voice down . . . Margaret sighed, as Simon nodded, amused, at her.

'We'll see you later,' he said, and he shut the door behind Margaret and her eldest daughter. They settled back down again to wait.

Margaret was determined not to be one of those awful stage mothers. But she *knew* Amber had talent: she'd been singing since she was tiny, she was always picked for the lead in the school plays. She loved singing. She was a quiet little thing, didn't speak much, but she sang all the time. Their showbiz friends who came to Bay Tree

House would often say that Margaret and George should encourage Amber to develop her talent professionally. Otherwise, it'd be denying Amber her chance, wouldn't it?

For this audition, Margaret had spent days planning Amber's outfit, but Chelsea – of course – had refused to change out of those awful tatty jeans and jumper. Margaret prayed, silently, that Chelsea hadn't ruined her sister's chances. Everything had to be perfect, and it often wasn't when her eldest daughter was around.

Margaret remembered only too well what it felt like to fail. She had auditioned countless times in her day, only to be told she'd *almost* made it. That was the worst. *Almost. Not quite.* It was meaningless, of course. You either got the part or you didn't. There was no *almost* about it. And in Amber's case, she would do everything, everything in her power to ensure she was never an 'almost'. She had promised to look out for her youngest daughter, to make sure she never felt the rejection she, Margaret, had endured. It wasn't going to happen. Amber was just too talented.

After ten minutes Amber suddenly reappeared, and Simon was with her again. This was unusual: it hadn't happened so far with any of the other girls auditioning. Was this a good sign?

Heart beating, Margaret put down her magazine and stood up.

'How did it go, then?' she said, as Amber came and stood next to her. She directed the question at her daughter, but she meant it for Simon, and he took the hint.

'Very well,' he said, looking from Margaret to Amber. 'But I have to explain, Mrs Stone – we won't be making a final decision today till we've seen all the girls.' He paused. 'We'll call later this evening, if she gets the part.' He opened his mouth to speak again, but changed his mind.

'Right,' said Margaret. 'What does that mean, exactly? Did she get it?'

She hated the high tone to her voice, the flat Sheffield vowels that showed through when she was nervous, no matter how well she'd learned to hide them.

Beside her, Amber whispered, in mortification, 'Mum!' Affectionately, Chelsea tugged on her sister's plait.

Simon pulled on his earlobe. 'Um – I'm not sure.'

'So that's a no,' Margaret said.

'It's an "unlikely",' Simon said gently. 'I'm sorry, Mrs Stone.' He paused. 'Look, Amber's a very talented girl.'

'I know that,' Margaret said, knowing she was behaving badly, but unable to hide her disappointment. Behind her, she heard Chelsea clicking her tongue in annoyance.

'She's good, I mean it,' Simon said, and he nodded at Amber. 'Honestly. You shouldn't be discouraged, Amber. It's just we're looking for someone quite specific for the part of Roxy, that's all. She's a misfit, a bit rough around the edges.'

Amber nodded, she understood, but Chelsea wasn't having any of it. She interrupted, furious on her little sister's behalf. 'That's crap!' she said loudly, and the girls down the corridor looked up again, fascinated. Simon's head shot up and he looked at Chelsea again. She pointed at him, her face glowering with anger, colour rising in her cheeks. Her blue eyes were dark, her pupils dilated with passionate anger. 'She's a brilliant actress!'

'I'm sure –' Simon began, but Chelsea was having none of it.

'You wouldn't recognise talent if it kicked you in the bloody arse!'

'*Chelsea!*'

Chelsea put her arm round her mortified sister. 'Listen, OK? If you're too blind to see how great Amber is, you can go and—'

'*Chelsea!* That's *enough*!' Margaret was furious.

She looked at Simon, who was watching her eldest daughter with something like horror mixed with fascination on his face. 'My goodness,' she said. 'I am so very, very sorry, Mr Moore.' She grabbed Chelsea. 'You apologise. How dare you speak to Mr Moore like that?'

But Simon shrugged it off. 'Don't worry.' He grinned at the fuming Chelsea, as if he'd found the whole thing funny. 'Like I said, I'll call you again if it's good news, Mrs Stone.' He nodded at Amber. 'Thanks again, Amber. It was good to meet you.'

'We should go now.' Margaret was picking up magazines, umbrellas and gloves, stuffing them into her handbag. She put on her Burberry mackintosh, tugging the belt firmly round her waist. 'Come on, girls. Th-thank you, Simon.'

Amber obediently followed her, Chelsea behind Amber. As she walked past Simon he winked at her. Chelsea stared at him, still flushed with annoyance, and then slowly she stuck two fingers up at him.

'See ya!' she said, rudely, and then broke into a beaming smile. He watched her, transfixed, as her face lit up. They turned the corner and she was gone.

Chapter Fourteen

The Stones still lived at Bay Tree House on Princess Drive, but it was quite a different house from the already spacious one they'd moved into. There was a garage, now, a pool out the back, and they'd built over the kitchen extension to make another bedroom and bathroom. There was a button you pressed to open the gates to the small drive, and the garden was seen to once a week. It was all very tasteful, though: Margaret was obsessive about that. No trace of anything that could be thought of as *vulgar* or *flamboyant*. No, not for her. She'd recently redecorated again; she and George felt the house needed freshening up. It was so important to keep up to date.

That Saturday afternoon, after the audition, the house was empty except for Margaret. George was up in town; lately, he seemed to spend most of his time working. There was even talk of him getting a flat somewhere near Regent Street, so he didn't have to sleep at the office.

The girls had gone to see their friend Emma, who lived down the road. There were lots of suitable playmates for them in this leafy, suburban paradise, children whose parents wore blazers and spoke with posh voices and went to the opera. George and Margaret liked that. As well as the rock stars and the celebrities:

since John Lennon and Eric Clapton had moved to Weybridge in the 1970s, it had acquired an even more glamorous cachet. Lots of rich people lived there. George and Margaret liked that, too. It was good for business; it helped for George to be able to say, 'Oh yes, I live round the corner from him,' when talking about some exec at a record label.

Yes, it was all part of keeping up the right appearances. Margaret sometimes thought to herself that it shouldn't feel like an act. They'd worked hard for this life, George especially, she alongside him all the way – they'd done it together. So why did it *feel* like an act?

On this particular Saturday, Margaret was alone, and she was cleaning, which always soothed her. She'd been ruffled by the audition that morning, annoyed beyond belief that Amber hadn't got the part – she knew they'd call, to be polite and to keep in with George, but she also knew they hadn't given the role to Amber. And the way Chelsea had behaved!

Margaret stopped, duster in hand, and looked round her spotless sitting room, breathing heavily. Sometimes it all got to her. Sometimes it was all a bit too much.

She closed her eyes and inhaled, taking in the smell of furniture polish, of the lilies standing in their huge glass vase on the grand piano by the french windows that led out to the conservatory. This room summed up why it was all worth it, why she had to keep going. She stroked the freshly polished glass coffee table, and fanned out the magazines she always kept arranged on it: *Homes & Gardens*, *Country Life*, the *Radio Times* and *Harpers & Queen*. The walls were decorated in a delicate blue and cream fleur-de-lys Laura Ashley print, with a dado rail running around the middle; the sofas were cream, with tasteful blue and oatmeal cushions; the curtains were heavy blue brocade raw silk, falling to the ground. On the mantelpiece, photos of the girls in silver frames, a couple of suitable family occasions: George's surprise fortieth birthday; Amber's first day at secondary school, all very tastefully done.

No wedding photo, though. Margaret didn't think the Weybridge elite needed to know that their reception was held in a smoky, stinking pub, when she was six months pregnant with another man's child – the groom's brother's, in fact . . .

Margaret breathed in again. For some reason the knot in her stomach wouldn't go away today. She wanted a drink. 'Happy hour' used to start at six, when George got back from work, but George rarely came home before eight-thirty these days, sometimes not at all, and happy hour had crept forward for Margaret, from five thirty to five . . . It was only three o'clock, but she'd kill for a gin and tonic.

There was honestly nothing more she could clean downstairs, even Margaret had to admit it was spotless. She moved out of the sitting room, duster in hand, trying to concentrate on the springy, soft immaculate carpet, the curving, smooth, white carved banisters, anything to stop the old feeling coming back again . . .

She would go to her room.

She knew what would happen when she was up there.

It was her only real escape.

At the top of the stairs, she paused, wondering if she should go into the girls' bedrooms and have a quick tidy-up, but somehow she couldn't face it. It was the only part of the house she didn't clean every week: she wanted the girls to take responsibility for it. They weren't going to grow up to be princesses, despite their address: they'd be hard-working, responsible, polite and well-behaved.

In control at all times, like their mother had worked so hard to be.

Margaret peered round the door of Amber's room, smiling a little. Everything matched: she herself had chosen the delicate pink rosebud-patterned curtains, duvet and pillow from Marks and Spencer: there was even a matching little heart-shaped cushion that rested on top of the bed. A desk from Habitat, a neat pile of books, a wicker stationery holder: Amber always wrote to say thank you promptly. A poster of Amber's favourite band, Take That, hung in the centre of the wall, next to a series of teddy-bear cards. It was all pretty neat. She was a good girl.

Next door along was Chelsea's room. Margaret opened the door, wincing slightly before she did. She always let her elder daughter get to her, and she didn't know how to stop it. It was, as usual, a tip. The bunk beds she had begged for only created more work, two different sets of sheets to change, beds to make. Music everywhere, tape cassettes and CDs lying out of their cases – *why couldn't she just put them away?* – huge, clompy Doc Marten boots, about four different pairs, taking up half the floor space. Black tights spilling out of the chest of drawers; posters of extraordinary-looking men with eyeliner and bare chests in black and white hanging on the walls, jostling for space next to an early shot of Marilyn Monroe, voluptuous and beautiful, leaning out of a window in New York. More and more music, records lying in a pile near the door. George had given Chelsea a record player, he said it was the only way to listen to music properly, and she was very taken with this idea, spending hours lying on the top bunk bed with an exercise book, doodling pictures of flowers, writing her thoughts down, daydreaming: it made Margaret furious.

She couldn't cope with Chelsea's room today. Quietly, Margaret shut the door.

She walked past George's room to her own bedroom. She and George had had separate rooms for years. It just made sense: he got up so early for work, and he didn't like to disturb her. They had separate bathrooms too: they had the room, in their vast house, and no need for endless spare bedrooms – there was no family to visit the Stones, after all, so why not?

Shutting the door behind her, Margaret sat down on the bed. She had a TV in her room. It was a new luxury, with a video player too, so she could do her workout videos every morning, keep in shape. She flicked through the channels, but there was nothing on. She picked up a pile of the secret gossip magazines she kept upstairs, as well as the *Sun*, to tell her what was really going on, to keep abreast of the new celebrities, the gossip, the stars, who was coming up, going down. It had always been one of her greatest talents, that ability to tell George who would be the next big thing. She was still doing it, years later. But today, she'd read them all, there was nothing to interest her.

The silence in the house was deafening. Margaret got up and opened her built-in wardrobe. She was going to do it. There was a full-length mirror on the door, that opened right out. She looked out of the window: only trees.

She was almost thirty-two. It made her laugh, sometimes. She felt really young, still, as if she had the whole of her life ahead of her, and then reality would come crashing around her: no. She was Mrs Margaret Stone, married with two daughters, living the perfect life in Weybridge. What had she got to be unhappy about? Why did she feel so trapped?

Slowly, she undressed. The drop-waisted Laura Ashley sailor dress: off. The expensive soft navy loafers: off. She was standing in her sensible white lace underwear. She took that off too, and Margaret forced herself to look closely at her reflection, staring at herself, unflinching, in the mirror, examining every flaw, every blemish.

She took good care of herself. Her stomach was still flat: she worked to make sure it was. She had a few stretch marks and her boobs were a bit saggy, but apart from that, she honestly felt she could say she was just as trim as she was when she ran away to London all those years ago, aged sixteen, with dreams of becoming a star.

The cassette player was next to her. She pressed Play, and 'Killer Queen' started playing.

Slowly, Margaret reached into the back of the wardrobe and pulled out an old outfit. It was a little party dress, a tiny, shiny thing, shimmering with sequinned stripes. She'd bought it in Camden in 1976, with Derek, for some party he had that night at an underground club in Hanway Street, just off Oxford Street. Dodgy as hell it was, but what a night . . .

The dress still zipped up smoothly, over her naked body. She dug out the platform wedges that went with it: nearly two inches off the ground, strappy blue and red. She strode over to her dressing table, fumbling in her excitement; her heart was beating, she was breathing heavily now, her eyes glittering with excitement. She put on the shimmering blue powder eyeshadow she used to love back then – not the subtle taupes or creams she now wore every day. She caked her lashes in thick mascara, and slathered on some shiny pink lipgloss.

And then, the final touch – from the back of the wardrobe, a long blonde wig to cover her own neat, highlighted strwberry-blonde crop.

The music changed: 'Can't Get Enough'. Bad Company. Margaret finished adjusting the wig and stepped back to look at herself, tapping her foot rhythmically.

And she smiled. Properly smiled.

She wasn't Margaret Stone any more. She was Maggie Michaels. With the whole world before her.

Maggie could feel the music pulsing through her body. It was the soundtrack in her head, the soundtrack to the life she ought to have had . . . She put her fingers to her collar bone, touching the smooth skin, and then slowly moved her hands over her breasts, stroking them lightly, flicking the already erect nipples. One hand moved down to lift up the short shift dress, feel the curve of her still-pert bum, and she smiled at herself in the mirror again, seeing a flush creep over her neck and breasts. She moved her hand between her thighs, stroking the coarser hair there, touching herself, while the other hand rhythmically squeezed her breasts. She bit her lip, as pleasure started to take her over . . . as she touched herself more firmly, gasping in pleasure, feeling alive. She took down her pants, so they dropped around her platform boots. She spread her legs, and as she slid her fingers inside herself, she closed her eyes and let her head fall slightly back, the long hair of her blonde wig brushing her shoulders, her back. She opened her eyes again and stared at herself in the mirror and continued to masturbate – this had become a regular, guilty pleasure for Maggie and she was amazed at how easy it was for her to satisfy herself. She moved to the rhythm of the music. She came, crying out slightly, as the music pounded through her, and she

84

squeezed her wet cunt with both hands as her body was still trembling with orgasm.

'*Mum!*'

The front door slammed, and Maggie jumped.

'Mum! We're back!'

There was a thud – the sound of Chelsea kicking off her shoes, and bags being dropped to the floor.

Calmly – because she knew panicking only wasted more time – she took off the sequinned shift and the wig, kicked off the platform shoes and put on her underwear, before climbing back into her old dress. She shoved the whole outfit in her wardrobe – she'd tidy up later, no time now. Looking in the mirror, she deftly wiped off the eyeshadow and mascara with some cold cream and a tissue – she still knew how best to do it. Turned the music off, slipped the loafers back on, ran a hand through her hair and licked off the rest of the lipgloss.

'Where are you, Mum?' Chelsea yelled again.

'Emma's got a puppy!' Amber called. 'Mum, she's so cute, can we have one? *Mum!*'

She looked in the mirror. Maggie had disappeared.

'I'm up here,' Margaret called. 'I'll be right down.'

She picked up the duster lying on the bed and went out, carefully shutting the bedroom door behind her.

Chapter Fifteen

George Stone poured himself another glass of wine and turned to his youngest daughter.

'So how did it go today, sweet girl?' He smiled, partly to hide a yawn: he was very tired.

Amber looked nervously at her mother, and put down her fork.

'Um – OK I think. Not great. I don't think they want me, Dad.'

George was only partly listening.

'That's good,' he said, shovelling another forkful of lasagne into his mouth. Margaret cleared her throat, sharply.

'She was fantastic, George,' she told her husband, raising her voice slightly so he'd listen. 'She looked wonderful, and they said she was very good.'

'They're idiots, though,' Chelsea muttered.

Margaret turned to her. 'I've had enough of you today, Chelsea.'

'What's this?' George said.

'I'm afraid Chelsea behaved ever so badly,' Margaret told him, with some relish. 'She shouted at the director. Drew attention to herself. Everyone was watching.'

'I was only standing up for Amber!' Chelsea tried to defend herself, but she could hear her voice echoing in the large room. 'They were being really stupid!'

The dining room where the Stones ate every night, spaced out around the huge dining table, was big, cream and soulless. Family meals there were often stilted. Next to Chelsea, Amber gave a small smile and squeezed her sister's hand. 'It doesn't matter,' she said. 'I wasn't right for it.'

'You were,' her mother told her firmly. 'You're a wonderful actress, and a beautiful singer, Amber dear. You're going to be a star, everyone says so. He was just wrong, that's all.'

'*Exactly*,' said Chelsea triumphantly.

Margaret was passing George a dish of boiled cauliflower and broccoli, but she turned to her daughter. 'You, young lady,' she said coldly, 'need to learn to keep your thoughts to yourself. OK?'

'OK,' Chelsea muttered.

'Behave like a young lady,' Margaret continued. 'Not like . . . some little tramp on the street. You don't think about anyone else but yourself when you open your mouth, sometimes, Chelsea, and it's not right. It's embarrassing for us all.'

'That's not fair,' George said, so loudly that they all looked at him. He took the dish out of Margaret's hands, holding it to himself. 'Chelsea was just trying to tell the truth, weren't you?'

'Yes,' Chelsea said uncertainly, looking from one parent to the other. 'I —'

'Like I said, George,' Margaret's voice was icy. 'That's all very well and good, but she needs to keep her thoughts to herself.'

'No,' said George. He put his hand heavily down on the table — not smacking it hard, he was a gentle man, but firmly. 'No, that's not right at all, Margaret. I don't agree.' The girls watched, astonished. 'You have to speak your mind. Don't be rude, Chelsea, don't call people names or be offensive, I don't mean that. But you've got to be true to yourself.' He looked down at the table, at his plate, at the congealing remains of the lasagne and vegetables. 'You've got to, otherwise what have you got?'

'I don't agree,' Margaret murmured angrily. 'You're giving that girl carte blanche to behave exactly how she wants!'

'Best that way,' George said simply. 'I've been thinking that lately. Only makes things worse in the long run if you lie.'

87

And he reached out and patted his daughter's hand, then squeezed it, almost fiercely. Chelsea squeezed his hand back, confusion on her face, but her eyes shining – she loved her father, adored him, in fact. 'Thanks, Dad,' she said, raising her voice at the end so it sounded like a question.

'It's OK, love,' he said. 'You're a good girl, Chelsea darling, don't let anyone tell you different.' He looked across at Amber. 'You're both good girls, and I'm very, very proud of you. You can get down if you want.'

Chelsea and Amber, relieved to be dismissed and away from their mother's smouldering rage, ran out of the room. In a few seconds, the sound of their feet thumping on the staircase made the glasses on the table rattle. Margaret turned to her husband.

'Have you gone mad, George?' she hissed. 'Undermining me like that, in front of the girls.'

'You're too hard on her, on Chelsea,' George said. 'You always are.'

Margaret was instantly defensive. 'I'm not. She's a handful. You don't know –' she began, and then trailed off. She couldn't explain how she sometimes felt about her eldest daughter.

George gulped down the rest of his wine and poured himself another glass. 'She's a good girl.'

'Some of the time,' Margaret said, desperately. She paused. 'Do you want her to end up like your brother? Eh?'

'Derek's got nothing to do with it,' George said, weakly.

'He's got everything to do with it,' Margaret said, looking through the door to make sure no one was there. 'He's bad to the bone. What's it this time? The fourth time he's been arrested, now?'

'It was one of the bouncers at one of his clubs dealing the drugs, not him.' George closed his eyes. 'Margaret, he's not to blame.'

'I can't believe you're defending him!' Margaret's voice rose, she was glad to prove her point, glad to be right about him. 'You know he was, George, don't make excuses for him. His fingerprints are all over it, they've closed down the bloody club, after all!' She wiped her hand over her forehead, tired. 'It's just so seedy, that's all. What if one of the neighbours found out?'

'They won't,' said George.

'They might. They might! You say that, but what's to stop them? And when Amber's a star, what happens when they find all this out? Drag her name through the tabloids, rake over it all, all because of your damn brother!'

George said, with a faint glimmer of humour, 'It's Derek. He'll be fine. He's got friends everywhere, and with the amount of money he's made with all those property deals over the years, I'm sure he can afford a good lawyer, Margaret.' He glanced at her. 'I'm sure he wouldn't want you worrying about him.'

'I don't worry about him,' Margaret said, standing up and collecting the plates. 'I worry about my girls, being infected by what he's done. He's a criminal, and I don't want him anywhere near us.'

'He's my brother,' George said, firmly. 'And Margaret, my dear, that's the least of it, as you know.' He stood up too, blinking. 'I'm going to go out for a walk, stop off for a quick drink, if that's OK?'

George's quiet, measured behaviour only made Margaret more conscious of how she struggled daily to keep her true self under control. She watched her husband now, a rush of fondness overwhelming her. He worked so hard, to give them this house and all these wonderful things. He wasn't Derek. He was a good man, honest and true.

'Of course it's OK,' she said. She gave him a kiss on the cheek. 'I'm sorry, love. You're right. Enjoy your walk. See you later.'

She didn't see the expression on his face as she walked into the kitchen, preparing to wash up.

Chapter Sixteen

The phone rang over an hour later. George was still out. Margaret was in the kitchen, going over the surfaces one more time, mulling over the day's events, trying not to think about how cross she was with Chelsea, with Simon that stupid director and with George, for failing to agree with her. She could hear the girls upstairs, crashing around in Chelsea's room, shrieks of laughter piercing the silence downstairs. They were dancing to some music, she thought it might be ABBA – they were huge again, Margaret couldn't for the life of her understand why; it made her feel extremely old that she remembered them first time round. They were doing some kind of routine, she guessed, judging by the thumping sounds coming through the ceiling.

As she walked briskly to the phone, wiping her hands on her apron, the noises grew louder. Margaret looked up, annoyed, and made a loud 'shh'ing noise, which they ignored.

'Good evening,' she said, majestically.

'Oh, is that Mrs Stone?'

'Speaking,' Margaret said.

'Mrs Stone, it's Simon Moore.' There was a pause. 'From the BBC—'

'I know who you are, Mr Moore!' Margaret said, trying to control the hysteria in her voice. 'Thanks for calling!'

The noises from upstairs grew louder, and she wanted to scream. Why was she the only one in this house, in this family, who cared about Amber's future?

'Oh, call me Simon, please. Look, we've come to a decision,' said Simon, and there was something in his voice that made her lift her head, as if scenting blood, victory. She stiffened. She hadn't realised till then just how much she'd been expecting a rejection. 'Mrs Stone – we really didn't think we'd be doing this, to tell you the truth. But it's good news.'

'Good news?' Margaret whirled around on the spot, almost mad with the effort of sounding calm. 'Well, that's great to hear—'

'Look, it might take a bit of persuading, as I for one really didn't expect to cast someone like this—'

Unable to bear it any longer, Margaret interrupted. 'Simon, please let me assure you, you've picked the right person. Amber will do a wonderful job! Oh, thank you!'

There was another pause. And then Simon said, 'Mrs Stone, I'm afraid I haven't explained myself very well.'

'What do you mean?' she said sharply.

'We're not giving the part of Roxy to Amber. We'd like to offer it to Chelsea.'

'Chelsea?' Margaret almost staggered with the shock. 'But you – you barely met her.'

'I saw enough, to be honest. I knew straight away, something just clicked. She's got everything.' Simon's voice was warm, excited: she wished he was there so she could kick him in the balls. 'She's got that spark that Roxy needs. She's tough, gorgeous, mouthy, she's vulnerable, she's totally compelling to watch. I've already talked to some other people here about it. I want to get her on film next week, show them what I've seen.'

Margaret was still reeling. 'Are you *sure*?' she said.

Simon sounded solemn. 'D'you know what?' he said. 'I've never been surer about anything. She's just got "it".'

'"It"?' she repeated, dully.

'Yes, I don't know what it is. She's great. Chelsea's going to be a star, Mrs Stone. I can guarantee it.'

This was all wrong. *All wrong.* Slowly, Margaret climbed the stairs to Chelsea's bedroom. She could hardly bear it. Poor Amber. Her heart twisted. She paused outside the door to listen to them singing along to 'Fernando', and tears filled her eyes. Chelsea was completely out of tune, singing wildly all over the notes and doing stupid impressions. But Amber's clear, sweet tones rang out – even at only twelve, she had a rich, beautiful voice.

How could this have happened? *How?*

Gently, Margaret opened the door.

'Hello girls,' she said.

They jumped at the sight of their mother. Chelsea stopped singing, and stood very straight. Amber smiled, waving her in, and Margaret wondered at the two of them, how she'd managed to make her eldest daughter nervous of her, driving a wedge between the two sisters.

'Hey Mum, come in, sit down, we're singing along to ABBA and Chelsea's being so funny, she—'

Margaret put out her hand, to make her be quiet. 'I need to tell you something, girls.' She felt like a criminal. 'Not a big deal, but I just got off the phone with Simon Moore.' She couldn't bear the look in Amber's eyes, the nervousness, the hope, the shining excitement. She turned to Amber. 'Listen, love. You didn't get the part.'

'Oh,' Amber said. She rubbed one eye with her hand. 'It doesn't matter, Mum. I didn't think I'd get it. He was more interested in Chelsea than me, I could tell.' She smiled at her sister.

Damn it! Margaret gritted her teeth.

'That's just it.' She smiled. 'I – yeah. It's just that – they want her to have the part.'

'Who?' Amber looked confused.

'Chelsea,' Margaret muttered.

'What?' Chelsea said behind her. But Margaret carried on looking at her youngest daughter. She stroked her cheek. 'I'm sorry, sweetheart.'

Amber's face was white. She swallowed, and suddenly burst into tears.

'I'm sorry,' she wept. 'Sorry, Mum . . .' Her little voice was heaving with sobs. 'But it's not fair . . . why didn't they want me? Why did they want Chelsea? She didn't even audition! I don't – I don't understand.'

Margaret watched her youngest daughter and felt as if her heart was breaking. She'd promised to protect her, to secure the stardom for Amber that had eluded her, and it was all going wrong.

Chelsea was standing stock still in the middle of the room, and Margaret was overcome with contempt for her. Her hair was straggly, her hands dirty with biro, her T-shirt filthy – she didn't look like a star, she looked like a tramp. In fact, she looked like Derek, the night he'd come running into the pub . . .

'I don't understand either,' she said, after a moment. 'How come I got it?'

How come indeed, I don't know. Margaret knew she had to be honest. 'Simon was very impressed with you this afternoon. He said you showed the spark they wanted for Roxy. He said you were great. Not what they were looking for' – she couldn't resist saying this – 'but absolutely right for the part now they've made their minds up.'

'It's wonderful, Chelsea,' Amber managed. 'Well done – you deserve it!'

And then her small face crumpled, and she burst into tears again.

'Oh, Amber,' Chelsea said, rushing to hug her. 'Please don't cry! It's so stupid, they don't know what they're doing, you'd be much better!' She squeezed her sister tightly against her. 'I don't even want to be an actor, you know that!'

At this, Amber's sobs grew louder.

'Get out, Chelsea,' Margaret said. 'You're only making things worse.'

Stunned, Chelsea left her room. She looked back, to see her mother cradling the sobbing, heartbroken Amber, crying as if her life depended on it. Chelsea watched them for a second or two.

'It's OK,' Margaret was whispering. 'It's all right, my darling. You didn't want this part anyway, did you? You're going to be a star, I promise. I know you are. It's going to be OK.' She was rocking her backwards and forwards, crooning softly. 'I'll make sure of it, don't you worry. You're going to be a star, baby girl, please don't cry.'

Slowly, Chelsea shut the door and walked away.

She sat in the middle of the big, cream-carpeted staircase, listening to her sister's muffled sobs in the otherwise silent house. It was huge, and she felt tiny, still insignificant despite this news, and she felt terrible for poor Amber. She wondered where her dad was. She wished he was here, so she could share how she was feeling with him. She was going to be playing Roxy, she was going to be starring in her own TV series! Her, dumpy, ungainly Chelsea . . . surely it must be some kind of mistake?

She gave a little giggle, still unable to believe it, and hugged her knees. Her eyes shone in the darkness, and she could feel a worm of happiness slithering through her. Something was waking up in her, something she hadn't even known was there. All her life Chelsea had been used to being in the way, and now she had won something.

Yes, she knew Amber was devastated, yes, she knew her mother was furious, and that she'd be paying for both these things for some time. But she couldn't help herself.

They'd chosen *her*. That Simon Moore – she'd liked him, annoying though he was. He'd noticed *her*.

For the first time in her life, Chelsea Stone felt the buzz of being at the centre of things, instead of always on the sidelines, watching her sister, her father's clients, the other prettier, cleverer girls at school. It was a huge, unexpected thrill . . . and she loved it.

And in that moment, Chelsea Stone knew she would do anything she could to stay right there, in the centre of things. She was going to be a star. She knew it.

Chapter Seventeen

1997

ROXY'S NINE LIVES ARE UP

News from the BBC is that *Roxy's Nine Lives* – the teen drama that launched Chelsea Stone on the path to fame, fortune and some wild, wild behaviour – is to be axed, after five years. Simon Moore, the director, said yesterday:

'We've had a great five years on *Roxy's Nine Lives*, but all great things must eventually come to an end. We've launched some wonderful new careers, too. Everyone's aware of the one and only Chelsea Stone, of course, who simply *is* Roxy, but there's also Gary Knox, who played her brother Bags and of course the marvellous Frank Lanchester as the headteacher, Mr Wells. We're all going to be sad to see it end, but there are some exciting new projects being lined up – including a replacement for *Roxy*'s teatime slot which the BBC will be announcing shortly.'

Everyone knows Chelsea Stone, of course, who as Roxy Jones gave parents nightmares at teatime. The programme became must-see TV, with children begging to be allowed to watch the often scandalous but always gripping story of Roxy's travails. Abortion, drug addiction, lesbianism, domestic abuse – *Roxy's Nine Lives* tackled

---

them all during its five-year run, and Chelsea Stone was at the heart of it, giving a devastatingly raw, compelling and sassy performance, shot through with honesty.

But what's next for 19-year-old Chelsea? Rumours of stardom going to her head and her wild partying are common knowledge, and the question on every TV exec's lips is: can she step out of the shadow of Roxy? Is she a lifelong talent or another child star who's burned out too soon? Only time will tell . . .

'Do it again, Chelsea.'

'OK, OK.' Chelsea cleared her throat, trying to ignore the throbbing pain in her head. She felt like shit and she was amazed it wasn't more obvious. Couldn't they see she was sweating? That the alcohol was probably oozing out of her pores, toxic and sour?

'Ready?'

Fuck it. Fuck 'em all. She didn't care. 'Yes! For God's sake, let's just get it over with.'

They were on the set for the Joneses' house, and Gary, who played her little brother Bags, was sitting on the threadbare sofa. It had been deliberately distressed when *Roxy's Nine Lives* first started but was now almost worn through with years of the cast sitting on it, not just during working hours but later, too, when they'd crack open the beers and wine after shooting was finished. Chelsea had almost lost her virginity on that sofa, to the assistant director, Paul, the previous summer, after the wrap show for series four . . . They'd done it later anyway, in the props cupboard.

And now it was almost over. Chelsea looked down at the tattered script one more time. She shifted impatiently, blinking hard to suppress the emotion she was trying not to feel as the make-up lady powdered Gary's greasy nose, her cork-soled wedge shoes cutting into her bloated feet. Perspiration pooled between her plump breasts; she was almost dizzy. Simon raised his hand.

'Action.'

BAGS
(Looking up in alarm)
'Roxy, what you saying?'

ROXY
'I'm saying, maybe it's time for Roxy Jones to live her own life
for once. Get out there, see the world . . .'
She gazes off, apparently unseeing, into the distance.

BAGS
'You ain't serious.'

ROXY
'I am. School's over, and it weren't all great, but it was some of
the best times of my life. Now it's over, and you know what?
I'm sick of being treated like a child. I'm nearly a woman. I
wanna see what's out there for me.'

BAGS
(Hesitating)
'We're really gonna miss you, Rox.'

ROXY
'I'm gonna miss you too, Bags. I love you, you know that, don't
ya? But yeah . . .' (*Pauses. Raises her chin, looks defiant.*) Look out
world. Roxy Jones is coming.'

THE END

'That's it!' Simon's voice came out of the darkness. 'Absolutely
brilliant.'
   'God, she's good,' one of the assistant directors muttered. (Paul
had been fired a few months after their affair, after it was discovered he'd popped the cherry of the Beeb's biggest – and most
volatile – child star.) 'Isn't she? Great bit of acting.'
   'She is good,' said Simon, taking off his headphones. He shook

his head. 'Damn, she really is.' Under his breath he said, *But that wasn't acting. That was really her.*

He started clapping as he walked past the cameras, his lanky frame suddenly appearing on the brightly lit set, and came over to a shaking Chelsea. 'You're all done now, Chelsea my dear. Time to give that hangover the attention it deserves.'

'It's your fault, Simon,' Chelsea said, her voice muffled, as he pulled her into a hug.

'You were the one drinking absinthe,' Simon said, squeezing her shoulder. 'You've only got yourself to blame.'

'Get off.' Chelsea pulled away from him crossly – lately, he'd noticed, she took criticism less and less well. He tried not to smile, but she did look pretty rough. Her dark hair was deliberately messed up, for the part of Roxy, her make-up heavy under the lights, but underneath it she was pale and trembling, a couple of spots blooming under her foundation, dark circles beneath her eyes.

This was not her first hangover. Not by a long stretch. For a nineteen-year-old girl, Chelsea Stone had done a lot of living. Simon couldn't help but wonder which way she'd go next.

Simon Moore had worked with a lot of child actors, but Chelsea was different. She wanted the limelight, wanted it more than anything, to a degree Simon found alarming sometimes. She loved being the centre of attention, the camera on her, the focus solely Chelsea Stone. It was when she was most truly herself, he sometimes thought. When he'd first known her, off-screen she'd been funny, self-deprecating, joyful, full of ideas and jokes and enthusiasm. And then the camera would come on her, and just like that she'd snap to attention, something in her face would change completely, an intensity came over her; it was as if she was intoxicated by the camera.

Lately, though, it was different. She'd grown out of her awkward teenage phase, as it was called, though Simon had always found her charming, great fun to have around, even if she was mouthy, a pain, hugely ambitious. These days, it had been replaced with something more sinister. She drank a lot; she was always out with someone from the cast and crew and the press had started to catch onto it. 'TOXIC ROXY' had become a bit of a heroine to the red-tops, always providing them with a news story when things were slow.

He patted Chelsea's arm.

'Hey, Chels. Listen to me. I heard about a part yesterday. It sounds perfect for you.'

It was a new drama, for ITV, about a group of prostitutes in Liverpool, and there was a role for Chelsea if she wanted it, the young girl from a children's home pimped out at an early age who's now desperate to make a better life for herself. It was a small part, but crucial, and at the heart of the story. Plus it would show everyone that Chelsea Stone was a grown-up now, that she'd left the teen stuff behind. Personally, Simon longed to see what she could do with it.

As he told her about it, he could swear he saw a light flickering in her eyes.

'What do you think?' he said, finally.

'No,' Chelsea said, petulantly. She stalked over to the corner of the set. Simon followed her.

'No? Chelsea, it's a great part.'

'I said no.' She picked up her bag, slung it over her shoulder and tossed her hair. She was still so young, he had to remind himself of that. 'I don't want to act any more, I told you. Anyway, I'm off now.'

'Chelsea, you can't just go.' He tried to sound firm. 'You're being childish. Cutting off your nose to spite your face – this is a great part.'

'I'm meeting the others in the pub.' She was fighting back the tears. 'Just leave me alone, Simon.'

'That's stupid.' Simon forgot himself for a moment; her blue eyes flashed fire at him. 'Sorry Chelsea, but you're mad. You've got the potential to be an amazing actress. This could be the perfect stepping stone for your career. I'm serious.'

'Oh, piss off,' she said.

'Listen to me, Chelsea!' He wanted to shake her, he was so frustrated. 'It's such a waste.'

She was standing in the threshold of the studio; the black paint was flaking off the woodchip door. Casually, Chelsea picked off a chunk and flicked it away with her fingers. She cast a lingering look round the studio and just shrugged.

'You only gave me the part as a fluke anyway.' He stared at her; did she really think that? He'd never met someone who had so much confidence and so little self-belief.

'That's rubbish,' Simon said. 'And you know it.'

He knew she was bluffing. He could see it in her eyes. But her teenage pride was too strong, and he knew he'd lost her. She shrugged again.

'It's their loss. If they liked me so much they shouldn't have cancelled the bloody show.' She sniffed. 'I really got to go. Hair of the dog for the hangover, that's what I need.' She reached up and kissed him on the cheek. 'Thanks for everything, mate.'

And she walked out, her bag slung casually over her shoulder, tossing her hair as she went.

Simon watched her go. He had to admire her bravado, but he felt very sad. He'd always thought Chelsea was a fighter. Perhaps he'd been wrong about her, after all.

He walked back to the director's chair, the studio almost deserted now. He thought of that first meeting at the audition, over five years ago now. Simon wondered what her parents made of it all. He'd always felt Margaret Stone had never forgiven him for casting Chelsea and not Amber. And as for George Stone: Simon liked the man, respected him a hell of a lot, not least because he clearly adored his eldest daughter, and to see them together was a joy – their banter, the light that came on in his otherwise rather dead eyes. But along with much of media London, he knew George's little secret. Did his wife know? he wondered, idly. He was pretty sure the tabloids knew, but George's powerbase was incredibly strong, almost impenetrable. He couldn't stop photos of his daughter appearing in the *Sun*, falling out of her tight sequinned boob tube, but he'd managed somehow to get them to conceal the little fact that Toxic Roxy's dad used rent boys on a regular basis.

He frowned. It all seemed wrong, somehow; George was such a nice man, and his daughter was nothing short of a star. That talent! To see it go to waste, that was what annoyed him the most. He'd thought with a mother like that behind her, Chelsea would have gone far . . . He thought of Margaret, and frowned. The truth was, she'd always been much more obsessed with that little sister, the quiet one – Amber.

Perhaps she was right. Simon sat down heavily in the chair, looking at the now deserted set of Roxy's sitting room. He had heard through the grapevine that there was a lot of buzz about Amber these days. She'd been in some cheesy near-paedo girlband, Frou Frou. They'd had one Top Ten number and then vanished without trace. But a couple of people had told him the record company was grooming her for a solo career. She could definitely sing, he'd heard her at Chelsea's eighteenth. She was shy, for sure, but when Amber Stone got up on stage and sang, she seemed like a different person. He wondered if she could be like that in real life, too. She was special, there was no denying it.

He shook his head. It'd be funny, wouldn't it, if little Amber ended up being the really famous one, after all . . .

Chapter Eighteen

He hated bloody Elton John. Hated him for the way he thought it was OK to be that way. As the traffic on the M25 slowed to a crawl, George fiddled with the radio station impatiently; they were playing 'Candle in the Wind' again, and he didn't want to hear it. Usually he liked listening to Capital, liked keeping up with the latest pop music, hearing what the DJs were playing to death, who was hot and who was not. Even after all these years, he was still as passionate about the business as ever.

But something had changed, lately. Somehow it all seemed to have got a bit harder. Business wasn't as good as it had been, and George Stone didn't know why. He was losing his touch, and losing money, more than he'd like, and he couldn't seem to get back on track, either. He knew he was the best manager in the UK. It just came naturally to him. He was great with numbers and had a very astute business sense and a creative flair.

But he got no thrill from it any more. Got no thrill from anything, apart from one thing, and it disgusted him still as much as always. He hated himself more than ever.

The old pain stabbed between his eyes. It was getting dark; it was September, and the nights were drawing in already. It was cold; he thought he should have gone through Richmond instead, this was taking ages. Dammit . . . George rubbed the bridge of his nose, wishing he was back at home already, a whisky in his hand, the day behind him, temptation avoided . . .

But what was there for him at home? All these years of working his socks off, and he'd come back to a vast house that never really felt like home to him, much as he'd tried, much as he was proud of what Margaret had done, grateful to her for how she kept it. But Margaret and Amber were away, recording in Sweden with some hotshot producers the record company were convinced would break her through to the big time.

George had heard a couple of the tracks; they were fantastic, he knew it. And Amber was a good girl, he thought fondly; a bit shy, always in the shadow of other people, but she'd find her own feet soon enough. She worked hard, she had a sunny, uncomplicated nature . . .

That pain again. How could he have created something so beautiful, so pure, when he was so vile, so disgusting?

The traffic was almost at a standstill. Here was where he'd start to think about turning off at the next exit, a notorious spot, giving in to what he wanted. George breathed deeply, trying to stay calm. He missed Chelsea, too, that was the problem. He would never admit it, but a lot of the joy had gone out of his life when, nearly two years ago, she'd moved out of Bay Tree House and found a flat in London, off Ladbroke Grove.

Margaret had been horrified, but George had agreed with Chelsea that she should move out, even though it broke his heart. She was wilful, independent – his beautiful, talented daughter. He loved her with a deep ferocity he could never claim to feel for his wife and biological daughter, though he never thought of his girls in that way, never admitted any of this to himself, like so many other things in his life.

Chelsea was a companion to him; they had the same sense of humour, liked the same US sitcoms, read the same books, they both drank whisky and liked red wine. He would meet her for dinner and they'd walk through the streets of London together, him pointing out the old landmarks, The Black Horse, his old flat in Marylebone, the Italian deli on Brewer Street, the only place back then you could get decent olive oil . . . Chelsea loved Soho in particular. Just like her father. In fact she was so like her father, it was a curious mixture of exquisite pleasure and pain to George. She looked just like him, behaved just like him — with a rod of steel from her mother running through her. George was incredibly proud of her.

He hadn't managed to mess that up, at least. One thing.

They were playing the Spice Girls now; George flicked off the radio, teeth gritted.

When had it suddenly become OK to be the way he was? Why couldn't he even say the words, why was he so fucking screwed up and repressed about it? Was it the years he'd spent building up layers to protect him against what he felt was the guilty truth? And then, all of a sudden, the walls had come down for everyone else, old friends of his were suddenly announcing left, right and centre that they were gay: film stars, pop stars, TV presenters, even their neighbour in Weybridge, a retired judge, had recently revealed he was leaving his wife and moving in with his boyfriend, for God's sake.

And old Georgy-boy was left fumbling desperately in toilets, furtively paying some boy to wank him off, crying with shame afterwards at the secrecy, the deception, how he felt no one could ever love him again if they knew what he was really like.

But George had made a decision, since Margaret and Amber had left for Sweden. At first, he'd been looking forward to them leaving, knowing he could indulge himself a bit more than usual; there was a sauna off Oxford Street he was partial to, he knew the best places to get what he wanted, the lay-bys on the main roads home where he could pull over if he wanted.

And then he'd realised it had to stop. He had to stop living this double life: no more. Apart from anything else, it was only half what he wanted — he wanted sex with men, but he also wanted companionship with them, a relationship, love, friendship — and he didn't get that from the glassy-eyed boys who sucked him off, let him bend them over and fuck them, wank over them as he came with cries of ecstasy mixed with shame, shame at how young they were, bored they were, how wrong he felt. Sometimes he really did just want to talk to them, and they were even more disdain-ful then; they wanted the money, they didn't want to engage their brains with these sad, pathetic middle-aged married men living double lives . . . So George had made a vow. No more. It was so easy, while he was alone, to get what he wanted when he wanted it, and it had to end.

Either be brave, leave Margaret, live the life he'd always wanted, or be a coward, carry on with his Weybridge existence. Work hard, take comfort in his daughters and his wife and his beautiful home.

He'd picked the latter. And he was going to stick with it. Yes, he was.

And then he saw him.

Standing by the side of the road. It was a lay-by he'd used before, where he'd got what he wanted in the bushes off to the side, labouring heavily over someone, silent, apart from grunting, sweaty, anonymous sex, the thought of which could make him hard for weeks afterwards. It was dark by now, and he could just make out the shape on the side of the road; it made him swerve, the flash of white T-shirt in the headlights.

George pulled over and rested his head on the steering wheel for a moment, and then he looked up and almost laughed with relief. This wasn't his type, this almost teenage boy, with his big dark eyes and furtive, sad face streaked with grime and tears.

'Hey,' he called, as he got out of the Mercedes. 'You nearly gave me a heart attack. Are you all right?'

Chelsea was having trouble focusing. She knew her wallet was in there somewhere, but she couldn't find it. 'Lanagastahro,' she called.

'Darlin', I don't understand a bleeding word you're saying.' The black cab driver was not fond of drunk people in his cab. 'Either you tell me where you wanna go, or get the fuck out of my cab. Got it?'

'Lanagastahro!' Chelsea said, more loudly. 'It's off Ladrook Gro . . .' She lolled against the seats as the cab lurched violently round a corner. 'Can you go more slowly please,' she asked him, imperiously. 'It's very fast.'

'Do you mean Lancaster Road, off Ladbroke Grove?' the cabbie said. '"Cos if you do, say it properly, else you're out on your ear, OK?'

Stupid wanker. 'Yes I do. Thanks.'

Left in silence as the cabbie swore under his breath, Chelsea slumped miserably down against the leatherette. She was drunk again, drunker than she'd meant to get, but they'd all been drowning their sorrows at a pub in the backstreets of Shepherd's Bush, near the BBC's White City studios. The hours she'd spent there . . . grown up there, really, and now it was all over.

The cab drove violently over speed bumps. She was sure he was doing it deliberately. Chelsea stared out at the anonymous houses, trying not to think about being sick. Her mum had lived somewhere round here, in a flat, when she'd first come to London, she knew. Chelsea tried to distract herself by wondering where it might be; she knew very little about her mother, she kept her past life to herself. It was just before she met Dad. They'd got married within the year, she knew that too; she knew her mother was pregnant with her. She was always rather tickled by the idea that her staid old dad couldn't keep it in his pants, had knocked prim and proper Margaret Michaels up. But she found it hard to imagine, if she was honest.

They were driving back into town, towards Ladbroke Grove. Chelsea could feel the cheap white wine she'd been drinking all night swimming around in her stomach; that and the tequila shots she'd done with Brian, the props guy, and Gary, who had been all over her like an octopus now his role as her brother was over. Fucking loser, Gary; she'd told him to fuck off, when he'd tried to put his arm round her, had pushed him off the seat onto the floor, and everyone had laughed. Good old Chelsea, life and soul of the party, drunk as a skunk and twice as much fun . . .

She stared blankly down at her lap, noting with disgust her – as she saw them – fat thighs, splayed out on the sticky leatherette seat. Who'd want her? She thought of Amber, perfect, blonde, polite Amber, with her bell-like voice and sweet manners, her slim, gorgeous figure, pert little breasts; that was what they wanted, now. Whereas she was washed-up, overweight, a stupid, ugly teen star with nothing to show for her years of fame.

Desolation washed over her, and she wished she were at home with a drink in her hand. She reached for her mobile phone; she'd just got her first one. She could call Brian; she'd been sleeping with him, in a half-hearted way, but Brian was married and lived in Loughton, Essex, and was probably on his way home . . . She put the phone down. She felt shame, as she always did, that she used people like him to distract her from the emptiness of her own life.

Anyway, she had long grown sick of him, sick of his red face with his greying hair flopping over her as she lay underneath him, desperately wishing he'd touch her, make her cry out, rather than just pumping inside her with an expression of ecstasy on his face, unable to believe he was fucking a nineteen-year-old, let alone the nineteen-year-old Chelsea Stone.

Tears filled her eyes. She felt desperately alone. And then, for some reason, she thought of her dad, her darling dad, and her heart leaped again. She'd go and see him. Amber and Mum were away, he'd be lonely. They could console each other; Chelsea often felt she was only happy when she was with her dad. He never judged her, always praised her, laughed at her jokes. He was the perfect companion.

She leaned forward, suddenly feeling a bit better, less drunk.

'Sorry, there's been a change of plan. Can you take me to Weybridge, please?'

The cab driver sighed. 'Look, love—'

Chelsea interrupted. 'If you don't want to, I'll get another cab.' He looked in the rear-view mirror; she was upright, eyes blazing, hair tumbling down her back; there was something familiar about her, who was she? Someone famous, he thought, scary, too.

She was waiting for an answer. He said, promptly, 'It's fine. Where you going, love?'

'Princess Drive. Weybridge.'

Chelsea sat back. Feeling happy for the first time in days, as the cab turned around, and headed for the suburbs.

Chapter Nineteen

'And when he found out I was gay, he beat me. Threw me out.'
The boy's bony fingers were wrapped around a cup of tea. George
nodded, sympathetically.

'And that's why you ran away from Glasgow, to escape your
stepdad?'

'Aye,' the lad said. 'And I don't care what happens now. Except
I'm away from all that, away from him. Bastard.'

'Didn't your mum care?' George was hugging himself, watching the young boy as he opened up, relaxed a bit more. They were
back at Bay Tree House, downstairs in George's 'den', his office in
the basement where he sometimes slept, had clients round to
brainstorm. It was a cosy room with a small kitchen set-up, a deep
well-worn leather sofa, a beautiful antique desk and a computer,
wall to wall shelves of books and CDs, and framed posters of his
clients. It was his space, untouched by Margaret's influence. He
even cleaned it himself; he felt totally at home here, like nowhere
else in the house.

'Mum? She didn't give a fuck, once she'd got herself a new
man,' said the boy.

'That's awful.' George wanted to reach forward, give him a hug,
but he didn't want him to get the wrong message. There was a
look in his young, dark eyes that he didn't like: could he tell

George's secret? It seemed mad, when George used that lay-by to get what he wanted, to be afraid of being found out.

But he'd brought Gavin into his home, they'd crossed a line, and it was vital now that secrecy was preserved.

Yet he couldn't have left him there, terrified, by the side of the road. He'd hitched down from Scotland and got as far as Staines, when he'd accepted a lift from a man who'd turned out to be 'a fucking perv'. Gavin had given him the slip when he'd pulled over in the lay-by and waited in the bushes till it was dark; when George saw him, it was nearly night and he hadn't eaten for twenty-four hours, didn't know where he was going to stay, what he was going to do.

Perhaps, George told himself, he shouldn't have helped him, but how could he leave him there, this vulnerable young thing, with enormous eyes and a shy, knowing smile that also seemed to say that its owner was aware of his own charms? George didn't go for young men, really, though in the course of his secret amorous adventures they were most often the ones who'd do it for money.

This one, though, made him feel protective. There was something about him that reminded him of Margaret, when they'd first met, when she'd just decided to stop being Maggie, though a delightful hint of ethereal wonder would peek through her armour now and then. She'd been so young, so vulnerable, soft: when, he wondered distractedly, had she become so hard?

George shook his head; he was tired, it had been a long day and the journey home was only adding to his fatigue.

'Nice place you've got here,' Gavin said. He took a sip from the whisky he'd been given. 'You sure it's OK for me to stay for the night?'

''Course it is,' George said robustly. 'My wife's away—'

'Oh, it's like that, is it.' Gavin smiled. 'And here's me thinking you weren't like all the rest, George. Shame on you.'

'Don't be ridiculous.' George was aware he sounded like a schoolteacher, blustering and pompous. 'It's not like that, not at all.'

'What is it like, then?'

And then Gavin walked towards him.

Very gently, he ran his finger over George's crotch, searching his flaccid penis out. He stared into George's eyes.

'I'd like to say thank you, that's all.'

His practised fingers gently groped at George's groin, and their eyes met as his cock hardened, almost immediately.

'Gavin.' George pushed him away. 'It's not like that. As I say.' He leaned against the sink. 'Really.'

And yet it was . . . He was so lonely, all he wanted was some human contact, really. The touch of someone else's hands on his body. Strong, male hands on his body . . . He closed his eyes. *No . . .*

'I don't believe you,' Gavin said. 'I think it is like that. You're ever so buttoned-up, aren't you, George?' He said it gently, kindly, and now his fingers were stroking the hard length of him as George struggled for breath.

Who was this boy, that he felt he had to say thank you like this? George shook his head, with one last desperate attempt to resist. 'You don't have to do this,' he said weakly.

'But I want to,' Gavin said. 'You're a nice man.'

A nice man. What a joke.

As Gavin sank to his knees, slowly, still watching George's face, he opened his trousers, reached into his neatly pressed striped boxer shorts where George's erect penis was straining to escape, and tugged it gently through the vent. The touch of his skin on George's was almost unbearable, and George sagged against the sink, as Gavin slowly put his wet lips against his cock and slowly, surely, sank his mouth over his thick, long shaft.

'Oh my God.' George choked the words out. He was in his own den at home, it was horrible, it was wrong . . . It was amazingly, incredibly good, had never felt as good as this! 'Oh. My. God.'

Gavin looked up again and smiled. He took him out of his mouth long enough to say,

'Don't come in my mouth. I want you to fuck me, too.'

110

He held him with one hand, cupped his balls firmly with the other, and started moving his head up and down, and George could do nothing else but give in to it . . .

As she sobered up more, Chelsea changed her mind about going to her dad's. Perhaps she should just go home, get some sleep, she'd feel better in the morning. But she'd already pissed the cabbie off enough, she thought if she told him to turn back again he'd probably deck her, or chuck her out in the middle of nowhere. So she stared out of the window, willing the journey to go faster; it was a long way to Weybridge, mentally and geographically.

When she arrived at Princess Drive, Chelsea took a minute to straighten herself up, make sure she didn't appear as lousy as she felt. The cold night air had hit her – she was still much drunker than she realised.

Her dad's car was in the drive, his natty Mercedes. Her heels crunched on the gravel as she walked to the front door, trying to stay steady, looking for signs of life; there were none. A light was on in the hall, but that was it. She let herself in, stumbling slightly over the threshold.

'Dad?' she called out, hating the sound of her too loud, harsh voice in the echoing silence of her childhood home. 'Dad, you there?'

She listened, but there was no reply, and then she heard something – music, coming from the basement. Of course, he was down in his den, working on something. Dad.

Chelsea walked towards the cupboard under the stairs, opened the door, the music getting louder as she did, Dusty Springfield . . . he loved Dusty.

At the bottom of the stairs there was a warm light, and she started to descend, gingerly. 'Dad?' she called again. She was sure she could hear something, someone?

And then she was at the bottom of the stairs, and something wasn't right. She stared blearily ahead of her, trying to take it all in. The music rang in her ears. There were clothes scattered everywhere. Her dad – her dad, naked, bent over someone, his back to her, what was he doing, what were those noises?

Her first thought in her drunken haze was that her dad was being attacked, that there was a burglar in the house . . .

She looked again, squinting, her heart in her mouth. Saw what was happening. That was her dad, having sex with another man.

George was grunting, the man underneath him was crying out, the two of them were moving in unison.

Then George looked up.

His face was covered in sweat. He stared at his daughter, his eyes dark, expressionless. She stared back at him. And she screamed, but no sound came out.

Chelsea carried on screaming. She ran up the stairs. Vaguely she could hear her dad calling her name. 'Chelsea! Come back! Chelsea!' He was running after her, she could hear his feet tramping loudly on the rickety stairs back up from the den.

She wasn't going to be sick. She just had to get out of there. *Now.* She raced into the hall, he was coming after her, she couldn't bear to see him. What could she do? The car keys to the Mercedes were lying on the pristine mahogany hall table. Desperately, Chelsea grabbed them, headed out into the drive. The night air again . . . She fumbled with the keys, climbed into the car. In the wing mirror she saw the outline of someone illuminated by the porch light. She revved up and sped away, screeching down the drive.

It was only three minutes since she'd entered the house.

Tears streamed down her face as Chelsea tried to breathe properly, but she couldn't. She was too drunk to be driving, she knew it. She was going too fast, she knew that too, but she had to get away, had to be as far as possible away from that place, from the sight of her naked dad, pumping backwards and forwards over some boy. The look in his eyes as he saw her . . .

Nothing would ever be the same. Chelsea looked at the clock.

Only forty? She needed to go faster, to get back to town, away from this!

The last thing she remembered was the car spinning out of control. She knew she was going to crash. She knew it, and there was nothing she could do about it.

Chapter Twenty

Someone had a terrible headache. It was near her, and it was so bad she wished they'd go away. They were moaning, crying . . . With a struggle, Chelsea swallowed, wincing – her throat felt like it was lined with razor blades – and opened her eyes. Everything hurt.

'Chelsea?'

A soft voice sounded nearby. Chelsea blinked, slowly, and realised the person with the headache was her, and the moaning she could hear was her own.

Slowly, she shifted in the bed. There were bright lights everywhere.

'It's so bright in here.'

'I'll dim the lights.' The person's voice was kind. The lights went down.

'Chelsea, I'm so glad you're all right. You've had us worried.'

Chelsea squinted. Did she have a hangover? 'Where am I?' She raised her hand to her forehead, felt a bandage.

'You're in the hospital.' She looked at the person speaking, trying to focus on them.

'Uncle . . . Uncle Derek?' she said, surprised. She hadn't seen him for at least a year. 'Wha – hello. What the hell are you doing here?'

He smiled, chuckled softly. 'That's my girl.' And his eyes filled with tears.

'How long have I been asleep?'

'Two days,' Derek said. 'You might remember some of it, but you've been pretty out of it. We were really worried at one stage . . . You've been stupid, Chelsea, driving your dad's car when you were drunk.'

'I know,' she said, her voice small. She tried to sit up, but couldn't. 'Wh-where's my dad?' she said, as the words got easier to say. But then she remembered.

Remembered where she'd last seen her dad, and how. She blinked, and shrank back into the voluminous white pillows. 'Oh,' she said, quietly. 'Doesn't matter.' But then she blinked again. 'Is he coming, though? Has he been to see me?'

And then, Derek took her hand.

'Chelsea, love. I've got something to tell you,' he said, and his voice broke. 'It's about your dad, darling. He's . . . he's dead.'

Slowly, he explained. How Chelsea had spun the car out of control and crashed in Addlestone, the next town. How the hospital had desperately tried to contact her parents, but with no luck. How they'd found her uncle Derek's number in her address book in her handbag, and called him. He'd managed to get through to Margaret, in Sweden, and she'd flown back with Amber, arriving the next morning.

Amber had insisted on coming straight to the hospital, which was probably a blessing. But Margaret had gone home first, looking for her husband. No one at work had seen or heard from George; it didn't make sense.

She found him in the den. Hanging by his belt from the open beams of the ceiling.

The tears were running down Derek's face as he held Chelsea's hand.

'Darling, I'm so sorry.'

Chelsea was crying too, every inch of her hurting, with bruises and pain, and with sadness too.

'When did it happen?'

She knew the answer, though.

'The police said he'd been dead for hours. Probably did it late the night before.'

'And there was no one else there?'

Derek shook his head, perturbed. 'No. Why would there be?'

'I don't know . . .' Tears slid down Chelsea's cheeks. Of course. She couldn't tell anyone. 'Just wondered if it might be something suspicious.'

Her uncle gave her a funny look. 'No, darling. He did it himself.'

'Was there . . . was there a note, or anything?'

'No note, nothing.' Derek squeezed her hand. 'I think your dad was just . . . a bit stressed. It's been going on for years, darling.'

'What has?' she said, sharply.

Derek sounded deliberately vague. 'All that stuff – he was working too hard, that's for sure. I think it just got to him, in the end.' He wrinkled up his face, swallowing down a sob. 'But he loved you very much, Chelsea, you mustn't ever forget that, OK?'

She stared at him, and then lay back on the pillow. 'OK.'

'I mean it,' Derek said. 'He really did.'

'Where's Mum?' Chelsea said weakly.

Derek couldn't tell her the truth, which was that Amber and Margaret were at that moment barricaded inside Bay Tree House, surrounded by paparazzi, and that the headlines in the tabloids this morning were, variously:

TOXIC ROXY'S TRAGIC SMASH

ROXY'S DAD SUICIDE – CHILD STAR NEAR DEATH
Chelsea Stone drunk driving family tragedy

CHELSEA DRUNK DRIVING SMASH
Washed-up child star's dad hangs himself

He didn't tell her that Amber had been at her bedside for the past forty-eight hours until, eventually, she was ordered home earlier that day by her mother and the head of her record company, who told her she had to eat and get some sleep or else she'd collapse too.

And he didn't tell her, because he didn't know himself, that George had left a note.

Please, please *tell my darling Chelsea this wasn't her fault. I had to do it, I know it now. I just can't lie any more. Tell my girls I love them.*

But no one told Chelsea it wasn't her fault.

Because when she found the body of her dead husband hanging from the beam, his face purple, his tongue bloated and swollen, and when she saw the note he'd placed neatly on the sofa next to where he knew he'd be found, the first thing Margaret did was tear it up and throw it away.

She didn't know what the 'lies' were that he was on about. And if she, Margaret Stone, didn't know, she didn't want anyone else finding out, either, even if it meant that her eldest daughter blamed herself entirely for her beloved dad's death. Even if it meant, for years afterwards, most nights she dreamed of the moment she went down the stairs to the den and saw him there. Even if, every day, she heard his desperate, sad voice, calling out to her as she ran away from him: 'Chelsea! Come back, love! Chelsea . . .'

Even if it meant, from that day forward, that something changed within her, something that could never be made right again.

Chapter Twenty-One

Amber looked around the gloomy Victorian church, trying not to cry again. She had never wondered what her father's funeral would be like, but she was pretty sure her dad wouldn't have gone for this. The incense, the huge choir, hundreds of mourners, one star after another getting up to talk about how much they loved George Stone, which she interpreted as: how much money George Stone had made for them.

She gave a ragged sigh; her throat was closed up, her eyes were raw from weeping. It was all wrong, them sitting here in this church – specially selected by Margaret, a couple of miles from Bay Tree House: the nearest church was deemed too ugly, modern and squat. Wrong that it was Dad's funeral. Wrong that Chelsea was sitting at the other end of the pew, battered and bruised, looking awful and on crutches, crying as if her heart would break.

It was wrong her mother hadn't let her see her, that she'd told her it was best if she leave Chelsea alone, she wasn't well enough. Amber had wanted to stay on at the hospital with her sister, help her through the first days after the accident, and she'd been firmly pushed away. Her record company had been funny about it too; they'd finally admitted it the day before, something about how it was best she steer clear of her sister, it wasn't good publicity to be linked with her, she was – quite literally – a car crash.

'But she's my *sister*!' Amber had said, incredulously. She and Margaret were at a meeting at their office, a glass and chrome building around the back of Carnaby Street.

Pale and tired, worn out through crying, Amber couldn't understand why the hell this meeting was necessary. The funeral was the next day, shouldn't they be planning for that? But her mother was on overdrive at the moment, and Amber, always the peacemaker, put it down to a grief reaction. She knew Margaret was tough, and perhaps she was dealing with her husband's suicide in the only way she knew how.

'We know you love your sister,' Gerald, the head of A&R, had said soothingly. 'But we have big, big plans for you after the debut album, Amber, a world tour, merchandise, perfume, a very clearly defined career arc. OK?'

Amber wanted to laugh. She felt almost hysterical. Her dad had been dead for four days, wasn't even buried yet, and here they were talking about five-year plans and career arcs – perfume? Jesus, what were they thinking, and why did Mum even *care* at a time like this?

When had all this become normal to Amber, not making decisions for herself? She'd got used to it, over the years, used to living in a gilded cage. Other people told her what to do, and she did it to keep them happy because she liked people being happy, she loved her mum and dad, and she loved singing. She was only truly happy when she was singing.

When she looked back, there was no one moment where she recalled ever saying, 'Yes please, I'd love to be an international pop star,' but while her dad had been alive it had been all right. There'd been a sense of stability and security about this career she'd been gradually growing used to. George was so calm and wise; with him you always felt everything was going to be OK.

And now he was gone, and she didn't understand anything about the world without him. Things were moving too fast, decisions about her career were being made in her name, and half the time she didn't really get what they were talking about.

She sat there now, numb with grief, as Gerald kept on talking and her mother, swathed in black, nodded gravely.

'We want to be very clear about who you are to the public. Someone new and fresh, Amber. Not linked with other things in your family. Your sister's behaviour, not just recently, but over the last year or so – and your father's suicide –'

'It was an accident,' Margaret said firmly.

Amber looked at her mother, appalled. 'It was suicide, Mum!'

'I'd rather you didn't use that word when you talk about it,' Margaret had said, quite calmly, to her daughter. 'Because you can think what you want, but I know what I think, too.'

Amber couldn't argue with her in front of them all, could she? She didn't get it, any of it. In less than a week, the whole world had changed, nothing would be the same. She glanced down the row at her sister as the vicar started droning on again, but Chelsea's head was bowed, she couldn't see her face, and so Amber just sat there, feeling completely alone.

Next to her, Margaret was doing her best to sit upright and not worry too much about whether her lipstick had faded. It was so important to look right, correct. It was so important this service went off well, so that when people talked about George Stone from now on, they remembered the good things – the success, the clients, the money, the loving wife and family, the beautiful home – and not the bad things. It was essential, not just for her, for Chelsea and more importantly Amber's career, but for George's memory too.

The bad things had taken her somewhat by surprise.

She'd vaguely understood, from a couple of little things George had let slip, that business wasn't as good as it had been. He'd lost his sparkle, somewhere along the way, but he'd started to take out loans to cover himself, and a combination of the recession and over-expansion had hit the company hard . . .

Oh, Margaret had discovered all sorts, going through her husband's possessions, down in his den. The house was mortgaged to the hilt. The company was practically bust.

And there was more.

Margaret wasn't sure, until she found the evidence, if she'd ever really understood that George was gay. Like so many things in her life, she'd just *chosen* to not know, and it had suited her – and George, she'd thought – very well. If she'd been completely honest with herself, had she known? It was impossible to tell: for all her veneer, Margaret was fairly unworldly. She'd cocooned herself in suburbia after her time in Soho, and she'd told herself it was what she wanted. What she'd found in George's desk told her otherwise.

Diaries, luridly detailing what he'd done and where, and with whom. Pulp books, featuring descriptions of men having sex that she didn't even understand. Magazines and photos that showed men doing things to each other that she could barely fathom. Especially coming from George, that was the thing . . . She knew they weren't close in the way some couples were close. They'd long ago agreed that a physical relationship was not for them. But she thought they'd got on well, that they'd loved each other, in their own way.

As she'd stood in the den, with autumn rain drumming softly outside, holding the evidence of her husband's secret world in her hands – the gay porn, the mortgage deeds, the diaries, the letters – Margaret cried. She could feel her face cracking, making strange expressions. She hadn't cried since Amber was a baby. She had spent her life trying to control her emotions.

'Just this once,' she'd whispered, as she bent over the desk, her sobs growing louder and louder, and she gave into her grief: grief for the world she'd lost, the husband who'd given her everything she thought she'd wanted.

The husband she'd never really known at all, as it turned out.

Margaret stood up, dried her tears and went upstairs to get the black bin bags. The evidence was being destroyed, life would go on, and even though financially things were bleak, she had the solution, and it lay with her youngest daughter.

Margaret had worked too hard and sacrificed too much to end up back where she'd started. It'd mean some tough decisions – especially about Chelsea – but she had no choice.

Nothing must stand in the way of Amber's success. Nothing. She paused at the bottom of the steps leading back up to the hall and she nodded, as if taking a vow by herself in this awful room where she'd found her husband hanging from the ceiling, and the secrets he was keeping. For George. For her, for Chelsea. And for Amber.

The service was ending; Margaret looked across Derek at her eldest daughter. Chelsea was on the aisle; Margaret hoped she'd be able to walk to the grave OK. It wouldn't look right if she stumbled, or started behaving hysterically. Amber was fine. Amber was always fine. Chelsea, though . . . Margaret bit her lip with concern. She was tired of worrying about her eldest daughter. She felt they were growing apart, and she couldn't stop it. It had been a long time, since before *Roxy's Nine Lives* started, that she'd last listened to what her mother said. Margaret hadn't been able to control her for years now. And look what had happened, Margaret thought angrily. Typical Chelsea; the night her father meets with this terrible accident, she goes and nearly gets herself killed as well.

Margaret knew she'd been at the house that night; she knew the note said 'tell Chelsea it's not her fault'; she knew something must have happened – it was her father's car she was driving, in any case! But she chose to say nothing. Let the whole thing settle down, as soon as possible. The less negative publicity for Amber, the better. She'd tell Chelsea soon, she promised herself. When all this had died down. Important, yes it was, that she didn't blame herself. She'd tell her soon.

Chelsea had made a pact with herself that if she got through the funeral without totally breaking down, she would treat herself when she got back home to the flat, alone. A stiff, stiff whisky, and two of the painkillers she'd been prescribed, instead of one. The whisky was for her dad, in memory. She'd killed him, sure as if she'd strangled him with her own hands. She gulped, and the tears started again. She'd flushed him out, he'd killed himself out of shame . . . She would get back home, and toast his memory with some good Talisker whisky – he'd given her some for Christmas.

The whisky and the pills were what was keeping Chelsea going.

She looked a mess, she knew it but she didn't care. She didn't really care what happened to her now.

The funeral was over: the congregation had dispersed, and they had been driven to the cemetery for the private burial, just the four of them. Her, her mother, Uncle Derek and Amber. Chelsea could barely walk, but she was determined to make it on crutches, determined to see her dad into the ground, so she could understand what she'd done, the enormity of how evil she was.

Amber had tried to help her as they walked slowly along the trim gravel paths in the weak October sunshine, but Chelsea had pushed her away, tears streaming down her face, wanting to do it herself.

After the burial, when the vicar and the undertaker were waiting respectfully at a distance, the four of them stood in silence around the grave, Margaret and Derek on one side, Amber and Chelsea on the other. Margaret fished around in her bag, looking for a mirror. Beside her, Derek squeezed her arm.

'You OK, darling?' he said. 'You've not said a word to me.'

She didn't want to talk to him, not Derek, not today. 'I'm not OK, no,' she said, sharply. ''Course I'm not.'

'Look, he was a good man, even if he had his little secrets,' Derek said, softly.

'What kind of secrets do you mean?'

'Weeell . . .' Derek looked shifty. 'I know he was in a bit of trouble, financially.'

'He talked to you about it?'

'Yeah, a bit. Look, Maggie, if you want a loan, anything – all you have to do is ask.'

'I wouldn't touch your money, Derek.' She was horrified. 'I didn't work all those years to be helped out by . . . by the likes of *you*.'

'Look, Maggie. I know it's bad. I know it must have been hard, living with George and his . . . his little ways, shall we put it. But—'

Margaret stared at him, dry-eyed and furious. 'You *knew*

123

George's secret all these years? And you never told me?' she hissed. 'God dammit, Derek.'

Derek looked stunned.

'You mean you didn't *know*? Christ, Maggie!'

'Margaret!' she said, far too loudly, and the girls on the other side looked up, distracted with grief. 'Margaret! No one calls me Maggie any more, Derek. *No one!*'

Amber used this opportunity, while her mother was whispering angrily with Derek, to put an arm round her sister. She squeezed her shoulder, but Chelsea winced and moved away. Amber looked at her, and a tear rolled down her cheek.

She said quietly, 'Oh, Chels. This is all so fucked up. I love you, you know that, don't you?'

Chelsea was silent. Amber pressed on.

'I mean, I know things have been weird between us, the last couple of years. We used to be so close!' She cleared her throat. 'Now we hardly see each other. I know you've been really busy with Roxy and stuff,' she added hurriedly. She didn't want to sound like she was accusing her. 'But I feel like people are trying to keep us apart, you know?' Was Chelsea even listening to her? 'We've got to stick together.' She paused. 'I love you,' she said again, and it sounded pathetic, even to her own ears.

And then Chelsea spoke.

'I'm bad luck, you don't want to be around someone like me,' she said. Amber looked at her sister, her green eyes searching her face. But Chelsea's mouth was set in a line. She looked stern. Remote – disinterested, even.

'I'm doing this for your own good, Amber.' And she limped slowly away. Amber stared after her in disbelief, fresh tears stinging her eyes.

Amber still didn't quite realise it, but everything had changed. She would not see Chelsea again for ten years.

PART THREE

Is That All There Is?

Chapter Twenty-Two

From *Stars!* magazine, April 1999, issue 20, page 45:

TEN QUESTIONS WE ALWAYS ASK:
MULTI-MILLION ALBUM SELLING GOLDEN-VOICED AMBER STONE,
WHO'S ABOUT TO LAUNCH HER SECOND ALBUM . . .

1. What are you most excited about at the moment?
My new album, *Amber*! It's my second album, and I'm really pleased
with it. Hopefully everyone else will be too!

2. What are you *not* excited about at the moment?
Getting up early to learn my routines for the tour! Marco, my choreographer, is a real slave-driver! We're going on tour for eighteen months
to twenty-three countries, and I can't wait to meet as many people as
possible.

3. Where do you live?
I'm all over the place at the moment – living in hotels, going back
and forth between LA and London because I've been talking to a

couple of people about film work. But when I can, I try to go back to my mum's. We go everywhere together, she's been amazing.

4. When did you last cry?

I cry all the time! But I guess it was when *It's . . . Me* went platinum, it was my first album and it was such an honour.

5. What's your secret ambition?

I don't really have one! I love singing. It's my life. I'm happy when I'm singing, it doesn't matter where. On stage, or at home into the mirror with a hairbrush, I don't mind!

6. When were you last naked and with whom?

With Marco, this morning! He stayed in my hotel room 'cos we were up late watching *Dirty Dancing* for the millionth time. But nothing more – he's not into girls, if you get me . . .

7. What do you dislike most about yourself?

That I haven't looked out enough for the people I love.

8. Where would you most like to live, and why?

On the beach, somewhere low-key . . . I don't really like hotels that much. I prefer the simple life, to be honest.

9. Who's your real-life hero?

My dad was.

10. What are you doing today?

Rehearsing for the tour, seeing my mum, practising the new songs, trying to get some sleep!

From *Stars!* magazine, April 1999, issue 20, page 68:

'You're wonderful, darling,' Marco said, handing Amber a towel. 'Honestly, wonderful. The way you take instruction –' he raised an eyebrow. 'You're going to make some man very happy one day.'

Amber laughed. 'Marco . . . You're the only man for me, you know that.' She wrapped the towel round her neck and took a big gulp of water from her bottle. She glanced at herself in the long mirror of the gym and frowned. Marco caught her expression.

'What's wrong with you? You're perfection, daahling.'

'Oh God, I'm not,' Amber said, sighing. 'I look awful. Look at me. I'm still carrying that extra weight from my holiday, and my hair's a mess, I wish I hadn't had those bangs cut when I was in the States.'

'"Bangs"?' Marco laughed. 'Hey, Lil' Miss USA, what's with the "bangs"? We say fringe here, you know.'

'Help,' Amber said. She looked serious. 'I'm always trying to say the right thing, it gets confusing when I don't know where I am.' She rubbed her hand over her forehead. 'Don't know who I am, even. I'm just tired, I suppose.'

'You're Amber, you're at the Dorchester in London, and you're Number One in the album and singles charts this week, that's who you are.' Marco came over to her and put his arm round her smooth, perfectly tanned shoulders. 'Darling, you're working so hard at the moment, and it's all going to be worth it. You just need to chill and keep focus, that's all. You're the hottest act in the world

129

right now, you're an amazing singer, your fans adore you and it's a totally brilliant, great album. This tour is going to be massive.'

She frowned again. 'Don't sweet-talk me, Marco.'

Marco looked at her. She was right. He'd never lied to her before.

'OK,' he said. 'It's all true, though. It's a good album, it's not a great album. Fine, if we had our way, it'd be just you up there with a guitar and your lovely voice, playing to forty people in a basement somewhere while I watch you with a large glass of vino and eye up the barman, but it's a good problem to have, the problem of international stardom, darling.'

She nodded, gratefully. 'You're always right. Bless you, Marco.'

'Bless you, my child. You're not going to ditch me when you're a huge movie star, are you? Even more famous than you are now?'

Amber laughed. 'Ditch you? Of course not! Marco, you're my only friend.'

He rolled his eyes. 'Liar.'

But it was true. Amber hadn't had many friends growing up – Chelsea was everything to her, and her mother was very particular about the little girls Amber was friends with, even in Weybridge. They had to be the children of Tory MPs, or the daughters of lawyers, doctors, nice respectable people like that. Marco was the one person in her life who didn't want anything, except to be with her. She hadn't had much of that before.

They'd known each other for two years now, since just before George had died, and had grown closer during that awful time as they worked together on Amber's choreography for It's . . . Me. Marco was Scottish-Italian, tanned and toned, absolutely beautiful, but he was a realist. He didn't bullshit Amber, he told it like it was, and he never abused his position, trying to use her to further his own career. It was partly why she liked him so much; he was his own person already. She wasn't so sure she could say that about herself, most of the time.

Plus, he was a brilliant choreographer, and she knew it. Amber had been groomed for stardom from such an early age, she'd worked with them all by now – and she knew who was good and who wasn't. She also knew it was about hard work, keeping your head in a good place, not letting all the shit get to you.

Sometimes she wondered, though – is that all there is? It was the title of her dad's favourite song. He'd loved Peggy Lee. Her mother had planned this all of Amber's life – now it had come into being, she felt curiously blank inside, and she could never tell Margaret. It had been her obsession these last ten, fifteen years.

But being a 'star' was such a strange thing. People treated you differently, laughed at your crap jokes, gave you more free stuff than you could ever use. Amber was only really content when she was singing – the rest of it she didn't care about – the interviews, premieres, photoshoots, the perfume named after her, the money . . . so much money.

She was happiest singing and strumming on her own guitar at Marco's cramped Primrose Hill flat, having a glass of wine and laughing with her best friend at whatever had happened that day. But those evenings were increasingly rare as a monster of a tour geared up and took shape, and what came next after the tour was already being discussed – things two years away. It was crazy. And she, Amber, was right at the middle of it, working away, and sometimes she felt as if it was nothing to do with her, nothing at all.

'Let's get some lunch,' Marco said. 'Then you've got that interview with the *Mail*, and some more costume fittings. Your mum wants you to get an early night tonight – we fly to Rome tomorrow morning for the first production rehearsal, remember?'

'Yes,' Amber said, plastering on a big smile. 'I remember.'

'Your mother called, by the way, when you were downstairs. That LA producer is chasing, he wants to see you again. Is this for the high-school film thing?'

'It's called *Prom Night*.' Amber rolled her eyes as they walked out of the private gym and onto the terrace of the penthouse suite, where the spring sunshine was warm. She gazed out over Hyde Park, at the daffodils bobbing in the wind. 'It's not going to happen. Who'd want to watch me in a film?'

'Plenty of people, apparently.' Marco picked up a menu. 'It's Leo Russell, after all, isn't that all that matters?'

'Mum thinks so,' Amber said.

'Wow,' Marco said. 'I mean, *Sir* Leo Russell. Isn't he, like, the best producer there is?' Even he sounded impressed, and Amber was annoyed.

'Oh, who cares about Leo Russell,' she said. 'Yes, let's get some lunch. I want to talk about our holiday. I asked Mum yesterday if I could have a week off, and she's looking at next October. Is that good for you?'

'*October?*' Marco spat. That's months away! Seven months away, in fact. You haven't got any free time before then? Come on, Amber, you're a huge star, you can do what you want!'

Impossible to tell him how untrue that was, how her mother had got everything planned out, how even a week in October was a huge deal to Margaret. Amber simply shook her head. 'I know, I know, but we'll get that week, I promise.' She smiled sweetly. 'I'll go mad if I don't have a holiday, anyway. Forget that for the moment. I want to hear how your date with the Russian dancer went. Hm?'

Marco put his arm round her and smiled down at her heart-shaped face, framed with long, wavy amber-gold hair. He adored Amber, she was like a little sister to him. She was so serious but funny, sweet, a real person, not full of bullshit, and he felt some-one needed to protect her from all those sharks. He worried about her sometimes. He hoped they didn't change her. He said, look-ing at her, 'I don't want to shock you, my darling. But get ready.'

In the adjoining room of the vast hotel suite, Margaret Stone sat at her desk, frowning. She could hear the shrieks of laughter coming from next door, Amber occasionally gasping in horror at something silly Marco was telling her, no doubt. She didn't mind Marco, but he was a bit frivolous. It was nice that Amber got on with her choreographer, but they were there to work, not have a laugh.

Margaret opened up the huge desk diary she always carried with her. She spread it out on the table and rubbed her fingers on the bridge of her nose as she pored over her daughter's schedule. Days like this were hard, for some reason. Days when spring was here and the sun was out, and you could see people smiling and you got a feeling of happiness, even high up here. She stretched out in her chair and looked round the room, her eyes gazing out onto the park.

She hadn't gone back to Bay Tree House after the funeral. Not once. She'd sold it and moved to a smaller place in Weybridge. She'd told people she couldn't leave the area her girls had grown up in. She and George had been so happy in Weybridge. But that was a load of crap – she was never there. Amber's career was taking off and she had to be with her daughter, not just as her manager now that George was dead, but to look after her. Amber needed it. If Margaret was honest with herself, she needed it too. Needed the distraction, a focus.

Because she missed George. She hadn't realised she would. She made a good widow; it suited her. After the numbness of his death, and the revelations which accompanied it; after the worry about Chelsea, who had been so ill, and sorting out the business, which had nearly collapsed and lost her everything . . . Margaret couldn't think about it all. And when it was all over, when the house was cleaned and sold and Chelsea was set up in her own flat again, and she'd got Derek off her back, told him to leave her alone once and for all, when that was over, Margaret sometimes found herself looking up from her desk diary on a beautiful spring day like this and realising she missed her husband, missed his kind eyes and quiet sense of humour, his love for the girls, his head for business. She'd never known him properly, and now she never would.

The sounds of hilarity from the next room grew louder, snapping Margaret out of her reverie. She frowned, but resisted the urge to go in and shut them up. Her pen hovered over the week in October she'd blanked out at Amber's request. The fact was, Amber wasn't going to get her holiday, not this year, not next year, and Margaret didn't have the heart to tell her, not just yet.

For though she may not have wanted it, there were even bigger plans afoot for Amber, after the tour was over. Plans to establish her as a star for all ages, not just a two-album pop star flash in the pan. To become the face of a major make-up brand, and the muse for an up-and-coming designer. She'd work with the best photographers, get edgy, arty photoshoots and videos done to get everyone talking. Launch a perfume – it already had a name: Nectar. Everything would lead her talented daughter down the path towards a career in Hollywood as the perfect package: actress, singer, perfect brand material for young girls, women, men of all ages.

Margaret had learned a lot from George, just as he had from her. She was a natural businesswoman, sharp, savvy and focused. Amber was her main asset, and now Sir Leo Russell was interested in this asset. Leo Russell, the biggest, most important movie producer in the world.

She didn't think about whether Amber really wanted any of this. It didn't occur to Margaret that she wouldn't. Amber was always so grateful, sweet and kind. She missed her dad terribly, to guide her career and look out for her best interests, and that's why Margaret had started talking to other people. Looking to the future. To LA.

What Amber didn't realise was how central Sir Leo was to those future plans. And how central he would very soon be in her life. But Margaret did. He wanted to work with Amber, wanted Amber quite desperately, before the competition got their hands on her – and Margaret knew she held the strings. She'd make him wait a little longer.

She picked up her pen and started scribbling on the empty week. She breathed in, nodding and smiling. Life was difficult sometimes, but Margaret had to admit she liked this part of it. So close to the main stage she could almost be on it herself. At the very least, she was in complete control.

Chapter Twenty-Three

'Sally!'

Sally Miller carried on typing. She'd had a manicure that morning, and she enjoyed the sound of determined clicking on the keyboard and the sight of her perfect nails, pink and shiny, smooth white crescents, exactly shaped.

Leo said a woman who didn't care about her nails was a woman who didn't care about herself, and why would he want to work with someone like that?

'*Sally!*' The voice grew louder, footsteps sounding along the tiled floor. Sally sighed indulgently and typed even faster. What would he do without her?

'Sally, did they call back?'

She looked up at her boss, standing in the doorway glowering at her, and smiled.

She didn't think a day would come when he didn't make her heart flutter, just a little, every single time she saw him. His thick black hair, which he was always pushing away distractedly from his permanently tanned face; the dark eyes, the smooth skin, the wolfish smile with the shockingly white teeth. She couldn't ever get enough of him.

Sally Miller was a girl with an obsession: Leo Russell. *Sir* Leo Russell, to give him his full title.

'No, they didn't,' she said. 'I'm sorry, Leo. I know how important it is. But she just started that tour of hers. You're just gonna have to be patient!' she said, trying to tease him.

He was in a sunny mood, and he let her. He flopped down in an armchair in her office. Leo's production company was probably the most successful independent in LA, and it had bought him a pristine white Mexican-style office suite in Santa Monica – a one-storey series of offices set around a lush private garden – and a courtyard with a pool, where Leo hosted screenings and parties. He could have chosen one of the anonymous office suites in Beverly Hills, downtown in the business centre, but he hadn't. That was part of his phenomenal success in the movie business: he was the best, and he knew it.

Leo Russell knew when to play up to the stereotype of the maverick, charming British genius – like the way he used his knighthood when he wanted to impress the Yanks, who lapped it up, but rarely when dealing with the Brits, who'd only think he was showing off – and his offices worked it to the hilt.

By the late 1990s Leo was at the top of his game. He was a self-made man, though he hid this, playing on his suave accent and looks. He had started out at the BBC many years ago (though he claimed to be in his late thirties, he was in fact forty-five), and had rapidly made a name for himself by bringing soap stars and stand-up comedians in to play in serious dramas. The critics hated it, but the public loved it.

The simple truth was that Leo had a near-visionary knack of knowing what worked for a mainstream audience and how to deliver commercial success. No one else could judge it like he could. And he was willing to do whatever it took to get what he wanted – he had no qualms about trampling over people who stood in his way. He was loathed by his peers, who despised the way he'd got to where he was, but adored by the people at the top. He delivered results, and that's what they wanted.

But Leo quickly grew tired of the rules and regulations governing the BBC and, when he'd used it to learn all he needed to know and to make the connections he wanted, he set up his own production company, selling his ideas back to the corporation and making millions in the process. It was enough to take the next step into film, and he had the perfect script: a romcom about an English girl and an American guy who meet in London and fall in love. And that was when he really hit the big time.

When *Jimmy&Jenny* came out in the early 1990s, it was such a massive worldwide hit that some sniping sections in the British press said it had to be a one-off, that this jumped-up TV guy Leo Russell had just got lucky. He'd cast a big American star and a well-loved British ingénue, plus the usual assortment of good character roles and stereotypes. He'd got his ducks in a row, they said. Nothing more.

Leo ignored them, jumped on a plane to LA and over the next five years went from success to even greater success, focusing mainly on lightweight romantic comedies that delivered 'boffo' – box office – and always, always had a star in them that girls and guys alike were going to fall for. He used British talent where he could, was a high-profile fundraiser for British charities abroad and these things – along with the fact that those in charge still loved him, whereas those underneath or alongside him knew what he really was – got him a knighthood, a few short years later.

There was no struggle with him, either. He hadn't grown up without shoes, or with an abusive, drunken dad. No, he was from a quiet, dull semi in Watford, on a street of quiet dull semis next to another street just like it. His mum and dad were still alive, but he'd long since paid them off. He felt no guilt; he had nothing to say to them any more; it'd be boring for them and him. He'd rather have the money if he was them.

Money was everything to Leo. It was at the heart of everything he did. It gave you power. He'd come from mediocrity, and he'd never go back to it. Money meant you were in control, in the driving seat. You could afford the best, and you wanted it because it showed how powerful you were: the most powerful man in the room. The general, commanding the foot soldiers. He had the dealers bring him only the best A-grade coke for his parties, none of the shit they sold on Sunset. And he didn't know the difference between Cristal and Lambrusco, if he was honest. He didn't care, either. It was the fact that one cost hundreds of dollars, that it got you the respect of the men in the room and got the girls wanting you to fuck them. Leo fucked women. They didn't fuck him.

Which was why he was excited about Amber. *Very* excited. It wasn't the lead role he was wanting her for in *Prom Night*, it was a teaser, a taster, with a song-and-dance number that would showcase her talent.

Leo was fascinated by this girl – he was a genius at knowing a good thing when he saw one. He recognised her likeability factor. He knew there was a gap in the market for a fresh, young star – at twenty, Amber was still young enough to play someone in high school for now, and then . . .

She was the complete package. A marketing dream – her hair was even fucking amber-coloured! She was exactly what he wanted, he could practically see the dollar signs, and when Leo Russell wanted something, he always got it.

So why hadn't they called back?

Sally's eyes followed him as he strode up and down her office and turned to face her. A pelt of dark hair was visible on his chest where the top two buttons of his thick white silk shirt were open. Leo always wore thick white silk shirts, he had hundreds of them back at his Beverly Hills home, hanging in a long, sandalwood-scented closet. It was part of Sally's job as his assistant to make sure they were immaculately cleaned.

He was goddamn near perfect, and he knew it. They both did. They both took immense pride in their success at holding back the years.

They had known each other for over a decade, when Sally was a professional PA, then in her late twenties, and moved over to the London office of the huge talent agency she worked for. Her boss was a pig, she was lonely in London and so one day, when Leo strode into their offices for a meeting, she made sure he noticed her.

He liked Americans: they were efficient and enthusiastic and they had good teeth and they loved the British accent. She was easy to get into bed – easy to pleasure, too. Sally took good care of herself then, as now, and her taut, slim body wound itself into any position Leo cared for. She only wanted to please, and that's what bored him. One afternoon, when she'd finished giving him a sensational blow-job – did they learn it in college over there, these Californian girls? – and before she tried to snuggle up to him, because he liked coming in her mouth but he didn't want to have to hold her afterwards, he broke it to her that he was seeing someone else.

Leo always found it was easier to be charming but brutal with women, when the relationship was over. No point in leaving them under any illusions, giving any hope.

But he'd liked Sally's attitude when he'd told her. 'Sorry, darling . . . it's not going to work out. I don't think you're the right one for me, and I can't lie to you about it.'

She'd been kneeling quietly next to him, still naked. She'd paused, swallowed a little, and blinked. As if she were controlling something within her, fighting some more primeval urge. And she'd said, 'OK, I can see that. That's fine.'

'Really?' Leo was amused, and a little impressed at how cool she was.

'Sure,' Sally had said. Her hands crept to her breasts; she cupped them, pinching the still erect nipples with her slim fingers. 'Just one little thing, Leo, can you do that for me?'

'Um –' Leo put his hands behind his head and looked up at her, assessing the situation. He never committed if he wasn't going to go through with something. He watched her, carefully. 'Yeah. OK. What is it, honey?'

She licked her lips. 'Will you fuck me once more, before I go? Because –' softly trailing one glossy fingernail down his still swollen but sagging cock – 'I brought these.'

And she'd produced a pair of fur-trimmed handcuffs, and looked at him imploringly.

Damn, she was good. Leo had felt himself getting turned on

again, though it had been only moments since he'd come. He'd raised one eyebrow.

'Sure, baby.'

'I want you to control me,' she'd said conversationally, as she lay back on the silk sheets and looked up at him, her fingers moving down between her legs to the downy hair that she waxed into a barely-there strip.

Leo Russell was not a fanciful man. He was a doer, not a thinker, and he had long ago stopped seeing Sally as a sexual being. But he sometimes thought back to that moment, to Sally's face as she offered him the handcuffs and then lay back while he took over. It was as if she were chaining herself to him. Accepting that she was totally subservient to him, that she would do anything for him . . .

She'd started out as a secretary at his newly formed production company, but over the years as he became more and more successful, Sally's role in Leo's life became more and more central. She moved back to California when he came out to LA and now she took complete care of Leo, looked after his house and his bills when he was away. She sorted out his dry-cleaning, bought his new suits, under instruction. If he crashed one of his sports cars, she arranged the repairs and the insurance.

At thirty-eight, Sally Miller was approaching middle age by Hollywood standards, but she'd been a beautiful young woman and had taken good care of herself. She was pristine, immaculate, every inch of her, from her pedicured toes to her highlighted hair. Sally knew Leo hated sloppiness, and that was why she made sure her make-up was immaculately applied, and reapplied at lunchtime, why her teeth were perfectly straight and gleaming white, and why there was not an extra ounce of fat on her body. Her skin might have been ageing badly with all that sun, and her once lithe body may have grown hard and sinewy after years of dedicated exercise and tanning, but Sally couldn't see that she looked a little too groomed, too much like a waxwork doll. She wanted to be perfect for Leo – she hadn't really realised that meant giving up her own life in pursuit of that perfection. She thought it was worth it.

Everyone who worked with Leo knew Sally, and she liked that she had that position in his life. She knew he trusted her, one hundred per cent. She was completely loyal to him – he knew she had very little life outside of his.

It didn't occur to her, these days, that she did a lot of his job for him. Not any more. That she was as capable and talented as any other producer, that she could have had a great career herself in the movie business. She would have looked blankly at anyone who suggested it. She'd long since given up her own personality to adore his.

She'd devoted her life to Leo. Converted any power she might have had into a great life – as she saw it – for herself. Looking after him.

And so Leo had long got used to telling her things, without caring what she thought. He confided in her, rather like a man confides in a priest, or a therapist. He knew all his secrets were safe with her – they'd been through a lot together, over the years.

Sally knew what this thing with Amber was. She understood Leo. Amber was hot. She was talented, and she was young – he liked them young. He'd put her in a film, fuck her and then move on . . . She was just like all the others, Sally thought. All the others except her – she'd stayed. Right by his side.

'Is this about Amber?' she said, trying to look like she was concerned. She tucked a lock of blonde hair behind her ear. 'Relax, Leo, they'll call. It's only been a coupla days. She'd be crazy not to take this part.'

'I've got a feeling about her, that's all. She's – she's got everything.' Leo's voice was deep, drawling, sexy. Sally sometimes listened to his messages twice, just to hear that voice again.

'Like what?' she said, smiling up at him, half teasing, half flattery.

Leo began ticking off on his fingers. 'There's a real gap in the market for someone like her at the moment. She can sing. She can dance. She's friendly. Girls like her. Guys want to do her. She's got that big, sweet smile, like a cute teenager, but she's all woman. She

141

can act, she's just got it. She's funny, bit of a klutz, but she has a sweet, serene look about her, that's what's going to get them. And she's completely malleable. She's hungry for it.' He paused. 'The mother's hungry for it, at least. And she drives the show.'

'Mmm-hm!' Sally said, nodding.

Now he got up, and began striding up and down. 'Dammit, she's really good. She's perfect, in fact.' He stopped, lost in thought, and Sally knew, with a stab of acid jealousy in her stomach, that he was thinking what it'd be like to have twenty-year-old Amber Stone astride him, her pert young breasts jiggling up and down as he thrust into her . . . She knew Leo that well. She had made it her whole life, knowing stuff like that.

He smiled at her, as if he knew what she was thinking, and shook his head. Sally was suddenly desperate to change the subject. She said, casually, 'Plenty more fish in the sea, Leo. Hey, Saul called. He wants your input on the latest draft.'

'I haven't looked at it. Tell him to fuck off.'

'I'm not going to do that,' Sally said smoothly. 'Why don't you go back into your office and just read those last couple of scenes? Joni says they won't go ahead without your say-so, and the studio's already in pretty deep. They need you.'

Leo looked up. He looked tired, she thought with concern, he hated not being in control. He had circles under his eyes and a five o'clock shadow, which she thought only made him look sexier. He smiled, slowly.

'What would I do without you, Sally?'

'I don't know,' she answered, honestly. 'I think you're really lucky, you know, Leo Russell.'

'I am, I am,' he said, his gaze shifting from her to the wall behind her, and she knew she'd lost him again. 'Damn, that stupid bitch of a mother's behind this, she's holding out on me.'

'Amber's mother?'

'She's her manager, she says what goes.'

The kid was managed by her mom. Of course — it was never going to work. Sally could have laughed with pleasure. 'What does she know, then?'

'Quite a lot, I imagine.' Leo's face was clouded over. 'She was married to George Stone – he was one of the best managers in the business for a while, late eighties, early nineties. Massive bender, topped himself. I worked with him when I was starting out.' His face cleared again. 'God, I remember now. He was looking for some new projects for his other daughter, Chelsea. Chelsea Stone. Wow, I'd forgotten all about her.'

Sally smiled brightly and looked fascinated. 'Who's Chelsea Stone?' she said, though she didn't really care.

'Oh,' Leo said dismissively, 'she's the sister. Some washed-up teen star – crashed a car and got fat, got into drugs.' He shook his head dismissively. Leo did coke frequently, but it was under his control. He despised people who couldn't control it. He looked out of the window into the yellow Californian sunshine, the blue sky, the white angles of the building dazzling in the sun, purple bougainvillea tumbling down the side of the hill towards the ocean. 'She was supposed to be the talented one. But they don't talk about her. She's been airbrushed out of the story. I wonder what happened to her?'

Chapter Twenty-four

'You made the papers,' the newsagent said to her, smiling happily as she handed him the *Sun*, the *Mirror*, an assortment of magazines, a pile of crisps and different sweets, a couple of Flakes, some ice creams. 'It's been a while. You're a star again, miss!'

Trying not to show her alarm, and thumbing through the notes she kept scrunched up at the bottom of her bag, Chelsea paused.

'Yeah, right,' she said. She gave a great hacking cough and scratched her bitten nails through her tousled hair. 'I'm a star, Azeem, you're a star, we're all stars. And . . . twenty Marlboro Lights, please. How much is that?'

'Twelve pound fifty-two, miss.'

'Jeez, how much?' Chelsea coughed again. 'Fucking prices these days!'

'Here's your change, miss,' Azeem said, ignoring this outburst. 'Lovely outside, innit? What you doing today, then?'

'What am I doing?' Chelsea looked up at him. Why did he care? 'I'm going back to bed, that's what I'm doing. And then I'm going out to get fucking wasted. OK?'

'Sounds good to me, miss,' Azeem was only asking to be polite. He always asked, but he wasn't really listening. Of course.

Chelsea stomped home, heart beating, terrified of what the pictures would be, desperately wanting to open the papers there on the street but knowing she had to wait to get back . . . She was shaking a little; she hadn't taken a pill that morning. It'd be waiting for her at home, it would make everything all right.

Chelsea looked at her watch; it was just after midday. What was she doing? She'd been out late the night before too, just drinking in her local, round the corner from her place at the cheaper end of Ladbroke Grove. Margaret had bought the flat for her with the money from George's will. Margaret oversaw, too, the monthly allowance Chelsea got, also from the will. It was what she lived on; she hadn't worked since the accident, since the night her father killed himself . . .

Once a week at least Chelsea would dream she was back at Bay Tree House again, opening the door to her father's den, walking downstairs in a drunken haze, seeing what she saw that night on the sofa, and her father's expression as he caught sight of her.

Before he killed himself.

Before she killed him . . .

It was impossible for her to forget it and move on. It was too hard, too hard for her not to blame herself – why had she run off? Why hadn't she seen it before? It was her fault, he would never have done it if she hadn't been so selfish, reckless, uncaring. It fuelled her self-pity, her sense of shame. She had had it all, and she had fucked it up. For her, and for the people around her. She was almost glad at how worthless it made her feel, to live off the money he'd left her. Because she *was* worthless. Worth nothing, good for nothing . . . living off her dead father.

Chelsea combed the newspapers obsessively as she ate her way through a couple of chocolate bars, occasionally pressing her hand to her sore head. The pictures were always the same: her, drunk, looking fat and spotty, with smudged lipstick, her tongue sticking out, coming out of another club at four the previous morning. She never remembered getting into these situations. She told herself all it took was one blink, that it was because the papers didn't want good photos, they took hundreds and only

145

used the bad ones. She'd been telling herself that for a couple of years now.

It had been a while since they'd featured her falling out of a club. She didn't know if the attention was a good thing or not. It wasn't news any more. More like a comic book. A joke. She was a joke.

These days, she was mostly just referred to in the press as the relative of Amber Stone: 'She has one older sister, troubled former child star Chelsea Stone.' At first Chelsea had been outraged – she was there first, she was the one they all adored!

But that was years ago. Eight years since she'd got the part of Roxy, and Amber was the star now. Part of Chelsea was pleased for her little sister – she had an amazing voice, even if Chelsea didn't love the stuff she'd been doing, didn't think the bland poppy stuff was right for Amber's soulful, sweet voice, with the catch of sadness at the back of it that was so alluring. But Chelsea didn't understand why it had to be either/or with the Stone sisters, though. Was it Margaret's doing? Of course not, but she couldn't help wondering. She didn't understand why there wasn't room for both of them in the world of celebrity.

It seemed not. She hadn't been offered a part since her father's death, and most of his friends and business associates had melted away. And her mum was completely wrapped up in her younger daughter's career, but then she had always been, so it made very little difference to Chelsea: she didn't miss her mother's support because she'd never really had it. It didn't mean she didn't wonder about what it would be like, though.

Chelsea had realised since her dad's death that she'd have to give up on her mother. She was sick of getting knocked back. She'd pushed Amber away too, pushed everyone away. She just wanted to be left alone. She'd told Amber that in no uncertain terms at the funeral. Told her they'd be better off apart.

They talked very occasionally on the phone, and by text and email, but it was tentative; they had increasingly little in common, and the phone calls grew less frequent. Amber was making another film; she'd already featured in one, *Prom Night*, and it had been a huge hit. Now she and Margaret were moving to LA to further her career.

It hurt Chelsea, she had to admit it. She knew Amber had talent, but when she'd seen her in the posters for *Prom Night* she'd nearly laughed out loud. She hardly recognised her. She didn't want to be patronising, but Amber wasn't an actress! She never had been. *She*, Chelsea, was the actress, she was the funny, talented one they'd all loved – it had been on the six o'clock news when Roxy came to an end, for fuck's sake!

Amber was . . . she was wet, if Chelsea thought about it for any length of time. Wet and wanting to please people, a simpering little 'yes' girl to their mum. Chelsea wished Amber would stand up to her sometimes – didn't she have any fucking backbone?

No. Chelsea caught her train of thought, running along the usual tracks. 'You're pathetic,' she said to herself. She *was* pathetic. The old familiar feeling of disgust washed over her. She hadn't worked in years, she had no life, unless you could count a few hardened drinking friends and the occasional judgemental phone calls and even more occasional visits from Margaret: who it was more painful for, her mum or her, Chelsea never knew.

She closed the last of the papers and stared out of the window into the grey afternoon. Everything was grey, everyone, she was completely alone and she felt out of control, rootless, empty, as bad as it was possible to feel. It was too early to go out, but she could still have a little drink here, to while away the time.

Shuffling across to the kitchen, Chelsea took another one of her pills. They were the painkillers prescribed for her injuries after the crash, but she still took them, two years on. She opened the fridge and got out a bottle of wine. It wasn't true that she was an alcoholic just because she had booze in the house, everyone said that a real alky never had anything in the house 'cos they'd drunk it all . . . she wasn't like that, yet.

She drank a glass of wine and a warm, lightheaded feeling swept over her. Everything was gonna be OK. Everything was nice. She wasn't a loser, she was Chelsea Stone! And it was all great . . . She went into the bedroom, lay down on her rancid sheets – she hadn't

147

hoovered or changed the bedding in weeks – and, wrapped up in her duvet, drank some more wine out of an old *Roxy's Nine Lives* mug. She would sleep, then she'd go out with Gary Knox, her old co-star. She was meeting up for a drink with him later. Maybe have some stuff beforehand to get her in the mood – the pills slowed her down, she'd need to come up . . .

Everything was good, it was good.

Chapter Twenty-Five

January, 2002

Amber had been living here properly for six months now, and she still didn't know how she felt about LA. On the one hand, it seemed so fake. So full of people who talked about themselves with huge pride, and openly said they liked her because of her fame. Because she was young and beautiful and successful. It was weird. People would come up to her at restaurants, once while she was lying by the pool of her hotel, even once when she was all tangled up in her headphones after a run and say, 'I just want to make myself known to you, I'm —' and then they'd give her their card: Agent, Producer, Publicist. I love your work. And go. No sincerity, nothing. Her mother was ecstatic they were here. Amber sometimes wished she could go back to London.

On the other hand, she could see herself loving life in LA. The warmth — she and Margaret had arrived to the Californian sun, when it was February and freezing back home. She liked the outdoor lifestyle, too. Marco had managed to get himself a job choreographing a talent show for US TV, and the two of them were like kids, roller-blading along the boardwalks by the wide, silvery sandy beaches, checking out the flea markets in Santa Monica and Venice Beach, eating Mexican food and sitting out by the pool of Amber's rental home in the Hollywood Hills, having a glass of wine and a laugh . . . Without Marco, she'd have gone mad. He knew how stupid it all was, how she shouldn't take it seriously. He also knew what she knew: that Amber was only really happy when she was on stage, singing – then she was truly herself.

Her second film was just out – *I Do* – a romantic comedy about high-school sweethearts who are reunited at their best friends' wedding. She had a couple of songs, and sang the theme tune, but it was her first main acting role. It was out in a few weeks. That was the one thing Amber was sure of, in a sea of uncertainty – Leo Russell knew what he was doing. She didn't know whether she *liked* him, but he was damn good. And when he was in the room, she felt safe – as if nothing could go wrong.

'Congratulations, Amber, my dear.' Leo's lips brushed her cheek, and she found herself blushing, unable to stop it. 'It's my biggest opening weekend, and it's down to you. You're wonderful.'

He gave her a sheaf of the palest pink roses and a magnum of pink champagne. Amber was sitting beside the pool of her white luxurious villa. She smiled up at him, and got up from her lounger, politely.

'Thanks, Leo. That's kind of you, but it was all you, really. You've met Marco, haven't you?'

'Sure.' Leo gripped Marco's hand enthusiastically, grin fixed firmly to his face, then dropped it immediately. 'So this is your place? I like it. Very clean.'

Amber wanted to laugh, but she remembered how obsessive Leo was about some things. Cleanliness was one of them. He had a kind of hygiene thing. Like Howard Hughes . . . She nodded. 'It's fine, but Mum thinks the pool's a little small,' Amber said, smiling. 'She's got ideas above her station. But I like it.'

'You can use my place whenever, you know that,' Leo said. Leo's sprawling, beautiful old-Hollywood Spanish-style mansion was high up in Beverly Hills, a delicious combination of old-world glamour and brand-new technology. It boasted three separate out-houses for the staff and guests, a massive pool tiled with dark blue mosaic tiles, ivy covering the walls and every last word in convenience. The sheets were changed every day, the bathrooms were all cleaned and disinfected daily and every surface in the place was wiped with antibacterial spray by Tina, his long-suffering house-keeper, twice a day. It was Leo to a T.

Leo was jangling his keys in his pocket. 'Sally can arrange a car or give you a set of keys and the code for the gate. You met Tina when you came over, right?'

Tina was one of Amber's favourite people in LA, for her sharp sense of humour, wicked tongue for gossip and welcoming hug. Amber loved her, and her daughter, and she found it funny that Leo didn't remember this. He was utterly uninterested in 'staff'.

'Sure, I've met her a few times now, and Maria.'

'Maria?' Leo looked blank.

'Her daughter,' Amber prompted him gently. 'She's a nice girl. Training to be a dancer?' Maria was only a couple of years younger than Amber, and Amber and Marco were giving her lessons. Maria was as much fun as her mother, absolutely stunning and wanted to be an actress. Plus she did a hilarious impression of Leo talking to her mother . . . Amber tried not to smile as she thought of Maria, stomping around the kitchen, shouting 'Get me a vegetable juice *now*, Tina!'.

After being in LA six months, she felt like Maria was the only person her own age she'd met who could be a friend.

'Maria . . .' Leo nodded. He knew Maria. Tina was always fucking rabbiting on about her to him, and he'd pretend like he cared. She was – what, sixteen? Seventeen? Definitely young, and pretty. He wasn't sure, but he thought he might have tried to kiss her once, put his hand up her skirt when she was in the kitchen late one night . . . He crinkled his brow, thoughtfully. Young. Smooth, caramel skin.

'Yeah,' he said eventually. 'I know her. She's a great girl. Brother's nice, too.' He raised his eyebrows at Marco, but Marco stared impassively back. Amber nudged him, embarrassed. She wished it wasn't so obvious how much Marco didn't like Leo.

'I have to go,' said Marco, picking up his car keys. 'I'll see you tonight, baby.' He kissed the top of Amber's head, patting her shoulder. 'Well done, lady. I'm really proud of you.' He squeezed her. 'The sky's the limit, if you want it.'

151

'She wants it!' Leo said, smiling broadly. Marco rolled his eyes, behind Leo's back, and walked slowly towards the drive. Amber watched him, wishing he would stay. On her own, she was always a little awkward around Leo. She didn't know why. He didn't ever flirt with her, and he was a huge flirt, she knew it. He flirted with her mum, with Tina, with the waitresses at restaurants, with the girls in the office and at the studios, on the lot – but never with her. Amber didn't know why, but she found it depressing. He treated her like a . . . like she was a niece he was fond of. Or a pet. It wasn't that she *wanted* him to flirt with her. She didn't have a thing for him, she was fairly sure, it was just . . . there was something about him. A charisma, a magnetic quality that meant she found herself drawn to him because he made her feel safe, looked after. Told her it was all going to be OK. Like her dad had. Only Leo was nothing like her dad . . .

'He doesn't like me, does he?' Leo said, jerking his head towards Marco's retreating form. He scratched his neck ruefully, pouting a little. 'I don't know why.'

'Oh, Leo,' Amber said. 'Don't worry about it. He's black and white about people. He'll change his mind, I bet.' She chewed a nail. 'He wants me to focus on my singing, that's all.'

Leo looked at her. 'You miss singing? I thought it was the acting you wanted to do now.'

Amber rushed to reassure him. 'Of course – of course! I love acting, it's my life now. I didn't like being a pop star much.'

'You didn't?' Leo sat down on a chair next to her, looking at her with interest. 'Why not?'

Amber looked thoughtful. 'It made me feel guilty. Like I was living someone else's dream, that belongs to some other girl who wants to be a massive pop star. I love singing. I don't love the stadiums, the publicity, the costumes, all that.'

'But you like acting? It's the same, isn't it?'

'No,' she said. 'When you're acting you can hide behind something. Behind the part you're playing. Shut everything else out.'

'Amber,' Leo said quietly. 'I didn't know you were that shy. Is that true?'

152

She blushed, unable to look at him, and stared down at the perfectly manicured lawn. 'Sort of. It's a . . . it's better, anyway.'

She couldn't tell him that she didn't like acting much either, that she'd rather just be in a basement bar somewhere with a guy on a piano and a mike stand, singing her heart out to anyone – or no one. She couldn't say, 'I don't want to be a film star, either' – he'd think she was the wettest thing on the planet. And she wanted him to like her, to be impressed by her. Amber wanted Leo Russell's approval.

'Look at me,' he said, his deep voice still soft. She raised her eyes to his, slowly. 'Listen, this is a great day for you. You don't need to worry. Amber, you are the hottest thing in Hollywood right now. Do you realise that, my dear? There isn't a studio in town that won't want you after this.' He smiled at her. 'And don't bite your nails!'

She smiled at him, gratefully, the thumping in her chest subsiding. It'd be OK if Leo was around, as ever. 'Thanks,' she said. 'You're – great, Leo. Thanks. It's all good.'

'It's all good? It's *wonderful*!' said a voice behind her. Amber turned around. 'Mum!' she said. 'Have you heard? Leo's just told me. *I Do* did thirty-five million dollars at the box office this weekend, it's going in at Number One!'

Margaret, still as trim as ever, elegant and neat in a purple silk shift, breathed in. She was silent for a moment. 'That's wonderful,' she said eventually. 'Sir Leo – that's amazing. What's next?'

Leo knew how to play Margaret – he knew how to play all women, come to that. He glanced at Amber conspiratorially, and stood up. He kissed Margaret's hand. 'World domination is what's next, and it's all down to you and your wonderful daughter, Mrs Stone.'

'Margaret!' she told him, smiling skittishly. Leo made Margaret feel young again – in fact, she had only just turned forty-one, and was younger than Leo, in spite of his insisting he was thirty-eight, not forty-five . . .

'Let me take you all out tonight,' he said. 'The Ivy. I've booked a table for four, Marco should come too if he's free, is that OK?'

'Of course,' Margaret said, answering for them all. 'That'd be wonderful, Leo! And we can talk about what she does next.' She beamed at Leo, her eyes shining. 'We owe you a lot. It's all down to you.'

Leo raised his hands modestly. 'No, no,' he said. He lowered his eyes, as if to the ground, but in fact he was staring at Amber's butt in that bikini.

It was down to him, of course, but by rejecting the suggestion that it was with the Brits, he looked modest, and they liked him more. And he was going to be working with Amber again . . . Leo watched her through half-closed eyes as she bent over the sun lounger to pick up her sarong. She wasn't under his skin – no woman got to him like that – but he wanted her, that was for sure. Wanted her sweet young flesh, her little breasts with their long nipples he could see poking through the bikini, her smooth skin and amber-gold hair, her green eyes . . . But he wanted her career too, wanted to exploit her – no, that was the wrong word. Work with her, to make sure everyone knew Amber Stone. She was the perfect package, in all senses.

'Please,' he said, as if modestly. 'It's nothing to do with me. But let me tell you something, Amber. In a couple of years no one's going to remember you were ever a singer. You'll be the biggest movie star on the planet. Remember this day. This is the day you started to become that person.'

Margaret beamed with satisfaction. Amber laughed, uncertainly.

'Thanks, Leo,' she said again because she didn't know how to say, *My best friend at school chose to be a vet. My friend down the road, growing up, chose to be a teacher. How did I get here, without ever choosing to?*

But she couldn't say that, to either of them. It was ungrateful and rude, and when she thought of what her mum and dad had done for her over the years, how proud her dad would be, she knew it was the right thing.

Chapter Twenty-Six

From *US Weekly* magazine, April 2003, page 2:

ROMANCING THE STONE?

Is Amber Stone sleeping with Leo Russell,
the British movie mogul?

A source, widely rumoured to be her best friend Scottish choreographer Marco Spinelli, claims that the silver screen's hottest young actress – star of I Do, *last year's* The First Date, *and this week's* Number One *at the box office,* A Hopeless Romantic, *is embroiled in a steamy affair with the legendary producer, who's nearly twice her age – and her size, if recent photos are to be believed (see above; taken last week of the two on Malibu beach). 'She's mad about him,' our source said. 'Amber's convinced if Leo dumped her, her career would be over. It's not healthy. Amber's always been easy to lead. She's known for being one of the most docile stars in Hollywood. She thinks she owes everything to him. He controls her – and her mom, too.'*

'How could you, Marco?' Amber didn't want to cry but it was hard. 'I trusted you, you broke that trust.' She gulped. There was a silence on the line and she carried on. 'I guess – I just don't understand why.'

Marco's voice was cold, exasperated. 'Jesus fucking H. Christ! I didn't do it, Amber.'

This wasn't the first time a story about her had been leaked; she, Margaret and Leo couldn't work out where it was coming from. This time, she knew. 'You took that photo, Marco babe. You showed it to me –'

'This is a fucking joke,' he said. 'You're too blind to see what he's done to you over the past couple of years, Amber. That's Leo!' His voice was hysterical. 'He's got hold of the photo somehow! He's made up the story! He's leaked it!'

Over the last year or so – and Amber hated to admit it – she'd grown apart from Marco. He was so down on Leo, called him Sir Dickhead Russell, wouldn't acknowledge his role in her success in any way. He said he was a wanker and he didn't want to hang out with him, that he was trying to take over her life. It was wearing Amber down. And it wasn't true.

'It's horrible about him, Marco,' Amber said, patiently. 'It's a horrible photo, horrible piece, it calls him fat and makes out he's a sinister control freak. Why on earth would he leak a story like that about himself?'

'Because he's a sinister control freak. And he's trying to get you to shut me out,' Marco said, spitefully. 'All that time you spend together, how you're always over at his house, you never spend time at yours, how he makes out there's nothing going on, and I see the way he looks at you, Amber. Like you're a possession of his.'

'He's never there,' Amber said, tiredly. 'I hardly see him, he's always away. I go to his house to see Maria. I'm sick of this, the same arguments again, Marco. What is it, are you . . .' She searched for the right words; she simply didn't get what it could be. 'Are you *jealous*? I don't understand. Leo's my friend, he's been a great friend to me and Mum, I owe him everything. It's *not* that he controls me!' Her voice was rising; she needed to stay calm, not lose it. 'You have to understand, I love you but you mustn't do this again. Ever. In fact, I don't know if I can see you for a couple of weeks, I need some time . . .'

'I'll make this easy for you then, darling,' Marco said, viciously. 'I'm not your fucking boyfriend. I can't help you any more, Amber. If you don't believe me, fine. You need to stop trying to please everyone. Grow a backbone. Goodbye.'

And then the line went dead. Stunned, Amber actually looked at the phone, as if to convince herself it was true. He'd put the phone down on her, said goodbye to their friendship, like he didn't care? She shook her head, tears coming into her eyes. Marco had been her best friend for so long – more than that, he'd told her she was like a little sister to him. Amid all the baloney, all the crap, he'd always been there for her, and she liked to think she'd been there for him, too. But now . . .

The fact was, she knew Marco had leaked the story. He hated Leo. It was so mad because she wasn't sleeping with him. No one would believe her now. It was such a spiteful, vindictive article. But that was the way it was – they could print what they liked, and if you tried to get them to change it, you looked like you had something to hide.

Everything should have been perfect, she thought. She was Number One again, and shooting on the next film was going well. Mum was happy. Chelsea seemed fine, back in London, though Amber felt a pang of guilt that she hadn't spoken to her in so long . . . She'd call her tonight.

Amber stretched out on the lounger by the pool; she loved Leo's house. He'd been away now for a couple of weeks; she really hoped he didn't see the article. It was just too embarrassing.

Sure, there was nothing between them, but it was still awkward . . .

Amber shook her head. She couldn't believe Marco would betray her like that. But that was the way it went, when you were a star. They'd warned her about it. There were always casualties along the way. Leo had warned her about that. In fact, she had to hand it to Leo. She'd thought he was hilarious when she'd first come to LA. But he'd never let her down, and everything he'd said was going to happen had happened. Just like he knew.

She heard someone moving behind her.

'Hey, Tina?' she called. She hadn't seen her in a while. 'Tina, is that you?'

Sally had a lot to do that day, and the last thing she wanted was to get embroiled in a conversation with Amber. She'd been trying to get the papers she needed from Leo's study and make her escape along the terrace by the pool without Amber noticing. She'd heard the conversation with Marco. Amber turned round, and saw her. She smiled brightly.

'Hey, Sally! Hi! I thought you were Tina.'

Sally came down the steps. She was immaculately dressed, as ever, in a perfect little grey Armani dress which showed off her tanned, toned arms. She swept her golden hair off her face and smiled back.

'Didn't you hear, Amber? I'd have thought you'd have known, you spend so much time here. Tina left.'

Amber sat up. 'Tina? Really? Where did she go?'

Sally shrugged. 'She just packed up and went back to Puerto Rico. Maria and José went with her.'

She looked closely at Amber. 'Like I say – didn't they mention it?'

Amber was embarrassed – Sally always made her feel like a little girl. She shook her head, flustered. 'I didn't know – that's awful. I mean, it's good for them. I – I'd just have liked to have said . . . said goodbye, you know.'

'I'll get you their new email, or their address,' Sally said briskly, making to leave. She turned back before she reached the steps. 'Though, Amber, if you don't mind me saying – I know Leo has always believed you shouldn't get too close to the staff.'

'But they were –' Amber dropped her hands in her lap. Impossible to try and explain to Sally.

'Tina was paid to do her job. Paid very well. You can't confuse that with anything else. Look at me! I'm staff!' Sally said lightly. She waited, and then delivered the killer blow. 'And Marco too, I guess. I heard about the article.'

Amber nodded. 'Perhaps you're right.'

She looked so forlorn, sitting there, when she should have

looked so glamorous: a script on her lap, an iced tea on the table beside her, huge sunglasses around her still childlike face . . . Sally relented, and patted her shoulder. Dammit, she couldn't help but like Amber, though she'd tried her best not to. 'Hey, kid,' she said, softly. 'Leo's back tomorrow, you can talk this all through with him then. Don't sweat it. That's the way the cookie crumbles, sometimes, OK?'

'OK,' Amber said, grateful to Sally for the first time. 'You're right. Thanks.'

'It's fucking embarrassing,' she said, twisting the newspaper over and over in her hands. 'And I'm sorry.'

Leo was sitting behind his desk, back at home, and he swivelled round to look at her. 'It really doesn't matter,' he said, practically. 'I never got Marco, I have to say. Turns out he wasn't a fan of me, either.'

'Well –' Amber chewed a nail. She'd had a couple of glasses of wine before she'd come in to see him, to get her nerve up for this conversation.

'Don't bite your nails, Amber,' Leo said, automatically. He'd been saying it to her for years now. She still ignored him, chewing away at the cuticles. It gave the make-up artists on set a real challenge.

'You see, that's what I mean,' Amber said, laughing. 'They don't get our relationship, do they?' She smiled at him.

'I know.' He smiled back at her ruefully. 'They think I'm an old Lothario, whereas in fact I'm more like your nagging wife.'

Outside, in the early-evening light, the sun was setting like a ball of fire, orange and fuchsia, flooding into the low-ceilinged office, illuminating everything. He stood up. 'I'm not wild about being referred to as twice your size.' She grinned. 'But let's not worry about it any more,' he said. 'It might not have been Marco, you know. Just don't let it get to you. You're a star. Rise above it.'

'Thanks.' Sometimes Amber forgot she was one of the biggest stars in the world. She shook her head, overwhelmed for a minute. Leo came round and put his arms round her.

'Hey, hey!' he said, softly. 'Don't cry, Amber. It's not worth it.'

Leo was big and strong; being in the circle of his arms was intoxicatingly comforting. Amber stared up at him, the tears drying on her cheeks. 'Thank you,' she said slowly, watching his face.

He didn't respond; he was smiling at her, kindly – but was there something else there, something beyond it? She couldn't tell, didn't know . . . Flushed with wine, and with a sudden longing that washed over her, more powerful than she could have thought, Amber closed her eyes, turned her face to his and kissed him.

Looking down at her, Leo Russell smiled for just a split second, and then started gently kissing her back.

Everything was going to plan.

The new housekeeper hadn't started yet – there was a daily maid service. Sally was back at the office, so they were alone. Quickly, smoothly, Leo led Amber to the bedroom, where he held her in his arms again, stroking her back and rocking her until she started kissing him again, suddenly wild with passion. Amber had dated a little since she got to LA, but it had been a while since she'd had sex, and he knew it.

Now she was his, was going to be his, and he couldn't wait.

He took her clothes off – the pretty embroidered white blouse, the elegant khaki capri pants – and watched her as she stood in front of him, breathing heavily, her chest rising and falling.

'Are you sure about this, Amber?' he said. He needed her to be sure – he wasn't going to make a mistake about it.

She came towards him, her eyes huge, pupils dilated with desire. 'I am,' she said. She sounded surprised. 'I really am, Leo. Please.' She shuddered, and put her thumbs on either side of the pale coffee-coloured lace knickers that clung to her perfect, peachy bottom. She slid them off and climbed on the bed, next to him.

Leo swallowed. This was better than he'd ever imagined. She was young and perfect and so fucking hot. He was hard, he'd learned to control himself, he thought, but this was going to be tricky. She knelt above him, her small, rounded breasts snug in their matching coffee lace bra, the dark rose nipples visible under the lace . . . Leo grunted, in his throat, reached up and undid the clasp, and then he moved his hand between her legs, kissing her nipples, checking she was ready for him. She was dripping wet and so tight, and she was moaning his name. Nice, polite, sweet Amber, he couldn't believe he was finally getting it from her . . . everything was going to plan . . .

He looked up at the newly installed, nearly invisible camera in the corner of the room. They'd been put in every room for insurance, after a spate of burglaries, his place and others nearby. He usually forgot about them, but he sometimes kept a couple of tapes back to watch . . .

He would definitely be watching *this* again tomorrow.

She stared down at him. Amber hadn't been with many men, but she knew this: Leo was enormous. He must be – what – ten inches? She gulped, even more aroused than before. 'Please . . .' she said again, and Leo lifted her on top of his huge, straining, hard cock and pushed gently inside her. She sank down the length of him, as he touched her, stroking her clitoris, staring into her eyes. Amber's mouth flew open, she gasped and then she started to rise and fall on top of him, squeezing his cock with her muscles, those perfect breasts with their long nipples juddering slightly as she rode him . . .

This was the fantasy. This was what he'd been working for, all these years. And Leo had to admit, as he came inside Amber, thrusting into her one final time with a long, low roar, that it was better than he'd ever imagined.

He'd got what he wanted. He always did. He gazed up at her, eyes glazing over, wondering where the next thrill would come from. As she climbed off him, slumping down next to him, Amber was thinking that perhaps what she wanted was right under her nose. It was safe with Leo. Thrilling, but safe. He was great in bed, he was kind, he had her best interests at heart and – she looked at his tall, muscular body lying next to her, his cock still hard, his broad chest rising and falling – yes, she could definitely do *that* again. Perhaps the two of them together made sense.

And Leo was thinking very much the same thing, but for

161

different reasons. He'd waited for a while to make his move on Amber. And the truth was, he needed to change his ways a little. A couple of incidents lately had scared him, made him realise that perhaps being with Amber could be more than just the fuck he'd been wondering about for years. He'd kept his hands off her till he knew she was ready but the two of them together – it could be good for business. Like the article he'd falsely planted had said . . . *She might be just what I need at this point. And she wants it. She's a nice kid, and I could make her mine, totally mine. She's the hottest star on the planet, and it's my name she's choking out as she comes . . .*

She'll do, for now. As long as he stayed in control he was happy, he told himself, as Amber tried to snuggle up next to him.

The next morning, Amber was shy, but Leo pretended everything was completely normal. He took her again, on top this time, moving inside her and gently kissing her neck, running his hands over her and murmuring her name till she cried out. And then he hopped out of bed, humming.

'I think Sally's downstairs.' He scratched his chest, foggily. Amber sat up, with alarm. 'Don't worry,' Leo said. 'I promise you, darling. She's paid to stay quiet. She won't say anything.'

Amber thought back to her conversation with Sally the previous day. 'Right,' she said.

'I mean it. You're a star, you can do what you want. Enjoy it,' Leo said, smiling at her worried expression. 'And come and get some breakfast downstairs.'

When they got to the terrace, the table was laid for breakfast – fresh fruit, oatmeal, fresh orange juice. Sally came through when she heard them. She didn't give any other preamble, didn't register Amber in Leo's dressing gown with any shock, just nodded at them both and said, 'Hi, Leo. Well, the papers are having a field day with you this week, Amber.'

Amber was pouring herself some coffee, trying to work out how embarrassing this situation was. Why it felt so right, yet why she was also uncomfortable.

'There's a problem. With your sister.'

Leo's head shot up. He had always been intrigued by the mysterious elder sister. Amber's hand flew to her mouth.

'What? Is she OK?'

'All over the British tabloids,' Sally sighed. 'I printed it out from their websites. Here's the *Sun.*' She smiled. 'Hope that's helpful!'

Leo grunted, and grabbed the printout. He started reading. Amber stood there, transfixed.

'She's been arrested, caught selling coke to a reporter,' Sally said. She looked from Amber to Leo. 'Time to finally cut loose, wouldn't you say?'

Chapter Twenty-Seven

AMBER STONE SISTER COCAINE SHAME

ACTRESS SIS CALLS STAR 'BLAND'

Chelsea Stone, perhaps the ultimate 'where are they now?' celeb – it's hard to remember there was a time when Amber's big sister was the star. It was over a decade ago she was the nation's favourite teenager in *Roxy's Nine Lives* – remember that? People who do will be horrified to see her in these shocking pics taken early yesterday morning, of the washed-up child star snorting line after line of coke and offering to sell some to our reporter. Looking badly bloated, she has piled on the pounds since her brief brush with fame ended many years ago. But Chelsea still thinks of herself as the star, she told our reporter.

'Amber's a singer, not an actress,' she slurred. 'She's a nice kid, but she's bland. One £$?%ing romcom after another, it's not acting.'

And in a sign that will show fans she has really hit rock-bottom, the out-of-it ex-starlet (above left) took a small bag from her pocket and begged our reporter to share it with her, for cash. (We declined, and handed our photographs to Scotland Yard.)

STONE SISTERS: IT'S WAR!

AMBER HITS BACK: 'ADDICT'
CHELSEA 'JEALOUS'

One of the UK's most successful film stars, Amber Stone, has been forced to issue a statement about her older sister, Chelsea Stone, recently embroiled in the latest of a series of drug allegations and wild behaviour.

'I love my sister, but I can't help her until she helps herself,' she wrote on her website yesterday. 'We have tried for years to support her, ever since she nearly killed herself in a drunk-driving accident, the night of my beloved father's death. I think she has serious problems and only she can address them by admitting her addiction and seeking counselling and support. When she does, I'll be there for her.'

The pictures were flashed around the world; it was a slow news week, being August. Amber had a new film out and was hotter than ever, and Chelsea had sunk so far that many people simply didn't remember that she'd ever been famous, much less that she was Amber Stone's sister.

They found her phone number, the press called her constantly. None of her friends got in touch; it seemed she didn't have any. Chelsea huddled in a duvet for a whole day, staring miserably at the blank wall opposite, listening to the sound of photographers jostling for space outside on Ladbroke Grove, occasionally someone calling out her name.

This was what rock-bottom felt like, then.

She didn't know what to do. She was still on the painkillers for the accident – she needed them, but they affected the booze and everything else. The past couple of years had been a blur, spending her inheritance on drugs and drink and late nights with strangers. She had nothing to show for it, nothing to show for her life. She had been such a fucking idiot, she saw that now . . . how had it come to this, for God's sake? Why?

Worst of all was what Amber had said. She knew she had hurt her sister, saying things she never meant to, but the way Amber responded – so cool and calm, so fucking up herself! Chelsea'd tried several times to get hold of her, but no success. Amber really was trying to distance herself, put more than just an ocean and a continent between them. It was as if they weren't even related any more.

Sniffing, Chelsea picked up the phone. She had to make this call, she knew it. But she wasn't looking forward to it.

'Mum . . . ?'

Margaret's voice was clear, all the way from a studio in LA, but Chelsea could hear the anxiety in her tone. 'Love – are you all right? You sound bad.'

Relief flooded over her. 'Oh, Mum – yeah. It's crap here, photographers everywhere . . . I was ringing to say how sorry I am, getting us all into this shit with the drugs and stuff.'

'Chelsea?' the voice said, sharply. 'Is that you?'

'Mum?' Chelsea sat up in bed. 'Yeah, I just said . . . How are you?'

'Oh.' Margaret gave a sniff. 'I thought it was Amber. You, then. So, are you happy? Mm?'

'Oh, Mum, listen,' Chelsea said. 'I'm getting help, I've already spoken to—'

'No, you listen, darling girl,' Margaret said, lowering her voice to a hissing whisper. 'I am on set, waiting for your sister to come out of hair and make-up. She is in the middle of shooting a new film, and this has not helped her at all, your bloody stupidity. Why d'you do it, Chelsea? I don't get it.' She made a clicking sound. 'Why have you always been like this?'

Cradling the phone under her shoulder, Chelsea hugged herself and rocked back and forth. 'I'm sorry, Mum – I know I've been stupid. It's – I don't know, everything seems to go wrong for me.' Her voice broke. 'It's just, I'm so—'

'I don't have time for this,' Margaret said. 'Ever since your father died, you've done nothing but fall out of clubs with your tits showing.' Her voice was rising; Chelsea never heard her lose her cool, these days. 'You're always drunk. You behave like a – like a slut! And now drugs. It's all over the papers, even here. People are asking Amber if she's ever had a problem with drugs too.' Her voice rose, near hysterical. '*Amber!* As if she would!'

Yeah, she's too fucking boring. Chelsea closed her eyes. 'Mum, please just listen to me. I didn't mean it about Amber, I was out of it . . . I want to speak to her.'

'No, I'm done listening to you, Chelsea. She bought you that car, she pays your bloody allowance each month, and what do you do in return?'

Chelsea's jaw dropped. 'She pays – *what?*'

There was grim satisfaction in Margaret's voice. 'Yes, my dear. You had to find out sometime, didn't you? There's no inheritance, there *was* no bloody money left at all when your father killed himself! It's Amber, she's been paying for you all this time. And how do you pay her back?' She was practically hissing, like a kettle full of steam. 'Y-you pay her back by dragging her name through the mud! You – Hello? Hello? Chelsea, can you hear me! Hello?'

But the line had gone dead.

As soon as she'd put the phone down, thousands of miles away from London, on a Burbank set, Margaret immediately felt guilty. She realised she'd been too harsh on Chelsea.

Margaret never liked being in the wrong. Perhaps she took stuff out on Chelsea that wasn't her fault. It wasn't her fault she was born when she was, or that every time she looked at her daughter she saw something in her of the only man she'd loved. Was it? Chelsea didn't know any of that.

They were carrying scenery around, setting up for the new set next door while they waited for Amber, and Margaret wandered out of one of the huge sound stages into the bright blue sky, the white of the hangar-like buildings dazzling her after the gloom inside. She was still for a moment. She remembered the night she found George, swaying from a hook in the ceiling, and she blinked, like she might faint, then and there on the set. And she remembered the note George had left, that she'd never shown anyone.

Please, please tell my darling Chelsea this wasn't her fault. I had to do it, I know it now. I just can't lie any more. Tell my girls I love them.

Please. Margaret swallowed, and smoothed out an invisible crease in her skirt.

Margaret never thought about George unless she had to. She'd trained herself to forget about him as far as it was possible, answering questions about her deceased husband with a mechanical politeness that meant she didn't engage her brain with what had happened the night of his death, and how, before or since, she'd never really faced up to who he was.

To find your husband's body is bad. To find that your husband was on the verge of bankruptcy is also bad – and then to find out he was gay . . . Well. The truth was, Margaret realised, she didn't know how she felt. She'd spent so long trying to make the best of everything and suppress her true emotions, that anything that didn't fit in with that plan soon fell by the wayside.

She didn't speak to Derek unless she had to. She ignored all the good memories of George, too. And, she now realised, she'd done exactly the same with Chelsea.

She picked up the phone to dial again. She did love her eldest daughter, of course she did, in spite of everything. And she'd been through a lot. Perhaps it was time to put the past behind her.

'The number you have dialled is not available,' the message intoned. 'Please check and try again. The number you have dialled is not available.'

She kept trying, both Chelsea's mobile and her landline.

There was no reply.

When Margaret got through to the phone company, a couple of hours later, because she was worried now, they told her the line had been disconnected. The mobile company said the same – the contract had been cancelled, the number was unreachable. Chelsea had left the flat and gone – who knew where?

In fact, despite her best efforts to try a bit harder, Margaret would not have been at all pleased to see what Chelsea did next.

The conversation was too much for Chelsea.

Here, right here, was rock-bottom. She realised that now.

She put the phone down on her mother's squawking voice and hugged herself even tighter, tears freely coursing down her cheeks.

All these years, she'd been living off her little sister. She was loudly contemptuous of how Amber had sold out, but she was actually living off her earnings, while she, Chelsea, stayed in bed, slept with strangers, got fatter and blotchier by the day . . . she was a fucking pig, she hated herself.

And her life was being subsidised by a sister who didn't really want to talk to her, who paid for her because she had to make sure she didn't die in the gutter, 'cos it would be a great ending to the tragic story of Chelsea Stone but it wouldn't make Amber look good, would it?

She stood up and looked around the small flat where she'd been living unhappily now for years, her life festering away. And she nodded, slowly.

It was time to make a change.

Perhaps she did have to hit rock-bottom to get her pride back. Swiftly, Chelsea moved from room to room, packing only the bare essentials of what she needed and leaving behind anything that could have been bought with Amber's money.

Then she closed the door behind her, and went downstairs to the shabby hallway, with the threadbare carpet and scuff marks on the old, torn wallpaper. At the front door, she stopped. The photographers were outside, she could hear them, humming malevolently like a wasps' nest. What was she going to do?

She knocked on the door of the downstairs flat.

'Joan,' she said, to the suspicious old lady who eventually answered. 'Joan, I need a massive favour.'

Joan rolled her eyes. 'Lost your keys again, dear?'

'No,' Chelsea said. She blinked; she mustn't cry. 'Nothing like that.' She hitched the large holdall over her shoulder. 'I need to get out of the flat. But the photographers are outside.'

'I noticed,' Joan said grimly. 'What you done now, then?'

'Nothing, nothing,' Chelsea said hastily. She looked at Joan's face. 'Oh, well, more trouble, I'm afraid. But no one got hurt. Thing is,' deep breath, 'I'm going away for a while, and I don't want them to see me go. I need to get out of here.'

She gave a gulp, and swallowed again.

Joan scanned her face. Chelsea was a nightmare neighbour – loud, drunk, terrifyingly random – sometimes she'd find her passed out on the dirty stairs, once even on the doorstep. She brought people home and they got up to all sorts, Joan dreaded to think.

But the truth was, she liked Chelsea. She just did. She had a big laugh and she was funny, and she didn't patronise Joan, put on a stupid 'I'm talking to an old dear' voice with her. She brought her doughnuts, they had cups of tea together, she asked Joan about the old days, as a Gaiety Girl up in the West End.

Yes, Joan liked her. She even reminded Joan of herself, when she was younger.

'Come in,' Joan said, looking at her tear-stained face, still lovely even though it was pale and bloated. She patted Chelsea's shoulder. 'There's a gate out the back of the garden, you'll come out just by the tube. All right?'

'Oh, thanks, Joan,' Chelsea said, scooping her into a big hug. 'Joan, you're a fucking legend, I'll pay you back, I promise.'

'Don't swear,' Joan said, removing herself from Chelsea's grasp. 'And don't you worry, darling. You just get yourself better.' She patted Chelsea's cheek. 'You're a good girl, all right?'

'All right,' Chelsea said, smiling for the first time in a long while. She slung the bag over her shoulder and disappeared into the garden.

When she emerged onto Ladbroke Grove, she took a cab to some swish Soho offices, just off Golden Square, all glass and concrete, and was shown up to the top floor.

170

'Hello darling,' the man said, coming towards her. 'So you've been in a bit of trouble, ain't you? What can I do for you, then?'

Chelsea knew how to play a scene. 'Hello, Uncle Derek,' she said. 'Your favourite niece needs something.'

She looked at him, and nodded. Derek didn't say anything, he just smiled and watched her, fiddling with his gold cufflinks.

'Yeah?' he said eventually. 'Tell me. I'd do anything for you, Chelsea. You know that.'

Chelsea cleared her throat. 'All right then. I want a job. Don't care what it is. I have to start paying my way. Make Dad proud of me.'

Derek watched her carefully. 'He always was, doll,' he said. 'Always was. And he is today. I just know it.'

Chapter Twenty-Eight

Derek Stone had aged well. He'd turned fifty that year, and it had forced him to take stock, and for the most part what he saw pleased him. Hardly any grey in his thick dark hair, eyes as blue as ever, he ran at the weekends and ate well to keep that spread off him. He could afford a nice suit, fat silk tie, gold cufflinks, the works. Yeah, Derek knew he scrubbed up all right, compared to most. Compared to the lags he'd done time with, most of the prison officers too. And compared to his old pals in Soho – the stallholders down the markets were wheezing and red-faced, bags under the eyes, years of early starts and cold mornings. The hookers were either dead or God knew where, the landlords and fellow businessmen either moved on or in the clink like him. He'd got out OK, got on, that restless quality he had serving him well.

Derek always made the best of a bad situation, turning everything to his advantage. Contacts in prison, friends made in pubs, those twinkling blue eyes that were the downfall of many a girl (and boy) when he wanted something out of them – he'd risen to the top, invested wisely, had a few lucky breaks. There'd been no one to share it with, over the years. He'd told himself he was a fortunate man, he could do what he liked . . . Derek didn't believe in regrets. But just sometimes, he found himself wondering how things might have been.

He was pleased to be asked for help by Chelsea. But he was a shrewd man, and he still took a bit of persuading.

'What does Maggie think about this?' Chelsea looked blankly at him, and he hastily amended himself. 'Your mum. Margaret.'

'*Margaret* can go to hell,' Chelsea snapped. Derek shook his head. 'Seriously, I don't care about her any more. Her or that wet rag of a sister. From now on I pay my own way. I have to stand on my own two feet. I just need a break,' she said, almost begging, 'I'll work like a dog, I'll do anything. Please?'

Derek looked at her, carefully. 'You're serious, aren't you?'

'Yes,' Chelsea said softly.

He saw the look in those sparkling blue eyes, one he hadn't seen for ages. Derek didn't see Chelsea often, and when he did he found it depressing. She was always drunk, maudlin, self-interested, embarrassing. Now he blamed himself, letting her get like this. After all, didn't he have responsibility for her? He wanted to kick himself, then and there. He'd been a stupid wanker again, avoiding his responsibilities, he should have done something about it himself. It was good to see that spark back in her eyes – she'd realised she had to make the change. He slammed his hands on the table.

'You're on, my darling. You can stay with me for a week till you get yourself organised. Now, let's sort you out with something, all right?'

Yes, against all the odds – or maybe because he'd fiddled them so they went his way – Derek Stone was a success. A big, fuckload-earning, multimillionaire success.

He sometimes laughed when he thought about it all. He'd learned his lesson, such as it was. He knew where to draw the line now, he wasn't a berk with no idea, like before, not paying rent, not keeping up appearances the right way.

The spell in the clink had taught him a thing or two, mostly from the other lags there. He'd networked with a couple of bent coppers who were doing time as well. Knew who to sweeten, who to avoid, where the money was. In the early 1980s, before the boom, he'd bought large chunks of cheap Soho property. Soho was still the dive it had been when he'd met Maggie, before the All Bar Ones and posh pizzerias came in and turned it into a middle-class fucking theme park. Now prices were sky-high, and he was sitting on a packet.

He still had the theatres, too. A few of them. *Amours du Derek* was a long way in the past, though. They were classier than that, not low-rent knocking shops like before. Not in his eyes, at least. He was the king of pole-dancing and lap-dancing, was Derek. He had a string of not-so-discreet places scattered around Soho and the West End, and they were full every night, come rain or shine.

Funny to think of it, how it had all turned out, but people had got hurt along the way and Derek didn't know how to put it right.

He'd been a proper dick, he knew it. Run off with that stupid bitch Camilla, not because he liked her but because he'd been ter-rified of being tied down with Maggie and her baby. Maggie was so serious, so innocent. When he looked into her sweet green eyes he felt worthless, not good enough for her. And he'd wanted the money Camilla's dad could give him. But he wasn't meant to be with a posh little cow like her, she treated him like dirt, made him feel as common as a dog.

Maggie, on the other hand, treated him like dirt because she still hated him, not because she thought he was common. And you know what? Derek liked that.

He still liked her, come to that.

And he loved their daughter. Loved Amber too, though she reminded him of George, and there was a sadness at the heart of Derek's life about George he couldn't ever get rid of. He missed his stupid nancy-boy brother, missed him more every day. Amber made him uneasy. Her smile was the same as George's – shy, diffident, lovely. It stabbed Derek in the heart.

Not Chelsea. No, not her.

She was *his* girl.

And now it was time to see what she was made of.

'This is it.' Derek pushed open the door and let Chelsea go ahead of him. She blinked, her eyes slowly getting accustomed to the darkness. 'Welcome to Safari Sammy's, your new place of work.'

He beamed as Chelsea advanced slowly into the room.

Chelsea was no snob. She liked to think she was a pub girl, not a fancy cocktail girl. She preferred the company of men to women, too. But this . . . no way. As she picked her way across the floor, she winced.

Sure, three in the afternoon was no time to see a pole-dancing club in all its glory, but Safari Sammy's was a bleak place no matter what time of day it was. The safari theme had been taken to extremes. Horrible green tentacles climbed the walls, shiny pink nylon tiger and leopardskin prints covered the banquettes and chairs, gleaming luridly in the dull light. Chelsea, who thought she loved anything decorated in leopardskin, felt quite sick. Up on stage, there were two poles and a scuffed, dirty floor. A lone girl, painfully thin, lank, pale blonde hair hanging over her shoulders, was swinging half-heartedly round one of the poles. Her fake tits didn't move – they looked like globes stuck onto her childlike, skinny ribcage. Chelsea looked down at her own ample figure and sighed. The whole place smelled of cigarettes and cheap aftershave. It wasn't kitsch, it was just depressing.

'Safari Sammy's should be doing well,' Derek explained once they were sitting at the bar, Chelsea holding a stiff rum and coke. 'It's just off Charing Cross, it's in a great location and there's loads of other places like it round here doing a roaring trade, but I can't seem to get it off the ground.'

'The decoration's shit, Derek,' Chelsea said frankly, trying not to watch the pathetic young girl on stage. 'It looks like someone vomited up a jungle.'

Derek waggled his drink at her, amused. 'You ain't in no position to be criticising, sweetheart. Listen to me. I'm not saying it's the classiest joint, but it's a good venue and it should be raking it in. I don't understand it. But I'm doing well, and I don't have time for this, I got other fish to fry, so I thought I'd turn it over to you for six months, see how you get on.'

'What?' Chelsea stared at him in disbelief. She'd been thinking she'd work behind the bar. 'I've never – I can't run a club, Derek!'

Derek jabbed his head over to an open door next to the stage. 'That's the manager's office,' he said. 'And I'm asking you to be the new manager of Safari Sammy's. I'm closing the place down by March if it doesn't work. Do you want it or not?'

Chelsea looked again at the large, airy stage, the well-stocked bar, the nice way the place was designed and arranged, intimate yet spacious. It was a good space, a good location, just badly done. She might not know the first thing about managing clubs, but she knew this was a good venue. So why didn't Derek? He couldn't know everything, she reasoned. He was good when things were straightforward.

She, however, was good when it was complicated. Screwed up. Going to shit. She nodded, and smiled.

'I think you're mad. I don't know anything about it.'

'That doesn't matter, Chels,' he said. 'I trust you. Give it a go.'

I trust you. Her eyes filled with tears. 'Thanks, Uncle Derek. I owe you one.'

Derek's eyes met hers over their drinks. He said softly, 'Sweetheart, it's my pleasure to help you. Always remember that.'

Derek wasn't expecting much from Chelsea at Safari Sammy's, if he was honest. He was actually on the verge of closing it down. It was running at a loss, what harm could it do, let her find her feet for a bit?

He had no idea what he was in for.

On her first day, Chelsea closed the place down temporarily. She set the bar staff and doorman to work, stripping the decor. She persuaded Derek to give her money to redecorate, and that was done in a record three weeks – she was used to getting her own way, she knew how to handle painters and decorators. Derek watched it all with a smile. She didn't take any crap from anyone, that girl.

While the club was shut, Chelsea fired all the dancers, giving them two months' pay. She brought in a mixologist from a smart

176

hotel who knew how to make cocktails and made him head barman, firing the disgruntled old lech who only came to work to wank off at the girls. She sacked the deputy manager, and brought in a guy she knew who'd just left a cabaret club she used to drink in, the other side of Soho. She hired new dancers, girls with curves, who did little routines with a dash of humour, a touch of burlesque, like the old striptease clubs. She paid them more, but they knew how to chat to punters, how to get them to pay for the private dances, knew how to do it with humour and panache, not because they were semi-starved Eastern Europeans with a violent pimp to pay.

And she changed the name. No more Safari Sammy's. She called it Roxy's. She couldn't think of anything else, and she liked the private joke only she knew about.

Three months after she took over Roxy's made a huge loss, as the old punters deserted the place and didn't come back.

Four months after that, the bookings were up, as new punters tried it out for the first time . . . and returned.

When the club had been open five months, towards Christmas, Chelsea gave out flyers in every pub in Soho, promising discounts for group bookings, and the office parties – girls liked Roxy's because it was fun, not sinister like so many other places – and boys' nights out kept them busy till the New Year.

By February 2003, six months after she'd turned up in tears in Derek's office, the club was a success. So much so that Derek gave Chelsea a pay rise, and a bonus.

'You've earned it,' he told her. 'You've got a real flair for business.'

Sitting in her office, where there was no natural daylight – just pictures of the club, wall charts, files and Rolodexes, and the odd feather boa – Chelsea took the cheque he gave her with a smile. She picked up her handbag and dropped it in. She wanted a drink, but she had a bet with herself these days – no drugs ever again, and no booze till she'd been awake for over twelve hours. It worked, bizarrely enough, or perhaps that was because she wanted to make it work. She had a will of iron, and she could bend it whatever way she wanted . . .

'Thanks, Uncle Derek,' she said. She smoothed down the tight-fitting skirt of the shapely, well-cut suit she always wore, accessorised with a red lace camisole and black fishnets so that people knew what they were in for. She knew enough to know she had to match the brand of what she was selling, and she was selling sex with a smile. 'You know what, I bloody have earned it. And let me tell you, it feels damn good.'

Chapter Twenty-Nine

Chelsea was one of those people who needed to throw themselves a hundred per cent into whatever they did, whether it was acting, boozing or running a strip club. She loved her new life, and Derek could only stand back in wonder as Chelsea took Roxy's from strength to strength. He kept trying to persuade her to take over other clubs, but she wouldn't.

'I'm good at this,' she said. 'I need to get better. One day.'

The truth is, she loved the club, loved the way she'd remade it in her own image. It was done out in zebra print and pink paint, vintage chandeliers and saucy posters of striptease queens of old, excellent cocktails and menus in the shape of a girl's silhouette. She wanted it to feel like an old French whore's boudoir – and she hoped she'd succeeded. But she didn't want to stretch herself, and part of her wondered if this was what she was going to be doing for ever. Only a tiny part – she loved it – but the thing that still made Chelsea tick was acting, and she couldn't quite give up on it.

Still, she got a huge buzz from the success of Roxy's. She loved being with performers, loved the late-night scene. She rented a place in Soho. It was great, walking through the streets early in the morning on her way back from work as the stallholders were setting up, red and pink dawn streaking the sky, seeing the city come alive again. She would sleep during the day and work at night. All of it suited her.

She was making friends, too. Gareth, the deputy manager she'd hired, had just split up with his boyfriend, and wanted someone to drink long into the night with. Chelsea was more than happy to oblige. Some of the girls and the barmen from Roxy's would come with them. They knew where to find a dodgy bar in some strange back alley off Hanway Street, or behind Beak Street.

And there was the Phoenix Club, a bar for actors and musicians in a smoke-filled basement lined with old postcards of variety acts, underneath the Phoenix Theatre on Charing Cross Road. You couldn't go in unless you were something to do with performing, the booze was cheap, it was open all hours and the crowd was always great. You got chatting to interesting people. It wasn't like the Groucho or Soho House, full of tossers snorting coke and jerking off about their latest advert for some expensive car.

Chelsea despised all of that. The Phoenix only let in people who made their living making music or acting or dancing. They didn't care how much money you made, or how well connected you were. She loved it.

She could stay anonymous – no one really cared about her tabloid travails or her famous sister. Instead, she could catch up with other actors, talk over ideas for new shows with people and relax with friends after a hard night's work, at home in a world she knew, where she could be accepted. It was good to be back.

It was Gareth who first suggested it. They were in the Phoenix, it was late on Saturday night – more like Sunday morning.

'Hey,' he said, gesturing to Chelsea, who was smoking furiously and chatting to Conor, an actor she fancied, over in the corner. 'Chelsea, get over here! He's not going to fuck you, so come here! I want to ask you something.'

Chelsea excused herself, her cheeks burning, as Conor smiled and turned back to Sara, the lithe, slim co-star of his musical. 'What?' she hissed. 'Jeez, Gareth, you're a fucking twat, you know

that? I was just – hello, Vicky,' she added, realising Gareth was talking to someone. 'How are you?'

'I'm good,' Vicky said, kissing her on the cheek. 'I'm just –'

'Darling, Vicky needs a place to rehearse, tomorrow, for that
new cabaret show she's putting on. They've got a spot in some pub
theatre round the corner, two weeks!' Gareth was easily excitable
when he was drunk.

'Yes.' Vicky nodded. She was a burlesque dancer who also sang,
and she had a great line in really filthy stories. Her stage name was
Marguerite. Actually, she was from Rochdale, and took no shit
from anyone. 'We need somewhere to rehearse, because we can't
get into the pub before the show.'

'Well, use the club,' Chelsea said. 'We're closed on Sundays.
You're welcome. What's the show?'

'It's just a cabaret,' Vicky said. 'Different stuff, who knows?
Jasmine's doing her trick with the Christmas-tree lights. You have
to see where she keeps them to believe it.' She rolled her eyes.

'You're joking,' said Chelsea.

'I bloody am not,' Vicky said, swigging the rest of her vodka
and tonic. 'And Conor –' she gestured over to the handsome actor,
who was still talking animatedly to Sara. 'Lovely Conor will do
some stand-up. There's about eight of us. I'll do striptease and sing,
I've got a new routine with some Union Jack nipple tassels. It's
great.'

'Cool,' said Chelsea, smiling at Gareth. 'I might come and
watch.'

'You should do something too,' Vicky said. 'Least we can do.'

'Oh, no way,' said Chelsea. 'I don't act any more.'

Vicky looked at her. 'That's mad,' she said. 'Think about it.
We'd love it if you did.'

Chelsea shook her head, politely. 'Oh, not any more,' she said,
though she didn't believe it. 'Not for me.'

From these humble beginnings, the Sunday Club, as they soon
called themselves, became an institution, a hang-out for actors.
After the show in the pub was over, they carried on meeting at

181

Roxy's on Sundays, just because it was fun more than anything else. They'd do stand-up, practise routines, sing old cabaret songs – mostly for each other. It was low-key, but there was a buzz about it, the chemistry worked from the beginning.

Vicky and Conor came up with a loose format, pretending they were all backstage at a show, so that the only part of the set was a tattered old velvet curtain, hung back to front. It was supposed to be informal, and the curtain kept it like that.

At first, they did it for themselves. Vicky wrote a few songs, Gareth's new boyfriend Max, a pianist, accompanied them. Some boyfriends and girlfriends would come along as audience, sitting politely on the zebra-print banquettes, while up on stage the actors worked around the poles that only the night before some girl had been sliding along.

And at first, Chelsea just watched, arms crossed at the back, drinking vodka, lime and sodas, smiling with contentment. But one day, Vicky made her get up on stage.

'Come on, Chelsea,' she commanded. 'This is Roxy's, we want to hear you. What can you do?'

Chelsea crossed her arms even tighter, laughing, as the group turned to her, yelling, imploring. 'No way,' she said, shaking her head. 'I'm not doing that. You carry on.'

'No.' Vicky stamped her foot. 'It's been four months, and I know you're better than most of us. Sorry guys,' she said, looking at the others. 'Come on up.'

It was a fuller than usual crowd that night. They started a slow handclap, and in the end she had no choice but to get up and begin walking towards them.

'I don't have anything . . . I don't know what to do,' she whispered to Vicky on the way up. Vicky shook her head, smiling.

Chelsea climbed onto the stage. Funny, she'd never been up here, on her own stage, all these months. She stood there, blinking into the spotlight. She cleared her throat in front of the mike.

'Hi,' she said, her voice croaky. 'I'm . . .'

She could make out vague shadows, not faces. An expectant audience. It had been so long. She bent down and whispered something to Max, waiting at the piano. And then she stood up, and sang 'Send In the Clowns'.

Her voice wasn't great, it cracked in places, but the song was written for someone who didn't have a strong voice. It was quiet, moving, poignant, about someone who's wasted chances and made mistakes. And it was devastating.

At the end, there was a pause, and then thunderous applause. She bowed. She wasn't used to a live audience, but she thought to herself that she could learn to like it. She thanked them, and then began to talk a little.

From *Time Out*, London, March 2004:

The Sunday Club

The hottest ticket for those truly in the know is Sunday night at Roxy's. A high-end strip club during the week, on Sundays a show you have to see to believe takes place. It's a kind of show within a show, featuring some of the West End's most exciting young performers. Originally started to give them a chance to try new ideas (it's not as much fun as you'd think performing *Les Mis* eight times a week, believe me), the show has become more and more popular, and the real sensation is Chelsea Stone – remember her? She sings a couple of songs, and talks a bit, and it's hard to believe she's still only 26 – her smoky voice and old-world glamour put you in mind of a mid-career Elizabeth Taylor, overweight, been through the mill, lashings of black eye-liner, but completely and utterly ravishing. Low-key, intimate, but we think a star is reborn. ★★★★★

Chelsea was sitting backstage, in the dancers' dressing area, which the performers for the Sunday Club used as a changing room and props store. She was about to change out of her black figure-hugging dress into jeans, for the five-minute walk back to her flat.

Her little club, her little empire, all the problems and stresses it gave her during the week melted away when she got up on stage, her long black hair twisted into a chignon, her dark blue eyes accentuated with 1960s-style eyeliner, and started doing her act, the one where the former child star becomes a delusional diva.

God, she loved it.

She looked at her face in the mirror. She was exhausted. It had been a busy week – a couple of Russian girls had started at Roxy's, and they needed a lot of training. Their English was non-existent, and Chelsea was wondering whether she'd been right to hire them. The liquor licence renewal had been tricky – Westminster Council were bastards, basically.

But everything was OK when she was on stage. She loved the stage; it terrified her sometimes how much she loved it.

She raised her hand to her head to release the pins that held her hair up, when a voice behind her said, 'Chelsea Stone, well, well well. Look at you.'

She swung round on her chair. 'Simon?' she said. 'Oh my *God*!'

Simon Moore, the director of *Roxy's Nine Lives*, was standing there in front of her. She hadn't seen him for years and years. He'd written to her after her dad died, but she'd dropped out of contact. He'd always been on her back; she felt he understood her a bit too well, and it made her uneasy – when things were bad. Now, it was just great to see him.

She leaped up and gave him a big hug. 'It's fucking great to see you, Simon! Did you see the show?'

Simon looked at her, into her beautiful blue eyes, at the woman she'd become. 'Yes, I did. It's been a long time, Chelsea,' he said.

'I know,' she said soberly, sitting back down again. 'How've you been? I saw that adaptation of the Beatles' biography – it was fucking brilliant. You've still got it, haven't you, man?'

Simon shook his head, smiling. 'That's kind of you. I could say the same of you, Chelsea. You were brilliant. You always were.'

'Oh, thanks,' Chelsea said happily. 'I love it.'

Some of the members of the Sunday Club were shuffling in and out of the changing area. One of them called out, 'See you in the bar, Chels?'

Chelsea yelled back, 'Sure, in a minute.' She smiled at Simon.

'Honestly,' Simon said. 'I'd forgotten how good you are, Chelsea. That same intensity you had the day I met you at the BBC, all those years ago. Tonight – well, it was just a sheer pleasure to watch you.'

Chelsea picked up her bag. 'All this flattery could turn a girl's head. Can I buy you a drink, Simon?'

'Sure,' he said. 'Hang on, though. Can I ask you something?'

She smiled at him. ''Course.'

'Have you ever thought you might take this further?'

'What?' she said, puzzled, looking around her.

'The acting, Chelsea,' he said, laughing. 'Go back into acting. Haven't you thought about it?'

'Oh,' she said. She shook her head, smiling. 'Silly me. No, Simon. No way. I'm happy as I am.'

'Really?' Simon said, incredulous.

Chelsea laughed back at him, contented. 'Sure! I love being on stage, but here, just like this. It's all worked out fine, and I don't want to jinx it.'

Simon opened his mouth, as if to protest, but she put her fingers on his lips. 'I mean it. Let's go and get that drink. They're waiting for my key to the till, the greedy bastards.'

Simon wasn't fooled by Chelsea. He never had been. Hours later, as he sat in a taxi on his way back to Chiswick, he stared out of the window, thinking about the conversation. He had always believed there was something about her, something almost frightening about her drive and talent. He was wrong if he'd ever thought it'd go away. And he didn't believe her when she told him she was happy as she was. Chelsea was something special. It couldn't be contained by doing a routine once a week for a cabaret club.

The next day, Simon was having lunch at Soho House with an old friend from the BBC, now head of drama at ITV, named Tristan Jones. He'd thought it would be a pretty thankless job, that, but word was they were throwing everything they had at one project – *Fortunes*.

Fortunes was a major new series, with a fantastic script, great production values and a big budget. It was to be a different kind of crime series for the twenty-first century, Martina Cole crossed with *Shameless* – gritty, urban, honest. The script was amazing. They'd been shooting for two weeks.

But it was all going wrong. 'It's a bloody nightmare, to be honest,' said Tristan. 'I think the whole thing might have to be shut down.'

'Why?' said Simon, helping himself to more Chablis.

'It's Jenny Simmons. She's fucking awful.'

'Isn't she . . . playing the lead?'

'Yep,' Tristan sighed, pushing his hands through his hair. 'But she's all wrong. Too pretty, prim, uptight. She's supposed to be a hardbitten cop from a tough, East End family. She's too sweet and soft.'

'Why did you . . .'

Tristan sighed again. 'Because we needed a big name, and she's a big name. And I thought someone like her might give the part a bit of humanity. She needs to be tough, but warm, you know?' He looked down at his plate. 'I don't know what we're going to do. They've got to be the right person. They carry the fucking show.'

And Simon Moore said, slowly, 'I think I might be able to help you there.'

At first, Tristan thought Simon had gone mad. 'You must be joking, mate!' he cried. 'She's a fucking druggie! Nutcase!'

But the more Simon talked, the more Tristan was prepared to listen. After all, there was no doubt about it: Chelsea had been around the block. You could see it in her face, it was obvious. She was twenty-six, but she looked older; years of late nights, of drink and drugs and cigarettes had taken their toll.

Yet she still had those incredible eyes, though . . . and that *something*.

And when Tristan came with him to see her at the Sunday Club the following week, he agreed.

186

'Christ!' he said, leaning over to Simon halfway through the show. 'She really doesn't have any idea how good she is, does she?'

'No,' Simon whispered. He looked up at Chelsea, her tragic smile, her glittering dark eyes, the almost magnetic power that drew you towards her, made you unable to stop watching. 'But one day she's going to realise. And then, God help us all.'

Chapter Thirty

Chelsea waited till she'd auditioned before she told anyone.

'It's no big deal,' she told Gareth, ten or so days later, at the club. 'This stuff happens all the time, you know. I'm not gonna get it, I know it.'

'They're *mad* if they don't give it to you,' Gareth said intently. '*In*sane . . . You'd be brilliant, Chelsea!' He rubbed his hands together in glee, and then looked at her. 'Don't you want it?'

Chelsea rubbed her eyes. 'Yes, of course I do.' They were in her office; it was a normal Wednesday night, not too busy. She shuffled some papers on her desk. 'I'm just tired, that's all. It's late.'

'But it would be—'

'It'd be fucking great, but I don't think it's going to happen. And I'm happy with things the way they are.'

Gareth looked at her doubtfully. 'Really? Doing this, for the rest of your life?'

It was after two in the morning. They looked round the dank, windowless office in silence. The faint sound of grinding dance music from the floor of the club could be heard through the thick office door. The club was about to shut. Chelsea pressed her fingers to her forehead. She didn't want to think about how much she wanted the part. Toni was a great character. The series had 'hit' written all over it. And just dipping her toe back into the spotlight these last few months had been great.

She loved the club, but sometimes it wore her down. She had to admit it; perhaps she'd let some things slide, but she was finding it increasingly depressing. There was only so much middle-aged men getting off on teenagers you could take in a lifetime, and she was reaching her limit. She had to do this. If she didn't . . .

Suddenly, there was a frantic knocking on the door and Oksana, one of the dancers, burst in.

'Oh my God, oh my God, Chelsea!' She ran towards the desk, clutching her hands. 'Come quick, oh my good God, what happened!'

'What's going on?' Chelsea stood up.

'Maya, she's bad – in the back room . . . I don't know what happened, he took her, she's bad . . .'

'Maya?' This was the other new Russian girl at the club, only nineteen, like Oksana. Chelsea and Gareth scrambled for the door.

They couldn't run around the stage, as they wanted to; they walked briskly, so no one noticed anything was out of the ordinary. Oksana led them to one of the back rooms.

Roxy's was not a knocking shop – Chelsea had been adamant about that. But for business' sake she had to turn a blind eye to what went on in the curtained booths around the edge of the club; they were private places where clients could take a girl and get her to perform a solo lap-dance; that was the way the club made a lot of its money. Any more than that, she didn't want to know about.

Chelsea pulled back the curtain of the booth nearest the door. Jonno, one of the bouncers, was standing guard inside. He nodded.

'Oh *fuck*,' she said softly, looking down.

'Shit,' Gareth said.

They both nearly gagged on the smell. Maya was lying on the floor, covered in frothing vomit, some of it around her mouth. She was pale, her skin glowing white in the gloom. Her purple sequinned two-piece was torn – the pants still on, but the bikini top half torn off, one triangle of tiny material hanging by her side, covered in vomit. Her eyes were hollow, her stomach was sunken in. She'd wet herself too, and the stale sweat, urine, vomit and stench of something else was almost unbearable.

'What happened?' Chelsea said. When the fuck had this girl last eaten? She couldn't take her eyes off her. She looked like a ghoul, she looked dead already.

Don't say it. She cleared her throat and tried to concentrate, as Oksana started to explain.

Maya had gone into the booth with a punter. Oksana wasn't sure what had happened, but they'd taken a speedball, she was pretty sure. This was a regular, a guy who had asked girls to do this before. Oksana had been in the booth next door and heard strange noises; Maya fitting, collapsing. The punter had disappeared by the time she got there. Of course he had. Back to his wife in Penge.

'Holy fuck,' Chelsea said again. 'Has she got a pulse?'

Jonno said, 'She did. Not sure any more.'

'I'm going to ask everyone to leave, nice and politely. It's past closing, anyway. You –' she turned to Gareth. 'Deal with this. Get someone here as soon as possible.'

Gareth nodded. 'Sure, babe.'

Chelsea patted Oksana's shoulder. They were both really young. Maya looked even younger than nineteen, lying there on the floor. Chelsea realised she didn't even know where she'd come from, she didn't seem to have any family. She'd been so busy lately, with Roxy's and the Sunday Club. Had she taken her eye off the ball? 'It's gonna be OK,' she said softly, but her voice was uncertain. She couldn't tear her eyes away from the heap of bones on the floor. She looked at Maya's face, saw that the side in shadow had an ugly bruise on it. Her lip had burst and was bleeding; it was swollen, a grotesque parody of those bee-stung lips. And she was completely still.

Calmly, as if there were nothing more pressing ahead for her than a cab ride home, Chelsea went around the club, chatting to the clients and getting them to leave with a combination of charm and veiled threats. It emptied in less than five minutes; when she came back into the booth, Gareth and Jonno were still there.

'Anyone around?' Gareth said. Chelsea shook her head. Oksana was crying quietly next to Maya.

'She's dead,' Gareth said.

'What?'

'Yep, Chels. Must have been for a while now.'

'Is the ambulance on its way, though?'

Gareth looked from her to Jonno. 'We didn't call one – is that what you meant?'

'Of course it fucking was!' Chelsea exploded. 'She's—'

'She was dead already,' Jonno said. 'Nothing we could do, trust me, Chelsea love.'

'But we should still call—'

Gareth came over to her. 'Chelsea, think about it.'

She shook her head, blankly. 'What the hell are you talking about?'

'We'll be done, the three of us.' Gareth gestured to himself, Jonno and Oksana, who was trembling in the corner. 'We didn't do anything to save her.'

Oksana looked at her imploringly. 'My visa – they send me back home.'

'And you, love,' Jonno was blunt. 'Council'll close you down in a fucking heartbeat, Chels.'

'Yeah,' Gareth said. 'And your uncle's other places too, I shouldn't wonder.'

'For sure,' Jonno said. 'They've been wanting to get him for years.'

Chelsea's stomach clenched, even tighter at the mention of her uncle. Uncle Derek had helped her when no one else would. She couldn't screw this up for him. Couldn't. She closed her eyes, and instantly the image of Maya flashed before her . . . the crusting blood on her lip, the curdling puke on her body, pooling round her. The bruises . . . the dreadful stillness. How had she let this happen? How would she explain it to Derek, to . . . to . . .

Gareth said, as if reading her mind, 'And that part you're waiting to hear about . . .'

Chelsea opened her mouth. 'Fuck the part,' she said hoarsely. But she didn't mean it.

Suddenly, she knew she was at a fork in the road, knowing she was taking one turning, and having to trust her instincts that it was the right one.

She wished the image of Maya flashing before her eyes would go. She cleared her throat: 'What do we do, then?'

Jonno said, without emotion, 'I know someone who knows someone.'

'Who can get rid . . .' Chelsea couldn't look down at the dead girl, couldn't finish the sentence.

'Get rid of the body, yeah. I'll call him, he'll come over.' Like he was talking about collecting the rubbish. He took out his phone, started jabbing the keys with his fat, sausage-like fingers. Chelsea watched him. Next to her, Oksana started sobbing, her shoulders shaking.

Chelsea wanted to put an arm round her, but she couldn't. Couldn't move. She forced herself to look down, one more time, at this fragile little thing lying on the floor. She was turning blue, the smell of drying vomit getting more rancid. The music from a nearby speaker pounded in Chelsea's ears, louder and louder.

She closed her eyes briefly. But she knew that sight wouldn't leave her. It was just one more image to add to her nightmares.

They got rid of the girl. Chelsea stayed in the office and didn't ask any questions. She never knew how. But when Jonno came in, a couple of hours later, when it was nearly morning, she handed him £3,000 in cash. He shook his head.

'Don't need bribing, love. I'm good.'

She pressed it into his hand. 'I want you to take it. Don't argue.'

'You're a good girl, Chelsea,' he said. 'That's bad luck, you understand? You don't need to keep me sweet. I wouldn't have told no one. Neither will Mikey. He owes me.'

She gave the same amount to Oksana, who looked at her dully, her red-rimmed eyes full of tears.

'I'm so sorry you've seen this. She was your friend – I don't know what we could have done—'

Oksana took the money without protesting. She folded it into her thin vest as if she'd been doing it for years. She said, 'I didn't know her well. She was sweet girl. This helps. Thank you.'

And she turned to leave.

Chelsea sat in her office, staring at nothing, for what seemed like hours.

When the phone rang, she jumped violently. It sounded harsh, cruel.

'Hello? Chelsea Stone, is that you?'

'Y-yes . . .' Chelsea said, passing a clammy hand over her forehead; it was seven o'clock, and she hadn't had any sleep.

The voice was public-school educated, smooth. 'Chelsea, I'm so sorry to call you at this hour, but I'm about to get on a plane for LA and I wanted to speak to you before I go.'

'Who is this?' she said, irritated.

'I'm so sorry. It's Tristan Jones. I just wanted to—'

'Oh, hello,' she interrupted, trying not to sound like the crazy person she felt she was.

'Hi. Look, I really just wanted to tell you myself. You got the part.'

'What?'

'The part of Toni. In *Fortunes*. You got it. I'm really pleased, we all are. You were terrific, you're going to be huge, Chelsea.'

Chelsea looked round the dank basement. There was a tiny slit that gave out onto the Soho sidestreet. Outside, she could hear a rubbish truck going past, and the bin men heaving sacks into the truck.

Time to clear out the trash.

A new start . . .

She gulped, blinking away the image of Maya's face.

'Wow, Tristan!' she said, as if she'd just woken up and was contemplating nothing more than going for a run. 'That's amazing. Thank you so much. I won't let you down. That's absolutely amazing.'

She put the phone down, feeling sweat pool in her armpits. She felt dizzy. She thought of last night, the fork in the road. A girl was dead. She'd covered it up. No one cared. Had she made the right decision? Was she really going to be allowed to get away with it?

Chelsea didn't believe in regrets. She couldn't. She'd made it to the fork, and she'd chosen her path last night. It was the right one, she knew it. She deserved a break. She had to take it. It was her against the world. Perhaps it had always been like that, since she was little. Amber was the favourite, she was the bad girl. The one her mother hated, and who as good as killed her father . . . Yes, Chelsea knew she was on her own.

Put it all behind you and move on. That's what she'd done before, with her dad, with her car crash, with the drink and drugs. And that's what she'd do now. Nothing must stop her.

Chapter Thirty-One

'Your big sister . . . Mmmm.' Leo's lips worked up from Amber's nipple to her neck. She batted him away. 'She sounds amazing.' He ran one tanned hand over her flat, honey-coloured stomach. 'I want to meet her.'

'I don't think that's ever going to happen,' Amber said. She was learning her lines on the day bed by the pool. Leo's probing fingers pushed aside the other triangle of her tiny aquamarine bikini and his lips settled on her other nipple, sucking, teasing, gently biting . . . Amber closed her eyes and gave in to the sensation, shuddering slightly.

'Come on, my baby girl,' he said, slapping her thigh. 'Get into it, will you?'

She looked down at him in surprise. 'I am into it,' she said. 'Don't stop; what are you doing?'

But he was frowning. That old look in his face again; she'd seen it more and more the last couple of weeks.

That was the trouble with Leo. She could stare across at him, smiling smugly in his sleep and, increasingly, realise she felt nothing. Or watch him on the red carpet, interviewed at a premiere, and want to smack him. Sometimes, Amber didn't know why she was with him. What was next, for her and Leo? How had it lasted three years?

The truth was, it had worked damned well for both of them, though Amber wouldn't have admitted it. Leo probably would have done, if not to Amber then to himself. The press he'd been getting since he'd started dating Amber had been much more positive. She was so wholesome, cute, beloved by all America, it seemed. He must be a nice guy if he was with her, the gossip magazines reasoned. He was so tall and masculine; on TV and in photos he was always seen looking so protectively and lovingly over small, sweet Amber who wouldn't hurt a fly, and without even trying to influence things, some of that goodwill bled through to the industry papers and to the power lunches at the top LA restaurants, and into the meeting rooms of the biggest studios.

And Amber knew he loved that. The truth was, she liked it too. It made her life easier. People were politer to her since she'd started dating Leo. Gave her more respect – she couldn't be just another stupid bimbo if she'd been with him all this time, could she? Even if she was . . . *Be nice to her, she's fucking Leo Russell, who knows when we might need him on board.* That was how the reasoning went, and she knew it.

It gave her security, too. She didn't have to negotiate her way through horrible paparazzi-strewn 'dates' with celebs of equal star power, set up by their respective agents. She'd tried a couple; they were awful. Leo looked after her, protected her from the crazy celebrity world. He made her feel safe. She could do her films and her interviews and then retreat, shut the rest of it out. Leo was the one who wanted to conquer the world, not her.

There was another reason she liked being with him, too.

Leo knew exactly what to do to get her off. He was a sexual magician. He could be gone for days, weeks, he could be distant and dismissive, making her feel like an unimportant little girl all over again, and then he would slowly slide his hand up her skirt at an industry party, and murmur, 'You know it makes me angry when you insist on wearing underwear,' his fingers gently sliding inside her till she stopped gasping in shock and started gasping in pleasure.

Then he would push her into the car and pull her on top of

him, tugging the straps of her dress off, pushing her skirt up, tearing off her underwear till he could come inside her. Or he would move her hand over his cock, so she was rubbing him, and then he'd lean back and close his eyes. 'Now,' he'd say softly, menacingly. 'Do it now.'

And Amber, trembling with lust, would open his fly, take out his erection and sink her soft lips over his hard cock, swirling her tongue round his engorged skin, glad to be told what to do, glad she had the power to make him choke, go red, call her name as he spurted into her mouth.

Amber had lived her whole life by rules. Be in bed by this time. Go to that audition. Practise this routine. And, because she wanted to please people in general, she didn't mind.

So it was nice to be naughty sometimes.

Other times, Amber found herself looking at her life in LA – she had been here for five years now – and was bewildered at the heights she'd reached. There were so many other girls desperate for it, who'd do anything for fame, take any terrible part, suck any warty old cock. Amber had worked hard to get where she was. She didn't feel guilty about her success.

It's just, she felt it should have happened to someone else.

Leo was good for that. She knew what he was like – or suspected she knew what he could be like – but it was good being with him, precisely because it allowed her to do two of her favourite things: please her mother, and have amazing sex.

The extra benefit was that there were no rules, no limits to their relationship, and it suited Amber to have just one area of her life that wasn't a hundred per cent boxed and tied up with a bow, set in stone for her for years to come. She loved Leo, didn't she? Yes, she felt she did. Amber had grown up with Margaret and George as her template for relationships. She loved them both, but as she grew older she had come to see that their marriage was anything but perfect. She had no idea what a good relationship looked like. She supposed her mum and dad had been happy – had they?

Amber had convinced herself, long ago, that this was just the way it went. You worked, you slaved, you were with someone who got what you did – just like her parents.

Real-life romance, falling properly in love, being with someone who understood *you*, not shooting schedules or box-office grosses – well, that was all very nice, but it wasn't actually true . . .

It just didn't happen to someone like her.

That was the massive irony. There were so many sharks out there, so many men who wanted to fuck her because she was Amber Stone the movie star, not Amber Stone the girl who liked playing guitar, roller-blading, hiking in the hills, watching cheesy old Ealing comedies like she used to with her dad, eating peanut butter out of the jar . . .

Leo undid Amber's bikini and cupped both of her breasts in his hands. He started licking her skin. She opened her eyes and looked down at the thick black hair without a single grey strand to be seen – she'd seen them increasingly round his cock and his balls – she was sure he dyed the hair on his head and chest. He was moving rhythmically against her tits and she groaned. It felt so good. She loved him when he was back to being like this – affectionate, playful, like a boy her own age. He could play her like an instrument, and she knew it: within seconds, his mood could change . . .

Leo's eye fell again on the *Variety* lying next to them, and he stopped working on Amber's skin and picked up the paper. 'Yes . . .' he said, licking his lips. 'So, my darling – that's really her, your sister? She's done well, hasn't she?' It calls her "the biggest star in the UK right now". Bit of a turnaround, isn't it?'

He was such a gossip, like an old woman, it made her laugh sometimes. 'That's Chelsea,' said Amber, looking over his shoulder at the photo in the paper of her sister, stunning in a figure-hugging dress, outside some awards ceremony at the Albert Hall. She tried to change the subject. She was uneasy with Leo's sudden interest in her sister. 'How's *The Time of My Life* casting going? Seen anyone for the male lead yet? When can I see the script?' She knew she was asking too many questions.

'Oh, I don't know, my love.' Leo's hand ran over her body. He

198

tried to pinch her, but Amber's flat, washboard stomach yielded nothing. 'So skinny,' he said, almost by way of reproach.

Yeah, Amber thought. *That's what happens when you work out two hours a day every fucking day of the year. You're skinny. Because the one time you kick back for a couple of months and put on a little bit of weight, you get told you look like a fat pig by your supposed boyfriend, OK?*

She glanced again at the picture of Chelsea. She looked amazing, Amber had to admit it. It was great to see her looking like that, though she did find it funny that Leo had never shown any interest in or concern for her sister before, unless it was in her druggie phase when she was an obstacle in the way of his plans for Amber's world domination. 'She always looked good in burgundy, it's a great colour on her.'

And then she looked over his shoulder again and started to read:

THE BEAUTIFUL HEAVYWEIGHT WHO'S MAKING AN IMPACT

Chelsea Stone, 27: The Brits love a good comeback story and it doesn't get much better than Stone's. A washed-up child star, she's battled drink, drugs, addiction to painkillers, a serious accident and the shocking death of her closet-case dad, to be the biggest star in the UK right now. Her show, *Fortunes*, has been a smash, reviving the 'fortunes' of ITV. Yet she's just announced she's leaving the show for a West End run in Chekhov's *The Seagull* and *King Lear*. 'I am a good actress, but I can be better,' she told reporters outside the BAFTAs, where she won best actress. 'I want to learn, and I love the stage. I'm thrilled to be appearing opposite Sir Derek Jacobi, and I'm just so excited to be having this experience.'

The British tabloids love her, that's for sure. There's one extra addition to the mix and that's her sister, who just happens to be Amber Stone. But as is the way, they're dismissive of Chelsea's younger sister. 'Pretty girl, but so lightweight', is the general theme in the UK. 'Bland Amber', one recent article said. 'She may have the looks, she may have the money, the golden hair, the perfect body, the even white teeth, but Chelsea's got something more. She's got the talent.'

'Jesus!' Amber exploded. 'I hate those papers! Can you get someone to put something else out over here, Leo?'

But Leo wasn't listening. Gently, he pushed Amber away, and was hunched over the paper reading greedily, grunting softly with approval. She watched him again, naked from the waist up, the bikini flapping around her ribs, feeling completely discarded and with a feeling of unease stealing over her. The one thing she knew about Leo for sure was that if he was bored, it was fatal. When he wanted to shake things up, you just had to let him.

Was this what it was, this thing with Chelsea? He'd done it with the casting of films, the hiring of directors, he'd done it with his staff – housekeepers like Tina would disappear, never to be seen again. He'd get bored of their sex life and give her ridiculous costumes to wear. Once, she'd had to whip him . . . Amber found herself thinking of his behaviour over the last couple of weeks as things started to fall into place. He'd had this on his mind for a while, she knew it. Once again, Chelsea had stolen her thunder.

And for the first time in her life, Amber found herself actively wishing her sister would just disappear back into a big, fat, Chelsea-shaped hole. She'd always said there was room for both of them.

Now she wasn't sure if it was true.

Chapter Thirty-Two

'I don't want to go to LA.'

The voice on the phone wasn't really paying much attention. She knew, in that goddammed perky American way, that she'd get what she wanted in the end, and she just carried on talking.

'We think it'd be so great . . . we're so excited to meet you, Chelsea. We'll book you into a hotel – you can stay at the Beverly Hills.'

'I have a sister in LA, that's fine. I can stay with her.'

The voice on the end of the line made a simpering noise. 'Of course you do! I know Amber, she's wonderful. OK, that's great. Listen, my name's Sally. I work with Sir Leo, and I'm gonna be looking after everything for you while you're here. Just call me. I'll email you my cell, call me any time. Wow, this is great! Leo is gonna be so excited you're auditioning. We all think *The Time of My Life* – well, we all think it's gonna be an amazing film!'

Who was *this woman? Why was she bleating in her ear like a wind-up Barbie doll?* It was teatime in London, but Chelsea was still hungover and grumpy. 'Fine, fine. What have you got to be so bloody pleased about?'

The voice on the end of the phone was silent, and then Sally said, 'Oh, I'm just so excited. Leo wants this very much, and I work for him, so . . .'

'Right, whatever,' Chelsea said. She didn't care, she wanted to get this – whoever she was, secretary person – off the phone. 'Thanks. Cheers. Catcha later.'

She put the phone down, lay back in bed, on her caramel silk sheets, feeling her glossy black hair like a pillow underneath her soft, dimpled back. She smiled up at the ceiling.

'Watch out, little sis,' she said. 'I'm coming to Hollywood.'

She still saw the dead girl in her dreams, but increasingly Chelsea learned to put it out of her mind, to add it to the list of images in her head she wanted to forget but couldn't.

And Chelsea had made a vow to herself, when Tristan had called her that morning to tell her she'd got the part. The night of Maya's death – she had to put it behind her. They'd covered it up, so they had to stick with it. Move on.

So instead she chose escapism: not drink and drugs this time, but hard work.

The years after *Fortunes* were golden for her. She threw herself back into acting with a ferocity that surprised even her. She was used to working completely by instinct, but she was starting to understand how to hone her skills. How to use her voice, her body, to do what she wanted, to change herself beyond all recognition. She did prestigious costume dramas, took a small part in an independent UK film. She played against type, good girls, old women, even a couple of young men, one year, in an all-female production of *As You Like It* at Shakespeare's Globe. The reviews were always amazing. Always.

She was in complete control of her craft, now. She could play anyone, anything.

It should have been enough.

But for someone like Chelsea, it was never going to be enough. She always wanted more: more fame, more adulation, more work, more money. She wanted to know – just how far could this go, how far could she take it? She was beloved in Britain, but everywhere else she was unknown, or known just as Amber's fat older sister.

And now she had the success she deserved, she wanted more.

Perhaps she wouldn't have done anything, if the timing hadn't been so perfect. But a couple of events, pushed together and ticking like a time bomb, made her jittery. Her newest TV series fell through when the director was fired, and ended up being cancelled – it wouldn't make the vital autumn slot, it was too expensive and it had to be perfect. So she was free for a few months, after what felt like years of hard work, moving from job to job, and Chelsea didn't like it. Like all great actors, she was hugely insecure. Then again, most actors hadn't been through what she had to get to the top . . . Chelsea had to keep striving, otherwise she'd start thinking, and thinking too much was fatal for her.

The second event was Leo, stirring things up, though she wasn't to know that. All Chelsea knew was that his office had called.

Asked her to come over for an audition.

It was to be a huge movie, *The Time of My Life*, a big part. They were seeing a ton of other actresses, they were careful not to get her hopes up but they wanted to see her. In strictest confidence, they said. She couldn't even tell her sister. Chelsea didn't know what they meant – she and Amber never really talked, these days.

The timing was perfect, though. She had a clear few months; she had to keep herself busy; she could see her mother and sister. She gritted her teeth and phoned her sister. Yes, she could stay in Amber's guest house – Amber was going to be away on a shoot for months after she arrived, which meant Chelsea didn't have to pay for a hotel. Again, like most actresses, she liked it when other people were paying her expenses, and she was clever enough to know the networking benefit of staying with her sister rather than in some anonymous hotel.

Chelsea knew by now that fame in the UK wasn't enough. She had one shot at becoming a star in Hollywood, and this was it. One shot at the big time, and she wasn't going to screw it up.

Chelsea wanted what Amber had. She wanted the world . . .

It was time to go and get it.

PART FOUR

I'm Still Standing

Chapter Thirty-Three

'So what the fuck am I supposed to do now?' Chelsea raised a puffy, hot hand to her sweating forehead to wipe the moisture away.

The woman at British Airways was not helpful. 'Ms Stone, like I say, we'll contact you as soon as your bags appear. I can only apologise most sincerely.'

'But –' Chelsea slung her big tote bag over her shoulder – the only bag she now appeared to own. 'I've got nothing! Don't you understand? Absolutely fucking nothing!'

'We will give you compensation, of course.' The girl blinked rapidly, like a robot on autopilot. Chelsea wanted to smash her face in. 'And we will inform you when your bags arrive, hopefully on the next flight? But in the meantime perhaps your sister could lend you some clothes when you get to her house.'

'Oh, yeah, right,' said Chelsea, laughing as a droplet of perspiration, like a slug, crawled down her spine. She looked at her shapeless pink T-shirt and ugly grey sweatpants, grimy and sweaty after a twelve-hour flight, and thought bitterly of Amber's boyish figure, her pert, perky little tits, her slim hips.

She, Chelsea, was a mess, a fat, curvy mess, in the town where being thin was a religion.

'I'll just borrow some of my sister's clothes. Great idea.'

'OK then!' said the BA representative. 'Thank you for flying with British Airways. And have a great day.'

'Oh, fuck off,' Chelsea muttered, turning towards the cab rank.

This trip was a mistake, she knew it. As the cab wound its way along the stunning Pacific Coast Highway, towards Amber's house in Malibu, she stared out of the window, fatigue clouding her vision. A billboard caught her eye, and she gazed at it, open-mouthed. It was about forty feet high, and bore the legend

AMERICA'S SWEETHEART IS BACK!
AMBER STONE
In
THE BACHELORETTE PARTY
OPENING MARCH 24TH!

There was a photo of Amber cut out above the hoarding, her teeth so white they looked radioactive, wearing a lame-looking hen-weekend veil and carrying a fake bouquet. One leg was up on a table, and you could see a garter, but it was all very demurely done, in pinks and baby blues . . . How naff.

The cab went under a bridge, momentarily blocking out the bright sunshine, and Chelsea caught sight of herself in the car window and groaned. She wasn't Chelsea Stone, biggest star in the UK, gorgeous, glamorous and super-talented, graciously consenting to audition for a film. She was porky old Chelsea again, the sweaty, hungover mess who'd drunk too much in First Class and was severely regretting it now. Her skin felt dull and greasy; her thick hair was escaping from its ponytail. And out on the road, palm trees fingered the endless blue sky. She felt as if she were in another world.

Unfortunately, when they reached Amber's road by the ocean, the trauma still wasn't over.

'I don't have your name here.' The security guard, standing at the black metal gates, ten feet high, was firm. 'I no let you in without your name on the list.'

'I'm her bloody *sister*!' Chelsea shouted. 'She's expecting me!'

The guard looked at her as if she was crazy. 'I can't do that. I can't let the car in.'

The taxi driver was already bored with Chelsea. She was clearly no one – no baggage, overweight and sweaty, yelling strange words at people. 'You get out here,' he said firmly, colluding with the security guard.

'This is a fucking *joke*,' Chelsea muttered as she picked up her tote bag and flung some money at him. 'Welcome to fucking America? I don't fucking think so!'

This Sally person had offered to put her up at the hotel, meet her at the airport – she couldn't believe she'd said no, that she'd rather stay with her sister. She was tramping down this empty road in the blazing sunshine – she, Chelsea Stone! If they could see her back home in the UK! This was all wrong.

Finally, she arrived at the gate of Amber's house, at one end of the secluded road. She buzzed the intercom, and thankfully the housekeeper had been told she was coming and let her in. At last, someone in this stupid town knew she was here.

Chelsea walked up the long drive through the lush, green garden, where the road side of the house was covered in jasmine. She passed a guest house. It was almost the size of Bay Tree House, their childhood home. She could hear a fountain or a hose, spraying peacefully somewhere. Chelsea took a deep breath, ran her hands awkwardly through her tangled hair and tried to calm down, suddenly nervous. Wow. Little Amber had done well for herself. And now she was here to get her share.

Chapter Thirty-Four

The nearly mute housekeeper greeted her at the door, wordlessly. Chelsea was led through room after room, all huge and immaculate. Was this really where her little sister lived? One room was a kind of study, with all her film posters, and Chelsea stared at them. *I Do*, *A Hopeless Romantic*, *The First Date* and, a new addition presumably, though it was interchangeable with the others, *The Bachelorette Party*.

How lame, she found herself thinking again. She shrugged, noticing the housekeeper was waiting for her at the door.

'You wait here,' the housekeeper said. 'I go and get Miss Amber. She doesn't know you're here.'

She looked at Chelsea as if she were a dangerous criminal. Chelsea wanted to snarl, bite, really scare her. This was getting worse and worse . . .

She waited.

Five minutes passed.

Then ten. Was she lost? How big was the damned house?

She waited in that empty terracotta room for what seemed like hours. By now she wasn't even angry, she was just depressed. Tired, sweaty, thoroughly demoralised and depressed. All she wanted was a shower, her luggage, a bed to rest her tired head. But no. LA hated her, she hated LA . . . And where the fuck was Amber?

But suddenly Amber was in the room, apologising profusely in the doorway. Rosita had forgotten to say she was here, she'd only just told her, the phone had rung and she'd had to fetch something for Leo, they were both awfully sorry.

'It's fine,' Chelsea said. Amber came towards her, her flawless features breaking into a smile.

'It's so good to see you,' she said, and she pulled her big sister into an embrace. 'Ten years! I've missed you, Chels.'

She hugged her tight, and Chelsea hugged her back, but in truth not as hard, because she was afraid she'd snap her sister in half. She was so beautiful, like china, perfect, her hair perfect, her skin, teeth – like she was kept in a museum. And she was so thin! Chelsea thought it was like hugging a bird. This wasn't her sister of old. It was crazy.

Amber was trying not to cry – it was much more affecting than she'd realised it would be, seeing her sister again after all these years. She'd forgotten how beautiful Chelsea was, how dark her blue eyes were, how cross she looked when she didn't realise it.

'All right, all right,' Chelsea pulled away, grumpily. 'It's good to see you too, *bella*. So far I've had a fucking nightmare time. I hope it gets better, that's for sure.'

Amber looked at the rest of her sister properly. Chelsea caught her expression. 'You're wondering why I look like a dog's dinner? Yeah. Wonder no more. The airline lost my luggage. And then your security guard wouldn't let me in, so I had to walk about ten minutes in these lovely grey sweatpants. I don't have any clothes or anything.' She held out her hands. 'I'm going to have to throw myself on your mercy.'

'Oh my God, you poor thing!' Amber said. Chelsea liked the fact her accent was still British, no mid-Atlantic twang, though she was always American Amber in her films. She scratched her head. 'Come with me. I'll lend you something.'

'I'm a UK size fourteen,' Chelsea said doubtfully. 'What size are you?'

'Er . . . a UK six,' Amber said, grabbing her hand. 'Don't worry, we'll find something. I put on weight last year. Leo wasn't happy about it. I have some clothes from that time. Let's see what we can find.' She squeezed her sister again and gazed almost anxiously at her. 'You're here, and that's all that matters. And I know nothing's going to have changed between us.'

Chelsea followed her. *Nothing at all?*

Chapter Thirty-Five

Leo was bored. It was dangerous, when he was bored.

He didn't like being at Amber's, in Malibu. She loved the privacy, how low-key it was, but Leo preferred Beverly Hills, the heart of the action, where there were no fucking hippies – albeit rich hippies – the cars were huge and it was A-list glamour all the time.

People who made money, who liked power. Just like him.

Malibu was like the fucking outback, as far as he was concerned, and though Amber loved her new ocean-fronted house, he didn't. She had decorated it in a homely, low-key Moroccan style, with cushions everywhere, sofas, a huge piano and guitar, a large terrace with a big old wooden table, enough to fit twenty people round – why? He didn't understand the obsession with homeliness, all of a sudden. She had virtually no friends; he was her closest confidant. Her mother wasn't exactly Mother of the Year, either. Perhaps he was thinking that now the sister was arriving, things would be different. Like they'd become best friends again and plait each other's hair.

We'll see. It was this side of Amber that irritated him. She never fully gave herself to him, always kept something back, and he felt like he didn't truly own her, after four years of on-off relationship – during which time he'd kept a steady supply of call-girls in

213

business, of course. This house was irritating, too – that steely streak of independence she had, going off and buying the property without consulting him. Making it look like some jolly old fucking coffee house out of *Friends* – it was pathetic.

He sighed and looked at his watch, growing impatient. They were off to Vancouver in a couple of days, shooting the next film, and he had a ton of stuff to do before then. He didn't have time for this, waiting for Amber to finish something with Rosita. They needed to go through her shooting schedule with Sally, for the new film.

Amber was irritating him at the moment, anyway. He was fond of her, yes, he was, and he loved the power trip it gave him, fucking the biggest star in Hollywood. Was she still the biggest, though, he wondered? Lately, the receipts had been down a little, the reviews weren't as adulatory.

And people were starting to say there was nothing to Amber – she was too polished, too smiley, that her life was boring, she was with some film producer, didn't fall out of clubs, didn't have much spark or personality. Leo wasn't sure. He only knew she kept herself so private, even to him – or perhaps especially to him – it was hard to know her, really know her, at all.

Things were difficult between them, at the moment. She wanted commitment. Wanted to settle down. He responded by wanting more distance.

The main clashing point was this film – she was continually bugging him for the script he was working on, *The Time of My Life*. This movie was going to be amazing. The buzz was already Oscar-worthy on it, and they hadn't started shooting yet. He was taking his time with it. *Everything* about it had to be right. The gestation period, pre-production, had been long, so he and his team could get every single detail perfect. The script. The sets. The crew. He was holding out for the best editor in town. And the cast . . . the female lead was crucial, and he hadn't found her yet. Amber . . . he frowned again. Amber was getting to him again; she and her stupid mother both were, Margaret with her big desk diary with Amber's schedule all over it. They wanted to know when shooting was starting; when would they see a script? The character of Maloney was going to be the best role she'd had yet – juicy, well written, fully rounded.

Leo had a problem.

He'd promised the part to Amber.

But it wasn't right for Amber. He was more and more sure of that. It was bigger, better than her. She was vanilla, she was peaches and cream, that was it. This was – something special. It was kind of magical realism, *Slumdog* meets *Meet Me in St Louis*, about a poverty-stricken girl from a small town. It was *Forrest Gump* without the fucking mentally retarded guy.

He wanted this to be the movie that would take him from Leo Russell, producer, to Leo Russell, legend. Everything had to be *perfect*.

He was moving on, moving up, taking himself to the next level. Amber couldn't be a part of that.

But maybe her sister could: for this was the movie he'd got Chelsea over to audition for. He'd made no promises, just wanted to check her out. Amber would know, soon, that she wasn't the only actress in town.

Because everything was riding on this film. Nothing could go wrong.

From the corner of the room, he looked out onto the terrace.

A movement caught his eye and he saw a girl – woman, really – leaning over the balustrade with her back to him, looking out at the ocean. She was in a coral jersey dress – he recognised the colour, it was Amber's. Her hair fell gently about her shoulders, her arse moving slightly as her head turned questioningly to take in the view, the material straining against her body. She raised a hand to push her hair out of her face and he saw the curve of her waist and the swell of a plump breast, squashed against her side, almost spilling out of the dress. Leo's cock twitched involuntarily, his fingers sliding over the condensation of his glass, all thoughts of the movie gone . . .

She was here. He smiled to himself.

Let the games begin.

'Chelsea?' Amber appeared, padding lightly over the floor. 'Rosita says we don't have any wine, I'm afraid. So sorry! I can offer you – gosh – how about a whisky? That's what Leo likes, and I—'

Chelsea. The big sister. Literally, Leo thought with a chuckle, even as his eyes raked over the girl's body. She turned around to answer her sister, and he saw with something like astonishment her rounded belly, the full, low breasts, her curvy thighs. He tore his gaze to her face, reluctantly, and recognised her at once. The dark, sparkling eyes, full lips, defiant stare. There was a dirt mark on her cheek; she was sweating into the coral dress. She looked a mess, he knew it. He suspected Amber knew it too. He said, lightly, from the corner of the room,

'I can recommend the whisky here, my dear.' He strode forward. 'I'm Leo. Good to meet you.'

He was doing his best 'lord of the manor' bit to relax her, and he was surprised to see a light in her eye – was it contempt? Amusement? She took his hand.

'Chelsea Stone,' she said, almost shyly. 'Excuse the near-porno dress. They lost my luggage. Amber lent me this.' Her cheeks were red, but she smiled at him. 'I mean, it's a great dress, but—'

There was, Leo realised with pleasure, something disarming about her. About the way she blushed, her dark, humorous eyes, her awkward manner – and the way he could see the outline of her nipples through the thin fabric of her dress. But she was wrong for the part. She was too big. Too scruffy, too raw. A shame – she was way, way more interesting than he would have thought.

Everyone else here was plastic. But she was fat! He hadn't seen anything like it for a long time, since they shot that picture out in . . . where was it? Somewhere in Texas, anyway, and everyone was fucking huge. OK, she wasn't obese, but she was in Hollywood. You didn't have a stomach in Hollywood.

Though what would it be like, he found himself thinking, to bury his head in those breasts, to hold that luscious, soft, smooth skin, to feel her rubbing that gorgeous body against him?

216

He shook his head, surprised at the force of his reaction. 'Don't be sorry.' He smiled at her. She smiled back, unimpressed, and he realised she wasn't scared of him. Wasn't even intimidated.

'So,' she said. 'I'm really excited about the audition.'

He waved his hand dismissively. 'We should talk. I'm not sure you're right for the part we discussed, but there's definitely something you can do here.'

'Not right?' Chelsea stared at him. 'You have to be kidding.'

Leo stared right back at her. 'What?'

'You're telling me I've flown all this way, and without even auditioning me for your stupid film you know I'm not *right*?' She laughed. 'Well, thank you. So far, so fucking great in the US of A.' She narrowed her eyes and stuck her chin out. Screw him! 'What the hell do you know, anyway? You haven't taken a risk in years.'

Leo didn't lose his cool, even though no one had spoken to him like that in a long time. He gritted his teeth. 'Chelsea, I'm sorry you feel that way, but we're auditioning a lot of people. May I make it clear, we never stipulated you would be—'

Chelsea tossed her hair and gave him a grin. 'Oh, don't get your frilly knickers in a twist, man,' she said. She licked her dry lips. 'Calm down. I won't bite you.'

Damn her! She wasn't even scared of him. Not one bit. She was fat, sweaty, she was a nobody in this town and here she was, standing in front of him, telling him to calm down! Leo felt foolish, for the first time he could remember. He smiled back at her.

'You're trouble, I can tell. Listen, enjoy your holiday. Take your time here in LA, relax, walk on the beach, all of that stuff.' He ran his eyes up and down her body. 'I'm away with Amber, as you know, for a couple of months. I'm seeing other people all the time. Let's talk about it when I'm back.'

It was a knockback, she knew it.

And knockbacks only made Chelsea more determined. Damn him. Fuck him!

'Right,' she said grimly. She tossed her hair, trying to keep her cool, unable to say anything else otherwise she'd lose it.

Leo watched her, appreciatively. He could see she was annoyed but still – she should look in the mirror sometime. He wondered what it would be like to fuck her. To bend her over that balcony, now. Grab that flesh – feel those tits – it had been literally years since Leo had been with a woman who had any spare flesh.

He realised, now, watching Chelsea, that he missed it. Chelsea Stone . . . bent over the balcony, looking out over the ocean as he pounded into her from behind, clutching her breasts . . . How would she sound when he made her come? He bet she was a screamer.

Leo could feel his cock getting hard. No. Control was everything. Without it, the games didn't work.

Sally emerged from Amber's office suite. She was reorganising Leo's schedule; he and Amber were leaving in a couple of days for Vancouver. 'Hey,' she said. 'Leo, can I get you anything?' Then she turned round, following his gaze. 'Oh my,' she said. 'You must be Chelsea.' She trotted over to her, light as a gazelle in her three-inch heels. 'I'm Sally Miller. We've been speaking.' Chelsea shook her hand dumbly. 'It's just so great to meet you!'

Then she turned back and raised a demure little eyebrow at Leo. He swallowed a smile.

In fact, he and Sally had a bet going on. Who'd come out on top. He'd already picked Chelsea, out of boredom.

But he'd have been interested to know that Sally was pretty sure she was right. She had learned not to underestimate the younger sister. She'd been around for years, and she'd counted them in and out again. She'd thought Amber would last a season and, a decade later, she was still here. On top of her game, on top of Leo again.

'Maybe I will have a whisky,' Chelsea said suddenly. She hated the way Leo was making her feel, like a blubbery whale in a too-tight dress. She was Chelsea Stone, the biggest actress in the UK, not the fat sister. 'I need a drink.'

'How do you take it?' Leo said, raising his eyebrows.

Chelsea didn't rise to it. Was that the best he could do? Cheap innuendo? What a loser. 'No ice. A sliver of water. That's it.'

'I knew we'd get on,' Leo said, nodding appreciatively. 'There's a nice bottle in the cabinet. I'll join you.'

Amber was hovering beside them in a white broderie anglaise vest and little pale blue Ralph Lauren shorts, her tanned, clear skin, her white teeth, her delicately streaked golden blonde hair making her look more than ever like America's sweetheart.

'Whisky?' Amber said, her voice rising slightly, even though she had been the one to offer it. 'No problem! Coming right up.'

She looked from Leo to Sally and then at her sister, and Leo, enjoying himself enormously now, looked at both the Stone girls, against the backdrop of the ocean. This was going to be fun.

Chapter Thirty-Six

All her childhood, Chelsea had wanted to go to LA. She'd always loved films, the stories her dad had told her of old Hollywood, the stars, the beautiful people, the sunshine, palm trees, Romanoffs, Sunset and Vine . . .

But LA in 2007 was not LA in 1938, she soon realised. It was a dog-eat-dog world, where people smiled as they stabbed you in the back, where dreams were crushed every day and where pretty girls from small US towns with hopes of being stars ended up sucking cock for $10 a time off Sunset Boulevard.

All in all, Chelsea thought, LA was like a pretty girl itself – a pretty girl hiding the clap. But she'd been around the block. She wouldn't let it get to her.

And she was determined to get what she could from it.

Two days after she arrived, Amber and Leo left for Canada. They were to be gone for three months, and after she'd waved them off, Chelsea realised she was relieved. It was awkward with her sister, though she was trying hard, they both were. There was something missing, and she didn't know if it could ever be repaired. Her mother was already in Canada when she'd got to LA, so she wouldn't be seeing her for a while, either. She'd gone on ahead to settle into the hotel and meet the team – she relished her role as Amber's de facto manager, but Chelsea wondered, couldn't she have waited two more days to see her other daughter? She'd been in the UK the previous year and they'd met up then, Margaret much nicer to her daughter now she had a BAFTA, an Olivier award and was generally acclaimed as the most popular, most accomplished young actress working in Britain today.

Chelsea had kind of given up on her mum, though she'd never have admitted it. It was Derek who'd sorted her out, and it was she, Chelsea, who'd pulled herself through everything else. She was a team of one, she had to be. She couldn't tell other people about the nightmares she had, the things she'd seen in her young life, and that was the way it was going to stay. Ever since she was a little girl, she'd felt second best to Amber. She didn't know why, and the last few years she'd kind of stopped wondering. It was something she couldn't explain, and now it was too late to do anything about it.

Leo's office continued to be vague about when her audition would take place. That only spurred her on. A few days in LA was enough to convince Chelsea of the size of what needed to be done. And she'd swiftly realised why Leo had looked at her like that: she needed to lose weight, and fast. She hadn't thought she was that big in London: in LA, it turned out, she was a freak.

She still thought Leo was a bit of a prick, but she liked him, she didn't know why; she'd seen the glimmer of humour in his eyes, enough to think he might be someone she could get on with.

And he was the best, she knew it. Chelsea hadn't really cared about this audition much either way, if she was honest. She saw it as her ticket to Hollywood. She had the talent, and now she just needed the looks to go with it. She had one shot at the big time, and this was it. She knew no one in town now, with Leo and Amber gone, and that was a blessing. Amber's agent, Dan Stein, had been in touch, but more because Amber had asked him to, Chelsea felt. She didn't need charity.

She was going to lose that weight, she was going to have that idiot Leo Russell eating out of her fucking hand, and she was going to enjoy it. No one was going to stop her! And so she got to work. It was when Chelsea had a plan that she was at her most effective – and her most ruthless.

Every morning, she swam in Amber's pool. In the evenings, she took Amber's two shitzus, Salt and Pepa, for a run along the beach. She didn't go out during the day, she burned easily and wanted to protect her pale skin.

And she stopped eating. Not altogether, but she found she wasn't as hungry in the Californian heat. She cut out the pastas and curries she'd been used to wolfing down after a night on the stage or shooting the TV show – God knows where she would have found them in LA, anyway – and started eating more fresh fruit and salads, grilled fish, nuts. She became obsessive about watching her body slim down – she used Amber's expensive body creams and oils, slathering herself with La Prairie and Crème de la Mer.

Slowly, surely, the weight began to fall off.

She tried on Amber's clothes, amazed after a few weeks at how she fitted into some of them. Every time she got hungry, she thought of Leo's face, his sardonic, polite voice. She knew it was an act, and that look in his eyes – what the fuck *was* it? Lust? It couldn't be, he'd as good as told her she was too big for him. For films, at least. What a fucking hypocrite, she'd think, and it would make her redouble her efforts.

And she made a friend, too. A fellow Brit called Jen, whom she met on the beach one afternoon. Jen was a make-up artist, working freelance for the studios and doing make-up for the stars for the awards shows. She was low-key and extremely cool, and Chelsea liked her for that – she was really ambitious, but she wasn't easily impressed. Didn't give away that she knew who Chelsea was, or that her sister was one of the most famous people on the planet. The second time they bumped into each other, when she was walking her dog Champion along the beach, she asked Chelsea if she knew what was happening in *EastEnders*.

'No fucking idea,' Chelsea said. 'I don't watch *EastEnders*.'

'You don't?'

Chelsea said, 'Look, love. I was too busy acting with Derek Jacobi every night to record some stupid soap.'

'Oh be quiet, you jumped-up cow,' said Jen, pushing her. 'I first saw you when you were a mouthy teenage bitch on a second-rate BBC kids' show, wearing eyeliner it looked like you'd applied on the back of a bumpy bus, so don't try and make out you're some class act. I know you, OK?'

There was a split-second's silence. Chelsea hadn't had anyone speak to her like that in years. But, she reasoned, since the Sunday Club had wound up and she'd left Roxy's, over two years ago now, she hadn't had any friends anyway. It'd be nice to say she had one here, at the very least.

She laughed, and put her arm round Jen. 'Come on,' she said. 'Let me buy you a drink. You're the only person in this weird town who hasn't crawled up to me since I arrived.'

For the first two months in California she was alone, apart from Rosita and Jen, but it was a life she liked. She came to love the outdoors, the warmth, the healthy lifestyle. She and Jen went roller-blading on the Santa Monica boardwalk, and Jen would tell her who was hot and who was not, who needed cover-up to hide their acne, who was fucking who. It made Chelsea feel she wasn't totally alone in this alien town. Jen was a good friend to have – free a lot of the time, cool enough to mind her own business, with a proper job and her own life. She wasn't one of those hangers-on you had to be careful about. Chelsea didn't want a best friend; she found it was best not to be reliant on anyone. But it was nice to know that Jen was there.

Every evening, Chelsea would sit on Amber's balcony with her one treat of the day – a chilled glass of Californian Cakebread from Napa Valley, and look out to the ocean, watching the joggers on the beach, the dog-walkers, the surfers and the pounding crash of the waves in the distance, the glorious coral, pink and amber of the setting sun. She didn't think about Amber, really.

What she was thinking was . . . *All this could be mine. And it should be mine. And it's going to be mine . . .*

223

Chapter Thirty-Seven

'Hi!' Amber dropped her bag on the floor, the chauffeur pausing behind her. Her mouth opened. 'My God, *look* at you, Chelsea! You look amazing!'

She hugged her sister. 'Thanks,' Chelsea said, returning the embrace, squeezing her sister back – it was easier to be enthusiastic about seeing your thin younger sister when you weren't four times the size of her. She stepped back and flicked her hair, self-consciously. 'It's great to see you.'

Amber took off her sunglasses. 'Wow!' Her eyes ran up and down her sister's body, taking in the glossy, beautifully cut and blow-dried hair, the creamy, glowing skin, the sparkling blue eyes, and that body – Chelsea was a UK size 10 now, and even that was baggy on her. It was still big by Hollywood standards, but she'd never been thinner. 'You're so hot! Look, your stomach's almost as flat as mine, and your boobs are amazing!'

She did look amazing in Amber's eyes. Almost *too* amazing. Her tits were still big, her body still pleasingly rounded, but her stomach was flat and her legs, which had always been dimpled and shapeless, were endless and lean. Her long, slender toes had had a French manicure, and she was dressed in a dark red heavy silk halterneck dress, which only emphasised her hourglass figure, her dark hair, her pale skin and the subtle make-up Jen had taught her to apply.

'Wow . . .' Amber was still staring at her sister. 'I can't believe the transformation. And that dress, it looks wonderful—'

Chelsea looked a little awkward. 'Oh, yeah. Sorry about that – I've been borrowing some of your stuff—'

Amber looked around the living area of the guest house, where clothes lay strewn all over the tiled floors and armchairs. She laughed. 'No worries,' she said. 'I'm not wearing them, am I? That colour looks great on you, I've always said so.'

There was an awkward silence, and then they both laughed, and Amber caught Chelsea's hands in hers. 'Good for you, Chelsea.'

Wow, can you sound a bit more patronising? Chelsea found herself thinking.

And then a voice behind them said, 'My God. Chelsea?'

Leo Russell stalked into the room holding his BlackBerry, still wearing his shades. He was laughing. 'You look fucking amazing, my dear, what have you been doing with yourself?'

She raised an eyebrow. 'Killing myself every day and not eating, that's what I've been doing. It's torture.'

Amber stiffened and looked at Leo, aghast. She'd been brought up in Hollywood to believe that you never, *ever* revealed that you worked to stay thin. If you were a star, you said things like 'I love my food!' 'I can't stop eating!' 'I guess I'm just lucky – I've got a really good metabolism, I don't keep the weight on, I never have.' On pain of death you did not reveal that you worked like a fucking dog, you denied yourself food, you ran and lifted weights, you took diet pills, made yourself sick if you had to – even someone like Amber, who was totally skinny by normal standards.

But Leo simply laughed, a great big laugh. 'Good for you, Chelsea. I love your honesty.'

Chelsea looked at him. He was the one she'd lost it for. He was the one whose look of horror, pity almost, had made her fight for what she wanted. And now she'd done it, he was telling her that he loved her *honesty*? Screw him!

She laughed. 'You don't give out compliments easily, do you? Want to audition me, then?' she said. 'I'm ready when you are.'

'Wow,' Leo fiddled with his huge platinum Rolex, still watching her. 'Yeah. Let's get that organised. Definitely.'

'Yes!' Chelsea nodded at him, her eyes sparkling. 'That's so great, thanks Leo.'

Amber gritted her teeth, but said nothing. What audition? She looked at her sister, glowing with excitement. *Have I ever been this excited about an audition? About making a film in LA?* She was struck again by the force of Chelsea's passion.

Later, back at her house, Amber was walking around her room settling back in after months away. Amber didn't like being away from home. She was tired of hotels: years of touring as a pop star and then shooting on location meant she'd spent more of her life in hotels than she'd care to remember. She wanted a quiet life – to be at home, to be at peace with her surroundings, do the things she loved.

But what *were* the things she loved?

She wasn't even sure any more. She hadn't sung for months, hadn't seen her dogs and run along the beach since she'd been away, hadn't laughed with a friend over some wine in she didn't know how long. Marco, Maria – they were long gone, she hadn't even tried to keep in touch with them. She didn't deserve friends. She spent her time shooting films she didn't really care about, films that were getting worse and worse (this one, with all the hallmarks of an Amber Stone romcom, was shaping up to be both limp *and* bloated, which was no mean feat, she thought). Thank God she was back, and could start thinking properly about *The Time of My Life* again. Surely Leo must be close to having a final script? Perhaps that would make her feel less jaded. Give her some of the fire she'd seen in Chelsea's eyes.

Carefully, Amber unwrapped her jewellery. She had a couple of really expensive pieces, but they were kept at the bank. These were simple things, but they meant a lot to her: a necklace George had given her when she was thirteen. A bracelet from Marco; it was cheap and tacky, deliberately so, spelling out her name in silver letters. Amber didn't tell Leo, but she kept it with her at all times. She still missed Marco.

Leo was on the balcony, staring ruminatively out of the window at the ocean.

'What are you thinking about?' Amber asked him, tentatively.

'Hm? Me? Oh, nothing,' Leo said, but too quickly. He came back into the room, clearing his throat.

Amber was struck with a feeling of unease, and she couldn't work out why. She said, hoping to keep her voice light, 'I love Chelsea, but she is hilarious. She's got such a fucking nerve. I don't know who she is any more. There's a bloody stranger in my guest house, wearing my favourite Roberto Cavalli dress.'

'I know,' Leo drawled. 'And it suits her much better, my dear.'

He'd told Amber she looked fat in that dress. That was the dress that had forced her into training with an army instructor seven days a week.

Highly irritated, Amber slammed the lid of her jewellery box shut. She stared at the bracelet Marco had given her, still resting on the side. From below, she heard Chelsea's throaty laugh as she chatted to Rosita by the pool.

Amber wondered once more about what she had given up to be here. And whether it was worth it.

Chapter Thirty-Eight

From the *Sun,* September 2007, page 3:

WHERE DID SHE GO??!

Look at this fine figure of a girl – recognise her? It's Chelsea Stone, three months into her stay in LA, and she's completely transformed. *Sun* readers will be particularly relieved to hear her biggest assets are still intact, as can be seen from the photo above, taken on Santa Monica beach.

This was a golden time for Chelsea.

So far she had kept her presence hidden, but when Amber returned, Chelsea started going out more. Once she'd made up her mind to do something, she did it. And she had made up her mind to love LA. So she did. She started jogging further down the beach, to the stretch where she knew the paparazzi hung out. Her picture began to appear in the UK tabloids – her agent in London was practically wetting herself with excitement. 'We could get anything you want here now, darling!' Joanna said, time and time again. Gareth, Vicky and Conor, her friends from the Sunday

Club, emailed her, as did other friends in London, telling her not to sell out, and by the way, she looked amazing . . . She ignored them, ignored the phone calls. She'd left England, left it all behind. It seemed like another lifetime.

She wanted the big time.

She was so clever, too. Amber watched her work it, work it with the paps, with people who came to the house, with Sally – and with Leo. Chelsea knew for damn straight she couldn't compete with the tiny, thin blonde starlets who crowded into the neon-lit ultra-exclusive clubs and bars of LA, the beaches and parties. Instead, she traded on the earthiness that had made her so loved back in the UK – the earthiness that had made Leo's hair stand on end – and his cock stand to attention.

And she began to socialise – she connected with her British contacts, made new friends, got to know the right places to hang out, where to be seen, who to be seen with. Amber was convinced she must be hiring a publicist, or something – she was playing some kind of game, always out running, or out at a party where she'd meet a darling old friend from BBC days, or a friend from the club scene back in London, or from TV, or the stage – Chelsea had had a varied career, to say the least, and now it was paying dividends. She had a past, too, and she was refreshingly frank about it to anyone who asked.

She was good company, modest, funny – and simply the most charismatic person her little sister knew. Sometimes, when they were together, at a pre-awards ceremony, at a dinner for an agent, or hanging out with Leo by the pool, Amber felt about as interesting as a blancmange . . .

One evening, Chelsea and Amber had gone for a run with the dogs, along Malibu beach. It was something they did together to try and bond, because it was easiest to spend time running than actually sitting down over a drink and properly talking. Chelsea had Salt, Amber had Pepa.

Their feet were pounding the hard sand, the surf sighing in the distance, when suddenly they heard someone running behind them.

'Chelsea, Amber! Hey! Stop a minute!'

Chelsea, alarmed, half turned round, but Amber carried on running. She was used to it all by now. She knew to keep on running.

She knew how to play the game, how to appear polite and friendly on *The Ellen DeGeneres Show*, while inside you were hating every minute, how to banter with David Letterman when you were nervously waiting to get in the charming, jokey, Amber-sweet line your publicist had strategised over with your agent for two weeks. How to smile at the photographers when you were coming out of Starbucks with the dogs in your running gear, not sweaty or rumpled, fresh as a daisy because the whole thing was staged.

Amber didn't mind premieres – a stylist put you in a shimmering gold, flirty little dress, threaded a cute little plait through your hair and all you had to do was exclaim in your still perfect British accent that you were really happy to be there, and they loved you.

Anything out of her comfort zone made Amber extremely anxious, though.

Turning round, she saw it was a slightly overweight guy in a black T-shirt, running after them.

'It's Zac Truman, I work for the *LA Times*,' he panted. 'Please, Chelsea, can I just ask you a few questions?'

'Oh, OK.' Chelsea stopped running, and turned to face him. Instantly another man materialised beside her.

'Jack Feather, freelance,' he said. He nodded at her.

'Hi, Jack.' Chelsea nodded at him.

Jack Feather was the bane of Amber's life, a weaselly man who somehow knew all her insecurities and was most likely to know when she was carrying that extra pound – his photographers seemed to have an almost psychic awareness of where she was going to be.

Amber was horrified. She slowed down, not sure what to do. But she couldn't leave Chelsea. She pretended to be adjusting the laces on her trainers.

'So, Chelsea,' Jack Feather said, sticking a recorder under her nose. 'Who are you these days? You've lost all this weight, you're running on the beach – shouldn't you be raising hell in some bar somewhere, shoving coke up your nose?'

He smiled, but his eyes were cold. Amber almost gasped at the insensitivity of it – it still got to her, how vicious they could be, all to get a reaction out of you. She thought of her mother's training, of how her dad had always told her to keep quiet and be polite.

But her elder sister just put her hands on her hips and laughed. 'Not any more, Jack. Those days are over – and thank God, too. I still enjoy a drink, though – just a glass a day at the moment, I'm really trying to lose weight and it's a pain.'

She looked so carefree, standing there with the setting sun behind her, loose tendrils of hair blowing in the wind. Amber felt a pang of something shoot through her.

'So you've embarked on this weight-loss programme,' Jack said. 'Don't you think it's a bit desperate, losing all this weight just to fit in with Hollywood? How about your fans back in the UK, won't they just think you've sold out?'

Amber stood up and walked slowly back to her sister's side. 'Hi,' she said, but they ignored her – without the make-up and the styled hair, Amber looked quite different, whereas Chelsea's personality shone through, wherever she was.

It had always been like that.

For a split second, Amber was mortified when they didn't see her, then she relaxed. It was nice, not being recognised. Standing in someone's shadow, for once . . .

'Oh, I'm sure some people will say it's desperate,' Chelsea said. 'But I've never been thin, and I wanted to try to be healthy. I'm still young, and my career is everything to me. I want my fans to be proud of me, and I hope they will, wherever I am, whatever I'm doing, don't you agree?'

Amber smiled – she couldn't help it. It was bullshit, but it was the perfect answer.

And then: 'So,' said Zac Truman. 'What about *The Time of My Life*, the new Leo Russell movie? Rumour is they've promised the part to Amber, yet you've auditioned for it, what's that about?'

Chelsea put her arm round her sister. 'Don't believe the rumours, Zac,' she said. 'We're sisters first, everything else comes second. Thanks, Zac. Thanks, Jack Feather.'

He stared at her. 'Call me when you need a friendly pap, OK?'

Chelsea ignored him. 'Have a great night, guys!'

She pulled Amber ahead, and they carried on running, back towards the house. Amber followed her, thinking, *Well*, that *was bullshit, too* . . .

She was right. Three days later, Leo called her up to his offices. It was business, he said, and when she arrived, he was dressed in his movie-producer clothes – silk shirt, black trousers, air of gravity around him. He met her in his office, with the BAFTAs and the other awards lined up behind him. He didn't kiss her.

He just said, with no preamble, 'Listen, Amber. I need to talk to you. That part in *The Time of My Life*. I'm giving it to Chelsea.'

'What?' Amber clutched the chair in front of her for support. 'Are you joking, Leo?'

'Why would I joke about something like this?' Leo said, as if he was curious.

'That part's mine!' Amber said. Her throat was closing up, as if she was winded. 'You know it is, Leo – you promised it to me!'

'It's Chelsea's,' he said. 'I'm sorry, but I'm giving it to her.'

'I thought –' Amber looked around wildly. She didn't know what to do, what to say next. 'I thought you were joking around with her about that part. I thought you were just trying her out with a couple of auditions.' She said again, weakly, 'That part's *mine!*'

Leo looked bored. He pressed the tips of his fingers together. 'Amber, please don't be like this,' he said, as if she'd just smashed a Ming vase and threatened him with a gun. 'Chelsea is a wonderful actress. I'm so excited about the future with her. You're one of the biggest stars in the world, Amber. I don't understand why you're being like this.'

She looked at the awards behind him, at the photos of him with various stars and studio heads adorning the walls, at the framed cutting from *Variety* which simply said 'UK's biggest / best export: Leo Russell'. Looked again, and realised that there wasn't a single photo of her anywhere.

'What is it, with you and me?' she asked, suddenly. 'I mean – do you love me? Or were you just using me, all along?'

'I can't talk to you when you're like this,' Leo simply said. 'Amber, come on. She's an amazing actress – aren't you pleased for her?'

Amber said softly, 'I don't know what you want me to do, Leo.' She felt totally blank. 'What do you want me to do now?'

She leaned against the wall of his office, breathing fast. 'I can't think what I should be doing any more.'

'Amber, darling, you have to calm down,' Leo said. 'You'll finish the new film, it's going to be fantastic. And there are many other wonderful parts lined up for you to play, we know that.'

Yeah, right, she wanted to yell. *The same old crap, regurgitated again and again for an audience that deserves better.* 'I wanted something different,' she said.

'Well –' Leo simply raised his eyebrows, and said nothing else.

Fuck him. Fuck them all. Yet again, Leo had manoeuvred her into the weaker position, so that to fight back would take more strength than she had.

'I don't know who you are any more,' she said, and she didn't know if she was talking to him or to herself. 'I don't know if I ever did.'

Leo nodded, looking at her sadly, and Amber knew she wasn't going to get anything more out of him.

She couldn't speak. She ran out of Leo's office, past an astonished Sally, hovering in the corridor, out into the sunny courtyard, and she jumped into her Bentley and sped off into the distance, revving as fast as she could, wishing she could drive away from here, away from everything . . .

This was all Chelsea's fucking fault.

Chapter Thirty-Nine

'I can't believe it!' Amber sobbed. 'Ever – ever since she came . . . she's trying to . . .' She sniffed. 'She's trying to take my place!'

'There, there.' Margaret patted Amber's shoulder and moved her face away a little – she was wearing a new Ralph Lauren linen shirt, and she didn't want it blotched with her daughter's snotty tears and make-up. 'Leo says it's her one big chance. And—'

'You *knew*?' Amber sat up, astonished, on the soft velvet chaise longue that stood by the window of her den.

'I – Leo called me yesterday,' Margaret said. She hadn't banked on Amber reacting like this, truth be told. It was a little . . . surprising. 'Your sister deserves a break, you know. She's been through a lot.'

'What the hell are you *talking* about, Mum?' she demanded, hugging a cushion closely to herself. 'You were the one who told me to cut all contact with her! To push her away! You made me put that statement out!'

Margaret stiffened. She looked down at her youngest daughter, not knowing what to say. Yes, she had done that. Yes, she'd pushed her own daughter away, she'd been doing it all her life. And she couldn't tell Amber why, couldn't ever tell either of her daughters the truth.

'I'm not saying she's perfect,' she said, struggling to find the right words, and unbidden, the thought of Chelsea's hysterical voice rang in her ears, crying down the phone after the drugs scandal had broken. She thought of how she'd rejected her then. She was so angry with Chelsea. She had been ever since she was born – and why? It wasn't her fault.

After the scandal had broken in the UK press, she'd had to preserve what she had with Amber. If she was dispassionate about it, she told herself, she'd say Amber was the product, Chelsea the distraction. Increasingly, though, it bothered her.

She had been frantic in the hours and days afterwards, when Chelsea had gone completely silent, no phone calls, nothing. The situation was completely out of her control, and she told herself that Chelsea was uncontrollable; that was why she'd had to leave her to do her own thing. Amber was a good girl, biddable and quiet, even now. Chelsea was a liability . . .

Two nights had gone by without a word from Chelsea and Margaret, in her little condo a ten-minute drive from Amber's, had not slept a wink, as she lay awake each night giving full rein to her terror. Chelsea was dead . . . she'd crashed again . . . she was lying in a gutter somewhere. London was such a dangerous place!

It was that bloody Derek who'd told her, ringing her after three days to tell her Chelsea was safe and that he was sorting her with a job. That man – Margaret frowned. She wished he'd stay in the past, where he belonged . . . Yes, OK, she'd been ever so glad to hear from him, but that had quickly passed. She couldn't shake him off. He was like a cockroach – impossible to stamp out.

'Look, I've seen her,' Margaret said, shaking herself out of the past. 'She's very upset you're cross with her. I don't think she thought for a moment she'd get the part –'

'Then why the hell did she audition?' Amber shouted. Margaret shushed her; Chelsea was over in the guest house, she'd seen her on the way in. 'I was desperate for that part, you know I was!' She was practically screaming; she never lost her composure. It was too much to think about, but this had brought Amber as close to hating her sister as she'd come in years – not since she'd got the part of Roxy and Amber hadn't. She shook her head. 'What's next, Mum?' she said, spreading her hands out. 'I don't know.'

'We'll talk to Leo.' Margaret nodded; she had complete faith in Leo, still. 'He'll be able to explain. There's a reason he wanted Chelsea for that part, I'm telling you.'

A cold, clammy fear was gripping Amber. She thought she knew what the reason was, though she couldn't even say it. 'It's like she's taking my life,' she whispered. And she believed it.

'Listen to me.' Margaret was brisk. 'You're being silly. She's not. Leo wants her for this one film. It's very different from your films. I bet it won't even—'

This was the part that was going to get me out of this rut. It was going to be the solution to what was missing . . . And Chelsea's doing it instead.

Amber closed her eyes and laughed. 'You're so wrong, Mum. It's going to be huge, I know it, and – look,' she said. 'You don't get it. I'm sick of the films I make.' Margaret looked horrified. Amber said frantically, 'I am! I'm sick of the stupid coy scripts, these dumb men I have to pretend I want to sleep with, the ridiculous situations I have to play. I wanted to try something else, something that *isn't* forgotten five minutes after it comes out.'

Margaret said sharply, 'Amber, there are plenty of girls who want what you've got. Be grateful.'

'I'm sick of being fucking *grateful* all the fucking time!' Amber shouted. 'I want to do what I want! Who *are* these girls, anyway? Why are you always going on about them?'

'I was one of them,' Margaret said, evenly. She stood up. 'I wanted this more than you can ever know. But I wasn't good enough. I didn't have it. "It".' She laughed, as if remembering some painful memory. 'Good God. Just remember, Amber, you're lucky. You're lucky!'

But Amber's face was grim and for once, she wasn't really listening to her mother.

'She'd better move out of that fucking guest house,' she said. 'She's come over here, she's moved in, nicked all my clothes, she wanders around using my stuff like it's hers, she's siphoning off most of my friends who all think she's *so* hilarious and *so* refreshing and *so* fucking *cool*, and now she's stolen the only part I've actually ever wanted from right under my nose!' She sniffed, and said, grimly, 'I just wonder, what else is there for her to take?'

'Nothing else.' Margaret said, firmly. 'I'll talk to her.' She got up, and brushed down her skirt. 'Don't worry, baby. I'll talk to her. I'll get you some tea. Where's Rosita?'

Outside, in the corridor, Chelsea heard her mother get up and ran softly down the stairs, biting her lip.

Nothing had changed, nothing.

Nothing she could do for her mother was ever right; even those few words of praise had been squeezed out of her like water from a wringer. And she was sick of Amber's whining. She'd tried so hard with her – perhaps she hadn't tried enough, or perhaps she just shouldn't have bothered at all? Just accept that she and Amber weren't ever going to be friends, now. Perhaps she shouldn't have auditioned, when Leo asked her to.

But he was hard to say no to, and there was something about him she liked – he was full of shit, sure, but there was a look in his eyes that told her he knew it was all a game.

Sometimes, Chelsea thought as she ran quietly back to the guest house, Leo Russell felt like the only person who really understood her out here in LA. There was Jen, the make-up artist, but they only saw each other once a week or so. Jen would laugh about this. Leo would, too – except she couldn't tell him. There was nothing going on with them! Chelsea felt embarrassed even thinking about it. It was playful, nothing more, and he made her smile. He called her Eliza, after Eliza Doolittle in *My Fair Lady*. 'When are you getting the accent sorted out?' he'd say, teasing her. 'You still sound like you should be in fucking *EastEnders* with Babs Windsor, darling.'

'And you sound like you paid someone to teach you to talk like a posh twat, when I know you're from bloody Watford, *darling*.'

'Fuck off,' Leo would say, smiling in amusement.

'You fuck off.'

'Hello, Eliza!'

Lost in thought, Chelsea jumped, and looked up. Leo was walking up the drive, throwing his car keys in the air.

Chelsea's hand flew to her throat. 'That's so weird,' she said. 'I was just thinking about you.'

Leo looked at her. 'You OK?'

'I'm fine.' Chelsea could feel herself blushing. She didn't know why – he really wasn't her type. Chelsea hadn't had any action in a while, it was hard when you were famous to find the right kind of guy, and she was usually attracted to low-life sleazes who sold stories about your penchant for oral sex and lacy red corsets to the *News of the World*. So she'd been on her own for a while. She wanted an equal. She wasn't anyone's arm candy.

Now, though, she was . . . what was it? She was in the mood. Horny. Up for it, she'd have said back in London. She wanted to show someone her new slim body, feel someone's hands on her skin, and she wanted to know who the candidates might be. Chelsea gazed past Leo, musing at the sight behind him. The gardener, Carlos, was top of the list – he was Cuban and could dance. Chelsea had told him all about her days at Roxy's, and got him to show her some of his moves – she wasn't sure of the ethics of fucking the gardener, though, was it exploitation, or was it OK? Surely it wasn't exploitation when the gardener wanted to fuck you too?

'What are you thinking?'

Leo looked mildly amused, as he always did when talking to her.

'Wouldn't you like to know,' she said, pertly.

'I bet I would,' Leo said, grinning. He had his arms folded, his hands stroking the muscles on his forearms, unselfconsciously. Oh, she *did* like him. She liked lots of things about him – he knew what she was thinking, what she'd like to do to Carlos. She liked the fact it was a blank piece of paper with Leo, every time they met. That they could be as rude to each other as they liked, spar and fling barbed insults at each other and still remain friends. It was all a game – he saw that, and she did too. She knew he was off-limits, for God's sake. He always had been. Which is why Chelsea felt she could push the boundaries with him, and it would be OK. Plus, he'd taken a chance on her, which was more than her own mother and sister had ever done . . .

'You look great today, Chelsea,' he told her, softly. He looked up at the house in the sunset, almost furtively. Almost like they both knew they had to keep quiet about the movie because of Amber. He lowered his voice. 'I'm looking forward to starting work.' Chelsea smiled again.

'I can't wait,' she said. She smiled that huge smile. 'I just can't fucking wait, Leo. Thank you so much.'

Her enthusiasm was infectious, her beautiful open grin flawless, and Leo breathed in. She had no idea how captivating she was; the camera loved her, it was quite extraordinary. He'd been in the edit suite with the other producers and the directors when they'd watched the audition tapes for *The Time of My Life*. He had never known someone light up the screen the way Chelsea Stone did. When she was in shot, you didn't look at anyone else. She was mesmerising.

She was looking behind him at Carlos, the buff young gardener, and Leo followed her gaze. But a figure was blocking the view, a figure clad in a tiny dark blue suit, minuscule skirt and tight-fitting jacket, hair perfect, scarf perfect, smile gleaming white, scampering up next to Leo holding a sheaf of papers.

'Hi! Hi, Leo!' she breathed.

'Oh. Hi, Sally,' Chelsea said. 'Great to see you.'

Sally was big on American-style courtesies, and Chelsea never knew if she loathed her or merely tolerated her. The chick was mad for Leo and he barely knew she was alive, that was for sure. 'It's great to see you too!' she said, smiling. 'Hey – we're here for a meeting with Amber, about the reshoots – is she around?'

'Oh,' said Chelsea. Reality sunk in. She looked up. 'Yeah, she's in.' She looked sober. 'She's – yeah, good luck.'

'Thanks,' Leo said, and a flash of something crossed his face. 'Look, we'll be in touch, I'm going to get you in to meet Paul and Bryan and the other guys we'll be working with.'

'You're not available Tuesday, are you?' Sally started tapping on her BlackBerry. 'Because I just heard from Bryan's office and he's good then, too.'

Leo turned to look at Chelsea. 'Great. Chelsea? I'll pick you up and take you to Culver City. It won't be so scary then, I promise.'

Chelsea was amused that he and Sally both assumed she must be free. That she had nothing better to do than hang around waiting for Leo Russell.

Well, she thought, they were right.

Amber was away most of next week, reshooting a couple of scenes of her film. It was best that she wasn't around to see Chelsea being picked up by Leo for the meeting on the film she'd desperately wanted . . .

'Tuesday's great,' Chelsea told them, and Leo and Sally nodded in the Californian dusk like they all knew what this was about. Like it was all OK, part of the plan, it was going to happen.

'I'd better go up and see Amber,' Leo said. 'She needs to know we still love her.'

'Right,' said Chelsea. 'Laters, then,' she said, nonchalantly. Leo's tall, masculine frame disappeared towards the house, as she stood next to Sally and watched him walk away.

'Leo really suits a tailored shirt, don't you think?' Sally said, dreamily. 'It's so great on him.'

'I wouldn't know,' Chelsea said firmly.

Chapter Forty

Did Chelsea Stone know what was going to happen? Did she know that she would fall for Leo Russell? If she had asked herself – which she wouldn't have: Chelsea wasn't given to introspection, not these days – she would probably have said no. He was Amber's boyfriend. She'd already taken the part in the film off her, according to Amber. She didn't want to do anything else to rock the boat.

The trouble was, Chelsea wanted everything. And she wanted it now. After years of despair and addiction after her dad's death, she had clawed her way back, come out fighting, right on top. She was making it work in LA, through her own efforts. She was young, thin, feeling gorgeous and she was ready for a good time, and she knew she had to take everything that was on offer.

In other words, she was ripe for the picking.

'Have another whisky,' Chelsea said.

She scrambled across the cool grass on her knees, giggling, holding the bottle as she went.

'I'm drinking with Chelsea Stone,' Leo murmured. 'My God, what am I getting into?'

'I shouldn't be drinking,' she said. She ran her hands through her hair. The meeting with the director and the other co-producers had gone well, and Chelsea was feeling that maybe this terrifying, scary film, maybe it was something she could do.

She had persuaded Leo back to Amber's and they were lying on the grass, drinking. At least, she was. He was sitting on a linen director's chair, watching her.

Amber had been away four days. She'd left without saying goodbye, spitting angry with both of them, and they felt like naughty children as a result.

Chelsea placed a wobbling hand on Leo's knees, carefully, and poured some more whisky into his glass. 'Don't be afraid,' she said, trying not to sound drunk. 'I won't hurt you.' She giggled.

There was a movement behind Leo, and she saw Carlos disappearing into the house. He'd been working on the garden all evening, trimming the hedges.

'Oh,' Chelsea said, shaking her head.

'What?' Leo asked. He turned to see what she was looking at, and his expression darkened. 'Oh,' he said, after a moment, his voice light. 'Someone's horny for the gardener, are they?'

She was drunk and carefree and it was late. 'Yeah,' Chelsea said frankly. 'Horny in general, but – yeah, horny for the gardener.'

Leo stood up. She couldn't see his expression. She scrambled to her feet, blinking heavily. 'I should go,' he said. 'I have a heavy day tomorrow, it's late.'

Chelsea was horrified. 'You can't drive like this.'

'This is LA, sweetie,' he said shortly, 'yes I can.'

She stared at him, breathing heavily. 'Stay a little while.'

Leo knew how to play them, each and every time. He breathed in, keeping his voice light, the line slack. Thank God he'd done that line of coke earlier. He felt on top of the world, unconquerable . . . He could take her, now. Later, he would reel her in.

'Do you want me to stay?'

'Yes,' Chelsea said slowly.

'Don't you want to go off and find that guy who trims your bushes?' He smiled, and touched her arm lightly.

Chelsea flushed as she felt his fingers on her skin. She moved closer to him, so that they were standing only a centimetre apart, almost touching, but not quite. She breathed in, her breasts rising, and they scraped the front of Leo's chest. He made a tiny sound in the back of his throat.

'Come with me,' he said, and pulled her by the hand towards the guest house.

When they were alone, standing in the doorway of her bedroom, he pushed her against the frame and said, 'I want you, Chelsea.'

He wiped the last of the whisky from his mouth and kissed her.

His hands moved over her body; Chelsea gasped. It had been so long since anyone had wanted her. *Leo?* It was scarcely believable. His tongue was in her mouth, probing her, jabbing against her; she could feel his hands running up and down her. He let out a kind of moan as he reached her breasts. Chelsea was wearing a sundress with no bra underneath. Gently, very slowly, Leo pulled the straps over her smooth shoulders and squeezed the fabric over her plump breasts, so that they were exposed for him. He shuddered as his hands reached for them.

'Your tits . . .' He looked up at her, holding her in his hands, squeezing the soft, cold flesh. 'You know you have amazing breasts, don't you? Please tell me you do.'

He kissed each one gently, then harder, cupping them, teasing the nipples, and then he was tearing her dress off her, and she was kissing him back, wriggling out of her clothes with an urgency that surprised her.

'God . . . you're so beautiful,' he said, his voice ragged.

She didn't know it, and she knew it was a line, a line to get her to do what he wanted, but Chelsea didn't care. She was past caring. He wanted her now, her, the girl he'd looked at a couple of months ago like she was a fairground freak. She wrapped her arms round his neck, feeling his muscular body against hers, his rigid cock jabbing into her pelvis. She kissed him, rubbing her rock-hard nipples against his bare chest.

'Don't lose any more weight, will you?' he said, panting a little as he nibbled at her neck. He ran his hands over her belly, dipping his fingers into her panties. 'You're perfect as you are.' He slid a finger inside her. Chelsea's eyes flew open, and she gasped in surprise. 'You're wet,' he said, his breathing getting even shallower. She felt as if she might pass out from wanting him. 'You're wet for me.'

'Leo –' Chelsea said, trying to ignore his fingers, moving towards her secret bud of pleasure. 'What about . . .'

'Don't,' he said, pushing her back gently towards the bed so that she was lying down. He was straddled over her, his hands at either side of her head. 'This is about you and me, Chelsea . . . I want you so much, but you're going to have to beg me to fuck you.' He whispered this to her gently as he proceeded to stick his tongue in her ear. He then slid his tongue slowly down her neck, down between her breasts and into her belly button. And every time she reached for him, he pushed her away. 'Not yet,' he said, calmly, as she writhed underneath him, desperate for him to be inside her. 'Not yet. You're mine, and I'm going to make you come till you scream.'

When she did, a few minutes later, she shuddered and called his name, weakly. He held her for a second and then lowered himself over her and wrapped her hand around his long, thick cock. She looked down at it, then up at him and smiled.

'I'm going to fuck you now,' he whispered. 'I'm going to make you come again, and again . . .'

She guided him inside her, inch by inch, gasping as she did. This was the first time she had ever experienced sex with a man whose dick must be a full ten inches.

She smiled as she looked up at him. His dick was so big she felt pleasurable pain. She moaned, as he slid further inside her. 'Oh my God, Leo!'

He smiled wolfishly down at her and started pushing inside her, long, deep thrusts that pressed hard on her G–spot, and they moved together in the small white bedroom, her cries and his together. When he came, he exploded into her and collapsed onto her chest. He flexed his dick a few times more, one hand resting lightly on her breast. He kissed her, and squeezed her bottom.

'Wow,' he said. 'I didn't expect that.' And then he fell asleep.

★

She had thought it would be awkward in the morning. But she woke to Leo's mouth between her legs, teasing her with his tongue. She clutched his head with her hands in pleasure. 'What the fuck –?' she said, still waking up. She groaned with pleasure, arching her back.

'Just a little morning pick-me-up,' he said, looking at her from between her legs.

Perhaps it was then that Chelsea fell in love with Leo Russell, loving him for going down on her, for surprising her, for fucking her with a dick that was the size of a stallion's. She couldn't believe this was the same Leo who'd lied and cheated and couldn't be trusted.

The same Leo who was with her sister. Who treated Amber like a commodity, a disposable plaything.

She froze a little as she lay there, his mouth working, lapping at her, his hands caressing her bum, her breasts, her thighs, and then pleasure overtook her as his tongue slid over her clit, pressing, teasing, and then he stopped and said, ' You've got the tightest pussy I've had in years.' He said it almost in surprise, staring at her with his dark eyes. And then he licked her again, long, luxuriant laps with the rough part of his tongue, and she cried out with pleasure, and couldn't think about anything else any more.

She didn't think about it as she went down on him, a few minutes later, almost gagging on the length of him, revelling in the way he overfilled her mouth, how thick, how hard he was. He was a man – she was used to boys.

Or when he came over later that evening and fucked her in the bathroom, rubbing frantically between her legs, pinning her arms to her sides until she howled like a wild beast and he thrust inside her then, smiling at how helpless she was in his arms, to his touch.

And she didn't think about it when he finally took her from behind on Amber's balcony, a couple of nights later, and she watched the ocean in front of her, crashing on the white sandy beach as Leo cupped her breasts with his hands, driving his big hard cock into her, nibbling at her neck and whispering her name as she choked his out.

She didn't know that had been what he'd wanted the first time he saw her, and now he was getting it, despite the risks, despite the fact that they were betraying Amber yet again . . .

She didn't know then that Leo Russell always got what he wanted.

Chapter Forty-One

It wasn't the unease she felt, whenever she saw them together.

The banter between them, the shared jokes, the sheer amount of time they had to spend together on set . . .

It wasn't the buzz that damn film got, gathering more and more momentum now it was finished and about to be released.

It wasn't the whispers, the kindness from her mother and from Sally, the encroaching paranoia, the feeling that the mask was starting to slip, and she couldn't control it.

No: the moment Amber realised something had to change was when she got the offer through from Dan Stein, her agent.

'Are you fucking *kidding* me?' Amber was yelling, so loudly that Rosita dropped the vase she was polishing in the cavernous hallway. 'Sorry, Rosita. Sorry. What the *fuck* do you think you're doing?' she hissed into the phone. '*I do* not *play the older best friend!*'

She tried so hard not to swear, but sometimes she couldn't help it. She couldn't eat cupcakes, drink more than one glass of wine – she couldn't smoke because it was so bad for her clean-cut image. She could swear like a trooper, though.

'Amber, sweetheart, listen—'

'No, *you* listen, sunshine.' Amber raked her nails across her neck, scratching so violently she could feel she was leaving marks. She padded into her study and kicked the door shut with her foot. 'I'm

Amber bloody Stone, OK? I don't play the support, I'm the lead. I'm America's fucking sweetheart, not America's washed-up nobody!' She stubbed her toe on an ornamental cabinet standing in the den. 'Fuck! *Fuck* it!' she howled, hopping round in agony.

Dan said, 'Hey! Amber, listen to me! They say you're perfect for it – of course you're not washed up, honey. Chelsea's older than you, it's no problem!'

'I don't need this,' Amber snapped. 'Chelsea's got nothing to do with it. You tell them to take that fucking script and shove it up their fucking arses till it comes out their throat. OK?'

She was almost enjoying this, the blood was pumping, she felt alive, *alive* . . .

'Well.' Dan sounded doubtful. 'If you really think—'

'Sorry, Dan,' Amber said. She gathered herself a little. 'Next?'

'That's all I have for you at this time,' said Dan.

'What the hell?' Amber frowned.

Was there a little note of triumph in Dicky Dan's voice? She didn't like him, with his soft lilting Southern accent and his lily-white, manicured hands; never had. He was a puppet of Leo's, completely under his thumb. 'Honey, you have to listen to me. This is a great part. Times are changing. America loves you, sure, but you're a woman, you're getting close to thirty. That's the reality, OK? I'm not going to be getting offers for you to play the bright-eyed lil' ingénue any more.' He cleared his throat. 'It's happened.'

'What's happened?'

'The tipping point, sweetie. Yeah, there'll be good films for you. But you're not playing the twenty-year-old from a small town again. You need to find something else. Other parts.' He paused. 'TV, perhaps.'

Amber said, awfully, 'I'm not going into TV, like some washed-up old . . .'

She trailed off.

'Just think about it,' Dan said. There was a rustling sound in the background.

'I won't,' she told him. 'Listen, Chelsea's nearly two years older than me, it's her first film here and she's the lead!' She felt as if she was bargaining for something.

'Yeah,' Dan was eating whatever he'd unwrapped; it was like he was trying to diss her. 'But *The Time of My Life* has been Number One now for a month. They're saying it's gonna win everything going. It's got the Oscar noms, for Christ's sake!'

'So? She's got no track record, it's the film, not her,' Amber said spitefully.

Dan sounded uneasy. 'And . . . well, Chelsea's Chelsea. She can do what the fuck she likes at the moment. You – you gotta understand that, sweetie.'

He hung up.

Amber stood in her study, looking at the soft sofa, the coffee table piled high with scripts to be read, the walls lined with posters for her films, photos of her at premieres, letters from fans, even one from the President's daughter, telling her how much she'd enjoyed *The First Date*.

Was this it?

She ran a hand over her forehead. She was trembling. She wanted to call Leo, and then she remembered. He was away with Chelsea again, more media training for the damn film – the awards season was in full swing, she'd already had to follow her lover and her sister up the red carpet.

Had to pretend to smile, when she wanted to run away, run to the ocean where she felt calm, at peace.

Pretend to answer the reporters' inane questions with a perky, sweet smile, that said she wasn't ruffled by anything.

Pretend she was happy for them both. Oh, she was, she was trying so hard to be. But it was hard. Really hard. And sometimes she felt like she was going mad. Was it just in her head, this feeling she had about them? Was she making it up?

She didn't know, and she couldn't ask either of them.

And lately, she didn't know how to talk to her mother, either. She looked in the mirror at herself, then around at her beautiful house. Tears fell down her cheeks.

The truth was, as Amber had begun to realise, she was completely alone.

Chapter Forty-Two

From *The Times*, February 2008:

CHELSEA STONE ON TOP AGAIN

In the end, it didn't win Best Picture, but that didn't stop Hollywood's new darling, Chelsea Stone (pictured) from stealing the show at tonight's Academy Awards. Dressed in Hervé Léger and making the most of the famous (albeit drastically reduced) curves that have seen her acclaimed as a role model for women everywhere, and beaming on the arm of her producer, fellow Brit Sir Leo Russell, the former wild child and drug addict said last night really was 'the time of my life'.

'This film (*The Time of My Life*) really has been life-changing for me, and for all of us who worked on it,' she said outside the *Vanity Fair* party, where she and other members of the cast and crew were preparing to celebrate their win for Best Original Screenplay. 'Working with Leo has been simply wonderful, as well as Bryan and all the guys. I loved playing Maloney. And I'm so lucky this is my first film. It feels a long, long way from *Roxy's Nine Lives*,' she added with a smile. When asked if she'd have liked to have won the Oscar, she said, 'It's honestly just wonderful to be nominated.'

Miss Stone need not feel her efforts have gone unrewarded, however. She was the mascot of the awards season, winning Best Actress at the Screen Actors Guild and Critics' Circle Awards. And the film has now gone on to gross $850 million already, after winning Best Picture at Cannes the previous year, and Best Drama at this year's Golden Globes. It is hard to think of another film in recent memory that has combined box-office appeal with such wild critical acclaim, and that is down in large part to the skills of the notorious Leo Russell and, of course, to the raw, almost unsettling talent of the girl who done good, Chelsea Stone.

The door was shutting behind them. 'Goodbye, y'all,' called out Ryan Peach, Chelsea's co-star, a sweet-natured Southern guy. 'Thanks for a great night, Leo!'

''Night!' Chelsea called. *Why the fuck wouldn't he just go?*

'Good night, then!'

'Yes, 'bye!'

There was a silence in the room.

A few hours after the Oscars were over, the parties were winding down and the huge hotel suite the studio had hired for everyone from *The Time of My Life* was empty, and Chelsea and Leo were finally alone. Outside, the lights of downtown LA glittered in the darkness. Dawn would be here soon – it was late, very late.

'So,' Chelsea murmured, slowly nibbling on a strawberry. She kicked off her dove-grey silk stilettos and ran her hands gently over her dove-grey silk dress. She knew she looked fantastic. 'Are you going to finish with me, now I'm a loser?'

She knelt up on the grey velvet couch, gently pushing the fleshy red fruit into her mouth, looking up at him from under her dark lashes, as Leo locked the door behind him, loosened his black tie and walked swiftly over to her. He put one hand on her neck, the other on her butt and sank onto the cushions, pulling her towards him, his tongue insistent in her mouth.

'At last. Take your dress off,' he said shortly, unzipping his trousers. He was always extra horny after coke, and he'd done a lot that night. 'Now.'

Chelsea's fingers fumbled with the straps on her dress. She was panting, as if she'd been running. She wanted him so much she could barely stand it. It had never been like this before, for her. She had never known sex could be this good. It wasn't just that he knew what he was doing – every inch of him gave her pleasure. And it was that he told her so; he made her feel sexy. Leo Russell, the man without a soul, whose teeth were fake gleaming white, whose films never had anyone more than a size 10 in them, who visibly baulked at a fat man, a blind person, an older woman – he was a total body and lifestyle fascist, she'd thought, and she'd always despised him for it.

From afar.

Now she was with him, and she didn't understand it. He loved her body. He couldn't get enough of her. He loved the little roll of fat on her tummy, her full breasts, her soft, luscious skin. She sometimes wondered whether he loved *her*, really, but she knew she couldn't waste time on that. He was with Amber. It was just one of those things.

But Chelsea knew she loved *him*. With all her heart.

Slowly, Leo's fingers slid up her legs, slipping beneath her dress and up inside her cerise lace underwear. He started stroking her, smiling into her eyes. 'You're still wearing your dress. Don't make me cross. Take it off . . .'

He bent down and kissed her collar bone as his firm, sure fingers unzipped the Chanel couture dress and her plump breasts were released from the silk. He threw the dress on the floor, kissing her nipples, and then he stroked her, gently at first, still touching her between her legs, then hoisted her onto his lap, so she was straddling him, and she could feel his erection, could hold it in her hands, all she'd really wanted to do all through this long damn night . . . He cradled her in his arms as she lowered herself onto him, and they rocked together on the couch, so she could feel him pulsing through her. She looked at him.

Leo was gritting his teeth, his eyes half closed, as if he was in pain. His nostrils flared. He gripped her shoulders as she moved with him more frantically, trying to help him along.

'No,' he said. 'Don't force it. Relax.'

She looked down at him, and he met her eyes and smiled, so genuinely, not his usual voracious, saturnine smile. He nuzzled her breasts, his hands clutching her almost protectively, and then he reached up and cupped the back of her neck, stroking her skin with his fingers. He was shaking his head. Chelsea could feel the orgasm breaking slowly, flooding over her . . . He came too, groaning quickly.

'I can't control it with you,' Leo said, hugging her to him as he sank back against the cushions. His handsome face was dark, his pupils slightly dilated. She didn't know if it was the drugs or desire. 'I don't know why. I want you all the damn time. All night, all through that fucking ceremony. I just wanted to take you into a corridor, fuck you right there.'

Chelsea blinked, still savouring the pleasure that washed over her. She sometimes wished he wasn't so upfront, more tender, more romantic, but she knew that was ridiculous. They had an unspoken agreement not to mention Amber, as if she didn't exist, so they didn't.

Twenty-five storeys up, she stared out at LA, twinkling below her. This was probably the biggest night of her life, and she was with the man she loved. Everything should have been perfect, but how could it be, when they were betraying Amber like this? Why did she care? She wished she *didn't* care, but she did.

She couldn't help wondering what Leo would do, eventually. What Amber thought of it all.

But right then and there, as she lay in Leo's arms, his cock sliding gently out of her, his breathing gradually slowing down, she didn't really give a damn.

'When do you have to go?' she said. She didn't usually ask, didn't want him to feel boxed in – what they were doing was awful. But she was drunk on him, and she wanted more.

'Not right away,' Leo said. 'I told Sally I wouldn't be in till later.' He rocked against her again and nuzzled her neck, her collar bone.

She could feel his five o'clock shadow rasping against her soft skin; she wished he wouldn't, she had interviews later and didn't want to look like she had stubble rash. She wasn't a fucking teenager, she was a world-famous movie star! She drew back, and looked out of the window again.

The dark sky was streaked with greying orange stripes. The night was nearly over, and he would leave her again. The film was over, the Oscars were over, and it seemed like everything was changing and yet she still couldn't have what she wanted . . . and she wanted Leo.

'It's getting light, look. Can we go and get breakfast?'

'Breakfast? Let's order room service,' Leo said, his arms still round her, stroking her spine.

'No.' Chelsea needed to get up, get out, all of a sudden. She'd been in this room too long, she didn't like air-conditioning. 'Let's go for a walk. A walk on the beach!' She laughed at his look of horror. 'Come on. I know a great place in Santa Monica. Baby, it's five o'clock and it's a tiny place. There won't be anyone there, I promise.'

'I don't do beach cafés,' Leo grumbled.

'Oh, come on,' Chelsea begged. She moved her breasts a little, so his head was directly in between them, and kissed his forehead. He grabbed her tits, like a boy, but she got up. 'Come on! If anyone sees us, they'll know it's because we've been at the parties all night, they won't read anything into it!'

'That's true,' Leo agreed, heaving himself off the sofa. She stared at his naked, powerful body matted with dark hair. He was so strong, so muscular. 'I guess. OK, let's go to your horrible beach shack then, Chelsea. But only because you're the biggest star in Hollywood right now. And I want you to suck me off afterwards.'

'I'll do it on the beach if you buy me breakfast,' she said, moving next to him and kissing him on the lips.

'I'll have a shower,' he said, after a moment. 'Then let's go?'

'Sure,' she said, sitting back down on the couch.

When Leo was in the shower, she picked up the hotel phone. It was time to move things along a little.

'Is that Jack Feather?' she said. Jack Feather was the paparazzo she was always meeting on the beach. They had an . . . understanding.

'Who's this?'

'You don't need to know,' she said, in a flawless American accent. 'Just wanted to tell you Chelsea Stone and Leo Russell are having an affair behind her sister's back. They're on their way to the Beach Shack, on Santa Monica beach. I think they'll go for a walk afterwards on the beach. No one else knows.'

She put the phone down, breathing fast. It was the right thing to do. Had to be.

'Who was that?' Leo called from the bathroom.

'No one,' she called back, pulling on the Chanel dress. 'Just you and me, baby.'

Chapter Forty-Three

From *The New York Times*, February 2008:

In a scandal that has rocked the LA-based sector of the entertainment industry to its core, sources at notorious website TMZ.com would not confirm who tipped them off about their scoop of the year. TMZ.com have posted pictures taken on a beach of Oscar-nominated actress Chelsea Stone and the producer of *The Time of My Life*, Sir Leo Russell, who were snapped kissing and embracing by Jack Feather, one of Hollywood's most feared paparazzi. Ms Stone's sister, the movie star Amber Stone, has been dating the mogul for the last five years. Neither Stone sister, nor their mother, manager Margaret Stone, would comment today.

The pictures have been sold around the world.

From *Heat* magazine, February 2008:

OMG! IT'S WAR!!
CHELSEA STEALS AMBER'S GUY!

The biggest rivalry in showbiz? It is now!

The Stone sisters are at it again . . . After weeks of rumours and denials, Chelsea Stone's spokeswoman has admitted that Chelsea and Leo Russell are an item, after the couple were spotted cavorting together on a California beach in the early hours of the morning after the Academy Awards. Leo . . . you've got the wrong sister!

What is it with those sisters, *heat* wants to know? Just three weeks ago Chelsea's sister Amber gushed that her 'on-off' romance with the serial love rat and film producer Sir Leo was 'on' again, when she talked about their five-year relationship, telling *US Weekly* magazine, 'I'm happier now than I've ever been.'

Everyone knows the Stone sisters have always been rivals. It's been especially chilly since Chelsea got the lead in the brilliant *The Time of My Life* – a part originally meant for Amber . . . 'Amber told everyone she was happy for Chelsea, but she was gutted,' our source told us. 'She can't stand the fact that everyone sees Chelsea as the talented one. Chelsea stole Amber's career, and now she's stolen her boyfriend as well. *It's the ultimate betrayal. But it's always been like that with Chelsea and Amber, right from the start.*'

So will Amber fight back? Our source thinks so. 'Amber may look sweet, but she's a fighter. She won't take this lying down. She's been second fiddle since she was born, and she wants revenge. *Chelsea had better watch her back.*'

We're guessing there's no chance of a family knees-up any time soon . . .

Are you Team Amber or Team Chelsea?
Vote now! At www.heatworld.com

Chapter Forty-Four

The news had broken on the Monday evening, the day after the Academy Awards. The pictures were extraordinary – she had hardly been able to tear her eyes away. It wasn't just that it was like a horrible dream coming true, it was that they were so . . . intimate. How could they post stuff like this on the internet? You could see Chelsea's *tits* in one of them, for God's sake, they were practically having sex on that damn beach. Amber didn't know whether to laugh or be angry.

How *could* Chelsea have done this to her?

Amber hadn't gone out on Tuesday – she hadn't been able to get out of the security gate of her complex. She felt bad for the other residents – she'd ordered a gift basket for each of them. It was crazy – photographers climbing up the gates, disguising themselves as delivery men. But thank God they hadn't got in, yet. No one had.

It was so public, this humiliation, and for a private person like Amber, that made it worse. She had never fallen out of nightclubs, never slept with people who sold stories on her. She was a private person, and she hated having her life served up as entertainment on a plate. She couldn't go out, so it was her, Rosita and Carlos, holed up in the house for two more days, and Amber had thought she was going to go mad.

Perhaps she *was* going mad – it would make sense. She had nothing to do, either – her next film didn't start for a week or so, she had no real friends to talk to, apart from her mother, and her mother wasn't a friend. There were millions of ordinary people around the world who liked her films, she was wealthy and beautiful and successful, and she hated herself for finding it all so worthless . . . for being so devastated that she had been betrayed in this way, by a sister who it seemed actively disliked her and a man whom, if Amber was completely honest, she wondered if she'd ever really loved anyway . . .

It was fanciful, but she felt as if she was in a terrible nightmare, the stage where you start to realise it's a dream, that you're asleep, and that all she had to do was wake up.

And then Sally called. Two days in.

'Amber, hi!' she trilled, as if everything was completely normal. 'How are you?'

Amber was lying on a huge creamy sofa in her den with a glass of wine, listlessly picking through the awful, hackneyed script for *Secret Sisters*, which she'd agreed to do . . . She didn't know why, it was the same old rubbish, only even more boring than usual. She was ashamed of it. 'How am I?' Amber said, slightly disbelieving. 'Well, er—' She didn't know what to say. She stared out of the window; it was a cold, grey day, so unusual out there, but it matched her mood.

'I would like to talk to you about something,' Sally said. 'Is now a good time?'

'Do you want me to help you kill Leo and eat him?' said Amber. She felt a bit drunk. 'Sure.'

'Ha!' Sally gave a tinkling but extremely forceful laugh. Amber jumped. 'Wow, you sure can laugh in the face of it all, Amber! And that's why the public love you!' She lowered her voice. 'Now, Leo would like to see you—'

'I'm not seeing him,' Amber said. 'I don't want to ever see him again.'

'He knows that,' Sally said. 'He's devastated by this, totally devastated. He really wants to sort things out . . .'

259

Something inside Amber snapped: the final thin cord binding her to Leo. She wasn't angry, though she knew she would be. She was tired. Tired of it all.

'I'll come over,' she said.

'They won't let you – there're photographers everywhere, outside his house too.'

'I don't care,' Amber said. She stood up. 'Tell him I'll be over in an hour. Tell him he's a fucking bastard.'

'Um . . . Sure!' Sally said.

Amber put the phone down.

'Wow,' she said slowly. She looked around the room. 'This is it, then. And it feels . . .'

She didn't know how it felt. She just knew she was getting angry, and that was a good thing.

She got in her brand new car, jammed her huge sunglasses on her head, got Carlos to open the gate to the compound as fast as possible and then – wham, she drove out of there, into town, up to Beverly Hills, to see her lover one last time.

Leo welcomed her gravely, as if she had a terminal illness. He put his hand on her hair. 'Hello, Amber,' he said in a sombre voice, nodding attentively at her, though she hadn't spoken yet. 'Thanks for coming over,' he added, as if he'd invited her.

'I just want to know something,' Amber said calmly, putting her bag down on the wrought-iron table by the pool. 'Are you happy?'

'It's not about me,' Leo said, gravely.

'No, it is, Leo,' Amber told him. 'It's *always* about you. What you want, and how you're going to get it. And I went along with it for years.'

'Amber, I feel terrible, you have to understand this.'

'You don't!' She couldn't even look at him. She could feel tears stinging her eyes, and it was so important to her that she didn't break down. 'You really don't. I just want to know – are you happy? Have you got what you wanted, fucking both of us?'

'It's not like that, my love—'

'I gave you the best years of my life, Leo. You were like a –' she was going to say *father*, but that sounded so fucking wrong. It was true, though. Wow. 'You were everything to me, Leo . . . How could you?'

Breathing heavily, Leo came stumbling towards her. 'Baby, this is all a misunderstanding.'

'Fuck you.' Amber looked directly at him and his I-know-I'm-so-suave smile, and she wanted to hit him. He was so full of himself, so sure he was king of the hill. She wished . . . she really wished she could wipe the smile off his face.

'Amber, I've never seen you like this!' Leo was almost grinning, she couldn't believe it. 'Have some tea. That'll calm you down.'

Amber gulped. 'Are you serious?'

'Yes, baby. Listen, you're not yourself. You need to calm down.'

Patronising wanker. She looked at him again more closely, this time seeing the paunch he tried to hide by sucking his stomach in, at the jowly face, the bloodshot eyes – he was doing more and more coke, she knew it, it was affecting him more and more. She didn't need this. She didn't need it!

One more piece of the puzzle fell into place. 'Wow,' Amber said slowly.

It seemed appropriate that they were at Leo's house. This was the house she had first come to, as a shy and awkward twenty-year-old. The big, Spanish-style house that was the first home she'd really known in LA. Where she'd hung out with Maria, and taught her the moves to 'Baby One More Time', right here on this perfect stretch of lawn. Where she'd gossiped with Marco. She thought about Maria, for the first time in months. What had happened to her? Where was Marco now? They had been her friends, and they'd gradually been sidelined. Because of Leo. Because of Leo, she'd stopped singing, because of Leo, she'd lost her friends, her identity.

And now she was losing her sister.

It wasn't the humiliation that got to her, though everyone else felt desperately sorry for her, and she hated the attention, hated the fact that she couldn't hide behind the mask of a character, like she could when she was acting. It wasn't the fact that she'd welcomed her own sister into her home and she'd stolen her film roles and her boyfriend.

261

It was that she was starting to see what she had allowed to happen. What nearly six years with Leo had done to her. She had put herself in a gilded cage and turned the key.

Who *was* she?

She had no idea. She, Amber Stone, had no idea. It was pathetic!

She held up the newspaper, one of many with the pictures of Leo and Chelsea on the beach, Chelsea's grey Oscar dress open at the sides, Leo's hands on her breasts, his expression one of childish delight.

'Look, Leo,' she said. 'Can't you see what you've done? It's all just a game to you, isn't it?'

Leo looked around the corner. He patted her on the shoulder and said, in a hollow voice, 'Look, Amber, I feel awful about this. But the fact is—'

She interrupted him. 'No, you don't. Don't lie, Leo. You don't feel awful.' She stared at him. 'I don't think you feel anything at all, for that matter.'

She was right. The truth was, Leo wasn't bothered. He didn't love Amber, hadn't done for years. He'd masturbated to the tape of the first time he'd fucked her many times, but it had been a while since she'd given him the same kind of pleasure.

He'd got what he wanted out of her.

He loved what she brought him, and he liked sex with her – not as much as with Chelsea, but hey – nobody was perfect. They'd had a good run, hadn't they? It had been a beneficial arrangement for both of them, for years now. It was hardly illegal to have an affair, was it?

And perhaps it was time for a change. He felt it was. He thought of Chelsea's porcelain skin, her jet-black hair, her china-blue eyes, all so vital, so sexy, so full of passion for him. He thought of her that early morning on the beach, when they'd drunk coffee and he'd wrapped his jacket around her, moving his hands up inside her dress, touching her, hoping no one could see, while the waves pounded on the empty beach. If only he'd known who was fucking snapping away in the background! Dammit! How had they *known*?

But still, he remembered Chelsea, too, that morning. She looked like an old-school Hollywood star, a real broad, not like her sister. And he'd started to think about how hot it was to have these two sisters, two of the most famous, most beautiful women in the world, fighting over him. He may have been a multimillionaire mogul, but Leo Russell was also a man. And when he thought about that, and when Chelsea had leaned forward, just enough so that he could see her plump breasts straining against the demure grey silk, Leo could only say, 'You know it's best with me, baby. You know we're the perfect team.'

And she'd reached down and grabbed his crotch, running one finger expertly along his flaccid cock, which instantly started to harden, and then she'd thrown her arms around him, pressing her body against his, and murmured, 'I want you so much, baby.'

And Leo had to say, 'Me too.'

Five minutes, they were on that damned beach, before they'd got into separate cars and gone back to Chelsea's new place, where they'd fucked each other's brains out for a pleasurable few hours. Five minutes, and it was enough to get photos that put him squarely in the frame with Chelsea. Once again, he wondered: how the hell had they known they were going to be there?

He was recalled to the present as Amber said, 'You're not even listening to me, are you? Where the hell is she?'

'Who?'

'Chelsea, you bastard,' Amber said simply. 'You know I mean Chelsea.'

'Oh.' Leo scratched the back of his head. 'She's – I don't know where she is. But we – we should talk this out, Amber, I feel as if—'

'There's nothing to talk about, and don't fucking patronise me by pretending there is,' Amber said. She stood up and walked towards him. 'I saw her car in the driveway. You're stupid, that's what. Or else you both just don't fucking care. Get her out here.'

'What?'

Amber was standing two or so inches away from him. He could feel her breath on his face. He looked at her, trying not to stare at her breasts. Christ, she wasn't wearing a bra. *Don't get an erection, Leo.*

'You piece of shit,' she said, sweetly. 'You deserve each other. My God. Just get her out here.'

Leo didn't waste any more time. Glad to step away, he went into the house.

When he returned, a minute or two later, Chelsea was following him.

The clouds had gone and it was going to be a clear, smog-free night. Stars would glitter like diamonds against the deep blue sky. The pool glowed turquoise, ripples reflecting on the terrace where the three of them stood.

Chelsea was in a vest and jeans, her hair tousled, no make-up. She looked younger than she usually did these days, and for a second, Amber felt a sharp pain in her heart. This was her family, this girl in front of her, looking like the stroppy, funny teenager she'd once been.

For a second, she thought about not going through with what she was about to do. For her mum. For her dad.

But then Chelsea said, 'Look Amber, I know you must be upset. But this thing is bigger than all of us.' And she smiled up at Leo, then looked defiantly at Amber, the same old Chelsea, like Amber was an annoying bug, getting in her way. And Amber knew it was time.

'I'm leaving,' she said. 'I'm getting out of here, going away for a few months.'

'But we're starting principal photography on *Secret Sisters* on Wednesday —' Leo, always business first, began.

'I'm not doing it.'

Leo looked at her. 'Oh, yes you are!' he said, and he laughed, like she was a silly little girl.

'So sue me,' said Amber. She stared at him, her eyes sparkling. 'That'll look good, won't it? First you fuck my sister behind my

264

back, then you sue me for pulling out of the film you're produc-
ing? I don't think there's a judge or jury in the world who'd give
you damages.'

She turned to her sister.

'As for you, Chelsea, I want you to know that this is it. It's over
between us. I'm glad to be able to say this to your face.'

'What?' Chelsea said, her hand on her collar bone, nervously.
'Amber, listen, I'm—'

'Hey,' said Amber, stepping back, and throwing her car keys in
the air. 'Sis, listen, it's too late. You've fucked me over for the last
time. Both of you. I'm going away, and when I'm back – you'll
both get it.'

'Get what?' Chelsea said, smiling nervously.

'Revenge,' said Amber.

She nodded, suddenly sure of herself. 'Yeah. Revenge. See ya.'

Chelsea followed her into Leo's big marble hallway, leaving Leo
still standing there.

'So, come on, Amber,' Chelsea said, walking towards her. 'Say
what you've got to say to me, and let's get it over with.'

And that's when Amber slapped her, harder than she'd ever hit
anyone in her whole life before. It felt absolutely fucking great.

She turned and walked away, through to the driveway, and she
got in her gunmetal-grey Bentley and drove off. For the first time
since she'd got the car, she put the roof down and let her hair blow
free in the breeze. She thought of the look on her boyfriend's and
her sister's faces.

She was going to have some fun.

PART FIVE

Somebody to Love

Chapter Forty-Five

Sometimes, when she was tired, or she'd had a glass or two at dinner, Margaret Stone would dream she was back in Sheffield, a young girl again. The tiny red-brick two-up two-down house was the same as ever. There was the outside toilet, with the worn linoleum floor her mother never cleaned properly; her father's jacket, hanging on the wooden pegs by the front door. The silence at dinner, the squalid tedium of her childhood.

And then she'd wake up in a panic, looking wildly around her, clutching her chest till she realised it had been a dream. She was in a beautiful white bedroom that was absolutely spotless. She was by the ocean, she could hear it in the distance. White and blue voile drapes would flutter gently in the night-time breeze, and she would lie back down, smiling into the darkness.

All Margaret had wanted when she was little was to be famous, but she saw now that it was a means to get the end she wanted: money, control, nice things, a clean house. OK, she hadn't made it as a star, but her two girls had, and that was entirely down to her, wasn't it?

It had all been worth it in the end, hadn't it?

Hadn't it?

But lately, everything had been going wrong. She'd ignored the rivalry between Chelsea and Amber: it had always been there,

Chelsea was a silly girl. Now, however, it seemed to have gone too far. There was a rift so deep Margaret couldn't simply order them to sort it out. She couldn't tell either of them what to do. Chelsea didn't need her help at all, really, though Margaret had tried to give it to her. No, she'd always been independent, and now she really was back on her feet. She had a lucky streak. Perhaps she got it from her father.

Reluctantly. She didn't much like being told she was in the wrong.

It was true, she'd pushed them, but only because she'd never wanted them to suffer the disappointments she had. If only someone had started earlier with her, what might she have become? Deep down, Margaret still believed that stardom had eluded her in some way. She had pursued it for her girls instead . . . And it was ironic, she realised, that she'd always pushed Amber, and Amber wasn't the tough one, the survivor. It was Chelsea. Amber's career wasn't on the rise any more. Chelsea's was. And now, neither of them seemed to want anything to do with her.

She was staying in Amber's guest house, where she'd been living since Chelsea'd moved out. She was still only forty-eight, a year younger than Meg Ryan! She'd kept her slim figure, her neat appearance. And she still felt she had something to give. But no one seemed to care.

Sometimes, she'd look in the mirror, smoothing her hands over the beautiful clothes she owned by the closetful, peering at the lines on her face, and she would think back to days gone by. To young Maggie back in Shepherd's Bush, full of hope and dreams, skipping along to the tube station, off to another audition, her whole life ahead of her. To crazy days and nights in The Black Horse, the whole cast of characters she'd known there, everyone from exotic dancers to well-known writers and world-class alcoholics, darling Nigel, who'd taken a chance on her, that bitch Camilla – where was she now, she wondered? It'd be funny to find out. And Derek and George, the two brothers. She'd loved both of them, and had never got the chance to say it to either of them. It was too late for George, now. She wished, with all her heart sometimes, that he could know that they were all well. That she could see him, put her hand on his chest and say 'It doesn't matter. None of it matters. You were a great father. You were a wonderful man.'

She never had. And he had died hating himself. Margaret couldn't help thinking that was probably her fault. She had stopped him being who he was. Had made the decisions for all of them. And of their children, one of them, Chelsea, had no idea that he wasn't her father, and still blamed herself for his death, and the other one, Amber, was . . . well, she was too like him, that was the trouble. Too reserved and shy. Too willing to hide her true self away from the world.

Had she done this?

Had she laid all this down, this lifetime of pain?

More and more, Margaret would wake up in the morning and wonder what she'd done it all for. Whether it really *had* been worth it.

And then one day, not long after Amber had disappeared, she was picking some flowers from the immaculately kept garden. It was a hot day, the sun was high overhead, it was deadly quiet in the house without Amber. The private compound where she lived was just that – private, with security so tight you never saw another person. It was nice, but sometimes . . . Was it that she was lonely? She didn't know, but Margaret jumped when Rosita called out to let her know her lunch was ready, and nearly dropped her secateurs. She made her way to the wrought-iron table on the terrace, where a place for one had been set. She sat down heavily.

She hadn't slept well – again. The dream of being back in Sheffield came almost every night now, and the details grew more lurid. The house grew more squalid, her father more threatening, the feeling of being trapped greater than ever. It was becoming a nightmare. Margaret passed a tired hand over her eyes, and smiled as Rosita appeared, carrying something.

'This looks great, Rosita,' Margaret said automatically. She was always nice to staff; it paid to keep the good ones on side so they'd

271

stay, and the bad ones would sell stories about you to the *National Enquirer* if you gave them reason. 'Thank you so much.'

Rosita stared. 'It's the phone, Mrs Stone.' She handed it to her. 'Lunch only a minute away, that OK?'

Margaret looked down at the phone Rosita was carrying. She blinked. 'Sorry,' she said, trying to recover herself. How embarrassing. 'Who – who is it?'

'I don't know,' Rosita said cheerfully. 'He said it was emergency from London.'

It irritated Margaret considerably that Rosita never found out who was calling. She couldn't believe Amber didn't say something to her about it, but Amber never seemed to mind. 'Thank you, Rosita –' Margaret began, but Rosita wasn't really listening. She thrust the phone at Margaret, and padded away. Margaret took it and said cautiously into the speaker, 'Hello? Who is this, please?'

'Maggie?' A voice, clear as a bell, a little distant though. 'Maggie, is that you?'

'Who's this?' Margaret said, her heart beating faster.

'You know who it is,' the voice said. 'How can you forget me? It's Derek.'

Of course she knew. She considered lying, saying 'Derek who?' But no, she must be civil. 'Hello, Derek,' she said. 'How – how are you, then?'

'I'm fine, fine,' Derek said. His voice was warm, low, it sounded as if he was smiling. 'How are you, Maggie May?'

'Margaret,' Margaret said automatically. 'I'm fine, thank you.' She traced a pattern on the clean white table. 'Everything's fine here. How can . . .' she trailed off. She wasn't sure what to say or do next. Derek Stone was probably the only person who had that effect on her still.

'I was only ringing to find out what's going on,' Derek said. 'What's all this about Chelsea running off with some fella? Amber's boyfriend, that's right, isn't it?'

'Yes,' Margaret said. 'It's rather complicated, Derek,' she added, in what she hoped was a dismissive voice. 'Everyone's fine.'

'I'm sure they're fine,' Derek said, and she noticed him slurring his words just a little. 'Just wanted to make sure you're all OK. My girls, see?'

She looked at her watch. Two o'clock here – it was evening over there. 'Derek, you're drunk,' she said.

'I bloody am not,' Derek said instantly. 'Just had a few glasses. How dare you insinuate, young lady.'

He sounded so like Chelsea sometimes, it was unsettling. Margaret breathed in, a ragged little sigh.

'You all right, Maggie May?' he said, softly. 'I been worried about you.'

Margaret couldn't answer. Her throat had closed up. She sucked her lips in and clamped her mouth shut.

Derek was silent and then he said, 'I still think about you . . . you know that, don't you? I'm proud of you. And Chelsea. She's done all right for herself, my little girl, ain't she?'

Margaret wasn't having any of it. She wouldn't ever let Derek Stone back into her life again, no. Never. She only had to think of the horrible bedsit in Shepherd's Bush, the armpit hair in the sink, the used condom on the floor, the way she'd cried over him, after he'd run off with that bitch Camilla . . .

She said, repressively, 'I'm fine, like I say, Derek. The girls are having their issues, but they're both doing fine. You know, they're both huge stars now. Life isn't always easy for them, I'm sure. But they're both very well. Now—'

'I don't believe a fucking word of it,' Derek said, and Margaret winced. Why did he have to swear? He cleared his throat. 'I want to see the girls. And I wanna see you. Shall I come over? Pay you a visit?'

'No, thank you!' Margaret said in horror. 'The last thing we need right now is you turning up, wreaking havoc!' She said this with relish.

'You really think that?' Derek said, his voice muffled.

He sounded so close, like he could be calling her from the beach below and suddenly, despite herself, Margaret wished with all her heart he was there. A friend, someone who knew her secrets, what she'd been through.

Derek was the only person in the world who did, she realised.

And, though it would be wonderful to know he was there, to share her burdens, rest her head on his chest and close her eyes and relax for just a few minutes, that was why she couldn't.

'It's fine, like I say, Derek,' she said again. 'All right? Thanks, though, that's a very kind offer, and I'll tell the girls.'

'Load of fucking rubbish,' he said. 'I've seen the paper. You don't even know where Amber is, do you? No one does.'

'Well—' Margaret began.

'Admit it, Maggie.'

'No,' she said, slowly. 'I don't know where Amber is.'

Chapter Forty-Six

There were cockroaches in her bathroom.

The trouble with being rich and famous was, you got used to things. Infinity pools, 800-thread-count sheets, Cristal champagne, free designer clothes, first-class travel.

If you wanted to go incognito, it was easier to downsize. People didn't look for A-list stars in Economy. But Jesus, it was so uncomfortable in Economy! On the flight out, Amber had been crammed next to a huge old Mexican lady and a vast young American guy, both of whom spilled over their armrests onto her, their legs squeezing hers. Amber was too polite to glare at them, to cast vicious looks at them for being so vast, especially the young man. She knew Chelsea would have muttered endlessly about it, but she didn't. Besides, she didn't want them to recognise her.

Amber's pretty, even features were unremarkable when she wasn't in front of a camera. She looked much younger, too. With a baseball cap on, and her hair tied back, face free of make-up and her training as an actress helping her to act low-key, she had found over the years that she could pretty much get away with it. Chelsea never wanted to – she loved it. She was a true star in that respect; she looked the part, and she was recognisable from twenty feet away.

The tiny hacienda Amber had booked herself into was on the

beach. She and Leo had been on holiday there a couple of years before, staying at Illuminate, an exclusive six-star hotel and spa retreat a mile away. Amber had gone for a walk one afternoon, by herself, and found this village nearby. It was a small, pretty place, with a little hotel that looked out over the ocean, slightly crumbling, with wrought-iron balconies painted turquoise blue and filled with cerise-pink geraniums, and terracotta pots of deep red chillies lining the steps up to the entrance.

Back then, she had wished she was staying there, instead of this soulless spa, where everyone was discontented with their money and their lifestyle, where they were overly impressed with her and Leo and they had to spend most of their holiday in their room, or on their private balcony. She had wished she was here, drinking in the tiny bar on the beach, eating fresh-fish tacos and watching life go by.

And when Amber had needed to run away, to go where no one could find her, it was here she chose to be.

She hadn't washed her hair in three days, and normally it was styled by someone else. She was eating and drinking exactly what she wanted, instead of being confined to a handful of food twice a day. She was sleeping eight hours instead of six, walking along the beach instead of being driven everywhere in a blacked-out SUV, watching convoluted but gripping Mexican soaps in her bedroom instead of going to screenings of mediocre films, lying on a sunlounger reading thrillers, instead of poring over scripts.

Amber had been controlled for so long, and now she was taking control.

But there were cockroaches in the bathroom. And a strange scuttling sound under the boards in the bedroom. And when her white trousers got dirty on her first day, no one was on hand to clean them.

The strange thing was, she didn't mind. She didn't want cockroaches in the bathroom; she'd called the manager twice about it, but for the first time in nearly a decade Amber was doing what she wanted, and she couldn't remember when she'd been happier. And the more relaxed she grew, the further away the others seemed:

276

LA, her mother, Chelsea, Leo . . . The further she was from them, the more she started to see how badly they'd treated her. They would pay for what they'd done to her.

But for the time being, she was happy.

A couple of weeks into her stay, Amber was finishing dinner one night at the bar on the beach. It was divided into two parts: a small taqueria restaurant, and a bar, where a pianist was playing old Motown songs, the sound floating gently in to where Amber sat, reading another thriller. She was completely absorbed, licking some chipotle sauce from her fingers, when suddenly everything came crashing down around her.

A voice said, 'Amber? Amber . . . Stone?'

She sat up straight, her eyes flickering in alarm. 'What the fuck . . .' she began.

In front of her was a man. Youngish, about her age, with soft dark brown hair and enormous black eyes. He was smiling at her, his hands in his pockets.

'It *is* you, isn't it?' He nodded his head, pleased. 'Yes! I *knew* it, man!'

Her heart was racing. It was over, it was all over . . . Amber looked up at him, imploringly. 'Please,' she said, and put her hand on his forearm. 'Can you keep your voice down? I'm trying to—'

The man looked down and saw the expression on her face. 'Of course,' he said. 'I'm sorry, I didn't realise.' He sat down next to her.

For a fleeting second, Amber was annoyed – then she realised she was being a prima donna. She grinned at him. 'It's OK.'

'Let's start again. I'm Matt Hughes,' he said, holding out his hand. 'And you're . . . ?'

'I'm Amber Stone,' replied Amber, shaking his hand. He had a tiny little mole below his eye, she noticed. His teeth were perfectly white and even, but one was slightly chipped. He was totally hot, but she liked the little flaws, imperfections. They made him more interesting. If he was in Hollywood, the tooth would be smooth, the mole gone.

'So I bet you're staying at the same place we're at,' he said. 'It's weird I haven't seen you there. Illuminate, yeah? Stupid name, I tell you.'

Amber smiled. 'I've been there before. I'm not there, no.'

He paused. 'I don't really like it, to tell you the truth, it's not my scene. Too many stuck-up people.'

'I know what you mean.' She nodded. 'How long are you there for?'

'I'm leaving tomorrow,' he told her. 'I'm going back to New York.'

'Shame,' Amber said. He raised his eyebrows and smiled, and then she blushed. 'Just that – you're the first person I've spoken to since I got here who doesn't work at the hotel.'

Matt wasn't embarrassed. He just said, 'That sounds pretty cool.' He leaned in. 'I'm here with some guys from work, a management bonding trip. And I wanna kill them.'

'Seriously?'

'Yeah, I escaped this evening. I've been playing the piano in the bar next door.' Matt scratched his neck.

Amber put her elbows on the table and put down her book. 'Wow,' she said. 'That was you, playing next door?'

They chatted for a while. Matt, it turned out, was a music producer, obsessed with all the same stuff she was. He'd done a couple of interesting things, and he loved music and talking about the old days. He had some of her wine, and then they had some more, still talking, and then they ordered tequila. Amber was getting drunk, but she didn't care, it was just so damn nice to talk to someone you wanted to actually have a conversation with . . . And when Matt got up and went back next door, she followed him, and when he sat down at the piano and started playing 'Somebody to Love', Amber stared at him. It had been one of her dad's favourite songs; in fact, the only time she could remember them as a family, back in Weybridge, doing anything funny together was when they were all in the car, and Dad would put on a tape, *Queen's Greatest Hits*, and they'd all join in together . . .

Amber bowed her head, grief overcoming her. She felt very alone, all of a sudden. The words of the song, so upbeat, were actually so sad. *Somebody to love me . . . Somebody to love.* That was all anyone wanted, and she felt she had no one, really.

Softly, slowly, she started singing along, and then she lifted her head and belted the lyrics out like her life depended on it.

Matt stopped, immediately. 'You've got a great voice.' He paused. 'Fuck. I'd completely forgotten. You used to be a singer, didn't you?' He played a few more chords and she sang along, smiling.

The locals in the bar either smiled indulgently or ignored them. It was a calm, still evening, a few people wandering past on the beach. The tequila was warming her inside.

Used to be a singer – yes, that was it. Amber said, 'Yeah, that was a long time ago, though.'

'You're great. You can really sing. Try this.'

He started playing Gladys Knight, 'Midnight Train to Georgia', and Amber sang. Again, after a few lines, Matt stopped. He looked at her.

'Why did you stop singing, Amber? You sound amazing. Amazing. That's something really special.'

Amber could only smile at him. She was so happy to be singing again, she'd forgotten how it made her feel; like a drug, and the mix of that with the wine and tequila was intoxicating. 'Play,' she said again, exhilaration washing over her. She tapped the top of the piano. 'Go on, play some more.'

He was in harmony with her; he knew how to accompany her, it was like magic. Knew when she was going to breathe, when she was taking an extra note or two, watched her intently. They matched, perfectly, and for a few glorious moments both of them were lost in the song.

When she finished, there was silence. And then applause. The whole bar had risen to its feet, old men and women, younger guys and girls, a couple of tourists. They were clapping, smiling at her, and Amber could only stand there and grin, as she winked at Matt.

'Thank you,' she mouthed to him.

'It was my pleasure, Amber,' he mouthed back.

They stood, staring at each other.

'That was amazing,' Amber told him. 'You have no idea . . . the most fun I've had in . . .' She stopped. 'Wow. In years.'

They were walking along the beach, deserted except for drift-wood and a few oil drums. In the distance, the lights of the spa and the town twinkled. If this was LA, the shoreline would be dotted with million-dollar condos. Here, in the hot Mexican night, it felt as if they were the only people for miles around.

They'd left the bar and gone for a walk. Matt asked the mini-mum of questions; she told him she was at a loose end, no films in the pipeline. She assumed he'd have read about the scandal with Leo, but he said nothing, and she was glad. It seemed a million miles away, all of that . . .

Instead, he asked her about her childhood, growing up in England. Matt was from Queens, the New York suburb. His dad was a truck driver, his mom a schoolteacher. Honest, respectable, not well off; they loved rock 'n' roll, the music of the 1960s and 1970s, and they'd instilled this love in both their sons. Matt had grown up listening to music all his life, sneaking into Manhattan for gigs, obsessively taping and recording albums – his dream was to work in music, with musicians, and now he was.

'People think I have this really full-on glam job,' he told her, his face serious in the moonlight. 'But it's not to me. I'm just doing what I love, what my mom and pop brought me up to love. I'm from Queens, now I live in Manhattan. It's not such a big journey for me. It just feels natural. Do you know what I mean? Making music? Don't you feel the same way when you're acting?'

Amber was walking alongside him, her leather sandals in her hand. She trailed her fingers through her hair, not sure how to answer. And then she thought, Why don't I just tell him the ter-rible secret, the truth?

'To be honest,' she said carefully, 'I've never really wanted to be this great actress.'

'What? Why do you do it, then?'

Amber shrugged. 'I think I've wanted to please people.'

Matt said, 'That is really sad, Amber.'

She wanted to laugh, he sounded so solemn. 'The truth is, I only really feel alive when I'm singing,' she told him. 'That's what I really love.'

She felt as if there should have been a thunderbolt, flashing down between them, for saying these sacrilegious words. But nothing happened.

'You should sing,' Matt said, after a moment. He looked down at the sand. 'Amber . . .'

'Yes?' she said, trying not to sound too eager.

'Would you think about something for me?'

'Sure,' Amber said, her heart beating.

'Would you think about coming to New York?'

'New York?'

'Trying to record some stuff, see if we could write together?' He was staring at her, intently. 'I really felt, tonight – when you were singing and I was playing – I felt like we had a good connection.' He cleared his throat and looked awkward; she felt herself blushing. There was something so honest about him, straightforward, cool, funny, but honest. 'I'm in Tribeca, downtown, there's a studio around the corner. We could play around, just see what happens.' He looked up at her. Amber was nodding, slowly. He grinned. 'Whaddya think, huh?'

Writing music. With Matt. Singing. Wandering through Manhattan, doing her own thing. Amber's eyes sparkled; she felt like she could burst with happiness.

'That – that would be . . .' she started to say.

Then she remembered.

'I can't,' she said.

Matt had been looking at her expectantly, a smile on his face. Now he frowned. 'You can't?'

'Yeah,' Amber said. She stopped, and jabbed her big toe into the sand. 'There's stuff I need to take care of in LA.'

'Come on,' Matt said. 'You can do that from New York, can't you?'

Amber thought of the last decade. How she'd lost her identity, how Leo had treated her like a fool, how Chelsea had stolen her best part yet, her lover, the awards she should have won . . . how she'd basically stolen her life. How she'd let them both do it. She thought of the look on her sister's face, that last evening. Pity mixed with contempt, that was it.

She'd come to Mexico to take time out. To work on her plan. Revenge.

It was still true. It came washing over her again like the waves lapping at the shore, the rage she felt, long hidden.

'I'm sorry,' she said. 'You've probably heard what's been going on with me. Have you?'

Matt put his head on one side. 'Well, I heard about that stuff with your sister. And that producer, your boyfriend. I'm sorry.' He touched her arm, lightly. 'But not a lot. I don't really read that kinda stuff.'

'That's fine. And I don't want you to be sorry for me,' Amber said. She shook her head. 'I'm serious.'

'But —'

She held up her hand. 'I just have some things to do that are connected with all this stuff. I have to make it right. For myself.'

'How?' Matt was still watching her. He looked bemused.

'Look, my sister needs to learn a lesson,' Amber said. She was getting impatient. She didn't want to get into it with Matt. She was being honest with him again, right? And the honest truth was, Chelsea needed to learn what she'd done wrong.

She needed to be punished, and Amber was going to do it.

'So I can't.' She swallowed. 'Not now.'

Matt let his hand drop back to his side. He looked a little sad. 'That's a real shame, Amber.'

He seemed disappointed. As if it was more than just that she wouldn't come with him, work with him. As if he'd thought she was a bigger, better person than that.

'I'll walk you back to your hotel,' he said, politely, and the moment between them was over.

Amber knew he was wrong, though. As they walked back

towards the Hacienda Santa Clara in silence, she wrapped her arms round herself, tightly. He stood at the gate leading from the beach to the hotel, and held his hand up in a farewell gesture.

'It was really good to meet you, Amber,' he said.

'Yeah . . .' Amber replied, fiddling for her key. 'Look – thanks again. I'm sorry.'

'Don't, it's fine.'

'Just, if you understand . . .'

'I understand you feel you have to do this,' he said, barely politely. 'I didn't think you were like that, that's all. Good luck, Amber. Goodbye.'

And with that, he turned and walked away.

Amber crept quietly upstairs, hoping the ancient creaking floors wouldn't betray her late arrival. She got into bed, fired up by the evening, and couldn't sleep. Perhaps it was time.

Perhaps that's the sign Matt had been. Yes, she'd wanted him to kiss her, but was that any surprise? He was cute, and good-looking, and they'd had a great evening. But it wasn't going to happen . . . Not now.

She was just falling asleep, when the cellphone by her bed rang. She jumped, and then picked it up.

'Hello?' she said. 'Hello, who is this?'

'Amber Stone?' the voice said. It was foreign, she didn't recognise it. 'I have something I think you want to know.'

'What?' Amber blinked, shaking herself awake. 'Who is this?'

'I know your sister,' said the voice. 'I know her from London.'

Amber was getting impatient. 'Look, how can I help you? What is this?' She suddenly had a terrible thought. 'What – is Chelsea OK? Is Mum – has something happened to Mum?'

'It's nothing like that, Amber,' said the voice. 'But there is something to say. About your big sister. You will want to listen, I tell you.'

When she put the phone down, five minutes later, Amber was shaking. Her eyes were gleaming in the darkness. Finally. It was like a sign, a fucking sign!

It was time to go home.

Chapter Forty-Seven

Chelsea should have been on top of the world.

She had a fantastic career, and she'd never looked hotter. She was fucking the biggest producer in Hollywood. He'd chosen her over her sister. Her – fat, older Chelsea. Everything she'd planned for, everything she'd worked for. It was all coming together now, and sometimes she couldn't believe it.

Why, then, was everything not that good? Why wasn't she happy?

After Amber left, Chelsea threw herself into her new film, a drama about drug-smuggling, with fierce commitment. She spent more money on the 1960s house in the Hollywood Hills, making it as cool, stylish, vintage, edgy as possible. She was away filming or at Leo's a lot, so she got Jen in to keep an eye on the place and to keep her company; she used to love being alone, but these days she couldn't stand it any more. Jen was a good housemate; they got on well but she did her own thing, and she didn't take shit from Chelsea. She'd done her make-up on *The Time of My Life* and Chelsea had got her other work, but Jen didn't crawl as a result. Sometimes, Chelsea thought, it'd be nice if she said thanks or made her a cup of tea . . . But hey, she wasn't her servant. She was her friend. And she didn't have many of those, these days, once news of the affair had come out.

Chelsea threw herself into her relationship with Leo, too. They were spending as much time together as possible – that'd show people who didn't believe their relationship was going to last! But it was only a month after Amber had left, and though she would never, ever admit it, Chelsea was starting to wonder what she'd got herself into.

Amber and Leo had had a more old-fashioned relationship; almost like she was a courtesan, and he'd come to visit her, or she'd visit him. He'd take her to dinner, they'd go back and fuck. With him and Chelsea it was different; wilder, more casual. They both liked to swim in the sea, to hang out, relax, watch films, eat brunch. And have sex: they both liked that, a lot. It was more free-form, and Leo loved it. He loved that he could turn up at her house, walk in and fuck her almost immediately, pushing her into the bedroom and closing the door firmly. Or that they could be swimming in his pool, and he could take her bikini bottoms off, slide into her in the water, as she gasped, laughing in his arms. Amber needed warming up, it was like bargaining with her; if you behave well, you'll get sex. With Chelsea, there were no rules.

And Chelsea started to notice things about Leo that she hadn't when he was with Amber.

Most of all, she noticed the drugs.

She'd always known Leo did coke; he'd offered her some a couple of times. He did it covertly; Amber didn't like it. Chelsea had said no; after the tabloid exposé of her drug-taking all those years ago, she'd sworn off drugs for ever. Drink, she knew when to stop. Cigarettes? Fine with her. Drugs: no way. It wasn't worth it any more. She still saw the Russian dancer, Maya, in her dreams. Nightmares. Oksana bending over her, her tiny frame blue, vomit everywhere . . . Drugs had done that to her.

But increasingly Leo didn't care. The coke was getting to him. He just used to do it before big evenings, when she'd first known him, or when they were starting to fuck, to spice things up. Now he was going to the bathroom to do it at work.

It was as if he'd let go, now that he was with Chelsea.

'You and me, we understand each other,' he'd say, before

slipping his hand into her bra, or up her skirt, in the car on the way back from a meal, a screening, a photoshoot.

He'd done that only last week. On their way back from the premiere of her co-star in *The Time of My Life* Ryan's new film, they were being driven back to Leo's place through the palm-tree lined boulevards in a blacked-out limo.

Leo was talking fast. 'Fucking bitch Ryan's manager, who does that fat cow think she is? Telling me she doesn't know if that's his kind of project, stupid twat. I make the rules, I made Ryan. She doesn't know.'

Chelsea was thinking about something else. She had a lot on her mind. She was staring out of the window at the lights on Sunset Boulevard. Red. Amber. Green. *Amber* . . . She wondered again where Amber was. Leo started scrabbling with something, and she turned to him. He had a line of coke out on the mahogany table in front of them.

'Come on, Chelsea babe. Take some! I wanna be high with you.'

'No, Leo,' Chelsea said firmly. She had an early call the next day, this new film was really tiring, the director was an auteur, a Spanish guy she kept being told she was really lucky to work with, but he was the kind of man who enjoyed making you feel fucking tiny so he was the king, you were just some dust on the floor. It was taking its toll, mentally and physically, and she needed to do her best for it.

Leo bent down and snorted the whole line. Chelsea watched him. It looked like a fat white slug disappearing into his face. He sniffed, rubbing his nose, his handsome lazy features twitching, his eyes huge.

'Yeah, that's good,' he said. 'Come on, baby.'

He slid his hand up her skirt. 'No, Leo,' Chelsea said. She pushed his hand away.

'Come on!' He was looking insistent. 'Yeah, baby, it's gonna be good in the car, you used to like it in the car!'

It was true, they'd fucked in the car, on their way back from another awards ceremony, when they were on top of the world.

She'd straddled him and he'd torn open her blue chiffon Elie Saab dress, grabbing her breasts, and they'd done it there, riding along the Santa Monica freeway back into town. The driver had ignored them – or pretended to.

Leo took her hand and put it over his crotch. 'Rub me, rub me here,' he said. 'Come on baby.'

He was flaccid. The drugs affected his performance, she'd noticed. She'd spent so much of her late teens and twenties out of it, Chelsea hadn't realised how tedious someone on drugs was all the time. She was tired. She wasn't remotely horny. She stole a glance at him, as he opened and shut his mouth, clicking his jaw, trying to remember how it used to be between them. Was she really in love with him?

It was then Chelsea started wondering about an exit strategy. For herself. She hadn't come all this way just to lose everything she'd worked for. It was too important.

'Baby,' she said, sliding her hand up his crotch and nibbling his ear. Leo rubbed his nose again. 'Baby, drop me off, OK? I need to get some sleep. I got my period, too, so . . .'

Leo was blinking hard, deciding whether to throw a tantrum, to push it, she could tell. In the end he just said, 'Is Jen at home?'

'Don't know,' Chelsea said, and Leo slumped back on the seat, annoyed.

She hoped she was. Jen was hilarious with Leo – she gave as good as she got with him, and he liked her, which made things easier. Chelsea had confided in Jen about Leo's drug-taking, how his behaviour was getting weirder, and she wondered if she was in tonight. It was good to have someone to talk to. A friend.

And there was something else, too, another reason she wanted to get back to her perfect little white house. She wanted to see if Todd, her agent, had called about *Pieces of Heaven*. She had to do *Pieces of Heaven*. She would kill someone if she didn't get the rights to that book.

She'd found an advance copy of the book in Leo's office, a few days after Amber left, when she'd been hanging around for him.

Sally had been giving her those patronising but sympathetic looks that drove her insane, so she'd picked it up and started reading. There was already heat around it: she'd heard Santi, the director of her new film, talking about it. It was a multigenerational story of three women coming to America, the Korean grandmother, her Italian daughter-in-law and her daughter Nicola, returning to the States after living abroad. It was a rich, heartbreaking, humbling epic. It was still only a book, but it had Oscar all over it. She devoured it the same day. And she had to get the rights to it. No way was Leo getting his paws on it; he'd turn it into a romcom starring Matthew fucking McConaughey.

This was the film that was going to make her a star for all ages. She had to buy it. She had earned a lot of money, sure, but this was going to stretch her. Todd was the best there was, and he'd do any-thing for her, she'd made sure of that. The first time they'd met she'd 'accidentally' let him see her naked, coming out of the pool house at Leo's, dripping wet, her nipples erect, the sun gleaming off her creamy, smooth body, and she'd noted with amusement his rapidly hardening cock in his pants, the whole way through the meeting.

Maybe, if he managed to get her the rights to *Pieces of Heaven* without Leo realising, she'd let Todd fuck her. Chelsea thought idly about what it would be like, how grateful he'd be. How long would he last? Would he go down on her? Leo had stopped doing that lately, she missed it. She bet Todd would . . .

'I want you to come back with me,' Leo said.

'I really can't, baby, please don't make me,' Chelsea said, putting on her best little-girl voice. She pressed the intercom. 'Martin, can you take me straight home? There's a change in plans. Thanks.'

'Sure, Miss Stone,' Martin replied.

They pulled into the drive of her house, and she leaned over and kissed Leo on the lips. 'I'll make it up to you, baby,' she said, not meaning a word of it. Leo was looking pissed off. She wanted to smack him. He was the one who was so out of it he'd be up all night trying to get hard, with no one to share it with . . . thank fuck.

'Is Jen in?' he said again. 'I wanna see Jen. She likes coke.'

'I don't know,' Chelsea replied briskly, deliberately misunderstanding him. 'I'll be OK, I promise. 'Night, baby, I love you.'

'You'd better,' he said. He looked at her lazily, one eyebrow raised, like he didn't believe her, and she shivered, reminded again of how dangerous he could be. Sometimes, she thought she had him under control, and sometimes, she didn't know . . .

She turned and walked into the house, relieved.

Everything was in darkness when she walked in. She had a maid, Marta, but she slept above the garage. Wearily, Chelsea put her bag down on the table in the hall. She rotated her neck, feeling the tension click out of her; Leo was really getting to her these days. She started upstairs, and then realised her sleeping pills were in the kitchen; she'd take one, she needed a good night's rest.

As she reached the kitchen, her cellphone rang. Fucking Leo, she thought, scrambling for it.

'Hello?' she said.

'Chelsea Stone?'

The voice was distant. An accent, she couldn't work out what. Some nutter. Or a fucking journo. She'd have to change her fucking number again. 'Who is this?' she said, imperiously.

'Chelsea Stone, you know me,' said the voice. 'My name is Oksana Demidova.'

Oksana . . . Chelsea stiffened. 'Hello? Oksana who?' she said, trying to bluff, she didn't know why.

'You know who I am. I am Oksana,' the voice said coldly. 'I was there, I was there when Maya died, you know it.'

'I'm sorry, I . . .'

'Don't lie to me, Chelsea,' Oksana said. 'You killed her, you all did. You should have got the doctor, instead you let her die.'

'Listen, this is –' Chelsea began.

'Let me finish.' Oksana sounded completely in control, though her voice was soft. 'You even bother to find out what those guys did with her body? Thrown in trash, that's what. Thrown away like piece of rubbish. No grave, nothing. They tape her up so she don't get stiff in that position, so she's curled up into small ball. She was thrown away, still covered with her own vomit. Did you know that? Did you know she was seventeen, Chelsea Stone, hey?'

'I—' Chelsea's heart was in her mouth. It was like she was back in the nightmares again. She could see Maya's body, her tiny, heart-shaped face, pale eyes sunken into their sockets . . . Was this a nightmare?

No, it was all real . . . it was really happening.

She had caused it, she had been the one, not checking her age properly, not checking who was doing what. She had let the fame of the Sunday Club and the adulation and everything else go to her head. And a girl was dead, because of her. Thrown away like trash.

She swallowed, trying to quell the nausea within her.

'Why are you ringing me?' she said.

'I'm ringing you because you need to pay. I read you don't like your sister. I read you stole her boyfriend. You're bad person, Chelsea. I wonder what your sister say if she found out about this thing? This is a bad thing, what happened with Maya. Would your sister like to know about it?'

It was dark in the hall, beams of light from outside falling into the den, silvery and sinister. Chelsea swallowed hard. She thought of Leo, driving back to the house.

Thank fuck she was on her own, now. Then she realised she'd always been on her own. She had to carry on. She had to get up tomorrow, pretend it was all OK, even though it was shit, fuck-ing shit. Then she thought of the role she was playing. A cop, a hardbitten, seen-it-all-before cop on the streets of Chicago, with two children to feed.

'Fuck you,' she said, her voice rising. 'How fucking dare you ring me up and make these threats? What do you want, you piece of shit? Money?'

'You can't talk to me like that—' Oksana began.

'I can talk to you however the fuck I want,' Chelsea said. 'It's you against me, and I know the others won't talk, even if it did happen, which I don't know that it did. You've got nothing on me, you little bitch. I'm not giving you any more money.' She was shaking, it was almost exhilarating. 'I'm Chelsea Stone, who the fuck do you think you are, talking to me like this?'

'Maybe I call your sister, then. Tell her all of that?'

Amber! What would she do with it? Whisper it to her My Little Pony collection before she went to bed, wherever she was, probably in some mental institution? Chelsea wanted to laugh.

'Call her, go on. I'd love to see you try. She's my sister.'

'Maya was like my sister,' Oksana said. 'We looked out for each other. You don't. You are making a big mistake, Chelsea Stone. I call again, see if you change your mind.'

'I won't. So don't bother. Stupid fucking bitch. Leave me alone,' Chelsea said, and she cut the call dead and turned off the phone. She threw it against the wall, and it bounced, shattering a crystal vase filled with lilies. Chelsea ran upstairs to bed, heart still beating fast, the sleeping pills clutched in her other hand. She'd better take two tonight. She needed to be at her best tomorrow, and that stupid bitch wasn't going to get in her way.

No one was.

Chapter Forty-Eight

'Oh my goodness! My little girl's back!'

Margaret leaped up from her chair, and gave her youngest daughter a big hug. 'Sweetheart, it's so great to see you!' She paused – it was hard to know what to say next. So many questions, she didn't know where Amber had been or what she'd been up to these last two months. She gripped her daughter's shoulders. 'Are you OK, dear?'

Amber put her Louis Vuitton travel tote on the ground. As she stood up, she flicked her hair out and smiled at her mother. 'I'm great, Mum. Really great.'

'You look beautiful,' Margaret was looking her over appraisingly. 'Really fantastic. Maybe—' she bit her lip. 'My goodness. You look wonderful, dear.'

Maybe you might need to lose a few pounds before your next film. That's what she'd been going to say, Amber knew it, but she also knew, ironically, that she'd never looked better. The sun had brought out the golden highlights in her amber hair – she'd been outside most of the day, reading by the beach, or running, or enjoying a glass of wine over lunch. She was more tanned than usual. She'd been getting loads of sleep, proper sleep, not because of sleeping pills Leo had given her when she was on a heavy film schedule.

And she was seeing clearly, for the first time in years. She didn't care any more. She was standing on her own two feet, she had a plan, she knew what she was doing with her life. In short, she had her sister and Leo exactly where she wanted them. And neither of them had any fucking clue . . .

'I feel wonderful,' she told her mother. 'It was really good to get away. Clear my head. Work out what I'm going to do next.'

Margaret still thought of Amber as a docile child. She had no reason to suspect otherwise.

'When does shooting start up again?'

'On what?' Amber said.

'On *Secret Sisters*,' Margaret replied. 'Didn't Leo put it on hold while you were gone?'

'I hope he didn't,' Amber said. 'I told him I wasn't doing it.'

'Not doing the film? But Amber!' Her mother was aghast. 'You can't—'

'I can, Mum,' Amber smiled at her. 'No way. I'm sick of those films. I don't want to do them any more. I never even liked it anyway. I want to start singing again.'

'What?' Margaret held onto the back of the chair, squinting out at her daughter in the midday sun. 'Singing? Amber, you must be mad, love, you've come all this way, you're a huge film star! You don't want to give all that up, love.'

She looked like she might burst into tears. Amber patted her arm. 'Mum, it's not up to you, it's up to me. You've been so supportive all my life' – that was the nice way of putting it – 'now it's time for me to do my own thing. And—'

Suddenly, a male voice behind her said, 'What's all this commotion, eh? My two favourite ladies, shouting at each other?'

Amber looked up. A stocky, handsome man in his fifties, black and grey hair, blue eyes, was standing in the doorway to the kitchen, looking out at them. His trousers and sleeves were rolled up. He looked like someone out of *EastEnders*, on a day trip to the beach. She screwed up her eyes, trying to work out—

'Oh my God,' she said. '*Uncle Derek*?'

'Oh lord,' Margaret said, under her breath. 'Listen, Amber, I'm sorry. He just turned up, last week. I tried calling you, but you never answered—'

'It's not a problem,' Amber smiled at her before she walked towards her uncle. 'It's great.' She embraced Derek. 'Uncle Derek, it's – wow, it's been years, hasn't it?'

Derek hugged her. 'It has, Amber darling. Look at you. You look fucking great!'

'Derek, don't swear,' said Margaret.

He smiled at her. 'Your mum's not changed either, has she? Still the same foxy little piece I first met back in seventy-six, working behind a bar—'

'That's enough of that,' Margaret said, shushing him. 'He's just come for a holiday, Amber. It's OK if he stays here, isn't it?' She said softly, 'I couldn't really turn him out on the streets.'

'Of course, it's fine. It's lovely. There's loads of room, and he can stay with you in the guest house or with me up here,' Amber said. She gripped his arm. 'Derek, it's so great to have you here. I'm so glad you've come.'

'I'm glad too,' Derek said. 'I've just been thinking, you know. Here's you, here's Chelsea, I'm so proud of you both, and I ain't seen either of you for years.' He looked at Margaret. 'It's time I made it all right,' he said. 'I want your mum to come back to London with me. Start her own life. You're a big girl, you don't need her, do you?'

Margaret looked horrified. 'Are you mad, Derek?' she said, almost shouting. 'You must be! Amber needs me here, I'm—'

'I think that's a wonderful idea,' Amber said, slinging her bag over her shoulder and pushing her golden-red hair out of her eyes. 'I'm probably taking a career break after I've sorted a few things out over here, anyway.' She nodded, encouragingly, at Margaret. 'Mum, you should go back. Set up your own agency. Name it after Dad, or something! You'd be absolutely brilliant, wouldn't she, Uncle Derek?'

Derek looked at his niece, then at Margaret.

'Come back to Soho with me, Maggie May,' he said, softly.

'Never,' Margaret said furiously. 'I'm here, I'm not going

back to London, I . . .' She trailed off and looked at him, breathless.

'Well, you can't blame me for trying. We're family, and that's the truth.' He stopped. 'Ah . . . Amber, you do look like your dad, you know. It's lovely.'

Amber hugged him again, tears filling her eyes. Dear old Uncle Derek. She was sure he'd come because he had a crush on Mum. They'd always joked about it, her and Chelsea. She sniffed, turning away from him so that he couldn't see she was crying.

'I'm going to say hi to Rosita,' she said. 'I'll go in and start getting unpacked. We'll have dinner here, yes?'

Derek hesitated. He looked at Margaret. 'Tonight, yes, but—' He cleared his throat. 'Day after tomorrow, Amber, we're having dinner with Chelsea and Leo . . . I thought you'd want to know.'

'They've both been working insane hours, this is the first time Derek's seen Chelsea since he got here,' Margaret said. 'You don't have to come. In fact, we'd completely understand if—'

'No,' said Amber, shaking her head. She was smiling. 'No, that's OK. I'd love to come. It's been two months, after all, and we need to put this all behind us. Don't worry, I won't make a scene.'

'Of course you won't,' Margaret said, patting her hand. 'You always were a good girl, Amber.'

Oh yeah, Amber said, as she put her head on one side and looked at her mother and uncle, both watching her complacently. *That's what you think.*

Amber spent the afternoon unpacking, moving around the house, sorting out her things. It was good to be home again, to have the luxuries she'd been used to. It was nice to wander round, catch up with Rosita, talk to Dan, her agent, call a few friends to say hi. It was all low-key, nothing earth-shattering, but somehow she felt fundamentally different; like she could feel the anxiety that used to accompany everything slipping away.

But later that afternoon, she was walking downstairs to the pool for a swim. Suddenly, she heard Derek's voice, beneath the spiral staircase.

'So we need to decide, Maggie. Am I staying in this nice room here, or shall I come into the guest house with you? Eh?'

'It's Margaret,' her mother said, in a low voice. 'Derek, don't. Please.' There was something in her tone of voice, something her daughter had never heard before. What was it? Amber shrank against the wall and listened, her heart thumping.

'Maggie, there's enough water under the bridge now, isn't there?' Derek's voice was wheedling, persuasive. 'Come on. Give me another try. Come back to London, we can work it out.'

She knew it! Amber had always suspected something had gone on with those two, before her dad was on the scene! She bit her lip. Wow. Her *mum*!

There was a long silence. Amber held her breath. She wished she could see them.

'I can't,' Margaret said. 'I just can't do it again, Derek. You – you hurt me too much.'

'I know, and I'm sorry . . .' He sounded desperate. 'You know how sorry I am. It was the biggest mistake of my life, running off like that.'

'You left me,' Margaret said. 'I – I was pregnant, with your baby. I loved you, and you left me.' Her voice broke.

Amber was frozen, she couldn't have moved even if she'd wanted to. She had never, ever heard her mother cry. Never seen the façade crack.

'But look at Chelsea now,' Derek said, and she could hear he was hugging her, his voice muffled. 'Look at our daughter, Maggie. She's beautiful. She's ours, and she's beautiful. It all worked out, didn't it?'

'I don't know,' Margaret said, sniffing quietly. 'I just don't know any more, Derek.'

Amber was unable to move, like she'd been hit with something. But she knew what that tone in her mother's voice was. She'd never heard it before, but it made sense now. It was attraction. It was passion. It was . . . love. She stiffened, gazing into space. She would stay there, immobile, till they moved. Had Dad known?

Did Chelsea know? What the *hell* had been going on? She felt like she was going a little bit mad, even though another piece of the puzzle was falling into place.

This dinner was going to be a night to remember.

Chapter Forty-Nine

Chelsea wouldn't have picked the Polo Lounge at the Beverly Hills Hotel for this family get-together. It was a place where you were *seen*, it was stuffed full of producers, deal-makers and A-listers. If she'd had a choice, which she didn't, it would have been dinner with just her and Uncle Derek, a nice quiet place like Morton's or Madeo's. She liked Uncle Derek. No Mum, watching judgementally. No Leo, trying to flirt with everyone and going to the bathroom every ten minutes. And no Amber . . . *definitely* no Amber.

She wasn't used to not having her own way, these days. She got what she wanted and it made it much worse, having to play this fucking happy families charade when she'd rather be in her lovely house in her sweatpants, watching *American Idol*, or something similarly trashy on TV. She loved American TV.

'Why do I have to go?' she complained to Jen, as Jen applied her make-up. She always did, before Chelsea went out; it was one of the perks of having her as a housemate. 'I don't want to go, why do I have to?'

'Because you fucked your sister's boyfriend and you have to do the penance,' Jen said, brushing her cheekbones lightly with bronzer. 'Sorry, love, you know it's the truth.'

'Jesus, Jennifer. You're supposed to be my friend.' Chelsea

298

pouted in the mirror. 'Anything else you'd like to tell me the truth about? Christ!'

Jen raised an eyebrow, but said nothing.

'It's just so fucking *humiliating*,' Chelsea said after a moment's pause. 'Like I care what Amber and Mum think. It's gonna be good to see Uncle Derek, but that's about it . . .'

Jen wasn't really listening. She was biting some dry skin off her fingers; Chelsea hated it when she did that. She'd asked her not to, when she was around, and Jen had simply stared at her and laughed. 'Who do you think you are, Queen Victoria? Get a grip!'

It was hard, having a housemate, especially one who answered back and didn't get you were the owner of the house and, well, a *film star* too. Chelsea was realising she didn't know Jen as well as she'd thought.

'And Leo,' Jen said. 'You haven't seen Leo for a few days, have you? He hasn't been over for a while, anyway.'

'Leo? Yeah,' Chelsea watched Jen in the mirror. 'Lay off the eye-liner, will you? I don't want to look like a trannie.'

Jen sighed. 'You're a real pain, you know that?' She patted Chelsea on the shoulder and the doorbell rang. Footsteps padded downstairs to answer it. 'There's Leo, Chelsea.'

Chelsea looked at her. 'Jen, darl, can you be an angel and go and tell him I'll be ready in five minutes? And can you get me a Diet Coke while you're down there?'

Jen sighed but said nothing, and went downstairs. 'Hiya, Leo!' she heard her calling, in a perky, polite voice, and Leo's answering tones, smooth, flirty, suave. Chelsea smiled at her reflection in the mirror. Jen knew she was lucky to be living in this amazing house for a fraction of the rent, Chelsea didn't need to spell that out. And she was getting to know Leo, and people in his circle. A man like Leo could make you, if he had the mind to. He could break you, too – Chelsea shivered. She had to play it careful with him, he was still one of the most powerful men in Hollywood, even if, for her, the mask had cracked long ago.

She spritzed a little Chanel No. 19 on her wrists, behind her ears – it was a classic, classy perfume, old school, permanent, not some shitty pop-star tie-in crap like Amber had done in her tatty poor-man's Britney phase . . .

She, Chelsea, was classic, classy, old school, a star for all ages, and no way was perfect, dull little Miss Amber going to make her feel guilty, not any more.

She knew she was right almost as soon as they arrived at the hotel, known to everyone as the Pink Palace. It was going to be a crappy evening.

Beside her sat Leo, taking charge as fucking usual. He was dashing in his black suit and thick silk shirt, his perfectly black hair more leonine than ever, his face smoothly smug – he still got off on two sisters fighting over him, and he loved a family showdown, he wouldn't have missed this for the world. He was courteous and friendly to everyone, especially Amber, like they were old colleagues, nothing more. He was kind and slightly flirtatious with Margaret, who almost quivered every time he talked to her; even after all these years, she was putty in his hands.

Uncle Derek had the measure of him, she was pretty sure of that. Leo treated him with a deferential, almost matey respect, and Derek saw through it, Chelsea could tell. There was no one in the world whose opinion she valued more. It was strange, after all these years. She wanted him to think well of her. He'd given her a chance when no one else would, when her mother and sister had totally shut her out. She knew he was a dodgy old git. But sometimes Chelsea wondered if some of the things she'd done would make him proud of her . . .

And Amber. Amber was being weird, no doubt about it. She was wearing a Chinese patterned silk dress, her hair piled neatly into a chignon, and she looked like a statue: classically beautiful, remote, like she was made of china and could crack at any point. She sat upright, answering people's questions like she was on autopilot, hardly touching her sushi. She could stand to lose a few pounds, too, Chelsea noted with pleasure. That heartbreak-break in Mexico had obviously been an enchilada-fest.

In fact, she, Chelsea, was doing most of the work, socialising, making sure everyone's glass was topped up, including her own, making polite conversation with her mum and Derek, stroking Leo's thigh, just near enough to the crotch to make him jump once and then keep him semi-interested for most of the evening. She was feeling quite horny this evening; perhaps it was knowing she'd beaten Amber in this particular competition. Towards the end of the meal, as Chelsea was subtly, gently kneading Leo's balls under the table, she looked up to find Amber staring right at her, like she knew, like she was judging, like there was nothing she could do about it.

Amber's green eyes bore into hers, unblinking.

Chelsea stared right back, gritting her teeth.

'Pass the butter, will you, Amber?' she said, cheerily. 'It seems to keep getting stuck down your end of the table, don't know why.'

Amber slid the butter dish across the cloth in a single, fluid movement.

Chelsea smiled to herself. She couldn't help it; having the upper hand after all these years was still a thrill to her. It felt fucking great, in fact.

Once the plates were cleared away, and the glasses were still on the table, Chelsea hoped they could skip dessert – no one ate pudding in LA, it was akin to incest on the Things You Just Didn't Do list. Get out of here, get back to Leo's, fuck him senseless. She looked around for a waiter, to order some coffee.

'Who wants –' she began.

And then it got weird.

'Wait a minute, Chelsea.'

Amber put her hands either side of her plate, and pulled herself up so she was standing, slowly, as if it was a big effort.

Her glass was in her hand. She bent her neck back, as if releasing some built-up tension, and Chelsea thought how commanding she was when she wanted to be. She never saw Amber take control. She was cool, calm, scary.

She didn't like it.

Chelsea didn't notice at first, till she started speaking.

301

'I want to make a toast,' she said, slowly. Derek and Margaret stopped their squabbling and looked up at Amber, proudly. Chelsea felt the knife twist, yet again. 'It's great to be here, isn't it?' She smiled, her eyes glittering, and Chelsea started to feel vaguely uneasy, she didn't know why. She thought Amber was a bit drunk.

'Yeah!' Leo answered, enthusiastically. Chelsea turned to him, in annoyance.

'Shut up,' she hissed.

'Yeah . . . it's great to be here, with Mum, *my* uncle Derek, Leo . . . and of course, my big old sister, Chelsea. Yeah.'

She raised her glass. Uncle Derek raised his, murmuring something, but no one else followed suit.

An unpleasant smile slid across Amber's pretty face. 'So, here's to you, Chelsea, darling. Wanted to toast a few things. Just mention a few little things.'

What the fuck's she talking about? Chelsea took her hand off Leo's thigh and wiped her sweaty palms on her silk dress.

Amber looked her straight in the eye. Like it was just the two of them. Alone, facing each other, the final showdown.

'Just – a few little things. One, I just wanted to welcome your real dad here this evening. Cheers, Uncle Derek. Yeah, he was fucking Mum before my dad showed up and picked up the pieces.'

'Amber!' Margaret croaked. 'Amber – no!'

Amber looked down at Margaret and shook her head. 'Sorry, Mum, but she has to know too. He's your dad, babe!' She laughed wildly, like it was great news.

Silence fell. They were in the corner of the restaurant. A waiter approached rapidly, and then stopped in his stride and backed away, mesmerised by the cloud of tension over the table.

'Wh-what?' Chelsea said, softly.

'Amber, listen—' Derek began.

'Oh my God, oh my God,' Margaret muttered, her slim fingers gripping her head. 'Amber . . .'

Amber ignored them all. 'Haven't finished! Haven't finished. Just a couple more things. Chelsea darling, I got a call last week, from a friend of yours in London. You remember Oksana?'

A trail of sweat, like an ice-cold knife, was working its way down Chelsea's back.

'She and I had an . . . *interesting* conversation.'

'Who's Oksana?' Leo was saying.

'I know *exactly* what happened to that poor Russian girl in your club.'

'What Russian girl?' Derek looked sharply round at her. 'What – Amber, what the fuck is this all about, love?'

'Russian girl? Chelsea, babe, what she's talking about?' Leo said. She turned to him, wishing she could scratch that smug, stupid smile off his bland face.

'Oh, Chelsea knows, don't you, darling?' Amber took another glug of wine. 'She knows what happened.' Her hands were shaking; Chelsea could see them. The bitch. The fucking little bitch.

'One more thing, just one more!'

Shut up, shut up, shut up!

Why wouldn't she shut up?

Chelsea breathed in and grabbed Leo's hand. She was going to stand up, walk out, she wouldn't take this.

'Sure you know this already, since you did it yourself. You know Leo's fucking that skanky make-up artist friend of yours, right? Jen, is it?'

Chelsea's hands tightened around Leo's, squeezing his bones so hard she hoped they might snap. A rage was coursing through her, a rage so hard . . . and then she stared across the table at her mum, and Uncle Derek, her face white with shock.

'You're making it all up,' she said uncertainly, looking round the table. 'You're jealous, you sad little bitch, you're making it all up.'

She looked at her mum's face, and then Derek's. And she knew it was true. She thought of her dad, who wasn't her dad. She stood up, trying not to fall over. She was in the middle of a flashback now, the night she caught her dad in the cellar with that man . . . not her dad, her uncle . . . George . . . who the fuck was who, she didn't know any more . . . Lies, all lies.

She turned and ran, just like she'd done that night.

Throwing his napkin on the table, Leo attempted to run after her. 'Chelsea!' he called, running through the doors. 'She was staff, for fuck's sake. She was just the staff! It doesn't *count* . . . I'm sorry! Look, what do you want me to do . . .'

But Chelsea kept on running, out into the night.

Back at the table, Margaret put her head in her hands and wept. She tried to keep it quiet, but her body was racked with sobs. 'This is all my fault,' she said softly, and then louder, as the crying grew in strength and volume, 'all my fault! What have I done?' Her hands were wet with her tears.

Next to her, Derek put his hand gently on the back of her head, stroking her hair. 'It's not your fault, my love. Please don't cry.'

She sat up and looked at him, golden blonde hair falling about her face, mascara smudging under her lovely green eyes. She sniffed. 'I've been a terrible mo . . . ther,' she said, gasping out the words. 'I tried so hard . . . And 1-look . . .' She waved her hand towards Chelsea. 'She hates me.' She turned towards Amber. 'So does she. I was only trying to do my best . . .'

She broke down in tears again. It felt to her, then, as if everything she'd been working for had come to this point, here, in this lavish restaurant, and it was all a mirage. It had all been a waste of time. All she'd done was make both her children unhappy, and possibly unstable – look at them! – when what she'd been trying to do was love them, make them be the best. Have the life she'd always wanted. And what was the *point*? Margaret gulped again, as the tears dropped heavily onto the linen tablecloth.

'I'm – sorry,' she said, in a small voice, but Chelsea was long gone and Amber wasn't listening – she was in a world of her own.

And then the same voice spoke: 'Don't cry, Maggie darling. I hate it when you cry.'

And for the first time in almost thirty years, Margaret didn't correct him. She looked up at him, her eyes brimming with tears. 'It's all my fault.'

She put her head on his shoulder, breathing out gently, and closed her eyes. As if she couldn't fight any more.

'It's not,' Derek murmured. 'It's time you stopped looking after other people, my love. I'm going to look after you now.'

'No,' she murmured. 'I'm fine on my own, Derek . . .'

And Derek said again, in her ear, so that only she could hear: 'Come back to Soho with me, Maggie May. We could be home tomorrow. It's time. Come back.'

Amber sat alone at the head of the table, shaking slightly. She felt hollow. She watched Uncle Derek comforting her mum. She knew that somewhere, Leo would be trying to catch up with Chelsea, talk things through with her. But she, Amber, had no one. Weeks of mulling over how badly she'd been treated, of plotting and planning, of deciding to change, from meek-as-a-mouse Amber to don't-give-a-fuck Amber and . . . and what?

She'd thought taking revenge would make it all better.

So why did it feel like *this*?

Chapter Fifty

The first thing she did was kick Jen out of the house, that night, when she arrived back home, having run all the way back from the restaurant, a crazy woman in her bare feet, just like the old days. She threw Jen's stuff out onto the sidewalk and pushed her, sobbing and shouting, out onto the deserted street, telling her never to come back, not caring who heard her. She may have been Derek's new daughter, but when it came to rage, Chelsea could give her mother a run for her money.

'You can't just kick me out, Chelsea – Chelsea! I've got nowhere to go!' Jen was scrabbling around on the sidewalk. Thank God no one walked anywhere in Beverly Hills. It was late, too.

Chelsea stood in the doorway of her house and looked at Jen, her stupid skanky black eyeliner smudged, a ladder in her leggings where she'd fallen on the drive on her way out. 'Why should I care?' she said, in genuine surprise. 'You're a pig, Jen! A fucking pig! How *dare* you do that? We were *friends*!'

'Friends?' Jen scooped the last of her clothes up into her arms, stuffing them into a bin liner. 'We're not friends, you stupid bitch. You treated me like shit! Or a housekeeper, depending on how you felt! I moved in with you because it was cheap and I'd get a leg-up.' She smiled, her eyes gleaming in the light from the street. 'And I certainly got a leg-up. Leo's given me loads more work.'

Chelsea shook her head, her heart thumping. 'Wow. You are a horrible person.'

'Maybe I am,' Jen said slowly. 'It's a tough town. You used me. It takes one to know one. You needed to pretend you had a friend, and that was me. But you don't want friends. You don't want anyone. You're dead inside, I think. 'Night. See ya around.'

And she turned and walked off, leaving Chelsea standing open-mouthed in the drive.

The second thing she did was break it off with Leo, and that took longer, a week before he got it, that he thought it was OK to do what you liked with a make-up artist because she was *staff* . . . but it wasn't OK with her, it was not OK with Chelsea.

'You can't dump me, darling,' he'd said, amazed, the next day in his office. 'You don't get it. Just calm down, sweetheart, you're overreacting.'

All she could do was stare at him. 'You don't think it's a big deal that you've been fucking my flatmate? Not a big deal?'

'I can see you're angry,' he said. 'I'm sorry. But Chelsea – she's a make-up artist! She's – I'm sorry to keep repeating myself, sweetie, but she's staff! She wanted it – you've been pushing me away a lot lately . . .'

He shook his head, like Chelsea was behaving childishly, and she stared again. And then he looked up and his eyes met hers, cold, suddenly. 'Don't do this, darling.'

She'd been unnerved by his expression, but she'd stood firm. Gazing at him. 'It's over, Leo. I'm sorry you can't see it, but it is.'

Imperceptibly, his eyes had flickered over her shoulder . . . she turned around swiftly, and saw Sally standing in the doorway, and for one split second Chelsea saw her look of sheer delight, mixed with an almost insane euphoria. Her eyes were bulging, like she was on drugs too . . .

Fuck it. Fuck them both! Sally could have her crazy fucking twat of a boss back now, and they were welcome to each other.

'See you around, Leo,' she'd said crisply.

'Yes, you will, babe,' Leo had replied, calmly.

Chelsea had stormed out of the office, trying to think positive.

She'd got something out of the relationship – a career in the movies, for sure. And it was in that very office that she'd picked up the copy of *Pieces of Heaven*, and Chelsea was sure *that* was going to be what saved her. The buzz on it was growing. She wanted to make sure it was all sewn up. She didn't want Leo finding out, getting his slimy hands on it.

She was Chelsea fucking Stone. And Leo wasn't going to get in the way of anything. It was the excuse to break it off with him she'd been looking for, she told herself. Though a part of her knew she would miss him. They were cut from the same cloth, the same kind of people.

But fuck it. He'd had to go. She had left his office, left him sitting in his chair staring after her, and she'd walked out, back home, alone again.

She made a vow. She wasn't going to go off the rails this time. It wouldn't be like when her dad died. Her real dad; she still thought of him like that. Derek may be her biological dad, but George . . . darling Dad, he was the one who'd brought her up, who'd taught her to love old films and classy music and given her a sense of humour, had smiled at her and made her feel she was wonderful, when her mother and sister were putting her down, planning their stupid plans.

How could he not be her dad?

When Chelsea thought about it, she felt as if her heart would break. It was as if she was losing her dad all over again. She'd killed him once, now the only tie they had was being taken away from her . . .

She knew something was going on with her mother and Derek, but she wouldn't take their calls. They phoned every day; Chelsea never phoned back.

He'd got her, just once, a few days after the dinner. The house was empty; Jen usually answered the phone, in case it was work, and they didn't have a machine. She was tired, she'd had too much wine that evening, slobbing in front of the TV and feeling sorry for herself, sorry and lonely. She was never usually lonely. Perhaps that was why she answered.

'Chelsea? Hello darling, it's me. Your . . . It's Uncle Derek.'

She'd blinked wildly, trying to sober up. 'I don't wanna talk to you.'

'I know you don't,' he said, 'so let's make it brief.'

Oh, he was a smooth talker. Perhaps that's how he'd got her frigid mum into bed. 'What do you want?' Chelsea said. She stuck out her lower lip. She could feel tears coming into her eyes. *Control it. Don't let him hear he's upsetting you.*

'I want . . . I want to say . . .' Derek hesitated. 'God . . . This is hard, Chelsea, you know? This is a bloody weird situation.'

'You should have thought about that before,' she replied. 'Before you knocked my mum up and ran off, and before you both decided to *lie* to me for the rest of my life . . .' She was crying now, but she wouldn't ever let Derek hear that. She breathed in, summoning every last ounce of courage and will. Couldn't let him see how much that hurt her. Couldn't let him see how everything made sense.

'You'll never be a dad to me, in the way my dad was,' she said, trying not to let her voice tremble. 'He didn't lie, and cheat, and run off. He was a good, decent man, and you two played him for a fucking fool.'

A picture of George came into her head. Singing next to her as they did the washing-up, him drying, meticulously polishing with one of Margaret's spotless tea towels . . . A great big smile on his face, in a neat oatmeal jumper, short, well-kept hair wet and sticking up at the front like a duck's tail, where he'd scratched his forehead with a soapy rubber glove.

'I hate you,' Chelsea said, her voice throbbing with passion. 'I hate both of you. At least it makes sense now . . . Why Mum's never loved me all these years. Funny, she's forgiven you. She never forgave me, did she?'

'Listen, Chelsea,' Derek said quickly. 'I know this must be very hard for you, but you have to understand a couple of things. First, I was an idiot. I ran off and left your mum when she was knocked – when she was pregnant. But good things came out of it, didn't they? She met my brother, and they fell in love and had a family together, you and Amber and the pair of them. Second, he was your dad.' His voice shook. 'He was your dad, and he was proud of you, girl. Like I am now. That's all I wanted to say. You know, me and your mum, we've screwed up. People make mistakes in life, that's what life is. But we're trying to put them right, now. Perhaps Amber did us all a favour, telling us what she told us that night.'

'Are you *joking?*' she interrupted. 'She's ruined my life!'

'No,' Derek said firmly. 'She's exposed the truth. And it needed to be said. Your mum and me . . . we got a lot of history. A lot we have to sort out.'

'When are you leaving?' she said. 'I don't want to see you, I don't want you around any more.'

'That's up to you,' Derek said. 'But it's your choice, darling. We're always here for you. I'm trying to persuade your mum to come back to London with me. She needs someone to look after her. She's been looking after other people all her life. She gave up on her dreams of being a star – she had you and Amber.'

'She didn't do a very good job of it,' Chelsea said.

Derek ignored her. 'All I'm saying is, she deserves a second chance. And we'd both love to see you. We always will. I love you, Chelsea. No dad could be prouder of their daughter, you have to believe me.'

Chelsea clutched the wall. She was breathing so hard she thought she'd explode.

'Fuck off,' she said. 'Both of you. I know you've done a lot for me over the years, Derek, and I'm grateful. But you've betrayed me. And Mum – she never loved me. I don't want to see either of you again.'

'Chelsea—'

She turned off the phone and stuffed it down the back of the sofa. She just wanted to be left alone.

Chelsea put her head down and focused on work instead. She finished filming the cop drug thriller, and then she started work on *Pieces of Heaven*. Thank God she still had that!

As autumn arrived in California, and the weather got a little cooler and the smog eased, Chelsea was completely single-minded. She had already hired a brilliant scriptwriter, Melissa Hershey, to work on the first draft, and when she delivered the script Chelsea was amazed – it was even better than she'd thought.

Nicola was the perfect role for her, too – the kind of role any star would kill for. In fact, Chelsea got a shiver just thinking about playing it: it was a once-in-a-lifetime opportunity.

This film was going to be huge. And it was going to get her an Oscar. She and Melissa worked long and hard into the night, polishing, perfecting. They had mentally cast every role, had started planning the shooting schedule . . . they were completely ready to go.

But something strange started to happen when she began to shop the script around town. No studio would take it.

No one.

'What can I say, Chelsea,' Todd Ritken said, his voice going up slightly. 'I've tried everything. Everybody loves this script. But no one wants to greenlight it.'

Chelsea did her best not to scream. 'Todd, honey, you're not doing your job right, that's all. This script is the fucking dog's bollocks. It's the best project I've ever seen, someone's got to be interested. What the hell is going on?'

Todd sighed. He was always so nervous around her, Chelsea thought. She chewed on her hair while she waited for him to speak.

'You've had a hard time, Chelsea sweetheart. I guess this is hard for you. I don't know what to say . . . I'm really confused.'

She interrupted him. 'I had a hard time, but I'm over it. It was months ago now. And this has nothing to do with it, Todd. I'm telling you, there's something else going on.'

'Something going on?' Todd sounded sceptical. 'Aren't you being a little . . . paranoid, Chelsea? What do you mean by that?'

'Listen, Todd,' Chelsea said, taking her hair out of her mouth. She took a deep breath. 'You're not listening to me. You can ask the question, surely? Say you're doing it on the down-low. Just make some calls. Find out what the reason is.'

'OK, OK,' Todd said, almost relieved to have something to do. He, too, thought it was an amazing project, he was as surprised as Chelsea at the result.

So he made a few calls, as high up as possible – Todd had a lot of influence.

And that was when Chelsea found out what was really going on.

He turned up one day when she was sitting on her daybed, out by the pool. Martha let him in, and Chelsea arranged herself on the cushions, seductively. She didn't want him, but she still wanted him to want her, definitely.

'Hi, Leo,' she said, in what she hoped was a friendly voice. 'How have you been?'

They air-kissed, he bending over to her as she reclined on the bed in her red polka-dot bikini, her long black hair hot from the sun.

'You're still looking wonderful, Chelsea,' Leo told her. He sniffed, and she wondered if he was high.

'Sit down,' she said. 'Can I have Martha bring you something to drink?'

'Chivas rocks, thanks,' Leo said to Martha. 'Thanks, honey.'

He turned back to Chelsea.

'It's good to see you again,' he said. He was fiddling with his cufflinks. 'I'd forgotten, you look great in a bikini, you look great today. Have you lost weight?'

'A few pounds, yeah,' Chelsea said. She licked her lips, trying to stay calm. She had to win this, had to. He was playing her, like a cat with a half-dead mouse. She wasn't going to let him win. 'Leo, thanks for coming over.'

'Oh, hey. It's my pleasure to see you,' he said, suavely.

Damn him, he was enjoying this, she thought. 'Look, I wanted to talk to you about something.'

He raised an eyebrow. 'Oh? What's that?'

'It's this film,' Chelsea began awkwardly. Why was she nervous? 'The film I was – I have a film I have a script on, for. Um – I'm explaining this badly. It's – you see, I found this book in your office, a proof copy, and I read it and I really liked it . . . Anyway . . . I . . .'

He put his hand on her wrist and she trailed off.

'Why don't I finish that for you?' he said, smoothly. She looked at him through her sunglasses, trying to disguise her loathing of him. 'I think I know how the story goes, will you let me?' She nodded. 'Right. So, this overweight British TV star gets really lucky with her first film in the States, and she starts fucking the producer, who, by the way, is going out with her sister. Now, she's a good lay, not great, but enthusiastic and grateful, and the producer likes her, so he goes along with it.'

'You bastard,' she said, wrenching her wrist away. 'You fucking *bastard*.'

Leo smiled. 'Please, let me finish.' He moved his face closer to hers. 'And then one day, when she's waiting for him, she starts snooping through his scripts.'

'I didn't fucking *snoop!*' Chelsea cried.

'We have CCTV in the office and my house,' Leo said smoothly. 'I have a record of every little thing, darling. How much you like giving head, how much you like it from behind, and how you went through my scripts and stole an advance copy and went behind my back to get it made yourself.'

His hand closed over her wrist again. With the other hand he took her sunglasses off, so that he was inches away from her face, their eyes locked. Close up, she could see the black pores on his nose, the burst blood vessels in his eyeballs . . . and the cold, cold look he gave her, and suddenly Chelsea was terrified.

'Todd was right to make a few calls,' he hissed. 'So you could find out that I've got the influence you'll never have. No studio in town will touch that project while I say so. You got that?' He tightened his grip, burning her skin. Tears filled her eyes.

'Listen to me,' Leo said. 'I made you, when I made *The Time of My Life*. I can make films. I know what works. You – you're a piece of shit I scraped off my shoe, don't you forget it. You were nothing before me.' He laughed, derisively.

'Wow, you really are furious I dumped you, aren't you?' she said. He flared his nostrils slightly. 'You know I'm the reason that film worked,' she said bravely, knowing it was dangerous to wind him up, but not caring any more. 'You'll have to go back to making that trashy schlock you were making with my sister. I think that's what you're best at, you know . . .'

'You silly little bitch,' he said. 'You have no idea, do you? It's really very simple. I make money. For the studios, for the guys that write the cheques. Therefore I can do what the fuck I want. And I want to make bigger films now. I want that script. I'm going to make that film.'

'No, you're not,' Chelsea struggled out of his grasp, and suddenly he released his grip on her. 'You're an idiot,' she said, thinking she'd won. 'Fuck off, Leo.'

Martha had appeared behind her – she hadn't heard her – and gave Leo his drink.

'Thank you, Martha,' Leo flashed a suave grin at her.

'Ms Miller's been calling you, Sir Leo,' she said. 'Said it was urgent.'

Poor old fucking Sally. Chelsea allowed herself a small smile. Had she made her move on her boss yet? She probably should – they'd be perfect together. She was the only person who worshipped him as much as he did . . .

'You need anything, Miss Stone?' she asked.

'No,' said Chelsea. 'Thanks, Martha.'

When the door closed behind her, Leo leaned over Chelsea, pinning her down onto the daybed. He held both her hands above her head and kissed her, a long, probing, sucking kiss. She squirmed underneath him, repulsed, terrified. He stopped, and ran his long, lizard-like tongue down over her chin, down her neck, her breast bone, and with one hand still clamped painfully over her hands, moved the fabric of her bikini aside to expose her right breast.

'You do have great tits,' he said, thrusting himself against her, as

314

he licked her nipple and then sucked it, harder and harder, until he gave it a sharp, agonising bite and she screamed, pushing him away with all her force.

She was shaking, pulling the bikini up around her. 'I'm going to call—'

'Who?' He stood over her, laughing, the circles under his eyes huge as he loomed above her. He looked like a devil to her. 'Who are you going to call, darling?' He brushed himself down, adjusted his cufflinks again, moved so he was standing over her and she could see his erection, bulging through the black wool Armani suit. 'Just listen to me. Why won't you ever listen to anyone, stupid Chelsea?' he said, softly. 'I am not going to be sidelined. I'm going away for a couple of months, but I'm doing this film. I'll give you a finder's fee to take the option out of your hands.'

She was panting. 'No way,' she snarled.

'If you won't do it,' he said, downing his drink and turning to leave, 'I'll destroy you.' He smiled down at her. 'You know I will. Think about it, Chelsea.'

Chapter Fifty-One

There was no denying it – Sally Miller was a happy woman these days.

Thrilled.

After ten years, Amber was *finally* out of the way, and Chelsea had sent Leo packing, though Sally reckoned Leo was relieved about it. Perhaps now her time had come. Perhaps now, after all these years, Leo would at last realise he and Sally were meant to be together.

The moment he left for the airport, a casual kiss on the cheek, quick stroke of the bottom – ''Bye darling. See you in a couple of months' – Sally had waited for the temp to arrive, and left the office too, for the first vacation she'd taken in a long time. A special vacation.

She'd pooled together all her money to pay for a range of extensive surgeries and beauty treatments: liposuction, botox, a facelift, breast augmentation – the works.

It was nearly twenty years since they'd met. Twenty years of loving him, looking after him, running his life, really! What would he do without her? And it was nearly twenty years since she'd been naked with him, and it was very, very important that she look as good now as she had done back then.

She knew Leo liked them young – he'd got his thing for Amber

316

when she was barely twenty. But he also liked women to look neat and presentable, and, as Sally peeled off the bandages in the downtown LA clinic a few days later, wincing at her swollen, bruised face, she told herself it'd all be worth it. She was going to look like a wife. He needed sex, he needed someone to look after him – she didn't really mind if he wasn't a hundred per cent faithful – you couldn't expect someone like Leo to sleep with just one person for the rest of his life.

So, Sally reasoned, as her body recovered, started to get back to normal – well, better than ever before. She was being realistic. Leo liked a plan, and this was a plan she thought he could get on board with.

Meanwhile, Chelsea was terrified for the first time in years. Properly scared, she hadn't felt like this since Maya had died. She passed from panic to uncertainty, but eventually, as the days passed, she started to realise what she had to do.

She had to get back at Leo, get something on him. He would destroy her for breakfast, and then have someone else for lunch, she knew it.

She mulled it over for days, brooding in the house, chewing her hair like a teenager till it was ragged at the ends. What could she do?

It couldn't be the drugs – it wasn't big enough, or obvious enough. He wouldn't get caught like she had, he wasn't that stupid. And anyway, she knew he had an incredibly clever lawyer on retainer for just that kind of eventuality.

Was there any way she could complain about him to the studios?

Of course not. Leo was still the golden boy independent producer. Perhaps the quality of his films had been going off in recent years; but then he'd come back again with *The Time of My Life*, and proved he really did have the Midas touch . . . No studio in town would want to piss him off. Only a fool would try – and she was no fool.

Leo had gone on an extended business trip, she knew – two

317

months away, filming in Wyoming. Last she'd heard of Amber, she'd run off to New York to do God knows what . . . best place for her at the moment, out of the way, one less thing to worry about. That bitch. And her mother – her mother had gone back to England! With – guess who? It was a fucking joke.

'I'm going back with Derek,' she'd said, when she'd come to say her farewells, a couple of weeks after the disastrous dinner at the Polo Lounge. 'He's in the car, do you—'

'I don't want anything to do with either of you,' Chelsea said.

Margaret was standing on the step of the 1960s house. Chelsea held the door half open. 'You're not even going to let me in?' she said, wondering.

'No, I'm not,' Chelsea said. She was tired with wondering about Leo, angry too. Angry with her mother, with Derek, with Leo. 'You're just leaving, without even bothering to—'

'Chelsea,' her mother interrupted, sharply. 'I'm sorry. I've called you ten times a day, you won't speak to me. I don't know what more I can do, neither does Derek.' She looked searchingly at her eldest daughter. 'I'm sorry.'

Chelsea looked at her, seeing her fleetingly not as her formal, forbidding mother, but as she really was to others – still young and beautiful, her green eyes full of life. She seemed to be glowing with something, alive for the first time in years. She looked out into the driveway, where Derek sat at the wheel of the car, watching her. He didn't say anything, just nodded. 'I'm sorry,' Margaret said again. 'I feel I've let you down, Chelsea . . . there are things I should have done for you. I don't think . . .' she gulped. 'I don't think I was the best mother I could have been. Amber – she made me see that. I tried, though. I only wanted what was best for you both!' She was crying now. 'I really just wanted you to do well, that's why I was tough with you . . .'

She paused. 'And – and your dad – George, I mean . . .'

'Don't talk to me about my dad,' Chelsea said. She was swallowing hard, swallowing down the rage and grief she felt. 'Get out.'

'I am getting out,' Margaret said sadly. 'It's time for me to leave you to get on with it. I just wanted to say to you – we'll always be here for you, Chelsea. Me, and Derek, we both love you.'

'Oh, that's nice to know,' Chelsea sneered. 'Thanks a bundle.'

'Derek wants to help you, Chelsea, love.' Margaret cleared her throat, nervously. 'We know you're having problems raising the money for *Pieces of Heaven*. He wants to give you a hand, he knows you're a good investment, love, look what you did with the club—'

'Yeah,' Chelsea said. 'I did, and I did it by myself.'

'I know you did,' Margaret said, stepping back. 'Look, just think about it. I know I'm leaving you, but we both thought this was the best way of leaving you with something to remember us by, out here. I'm not saying it's a substitute for us, but . . .'

Chelsea wanted to laugh. A substitute for those two, like they were proper parents? She'd take the money any day. Her mind was whirring, though. What couldn't she do with Derek's money? Start to plan her revenge on Leo. Get that film made. Derek was rolling in it, she knew . . . Should she, *could* she swallow her pride and take it? She looked at her mother, twisting her plane ticket round in her hand, and she hardened her heart. Not yet. She still wanted to hurt her a bit more.

'We are proud of you, Chelsea,' Margaret was saying. 'I know you think we're not. And your dad, he would have loved you too, you know he—'

Margaret was trying to get the courage up to tell her what she'd been meaning to tell her for a while now: the suicide note George left. Try to convince her it really wasn't her fault.

Please, please *tell my darling Chelsea this wasn't her fault. I had to do it, I know it now. I just can't lie any more. Tell my girls I love them.*

She swallowed, and opened her mouth.

But Chelsea just said, 'I don't want to see you again. Either of you.'

And she shut the door, shut it on her mother and bolted it. Like she was shutting something out, and it felt great.

A couple more weeks went by, and still Chelsea sat in her house, brooding, wondering how she was going to get Leo. Get what she wanted.

Gradually, she came to the conclusion that there must be *something* out there. She knew Leo, she understood him. Partly because she was good at getting under people's skin, but also partly because he was, quite simply, like her. She had secrets in her closet – George's death, Maya's death, the cover-up – and it became apparent to her that he must, too . . . She had to find something dark, and with Leo, she was just sure it must be out there. But what was it? Who was it? And who would help her?

Luckily for Chelsea, fate was about to smile on her. Because the perfect opportunity was about to present itself.

Chapter Fifty-Two

By the time Leo returned from Wyoming, the swelling and the bruising had gone down, and Sally was ready.

It was a Tuesday morning soon after Thanksgiving, early December. It was cooler in LA, still warm and sunny, though. Sally had chosen her outfit with even more care than usual. It was a brand new cream, black and red Diane von Furstenberg dress, a tiny silk DKNY cream cardigan and one of the brooches Leo always gave her for Christmas – last year's gift, in cream and black, just like the dress. She had new dainty red Manolo Blahniks strapped to her tiny feet. Her hair had been blow-dried that morning, her make-up fresh but light to emphasise her new-found youth . . .

Her palms were sweating as she sat with the cardigan draped over her slim shoulders. For the first time in years, Sally Miller was nervous. This was it.

She heard the car door slamming out in the office drive. Footsteps on the gravel. A call out to the security guard. And then he was there, walking down the corridor with Mike, another producer. She could hear them talking, see him on the CCTV . . .

And then Leo sailed in.

'Hello, darling! I'm back!'

'Hi, Leo!' Sally said, her voice squeaky. Dammit. This was *it*! Stay calm. 'How are you! It's so good to see you.'

He stopped, looked her up and down. Squinted. 'Hm, darling. New haircut?'

Sally, crestfallen, ran a shaky hand through her hair. 'Yes . . . do you like it, Leo?'

'Not really,' Leo said casually. 'Makes your face look fatter. Never mind. It'll grow out. I'm leaving these scripts here, darling. Get them over to Walter, will you? Fast. I'm going to find Mike, he was just about to leave again.'

And he tossed a pile of amended scripts onto her desk, scattering the rest of her things, and wandered out into the hallway.

Sally was left alone in her office.

She ran her hands carefully over her smooth, smooth face, pressing lightly on the skin, forcing herself not to allow any expression. She was worried something might crack if she did. She felt – she didn't know what she felt.

Yes – that was the word. '*Idiot*,' she muttered to herself. 'Gosh . . . what a stupid *idiot*.'

Had she *really* thrown her life away on this man? Twenty years, on . . . on *him*?

Then she gathered herself, sharply. It wasn't Leo's fault. He was just like that! She had to try harder, be more efficient than ever, make him realise, now he was back, back in LA with the potential to be lonely, just how much he needed her.

She trotted after him, down the corridor to his office. The door was closed, but they had intercom. Perhaps he needed a coffee, maybe something stronger . . . Sally would get him anything he needed; whatever Sir Leo desired.

She went back to her desk and switched on the intercom. She heard his warm laugh; he was on the phone to Mike now. Sally sat there, transfixed. She knew she shouldn't listen, but that deep, rich voice, it still went right through her, even after all these years . . .

And she carried on listening. Which was a mistake. He was talking about her.

'Silly little cow. I know, Mike, I know. She thinks I don't realise she's got the hots for me. After all this time . . . begging for it, she is. It's sad, really. Yeah . . . ! I know. She'll get over it. I'll buy her one of those goddamn awful brooches she likes so much. I know! She's wearing it today. Seriously, mate, the staff! These *women*! They're fucking impossible.'

Back home in her modest condo, a few hours and several drinks later, Sally made a phone call.

'Chelsea?'

'Who is that?'

'Chelsea, it's me. Me, Sally.'

'Little Miss Sally?' Chelsea sounded amused. 'What can I do for you, then?' Her tone was almost rude.

'I want to see you,' Sally said calmly, amazed at how cool she could sound. 'I think we should meet. There's something very interesting I think it's time I shared with someone. And I've picked you. It's a secret. A big secret.'

Chelsea said calmly, like she was reciting something, 'About Leo.'

'Yes,' Sally said. 'About Leo.'

Chapter Fifty-Three

She hadn't had a manicure for three weeks, didn't want one. Or a Brazilian, or a hair tint, or an eyebrow shape. But there was this one nail that kept catching on stuff, every time she pressed the button on the lift in her hotel it ached. She didn't bite her nails any more, hadn't for a while, but this one was driving her insane. It was fucking irritating.

'Look,' Amber said, nibbling at her jagged cuticle. 'I know it's strange, me calling you out of the blue, it's just, I thought –'

'Yes?'

She cleared her throat and stared out of the window, out over Lower Manhattan that was covered in snow, the lights from the bars and restaurants dotted around beneath her hotel red, golden, welcoming.

She was so nervous, it was weird; nice, almost, to feel like this, like she was *feeling* something, for the first time in years. 'Look, I'm sure you're busy? But I was just wondering if I could buy you a drink. Explain why I was so . . . weird in Mexico.' But she didn't want to make it sound like he should remember it – what if he didn't? He'd probably forgotten all about her by now. 'Look, or just buy you a drink anyway.'

This was horrible. No wonder her love life was confined to a few disastrous flings and Leo, who'd practically hypnotised her into it anyway . . . It was hard, being out there like this. Amber pulled the tuft of cuticle out of her nail in rage, giving a little howl of pain.

'Wow, are you OK?'

'Yeah – yes,' Amber said, rolling her eyes. 'Um, so – what do you think?'

There was a pause.

'Yeah,' Matt said into the phone, and she could hear him smiling. 'A drink'd be great. Do you know a bar in the West Village called Lance's? Horatio and Greenwich Street. See you there. Twenty minutes?'

Amber loved New York; she had been here a lot in the early stages of her pop career, rehearsing and recording, hanging out with Marco. Where was he now, the lovely, kind, hilarious Marco? He loved it here, too.

Lance's was in an old red-brick townhouse, a cool, dark, laid-back place full of low-key locals, a couple of them as famous as she was, Amber noted. She picked out a British pop star who'd just broken through in a massive way in the States with her first album and a beautiful, quirky actress who'd won a Best Supporting Actress Academy Award the same year Chelsea had been nominated, and her director boyfriend. And yet they'd just walked in off the street; they hadn't driven in a blacked-out car with security, with someone having already ordered a roped-off area for them. They weren't wearing sunglasses and flashing their C-sections to anyone who cared to see. They were sitting there, with the other patrons, low chatter floating across the bar, condensation steaming up the windows. It was cold outside, Christmas was the following week.

She'd made films about couples who get back together for Christmas in New York. They'd dump tonne after tonne of fake snow onto a lot in Culver City, and she'd have to wear cute matching scarves and hats, all the while sweltering in the Californian sun. But it had been a while since Amber had been anywhere snowy, Christmassy, in December, where you had to button up your coat before you went out, somewhere more real than LA. It was for family. She didn't really do family any more.

She and Matt drank mojitos. They made polite conversation for the first cocktail, how's the record business, what's your next project, did you see that X is going to make Y with Z, standard low-level entertainment-industry chit-chat they could both manage.

And then, halfway through the third drink, Matt asked about her sister.

'I just wondered what happened,' he said, staring into his drink. 'You were really bent out of shape about it.'

'You only met me that one time,' Amber said, amused. 'How do you know I'm not like that all the time?'

'I just know,' Matt said. 'It sounded pretty heavy. I kinda wondered . . . it seemed so important to you and when you talked about it, you seemed to change.' He stopped, embarrassed. 'Sorry,' he said. 'That's outta line.'

'It's not,' Amber told him. 'I was obsessed about it, it's true.' She remembered what she'd liked so much about him in Mexico. He was incapable of telling a lie, she thought. He just couldn't do it. No bullshit. For Amber and the world she'd been in, that was a revelation. 'Yeah . . .' she said. 'My sister. Well—'

So she told him. She told him about the Russian girl and the overdose, about how Leo would fuck anything else that moved, about who Chelsea's real dad was. She told him how she'd got her revenge on her big sister, finally, after all these years.

And she told him how it didn't make her feel any better.

'I thought it would,' she said, quietly. 'But I just felt shitty. My mum's so upset she's gone back to England for a while. Chelsea's split up with Leo – that's a good thing. And that poor dead girl – there's nothing anyone can do about that now.'

'Is she still calling? The friend? Is she going to cause trouble? Go to the papers?'

Amber bit a nail. Oksana's calls were more regular and more threatening. 'She says she will, yeah.'

Matt nodded. 'Wow.' He sat quietly for a moment. 'And if she did, that'd blow the whole thing up.'

'She'd be arrested,' Amber said. She watched him. She wasn't sure why she trusted him: it was an explosive story, he could stand to make a huge amount of money if he went to the press. It could set him up for life.

But she knew he wouldn't. There was just something about him: she could trust him. He wasn't really interested in celebrity, she'd known that the first night they'd met. He was interested in music.

'That's tough on you,' he said, quietly. Amber stared at him.

'You must think I'm a terrible person.'

Matt looked a bit bemused. 'You? No way. Why?'

Amber looked out of the window, watching the buttoned-up New Yorkers, swaddled in thick coats and ear muffs, sliding, hurrying through the snow. She tried to explain. 'Well, I've behaved really badly . . .' she said.

'I'm sure you felt you had to do it,' Matt said, shaking his head. 'That's crap, Amber, and you know it. I'm so sorry. Look, they're shovelling the snow again.' He drained his drink and leaned forward, while she stared out of the window, like a child amazed at the snow.

'It's beautiful,' she said, laughing. 'So sad of me, but I love it.' She turned to him, and he was looking at her intently.

'Listen, Amber,' Matt said. 'I wanted to see you again, you know.'

'Me too,' Amber nodded.

'I wanted to talk to you – about your music –' He broke off. 'About us . . . you singing again.'

'Wow.' She cleared her throat. 'Wow – yeah. Yes, so did I.'

It was amazing, and yet she was a tiny bit disappointed. Did he just see her as a new recording contract, or was it more than that? Amber shook her head, impatient. Stupid girl. She was lucky to be here at all, with this cute guy who just seemed to get her, without any other complications than that . . .

Matt was still talking. 'I was thinking – do you wanna get another drink, talk it over, go dancing a little, maybe? I know a great club up a block from here that plays really cool soul stuff.' He paused. 'Of course, I guess you're probably tired . . .'

She looked at him. 'I'd love to,' she said, smiling into his eyes.

'Great,' Matt said, slapping the bar enthusiastically. 'That's great!'

The club was tiny, down some rickety, rusty steps, in the heart of the Meatpacking District, its cobbled streets grey with old snow dotted with grit. Inside, there was the scent of mildew mixed with sweat, and some exotic scented-candle fragrance, presumably to hide the odour. And it was packed, with old guys in caps, tapping along to the music, couples sitting around minute tables with lights and flimsy lampshades that illuminated the little dance floor. There was an old, old bar with a scary-looking tattooed barman behind it, and a DJ, around Amber's age, shut away in the corner in a black booth, with piles and piles of LPs – not CDs, no iPods by his side – almost obscuring him. And the music – wow, the music! Marvin Gaye, Jimmy Ruffin, Aretha, James Brown, Smokey Robinson, more Marvin, Gladys Knight . . . Sweet soul music, like James Brown said, and Amber and Matt simply put their jackets down on a spare chair in a corner and danced and danced and danced, and they took it in turns to get drinks, leaving the other to dance. No one recognised Amber; she didn't want them to, she wanted it to be just her and Matt, dancing together till they kicked them out.

Eventually, they were sitting at one of the little tables, finishing off another bottle of beer. Amber was panting, sweaty. She knew she looked a fright, and she didn't care. She couldn't remember the last time she'd enjoyed herself so much.

'Thank you,' she yelled to Matt. 'This is – this is amazing.'

He smiled, and took her hand. 'It's my pleasure, Amber. You really know your Motown!'

'It's my dad,' she told him, pleased, lowering her voice as the music paused. 'He loved that stuff . . .' Her eyes filled with tears at how far away her memories of him seemed now, how much she still missed him, every single day, darling Dad in his funny den in the house polishing his records and pottering around, the light in his eyes when a new song came on, or when she'd sit on the edge of the crusty old sofa and ask him questions, about what happened

328

to Tammi Terrell, or Marvin Gaye; why Gladys left Motown and went to Buddha, who was better, Aretha or Diana Ross.

Her eyes were brimming over, and she looked away, swallowing. Matt squeezed her hand, moved a little closer.

'Hey, baby,' he said softly. A new song came on, 'Let's Stay Together' by Al Green, and she looked up, almost unable to believe the strangeness of the coincidence, but then accepting that perhaps, sometimes, these things were meant to be.

'This was . . . this was his favourite song,' she said. 'His favourite. Wow!'

'Let's dance,' Matt said, and he took her hand and they stood up and swayed, gently. 'Let's . . . stay together . . .' he hummed in her ear, and she breathed in at the comforting, solid strength of him, his arms around her, his breath in her ear. She pulled back a little and looked at him. He was smiling gently at her, his face millimetres away from hers . . . and then he put his lips to her ear again and said, so only she could hear, 'I know it's gonna sound strange, it's been no time at all, but . . . I think I'm falling in love with you, Amber.'

And she smiled, and he kissed her gently. 'Me too,' she said. 'Me too.'

They danced, melded together, holding each other tight as the music played on, and Amber couldn't remember when she had last felt so safe, so happy. So . . . normal.

Chapter Fifty-Four

By the end of that night, Amber knew she was in love with Matt Hughes. She stayed over at his apartment, also in the Village, though they didn't have sex. It was four in the morning and they were both exhausted. They simply crawled into bed, and Matt wrapped Amber in his arms and they were both asleep within seconds, like they'd been together for years, an old married couple.

They had breakfast the next day at a café nearby, before Matt went off to work with some band from Brooklyn. He wasn't looking forward to it.

'They're fucking slackers – middle-class kids who think they're gonna rule the world because they went to college and they've got some kind of manifesto about the band,' he said, hungover and grumpy. 'I hate those kind of guys. Their first single is great, it's pop-guitar stuff, and the rest is totally mediocre, and they're already doing coke and fucking hookers and behaving like they're Led Zep . . .' he trailed off. 'Man, sorry, that's too heavy.'

'Too heavy for my hangover,' Amber said, wrapping her hands round her coffee mug and taking a huge gulp. She leaned over and kissed him.

'I just wanna stay here with you,' he said, simply. 'I'm sorry, I don't want to sound so heavy today, but with you it's—'

'I know,' she said, trying not to smile like an idiot, she was so happy. 'Don't worry, baby. I know.'

'I'm talking to Carrie today, and we're gonna start putting together some songs. Get you in to talk about what kind of thing you wanna do on the album. We should start recording in the New Year.'

'But that's a couple of weeks' time!' Amber was aghast.

Matt ignored her, and carried on. 'I think it should be new stuff, but with a bluesy edge. Maybe a couple of covers. Do some Dusty, perhaps.'

Amber winced. 'I'm too in awe of Dusty,' she said. Her mum loved Dusty Springfield. She wondered about her mum, about Uncle Derek. What would Mum say when she learned of her decision, that she was giving up film for ever, doing music now, and that she really didn't care what anyone said about it? She wondered about Chelsea, too . . . what would Chelsea think? How was she?

Matt called her out of her reverie. 'You're hugely talented,' he said. 'We don't need to rip anyone off. You're not Amy Winehouse, you're not Dusty. You're Amber. You've got something all of your own. And you'll carry it, I promise. I wanna show people your soulful side.' She laughed, and he put his hand on the back of her neck and pulled her towards him, gently. 'It's true! And we're in it together, aren't we?'

All this time, Amber had been wanting to show another side of herself with her acting, and now she realised she couldn't ever go back to it and do that. She'd spent most of her life pretending to be something she wasn't.

Now she could just be herself.

'That sounds great,' she said. She kissed him again, and he slid his fingers around her neck, his tongue pushing slowly into her mouth, his lips on hers, his other hand gripping her thigh . . . Amber was used either to kissing her co-stars or Leo, and both experiences were fairly mechanical. She hadn't been kissed properly for years, not like this, not by someone who wanted to, who wanted to run his hands through her hair, pull her closer towards him so that she could feel his heart beating, his warm body against her . . .

He broke away first. 'I want you,' he said, whispering softly in her ear. 'I want you so much, beautiful girl . . .'

He tucked a lock of her hair behind one ear, and she smiled at him.

'I can't believe this is happening,' she said, simply. 'Me too. Oh, me too.'

Self-conscious all of a sudden, as she realised a man was staring at them curiously and she didn't want to be recognised, she took a large gulp of coffee, head bent down.

'So you're moving to New York, staying here?' Matt said, shovelling some more eggs into his mouth. He said it like it wasn't a big deal.

Amber looked round the diner, with its checked red tablecloths, white oblong tiles, the caramel coffee-cups, the low windows with the street outside, muffled New Yorkers bustling along the sidewalk, going to work, and she felt at home. She was here, leaving the past totally, completely behind.

'I'm staying here,' she said. 'I just have one more thing I have to do. Do you mind if I make a quick call?'

'Sure,' Matt said.

'I'll just go outside.' She put on her coat.

'Are you crazy? It's freezing out there. I won't listen.'

'It's OK,' Amber told him. 'I have to go outside. It's best you don't hear this.'

Matt looked up at her. He could have said, *What?* Or, *Why, don't you trust me?* Or, *Is there someone else you need to break off with?* But he didn't, and that was why she loved him. He reached down onto his banquette and threw her his scarf. 'Don't be long,' he said.

Amber dialled the number and stepped outside, the cold air like a knife in her chest.

'Hi,' she said, when the phone picked up. 'Hi, Oksana. It's Amber Stone.'

'Hah.' Oksana's voice betrayed no emotion. 'You see sense? Your sister, I tried her again. She tell me to fuck off. I am going to police, Amber. OK? You're too late. I am going back home, to Russia afterwards. I don't need this any more.'

'Sure, sure,' Amber said, placatory. 'Listen, Oksana. I don't agree with what you're doing. You need to understand that. I know you're angry with Chelsea. But I know that Chelsea is very upset by what happened. It still gives her nightmares.'

And as she said it, she knew it was true. She'd heard her sister crying out in her sleep, sobbing one night in the guest house, when Amber had been looking for some sleeping pills. She felt for Chelsea, now she was thousands of miles away from her. Dad's death and this . . . it was more than most people had to bear.

'Hah,' Oksana said again, and this time she sounded scornful. 'I don't care about her. She's a bitch, Amber. A bitch. Evil. She doesn't care about anyone any more.'

Amber cleared her throat. She didn't want to tell Oksana that people in glass houses really shouldn't throw stones . . . She looked back into the diner, at Matt reading the *Times* and drinking coffee. She wanted to be back inside with him. 'How much for you to go away, permanently?' she asked, bluntly. 'To never bother my family again, any of us? And I mean it,' she said. 'If I hear from you again − I know people. My uncle Derek knows where to find you.' This was a bluff, and she hoped Oksana wouldn't see through it. 'Just tell me how much. A hundred thousand dollars?'

'Two-fifty,' Oksana said immediately. 'Two-fifty thousand dollars.'

Amber had spent that much the previous year remodelling the pool and guest house. 'Done,' said Amber. 'It's a deal. OK?'

'OK,' Oksana said. She didn't say thanks. 'You take care of it, yes?'

'I will. I'll have it to you within a week.' Now she could rest easy. Now, perhaps, she'd started to make amends for taking revenge on her sister so cruelly. Chelsea was free to get on with her new life.

And Amber just hoped it'd make her happy. No more revenge. No more plots.

Chapter Fifty-Five

Chelsea opened the door herself.

'Come in,' she said.

'Hi.' Sally Miller smiled at her perfunctorily. There were circles under her eyes, and she was dressed in a T-shirt and jeans – Chelsea had never, in two years, seen her in jeans. 'Thanks.'

She wandered into the hall, almost sloppily. Chelsea wondered if she was drunk. 'Shall we go in here?' she said, indicating the cosy sitting room which doubled as a den. She'd hardly spent any time in there before everything had gone wrong – she was either out by the pool, out at meetings or out filming. And now that her world had kind of crumbled, she didn't have so much to do. She spent a lot of time watching TV and trying not to eat crappy food.

The room was a mess: gossip magazines, cans of Diet Coke, empty packets of crisps littered the floor. Out on Rodeo Drive the designer boutiques were draped with elegant boughs of holly and pine and twinkling lights, and the highways were full of flashing Santa illuminations. Here, it was as if Christmas didn't exist. Sally stepped over the rubbish and sank down, her tiny frame almost lost on the large sofa. Chelsea looked at her. She and Leo had fucked on that sofa, the day it had been delivered, with the plastic wrapping on, and then again when she'd taken it off . . .

'Can I get you a dri—' she began.

'I'd love a vodka tonic,' Sally said. 'Thanks.' She smiled again, automatically, and pushed a hand through her lank hair.

Chelsea walked away, raising her eyebrows. Wow, this chick really was in some kind of state. She mixed the drink and poured one for herself, making them strong, and handed one to Sally. Before she'd even sat down, Sally said, 'So, I guess we both wanna get even with Leo.'

Chelsea said, 'What happened with you two, Sally?'

'It's no big deal!' Sally smiled elastically. 'I have realised just now that he's a piece of shit.' She paused and said, as if referring to a boyfriend, 'I walked out on him yesterday.'

'Wow,' Chelsea said. 'What—'

'Yeah, we had a big, big fight.' She said it quietly. 'I told him a few home truths. Told him a couple of things he should have heard a while ago. And he said . . .'

Her face cracked a little bit.

Chelsea wasn't into hugging and hand-holding, especially not with that fembot Sally. 'What – what did he say?' she said, in what she hoped was a soft, caring voice.

Sally gave a small sob, a noise like an animal in pain; it was uncomfortable, watching her, and then she looked up, baring her white teeth. 'He said some really very unkind things to me.'

You sad, sad, dried-up old bitch, Sally. Don't speak to me like that. I hired you, no one else will want you. In any possible way, darling. Who'd want to fuck you? You're like a piece of leather that's had a facelift. You're pathetic. You're pathetic . . .

'Like what?'

'I can't say,' Sally said, so sharply Chelsea didn't ask again. 'All I can say is I feel like I've come to my senses. For the first time in years.' And then she looked up and said frankly, 'Leo doesn't know it, but I've got something on him. And I want my revenge. I want him to pay, for everyone to know how evil he is.' Her hands were twisting in her lap. She clamped them together and stood up. 'I need your help to do it, that's all.' She looked round. 'You have a VHS player somewhere?'

Chelsea nodded towards the huge, shiny black entertainment

console, slightly ashamed. 'It's there, actually.' She didn't want to tell Sally she'd bought it so she could watch the tapes her mother had dutifully recorded of her fourteen-year-old self on *Roxy's Nine Lives*. When she couldn't sleep – most nights now – when she felt like she was living some kind of nightmare, didn't know who she was, how she'd got there, she'd curl up on the sofa and watch an episode of Roxy getting into some minor scrape, being rude to a teacher, dissing a bully, something like that, and the comforting theme music, the almost am-dram way the sets slightly rocked in the background, the set of Roxy's home with the sofa where she and Gary, playing her younger brother, had sat and taken the piss out of each other for hours . . . It was like watching a version of her reality that she wished she actually had. Toxic Roxy . . . those days were a long time ago.

She couldn't explain that to Sally. No.

'That's good,' Sally said. 'I have a tape I need to get hold of.'

'Why? What tape?'

'Did you know Leo has a camera in every room in his house?' Sally sat back down, all business.

'My God – no way . . .' Chelsea felt the colour drain from her face. 'Why the fuck—'

'They wipe after twenty-four hours,' Sally reassured her. 'It was insurance, originally. He had like, three, four burglaries in a year, and the insurance company recommended it.'

'You're not serious.'

Sally nodded, and then a strange look crept over her face. 'Oh, yeah. But you know, the guy's a deviant. He liked having them. I know he'd keep some stuff back and watch a couple of things over, before they got wiped.'

Chelsea had her head in her hands. 'Fucking *bastard* . . . I should have known.'

'Yeah, you should have,' Sally agreed. Her tone wasn't harsh, just factual. 'You should have known more than most, Chelsea, you're a smart girl.' She leaned forward. 'But he should have known better. He thinks he's so clever, but we've got him now. If we can get hold of some tapes I kept back, we've got him.'

'What's – what's on them?' Chelsea almost didn't want to ask.

'Did Amber ever talk to you about Tina? Or Maria?'

'Who?' Chelsea looked blank.

'Tina was Leo's housekeeper. There for years. She had a daughter, Maria. Did she never mention them? They were both kind of friends of Amber's when she came to LA. Her only friends, really, after Leo got rid of that gay dancer guy.'

'We weren't talking so much then,' Chelsea mumbled. 'Maybe.'

She vaguely, vaguely remembered, in the early days of Amber's almost childlike enthusiasm about Leo, her rabbiting on about his house, how cool he was, how great the people were there, how she'd go swimming and hiking with some girl that had something to do with the house . . . 'But the daughter – she was like a kid, wasn't she?'

'She was fifteen.' Sally's voice was grim. 'Just listen,' she said. 'Just listen to what he did.'

And Sally starting talking.

Yes, Leo had a secret. A very dark secret.

Seven years ago, he had been very frustrated. Amber had just come to LA, she and her mother were staying there while they found a place to rent. He wanted her – he always wanted what he couldn't have. She was young, she looked younger, and she was hot, physically and career-wise.

Only Sally knew how bad it got when Leo had to deny himself anything.

But Leo knew he couldn't have Amber, not just yet. She was off-limits – Margaret was charmed by him, but Margaret wasn't stupid. She'd been around, she knew what guys like Leo were like. Anyway, Amber was worth too much to Leo as an asset for him to spoil.

But *staff* . . . the staff were different.

And one night, when Amber and Margaret were away, when he was frustrated, lonely, in the mood to test himself, it happened. Maria's mother Tina was out at the cinema, and it was easy for him to persuade Maria to have a drink with him, by the pool.

Maria was hugely flattered. Leo was a big shot, so handsome too, so much fun, that twinkle in his eye. And she dreamed of being a star, just like her new friend Amber. Leo, watching her, trying to control himself, got to work.

One drink, then another. All spiked.

And then it got bad. Very bad.

Tina came back from her night out and found Maria lying in a heap, blood under her fingernails, blood by the pool where she'd fallen over, banged her head . . . her clothes torn . . .

Leo called his private doctor. They got her to hospital, he paid the guy off. You could pay anyone off with enough money. She'd had an aneurysm. She was a vegetable. Fifteen years old, never going to wake up, hooked up to machines, bills every month costing thousands . . .

Even in her grief, Tina wasn't stupid. She guessed the truth. She knew Leo, she knew her daughter had caught his eye. Now she would never wake up, and Leo was going to pay.

But what could Tina do? She was there without a proper passport. They'd deport her and keep her daughter there. She had to go along with him.

Leo paid all the hospital bills and set up a fund to pay the family each month. And that's why Sally had to be told, the day after it had happened.

But Leo didn't tell her everything.

So Sally never really knew why, that morning, she went back and found the security tapes for that previous night. She didn't know why she took them out and replaced them with fresh ones, and why she hid them, in a safe in her office. Leo had no idea they were there. Sally had no idea *why* she was keeping them there . . . all those years.

'Insurance,' she told Chelsea, with a half-grimace. 'Perhaps I always knew it'd end like this.'

Chelsea smiled. 'I think we've got him,' she said.

'We haven't,' said Sally, matter-of-fact. 'We need the tapes. And they're still in the office.'

'So go back and get them!'

Sally gritted her little teeth. 'I can't. He's changed the locks. To the house. And he won't let me back in the office.'

'Seriously?'

'Yeah. I tried to go back today, pretended I'd got one of his stupid brooches still there . . . they wouldn't even let me through the gate.'

Chelsea balled her hands into fists. 'Fuck,' she said. 'Fuck. Is there anyone who—'

Sally shook her head. 'Um – not really. I don't have many friends there, you know. I wasn't really working there for that.' She looked down, as if fascinated by the oatmeal fabric on the sofa. 'Yeah. I was all about him, you see. Didn't care about the others.' She looked up and her eyes were full of tears. 'I have to get back at him,' she said. 'So do you. Not just for me, not just for you, but for what he did to that girl. Poor Tina. She's a fucking idiot, she should have taken him to court, got millions off him.'

'So what do we do now?' Chelsea said.

'We? You wanna help me?'

'Yes,' said Chelsea, and she uncurled her fingers and shook Sally's hand. They didn't smile.

'We need someone he still trusts to go back into the office, get the tapes.'

'You don't mean me,' Chelsea said, almost laughing. 'I stole *Pieces of Heaven* from right underneath him. He says he'll crush me.' She was remembering the look in his eyes, almost mad, the agony of his teeth biting her breast . . . She shivered. 'I'm the one person he likes even less than you.'

'No,' Sally said. 'You're right, I don't mean you.' She paused. 'Chelsea – we need Amber.'

'But I don't know where she is,' Chelsea said. 'She changed her number. I think she's in New York but I don't know.'

'So, we'll find her. This will keep. But not for long,' Sally said. 'We have to get into that safe before someone else realises what's in there. You start looking for her, OK?'

'OK,' said Chelsea.

Chapter Fifty-Six

It was her first day in the studio. And for the first time in a long time, Amber couldn't wait to go to work.

She was still staying at the hotel. She told herself that's because it was handy for the studio, for the bars and cafés of the Village, but that wasn't true . . . it was handy because Matt was only a few blocks away from her. It was the first week of the New Year, she'd been in New York for a month now, and everything had happened faster than she'd thought possible. The album deal was done; her agent Dan was furious. He knew when Amber Stone was serious, and she was serious about this.

'You're throwing your fucking career away, sweetie, you know that?'

She could hear the echo of his voice, in the cavernous corner office suite he insisted on, with views over the whole city. Could hear the clatter of his Gucci-shod feet as he swung them up onto his glass desk, swivelling in his thousand-dollar chair to stare out the window, the flick of his fingers as he checked his BlackBerry while he talked to her.

'I don't want the kind of film career you want me to have, Dan, honey,' she told him. 'I'm not going to play anyone's sister.' She felt it was especially inappropriate for her. 'It's a short step from that to playing someone's mom, and then I'll shoot myself.'

'You're making a—' Dan began.

'No,' Amber said gently. 'You're trying to make me do stuff I don't want to do. It's not your fault, I'm just not doing it any more.'

No more balding, doughy studio execs with facelifts, no more sharp, Prada-suited development execs and agents with their shark-like smiles, no more perky, fake-breasted girls everywhere, serving at the bar, greeting you at the restaurant, eyeing up whoever you were with – would this be the one they could use to make it big?

She was over it. She wasn't kidding herself, she knew the music business wasn't perfect. But it didn't all hang on appearance to quite the degree the film industry did. And there were still people working in music who loved music.

Amber knew she had one shot at this. And so it had to be perfect.

She chose what she was going to wear carefully. Jeans, a pretty, flirty top, carefully accessorised jewellery – she wanted to look like she'd thought about it, but low-key as well . . . she picked up her grey Mulberry Bayswater, which doubled as a music briefcase, and was just heading out the door when the hotel phone rang.

She nearly didn't get it, but something made her turn back; had the recording plans changed?

'Hello?' she said quickly.

'Amber? That you?' Her heart skipped a beat, she knew that voice so well, rasping, dripping with a curious combination of sexuality and sarcasm . . .

'Chelsea?' she said. 'Hi . . . hi. How are you?'

They hadn't spoken since the showdown at the Beverly Hills Hotel. Amber had changed her number so they couldn't get hold of her.

'Fine, yeah, fine. Listen, can you talk?'

'How did you get my number?'

'I've been ringing people for ten days now. Tracked you down.' She sounded breathless. 'So – can you talk?'

'Not really –' Amber looked at her watch, she was due there now, at ten. 'I'm on my way out somewhere. Is it important?'

'You could say that, yeah,' Chelsea cleared her throat.

'It's eight in the morning in LA, Chelsea, what are you doing up so early?'

'I wanted to catch you,' Chelsea said. 'Say hi to Sally.'

'Hi, Amber!' A perky voice trilled thousands of miles down the line. 'How are you doing?'

'Am I on speaker?' Amber said, bewildered. 'Sally . . . ? Leo's Sally? What do you guys want?'

There was a pause.

'Tell her,' she heard Sally whisper. She felt the hairs on the back of her neck rise; she was scared, and she didn't know why.

'We need your help, sis,' Chelsea said eventually. 'We need to nail Leo, once and for all. And you're the only one who can help us do it.'

At first, Amber refused to help them. She said it over and over again. 'I'm not interested. You won't tell me what it's about, why should I drop everything in New York and fly back to help you two? After everything that's happened?'

'I could say the same to you,' Chelsea said. 'After all, Amber, wouldn't you say you owe me?'

Amber was silent: chilled, once again, by what she'd done, how she'd ruined her sister's life in a few sentences, how she'd been consumed by revenge . . . wasn't this just the same thing, weren't they just eating themselves up over getting back at a man who simply wasn't worth it?

As if reading her thoughts, Chelsea said, 'Listen, we can't be sure what's on the tape, but that's why we need you to get it. We know the state he left her in, after he was finished with her. And you liked Maria. She was a sweet kid –' She paused. 'She was fifteen, she didn't deserve this, Amber.'

How do you know, you weren't even there! Amber thought, but there was no point in antagonising her. Whatever it was, it sounded pretty bad. She put her hand on her chest. This was horrible, horrible. Poor Maria. Poor Tina.

'And—' Chelsea paused. 'You know, it doesn't look good for

you,' she added, casually. 'You were technically living there at the time. You need to make sure, if this ever comes out, that there's nothing attached to your name.'

'I knew nothing about it, you know that,' Amber said calmly, but her heart was racing.

'Well, *I* know that, and so does Sally!' said Chelsea, as if Amber was the one suggesting it, casting doubt on herself. 'But other people won't, will they? They'll think, you were with him all this time, did you really never ask where she went? Not suspect anything? I mean . . . what were you thinking? they'll say.'

What had *she been thinking?*

It was a good point. What the hell had she been doing, not to see what Leo was like, all that time . . . Amber thought of Margaret again, back in London now. How could *she* not have seen it, what he was like? She was supposed to be a mother, not a career manager . . . But no point blaming her. Amber shook her head. It was time to take control herself, instead of blaming other people. She took a deep breath.

'I'll come.'

Chelsea whistled, relieved. 'That's good. When?'

'As soon as possible.' She wanted this over with. 'I'll get on a flight today.'

'But your recording session, and all that stuff?' Chelsea sounded concerned. It was so fake, Amber bit her tongue. She wanted to tell her to fuck off.

'I'll get out of it.' She couldn't think of Matt, now. 'I'll make something up. This is the last time, though, Chelsea. The last time.'

'Yeah, yeah,' Chelsea said. She was clapping, now. 'This is fucking awesome. We've got him. We've got him where we want him. He's going to pay.'

As Amber hung up and put her bag down slowly she thought, pay for what? She didn't think any of them were in this to avenge what happened to Maria. No, they were in it for their own ends.

She began to pack, dialling the studio. Matt'd wonder why she wasn't turning up. He'd think she was a flake. But she didn't have any choice; she could see that now. She certainly wasn't going to tell him what was really happening.

She was going back to LA, though she wished with all her heart she could stay in New York . . .

Chapter Fifty-Seven

'Amber! My favourite little girl. This *is* a nice surprise, how are you? What can I do for you today? Here, back in LA, right? When did you get in? Where have you been? Off my radar, that's for sure! Probably you were glad though! Ha, ha!'

Amber submitted to Leo's embrace and stood back, trying not to show her alarm. Had he always been this manic?

'Sit down, sit down . . .' Leo clapped his hands. 'Let's get some drinks, shall we? What do you want? When did you land?' He leaned over the desk and smiled wolfishly at her. 'What do you want?' he asked again, as a woman in her twenties appeared. 'Lotte,' he said, smiling at the tall, pale, blonde girl in the doorway. 'Lotte's going to bring us some drinks, isn't she?' Lotte's hair was almost white, so were her eyelashes. She wasn't smiling back. She looked like an angel, a very young angel . . .

Amber swallowed. It was so weird being back in this office, where Leo and her mother and she had plotted her career nearly a decade ago. What was she doing here? How was she going to get to the safe? Sally had given her the combination, but how on earth was she going to do it? 'Um – just some green tea, thanks, Lotte,' she said, smiling at the girl.

'Where's Sally?' she asked blithely, after the door had shut behind them.

'Who?' Leo was fiddling with his wallet. 'Oh, Sally – well, poor old dear. She had to go. Went a bit . . . off the rails, let's say.' He looked up at her, sorrowfully. 'I should have seen it coming. She needed a break . . . I'm really sorry. I miss her, of course.' His face assumed an expression so sincere that Amber stalled, until she remembered what a very good actor Leo was. He'd had to say this to everyone in the last few weeks, of course he'd got good at it! She smiled.

'But now, you,' he said, changing the subject. 'You, *you*! What are you up to? Want a part in *Pieces of Heaven*? It's going to be great, going to be great, my dear . . . your conniving little bitch of a sister isn't getting anywhere near it, that's for sure. Speaking of sisters,' he broke off and said, so magnanimously she wanted to punch him, 'babe, I might have something for you . . . do you want to play the sister? I could get an audition, and you'd need to dye your hair but it's all cool, all cool.'

He was on something, he had to be . . . she'd known him be up, be high, but never as bad as this, or had she just always been in his thrall? She didn't know. Amber smiled. 'I told you before, Leo. I'm not playing anyone's sister. I want the lead, or nothing.'

He looked at his hands. 'Amber darling, I'm afraid, my sweet, that that's just not possible.'

'It's OK,' she said, wanting to get in there before he humiliated her by gently letting her down. She didn't care, anyway. 'Listen, Leo, I just came back to LA to sort out some stuff of Mum's now she's moved back to the UK.' His eyes glazed over; he wasn't listening the moment it was out of his control. 'I'm not back to audition for anything. I'm living in New York now.'

'Right, right. So . . . What are you doing?' he said, stroking the onyx paperweight on his desk and not really looking at her. She felt he was already wishing she'd leave, so he could go and do more coke.

'I'm quitting the film business, Leo,' she said, sitting up straight. 'I'm going back to singing.' She laughed, trying to sound convincing. 'Breaking out the guitar again. I'm working with a producer, we're recording an album.'

She thought she'd lost him completely, as there was a silence when she'd finished, but then he looked up at her.

And smiled. And then he laughed. Laughed out loud.

'Ha ha ha! You serious?'

'Er – yeah,' said Amber, nodding.

'You? You're "going back to singing"? *You?*' Leo's voice dripped venom. 'Amber, my dear, my darling, what the fuck are you *talking* about?'

'I just said, Leo. I'm—'

'I heard you.' He was smiling again, looking hugely pleased with himself. 'That's a laugh. You! Oh, Amber, that's hilarious. Please, don't be offended, but let me tell you a few home truths, darling. You've got no voice, no voice at all. Are you mad?'

'I've got no voice because you took it away from me,' she said, bravely, but he wasn't listening, didn't even seem to care.

'Listen to me, Amber,' he said, and he laughed again. 'No one wants to buy *Amber Stone*'s records. That's hilarious. Forgive me.'

Amber stood up. She felt like she was watching herself, from up in the corner of the room, like one of Leo's security cameras, recording everything. She was amazed at how calm she felt, how clear it all was to her. She thought how this would have crushed her once, how much in his power she had been.

But she was stronger now. Matt believed in her. He trusted her, and she trusted him: his tastes, his way of looking at the world, far more than she could ever trust Leo.

'I'm sorry you think that,' she said, and she looked down at him. His pupils were huge, he was sweating. 'I'm sorry for you, Leo.'

'Oh, get out, you stupid little bitch,' he said, like he couldn't be bothered any more. 'Fuck you. Fuck you! Actually, I don't want to fuck you. You were hardly worth it. Your sister either, at least she wanted it, the fat cow, I don't know why I . . .'

Amber turned and walked away. She walked down the corridor, towards Sally's old office. She poked her head in the door.

'Lotte – I'm just leaving now. I told Leo I'd let you know – he wants you in his office.'

Lotte stared at her. 'He said right away,' Amber added sharply.

'Oh. OK.' Trying not to look scared, Lotte grabbed a notebook and her iPhone and skittered out as coolly as she could.

Stay calm, stay calm. Perhaps they wouldn't be there, perhaps . . . Amber pulled the piece of paper out, swiftly turned the combination lock of the safe, back, forward, forward again, back . . . click . . . click . . . click . . .

She was in luck. No one had touched the safe since Sally's departure, either because they didn't have the combination or, like so many things in an office, because they'd just got used to the safe in the corner with the in-tray and the rubber plant on top.

Three video tapes, stacked neatly at the back of the cold metal interior.

Amber picked them up, stowed them in her bag and walked quickly and calmly out of the building.

'Real nice to see you again, Amber,' Alice the receptionist called out.

'And you, Alice,' Amber told her. 'See you soon, maybe.'

She walked out into the sunshine, flipping her sunglasses back down over her tired eyes. Yes, she was quitting the movies, but that didn't mean Amber Stone wasn't still a great actress . . .

Chapter Fifty-Eight

She called Chelsea to let her know she was on her way over, hugging the tapes to her body.

Amber hadn't really thought about where she was going to stay, for the brief time she was in LA. She couldn't go back to her house; it felt too weird, she hadn't warned Rosita. And she wasn't ready; it'd be like saying she was back in LA for good, rather than just for a couple of days . . .

Perhaps she'd stay the night at Chelsea's? Shaking slightly with the tension of what she'd just done, Amber drove the hire car she'd picked up at LAX to Chelsea's place, and as she pulled in she saw her sister was waiting in the driveway. It was early evening. She'd flown in from New York that morning, the time difference in her favour, but it had still been a long day. A long, long day.

She blinked as she got out of the car, trying not to yawn, stress and fatigue catching up with her.

'Hi,' she said, walking towards Chelsea.

Chelsea was in tracksuit bottoms. She'd put on a bit of weight. She was holding a packet of potato chips, munching on them. She stared at Amber, at the huge grey Mulberry clutched in her hand.

'So . . . ?' she said.

'I got them,' Amber told her.

Chelsea punched the air. '*Yesss*,' she said, looking up to heaven. 'Thank fuck.'

'We don't know what's on them, though, do we?' Amber pointed out. 'Sally never watched them. Could be grey static. You know what CCTV's like.'

Chelsea wasn't listening. 'Come in, Ambs, come in babe,' she said, padding back into the house towards the den. 'I'll call Sally, get her over. We'll wait till then to watch them.' She shook her head, blinking. 'I can't believe you did it. Well done,' she said awkwardly. 'Thanks . . . Thanks a lot.'

Grateful, Amber patted her shoulder. And then the two sisters went inside.

'I'm nervous,' Amber admitted after Sally arrived thirty minutes later, as the three women sat down on the large sofa together, and Sally pushed in the videotape.

'I know, honey,' Sally said pragmatically. 'I am too. But we have to watch it. It's gonna be for the best.'

Amber squeezed Chelsea's hand, and Chelsea squeezed it back, but her eyes were fixed to the screen as Sally pressed Play.

And they sat back to watch.

The first videotape was of the camera outside, by Leo's vast pool. They watched, each rigid with tension, as the screen flickered into life.

Some feet walked past, the body out of shot. A few shadows, on the edge of the picture.

'There's no sound,' Chelsea said, disappointed.

'I know.' Sally pressed Fast Forward. 'There isn't. Sorry.'

'We don't need sound,' Amber said. 'If there's anything on it . . .' she trailed off.

Sally kept her finger on the Fast Forward button and they watched in silence, focused on the flickering grey screen.

'Stop!' Amber screamed at one point, and Sally rewound and they watched . . . watched Leo walking across the screen, drink in hand, white linen shirt, baggy linen pants, open shoes. The time was 9.37 p.m.

'That's his "relaxing at home" outfit. The bastard,' Chelsea said. The other two nodded. All three knew his wardrobe inside out. 'That doesn't prove anything, sadly,' Sally said. 'Let's keep going.' And she pressed the button again.

By the end of the second tape, the camera in Leo's bedroom, they were growing panicked, depressed, but no one wanted to admit it. They'd stopped the fast-forwarding countless times when some object flitted across the screen, hoping against hope this time would be the one when the action would begin . . . and it was always nothing. If it wasn't there, where would it be?

'Are you sure there were only three tapes?' Chelsea murmured to Amber.

'There were only three,' Sally said loudly. 'I only took three.'

'But were they the right ones?' Chelsea demanded.

'We don't know where it happened, do we?' Sally snapped. 'It could have been anywhere in the house . . .'

'There were five cameras, you said,' Chelsea said.

'OK, OK, I know that. But one overlooks the cars, and the other's in the kitchen, and unless you think he did it there . . .'

'He might have,' Amber said soberly. 'It's Leo.'

'Let's try the third tape,' said Sally.

'Where was that, then?'

'His study,' Sally said.

It wasn't looking good.

She put the tape in and pressed Rewind, and the machine started whirring. Chelsea picked up her glass and downed the rest of her wine; Amber chewed her nail. As Chelsea was putting her glass back down, her hand slipped on the remote. Sally said, 'Don't, Chelsea – it's still –' She trailed off. 'Oh. Oh no.'

She had pressed Play, halfway through the tape.

The black and white screen had flickered into life, the scene Leo's office at home, the big carved wooden desk he said was like the one in the Oval Office. Leo, bent over something . . . someone.

They could see his back, curved. See the perspiration grey on

351

the back of his shirt. He was pumping, rocking against the desk, and Amber had to squint to work out what was going on . . .

'Oh shit,' she said, and her hand flew to her mouth. Sally dropped the remote.

Almost like a sack, they could see Maria lying on the desk, so thin and tiny, so *young*, she was almost obscured by Leo. Her eyes were closed, her mouth was open, crying out, she was hitting him, scratching, but Leo had his hand on her breastbone and was pushing her down on the desk.

Her thin legs dangled like sticks on either side of his black trousers.

He was holding her down as she struggled, pressing so hard on her chest, and suddenly, she went limp. Stopped struggling. And Leo didn't stop, carried on pumping into her.

The three girls were silent.

'Let me rewind a bit,' Sally said. 'Just to see how much we've got.'

She rewound, biting her lip, to a point about ten minutes previously, and they fast-forwarded till they found Leo, pushing Maria into the office. She was wobbly on her legs, almost as if she was drunk.

'Drugged out of her mind,' Chelsea said, hoarsely. 'Fuck.'

They saw Leo push her onto the desk so she was sitting. He stroked her cheekbone, and then pushed her back. She was laughing, and then her expression changed.

Sally pressed Stop. 'I don't want to watch any more,' she said, putting the remote down quietly on the desk. 'We've got enough.' She ran a hand through her hair.

'Just let me see something.' Chelsea pressed play, watching it again. She laughed. 'This is going to fucking destroy him. I've done it!' She clenched her fist. 'I mean, *we've* done it, girls. We're going to bring him down.'

She poured herself some more wine and laughed again, her eyes more alive than Amber had seen them for a long time.

Amber watched her, and she didn't know what to say. As Sally stopped the tape again, got up and pulled it out, Amber carried on staring at her sister.

She realised the Chelsea she once knew had gone.

Because this Chelsea was a monster – someone who could watch a video of a girl being raped, and think only about how she could use it to get her revenge.

She cleared her throat; she wanted to cry, curl up into a ball and sob for Maria and Tina at what she'd seen. She hadn't really believed what Chelsea and Sally had told her till then. How could she not have known? How could she have been so naive, so stupid?

'I'll take this to the cops tomorrow,' Sally was saying. She didn't look happy, or triumphant. She looked grim, like someone who's finished a marathon, completed a tour of duty. Done what they had to. She suddenly looked much older. 'I know who to go to. It'll take a while to verify everything, I think.'

'Do it before the Oscars,' Chelsea said, bouncing up and down on the sofa. 'He's gonna be presenting an award, I heard. The sick fuck. Do it before then. You've got to.'

'Yeah, you're right.' Sally put the tape into a jiffy bag. 'Where can we hide this? It's the most valuable thing you've ever had, Chelsea. I'm staying here tonight to make sure.'

'Sure,' said Chelsea. 'Sure, sure. I might just get some more wine. Amber – you want some?'

She turned around.

'Amber?' She looked at Sally. 'Where'd she go?'

Sally looked up, as if she expected to see Amber hovering in front of her. 'Don't know. She was just here . . . Where shall we hide the tape, Chelsea?'

They were so engrossed, they didn't even hear the car pull out of the drive.

Chapter Fifty-Nine

Amber got on the Santa Monica freeway and drove to the airport as fast as she could. She was swallowing hard, staring into the night at the slow, five-lane snake of traffic lined with palm trees. She thought she was going to be sick. She would never get the images she'd seen that night out of her head, ever. Perhaps almost as disturbing, though, was the way Chelsea had reacted to them. She simply didn't care about what she was watching. It was on the screen for her, and Amber realised, perhaps for the first time, that that was why Chelsea was such a great actress.

Better than she would ever be.

Chelsea had managed to cut herself off from everything else, to see only what she needed to see. Amber carried on driving. There was a flight at ten; she might still make it. She could be back in New York in eight hours; she could still make that rehearsal with Matt the next day. He would never need to know what had happened.

She could tell him; she knew he'd understand.

But she didn't want to. He was pure for her, he wasn't marked with the dirtiness of what had gone on in LA.

He was part of the future.

It seemed fate was on her side that night. At the airport she joined the queue for stand-by tickets, drumming her fingers impatiently against her bag, her sunglasses still on her face. She was bone-tired now, and she felt hollow inside, the strip lighting and aircon making her feel as if she were in a film, a dream – no, a nightmare . . .

When she got to the front of the queue, the woman behind the desk took a look at the name on her platinum Amex and said, 'Yes, Ms Stone, we definitely have a space for you on this flight . . . if you'd called before, we would have had someone come pick you up,' she added, obviously horrified that a *celebrity* had had to stand in line with *normal* people . . . how terrible!

Amber didn't mind. She liked being normal again. She was shedding her fame, a layer a day, and it felt great. But there was still no way she'd ever fly coach, that was for sure.

She was ushered through to the First Class Lounge, and took a glass of champagne from a hovering waiter. It was a calm, beautiful space, dimly lit and scented with flickering, gentle candlelight . . . Amber sank gratefully onto a soft leather banquette, and took a sip of her drink. 'Ahh,' she said, lying back and closing her eyes. It had been a long day.

A soft, Scottish voice behind her said, 'Jesus. Amber?'

She turned to the table next to her, and her jaw dropped open.

'You don't recognise me, do you?' said the man, flipping his laptop shut.

'Of course I do,' said Amber, sitting down next to him. She threw her arms around him. 'Marco, how the fuck are you? Oh my *God*!'

'I'm well, little Miss Amber, I'm well,' said Marco gruffly. 'It's been a long time, hasn't it?' He pulled himself away.

'It has.' Amber said, and she stared at him. He was the same old Marco: shaved head, high cheekbones, beautiful dark eyes; a little older-looking, perhaps, but the years had been kind to him. He was wearing a grey cashmere hoodie, and a Louis Vuitton overnight bag was slung over his shoulders. He was drumming his long, sensitive fingers in a perfectly timed rhythm on his MacBook, and she remembered with a sharp ache the fun they used to have, how he'd taught her about rhythm, movement, so much more about music. What a friend he'd been to her, how much she could have used a friend like him over the years . . . 'I missed you,' she said simply.

Marco curled his lip. 'Darling, you were the one who—'

'I know,' she said. She pushed her golden-red hair out of her face and looked directly at him. 'Listen, I know that wasn't you, leaking that story about me all those years ago.'

'I know it wasn't too,' Marco said, tersely. 'I told you that. Many times. And you still went ahead and dumped me. Cut me out altogether.'

She couldn't say anything, so she just put her hand on his. 'Yes. Look. I was young. I was naive and stupid and willing to listen to people I shouldn't have. Wow . . .' she brushed tears from her eyes. 'Wow, Marco, it's so good to see you . . . Where are you going?'

'Back to New York,' he said, slightly mollified. 'I've got a dance studio there, I'm a choreographer for musicals.'

'I know, I know,' she said, smiling. 'You're doing so well.' After several years not knowing what had happened to him, she'd managed at last to catch up with his career in the press, bringing a small pain to her heart at the thought of how much she missed him. 'Listen, Marco—'

'Madam, can I offer you a menu?' A waiter appeared at her arm. 'We have a range of snacks and meals . . .'

'I'd like another glass of champagne for my friend, please,' she said. 'And some Eggs Benedict with extra bacon.'

Marco's eyes widened. 'She eats food? Last time I saw you it was egg white omelettes and raw carrot, and that was it.'

'Yeah, well . . . Things change,' she said, smiling. 'And I'm hungry. We've got a lot of catching up to do . . .' and she linked her arm through his.

'We have, Amber,' Marco said, and he squeezed her arm. 'You know, I missed you too. No one quite like you, darling. I've never known someone less suited to stardom than you. Perhaps that's why I was so furious with you when you thought I'd leaked that story.'

She shook her head. 'I'm so sorry,' she repeated. 'Marco, you don't know—'

He nodded. 'Let's forget it,' he said. 'For now,' he added ominously. 'So, how are you? What are you up to?'

So nice to tell this to someone who wanted to hear, not someone who wanted to know if you were hot or not . . . The waiter brought another glass of champagne, and she clinked her glass against his, smiling into his eyes.

'Well, I live in New York now,' she said. She was saying it almost to herself. 'I'm a singer again.'

Marco laughed. 'No way! Wow, I didn't realise. So what were you doing back in LA?'

There was a pause.

'It's a long story,' Amber said.

Chapter Sixty

'Hi, and welcome to E! Entertainment News, *with you this evening and all night as we follow the stars arriving for the 81st Academy Awards here at the Kodak Theater in the heart of Hollywood. I'm . . .'*

Burritos, delivered from her favourite place in West Hollywood.

A box of cupcakes, ordered from Sprinkles on Santa Monica Boulevard.

And a bottle of Cristal champagne. With only one glass.

That was all she needed, for this evening. She wasn't going to the Oscars, she wasn't invited. Instead, Chelsea Stone had a ring-side seat, in front of the TV.

'And the first stars are arriving . . . I see the winner of the Golden Globe for that wonderful film Dressed to Kill, *October Donahue, we're just gonna get over there and interview her . . . What a great dress! Are you excited to be here tonight? It's the biggest night in the Hollywood calendar, isn't it?'*

Chelsea had got dressed up, had someone come in to blow-dry her hair. Since they'd found the tapes, she'd gone on a strict diet again, and the weight was dropping off her. This was a night off. She was wearing a red draped Vivienne Westwood gown that pulled her in in all the right places, making her still voluptuous figure as devastating as possible. She'd applied her make-up carefully.

She didn't know why, quite. She just knew she wanted to look good when the moment came, the moment of her triumph. When they took him away, she didn't want to be picking Cheetos out of her teeth.

'Well, ladies and gentlemen, welcome back from the break . . . I can tell you it is chaos here on the red carpet, and we're trying to get the stars to come by and talk to us . . . I've never seen so many people here, it's a fabulous night, so many wonderful films out this year. Just take a look at the cameras down the carpet – I'm told there are representatives from thirty-eight different countries . . . Next up, we're gonna be talking to—'

And so, at six-thirty on a balmy February evening, Chelsea Stone sat down alone on the sofa in her house and prepared to watch.

'Great, great, thank you! Wow, I've got a real British gent for everyone at home, now. This is Sir Leo Russell, coming up the red carpet now, the dapper producer of all those wonderful Amber Stone pictures, and of course The Time of My Life. *You'll remember he's been having a little local difficulty with those Stone sisters lately, but we won't mention that! Hello, Sir, how are you doing?'*

There he was, on the small screen. He looked small. She found it comforting, knowing he was there, not some shadowy presence who could appear at any time. Tonight's the night, Leo . . . She looked at the screen again, to see him pushing a stick insect in a dress towards the camera, an incredibly young-looking starlet decked out in the finest haute couture and looking curiously blank. 'My God,' said Chelsea. 'She looks about fifteen.'

'This is JoAnne Cohen, Jim. She's a new friend of mine.'
'Typical Leo Russell . . . It's delightful to meet you, miss! You're a

lucky girl, for sure, we all know how popular Sir Leo is with the ladies . . . How long have you two known each other? You make a beautiful couple.'

'We're working on a film together, Jim. It's a great script, really a lot of fun, a great romantic comedy called Marie's Marriage. *JoAnne's a remarkably talented young actress, and she's going to be America's new sweetheart. I promise you'll remember the moment you first laid eyes on JoAnne Cohen, Jim.'*

Chelsea stared at him with loathing; the smug way he smoothed his hands over his chin, staring at JoAnne like she was a prize cow at a fair, the respectful, serious way the fatuous interviewer was listening to him, like he was the Dalai Lama or the President, for fuck's sake. Oh, she hated him . . .

'Well, thank you very much indeed for sharing your time with us, Sir Leo – and JoAnne, too! Good luck with everything . . .' They're moving off now, and I see someone approaching Sir Leo Russell, wanting to do a deal of some kind I expect . . . Excuse me, sir! Don't push! I said – no, out of my way! Oh . . .

Wow, ladies and gentlemen, something seems to be happening here . . . We're not sure what's going on . . . The LAPD has appeared and they're – wow, yeah. They're talking to Leo Russell. I wonder what they want?

Chelsea leaned forward and reached for the bottle, chilling in its silver ice bucket. She popped the cork – gently, gently . . . and it slid out, with barely a puff.

'Well, this is most extraordinary, let me try and explain what's happening for the viewers at home, if you can't see it on your screens. It's a real mess over there. It looks like the LAPD are arresting Leo Russell, they're saying something to him and he's looking kinda angry about it, he's gesticulating to the police who are putting him in handcuffs . . . I don't know how much you can see on your screens – he's looking extremely shocked and alarmed by this, ladies and gentlemen . . .

360

They've escorted him to a car . . . Ladies and gentlemen, these are incredible scenes here on the red carpet, as the police mix with A-listers, there are stars arriving all the time . . . His date, er . . . JoAnne, I think? She's standing there on her own . . . Look, Sir Leo Russell is being driven away, I can hear helicopters, sirens wailing in the distance and – oh my goodness, I see there are at least five, ten police cars backed up outside, indicating this is a major operation . . . I hope you saw that. We'll have to find out what that's all about and get right back to you . . .'

She poured herself a glass of champagne. The frothing liquid bubbled into the flute like molten gold.

'Cheers,' Chelsea said, and she drank, smiling.

Chapter Sixty-One

The whole thing was so ridiculous.

Just stupid, really. Leo smiled, wide-eyed, at the cop who was in the room with him.

'You know you guys are going to get your asses sued, right?' he said. 'You'll be paying for this for years. My lawyer is the best in town. You're going to regret this, fellas, I cannot tell you how much.'

He was bluffing, just a bit. The truth was, Leo was slightly embarrassed to be carted off by the cops, live on TV, even though his bad-boy image wasn't harmed by it. Deep down he was relatively unconcerned. He was pretty sure they were busting him for the drugs. He was a high-profile scapegoat.

OK, his lawyer would get him off, or at worst he'd have to do community service, maybe a stint in rehab – he'd screwed up, for sure, he'd just have to be more careful. So stupid! He wondered to himself, as he turned the platinum Rolex round and round in his hands, watching the seconds pass, whether it was time perhaps to ease off a little on the coke. Was it? Not if Kevin could get him off, for sure . . .

The door opened again, and Kevin came in, followed by a detective. Slick, thin guy, trying to be like someone off a cop show, what a loser . . . Leo looked up, smiling, ready to be contrite, ready to sort this whole thing out.

He saw Kevin's face, though, and paused. He was white. He wouldn't meet Leo's eyes.

'Sir Leo.' The detective couldn't remember his name, nodded at him and sat down in front of him. He pulled out a sheaf of grainy stills, enlarged from video footage. 'We want to talk to you about these. Please look at these images.'

Leo looked down angrily at the stills. This was fucking ridiculous, this whole thing . . . and then his eyes focused on what was in front of him. Stared, in mounting horror, as he took in the images.

Stills of Sir Leo Russell raping an underage girl. Her hands pushing him away in one shot, covering her eyes in another. Stills of him handing her drugs. Stills of her overdosing.

'Where the fuck did you get these?'

His mind was racing, he couldn't quite remember, it looked like something out of a nightmare, and then he knew. Maria. That stupid girl. The night that had gone badly, badly wrong.

'I want to know what you have to say about these pictures,' the detective said, ignoring him.

'I urge you not to comment at this stage,' Kevin said, breathing heavily. 'Do you understand?'

'*Where the fuck did you get them?*' said Leo. He crushed one of the A4 printouts in his hand and stood up.

'Sit down, sir,' Detective Shelley said. Leo raised an eyebrow.

'OK, OK,' he said. He sat back heavily in his seat and untied his black tie. He was going to be here for a while, he guessed.

'You have nowhere to go, Sir Leo,' the detective told him. 'Now, you can make this easy on yourself, or you can make it very, very hard.'

There was an eerie silence in the dank interview room.

'Now,' he continued. 'Tell me. Is the girl in those photos your ex-housekeeper's daughter, then aged fifteen?'

'Yes,' said Leo.

'And sir . . . Is the man in these photos you?'

Leo Russell had got where he was because he had a knack for predicting what was going to happen, looking at all possible outcomes and selecting the best one himself.

But it hit him that evening, right then and there. He couldn't escape. The game was up. The game, in fact, was very much over . . . He wasn't a stupid man. He knew when he had to admit defeat. For the moment, anyway . . .

'Yes,' he said. 'That's me.'

'Sir Leo Russell,' Detective Shelley continued, 'I am arresting you on suspicion of rape, sexual assault and battery, sex with a minor, possession of Class-A narcotics and obstruction of justice. You have the right to remain silent. Anything you say can and will be used against you in a court of law . . .'

Leo wasn't listening. His mind had gone elsewhere, thoughts racing through his head. He knew who'd done this . . . he just had to let the card file in his brain flick through a few more combinations.

The video, the safe, the girl. Sally, Amber, Chelsea.

Damn, damn, damn. He knew who to blame, though. He knew Chelsea was the one behind it all. Oh, Sally might have the evidence, but she was still his, he knew it. Amber was weak and pathetic – singing career! He smiled, even as the cops looked at him in disbelief. No, it was Chelsea, that damn bitch. She had brought him down, and she would pay; it would take a while but he'd get revenge, no doubt about it . . .

Outside, in the LA night, the parties went on till dawn, limos and SUVs blocking the streets as the world's most famous stars were ferried from Morton's to the Governor's Ball, from *Vanity Fair* to Elton John's party. The palm trees were floodlit, helicopters whirred outside, photographers jammed the sidewalks. As he was handcuffed, shoved into a cell, handed a blanket and stripped of his belt and shoes, Leo didn't know it, but one of the only people sleeping soundly that night in town was Chelsea Stone, passed out on the sofa, still wearing her brand new dress and heels, a happy smile on her face . . .

Epilogue

Nine months later

'Mum? Mum, are you there?'

'Yes, of course I'm here.'

'You're not listening.'

'I am listening, love. It's just, Derek's making a right clatter in the background. *Derek!* Would you please be quiet out there! No, I don't care! I'm on the phone to Amber, love!'

Amber smiled, and rolled her eyes at Matt, who was flicking through a magazine on the couch, his feet up on the worn leather arm. She was sitting in a window seat of their new townhouse. Sun glinted off the skyscrapers of lower Manhattan. In the distance, walkers straggled along the newly opened Highline, the grasses and rushes waving gently in the summer breeze. It was late June, and New York was still beautiful, not the smoggy, fuggy mess it would become in July and August. 'How's the flat?'

'Well,' Margaret sighed. 'It's not LA, I'll tell you that much, love. Dirty, cramped, it's dead annoying, drunk people every moment of the day and night . . .'

'Bet you love it, Mum.'

'I bloody do not,' Margaret said hastily. 'Now,' she said, changing the subject. 'We wondered when you're coming over here. On tour. Surely you must be?'

'We're just finalising it at the moment,' Amber said. 'We want to find the right places. Might be doing a gig at the Roundhouse, Mum, how about that? Your old stomping ground, eh?'

'Tell her!' Matt hissed in the background. Amber picked up one of her CDs, stacked on the desk next to the seat, and threw it at him. It narrowly missed his head.

'Not fair!' he said, getting up. 'I can't throw stuff at you, now.'

'. . . Important to get the right venues,' Margaret was saying. 'Is the Roundhouse big enough? You're a star, love. You're not some crummy band that can only get a few dozen along to a gig. You need the O2! Or Wembley. Are your management talking to Wembley? Are they—'

'*Mum!*' Amber interrupted, smiling. 'You're not listening! We want to keep it small. I haven't done a live gig in years. I don't want to stretch myself, and we want to keep them intimate . . .'

'But the album's been Number One for weeks, you silly girl!'

Amber raised her eyebrows and let her mother talk on. She covered the mouthpiece. 'She's mad,' she said to Matt.

'She is,' Matt said. 'So just tell her and get it over with.'

'Mum,' Amber broke in again. 'I wasn't calling about that. I was calling to tell you something.'

'What?' Margaret sighed, obviously preparing herself for the worst. 'Oh dear, what?'

'It's good news, I hope,' she said. 'It's good news. I'm having a baby!'

'What?'

'I'm pregnant, Mum!' she shouted, like it was a faulty line. 'You're going to be a grandmother!'

'Oh –' Margaret made a strange sound in her throat. 'Oh, Amber dear. You're—'

'Yes. And if it's a boy, Mum, we're going to call him George. After Dad.'

'I know who George was,' Margaret said. 'I may be old, but I'm not stupid.' She was silent for a moment. 'Well, love,' she said eventually, 'you're not married, but I suppose in this day and age—'

You're in no position to lecture me, Mum! Amber wanted to say, but she knew there was no point, and instead she just smiled down the phone and said, 'I know, Mum. I know. Now, tell Uncle Derek, will you?'

Margaret Stone put the phone down and stood still, smiling at nothing.

'What was that about?' Derek came through from the tiny front yard where he'd been fixing his motorbike. Six months before, they'd moved in together. Nothing permanent, Margaret had said. But the four-storey, tiny Georgian house in a sidestreet off Wardour Street, in the heart of Soho, was very convenient. Derek could walk to his offices and Margaret could come with him, as one of his newest employees.

Margaret had always thought she didn't like old houses, but there was something reassuring about this place. Darling Nigel, her boss at The Black Horse all those years ago, had always said he could see her in a cottage with roses round the door and she'd laughed at him, young and knowing better, or so she thought.

Perhaps he was right, though. Dickens had probably walked down this street any number of times. She had too, when she was a young thing, just arrived in Soho, all those years back . . . The house had been here then, and it'd be here long after she and Derek were gone, and she liked that. The floorboards were uneven, and the chimney was blocked, and she was sure mice and even worse could get in through the back door, though she was damned if she'd let them.

She cleared her throat. 'Amber. Amber's pregnant . . .' She trailed off. 'She's having a baby!' Her eyes filled with tears.

'Maggie, that's wonderful news.' Derek came nearer, his blue eyes sparkling. 'You're going to be a grandma. The most glamorous grandma there ever was, Maggie May.' He walked over and put his arm around her.

'Get your filthy hands off me, Derek Stone,' she scolded, pushing him away. 'You're all covered in oil, I won't have it!'

But there was a smile on her face as she said it, and he leaned over and kissed her anyway. 'Did she say if she'd told Chelsea?' he asked, after a minute.

'No,' Margaret said, stroking his cheek. 'She hasn't spoken to her for months now, love.' She hated how it hurt him. 'She'll be in touch, Derek. She has to be. She owes you a small fortune, apart from anything.'

'Yeah,' he said. He hugged her again. 'I just want to make her happy.'

'I don't know if you can,' Margaret said, carefully. She watched him, and he looked at her. She couldn't be doing with all that, now. She was going to be a grandma! 'Come on,' she said. 'Let's have a glass of champagne, I want to celebrate. Wash your hands, Derek, don't come near me till you have.'

The trial had taken no time – one day, and two weeks to wait for sentencing. Leo had pleaded guilty – as he said to Bryan French, co-producer on *The Time of My Life* and one of the few who hadn't dropped him, when he visited him before he was sentenced – 'I did it, I just need to get it over with, come back stronger. This way, I spend less time in jail.'

'Yeah,' Bryan had said, nodding uneasily. He leaned forward, his voice distant over the microphone, face blurred behind the Plexiglas. 'Leo, you need to accept what you did, though.'

'Yeah, yeah.' Leo waved his hand almost airily, as Bryan stared at him. 'I did a really terrible thing. They've taken away my knighthood, Bryan. I'm just plain Leo now. I know how serious this is. And now I'm paying the price.'

It was almost as if he couldn't bear to acknowledge how bad it was. That the game was over, and he had lost.

Even as the armoured van pulled up outside the LA County Jail, way out towards Culver City, and as they were discharged, Leo wasn't really paying attention. He knew this would be a long stretch, he knew he'd done wrong, and he just wanted to keep his head down and get it over with. They gave him a uniform – blue, baggy, horrible. They examined him for lice, other indignities like that. He was stripped and hosed down by a bored guard chewing gum – in any other circumstances, Leo would have been a little turned on by this; with a little imagination it could have been kind of hot . . .

He was put in a holding cell, before they took him to the governor.

'Can I get something to read?' he called. Had to keep his mind off things, that was the way it worked. The guard who had taken him there looked at him, smiling.

'Think they left something in there for you already, scum.' He jerked his head over to the bench, where a magazine sat, a brightly coloured gossip magazine, its colours tawdry in the pale fawn room.

'This?' Leo picked it up, and the guard gave him a sly look and started laughing.

On the front was a picture of Chelsea, stunning in a white bikini and cavorting with a handsome young basketball player on board a huge yacht.

SHE'S GOT IT ALL ran the headline.

He flicked through the pages, almost tearing them in his impatience to read what they said.

Last week Chelsea Stone made a swift land-grab, buying Lion House Productions from creditors at a knock-down price and immediately renaming it Roxy Enterprises. After the collapse of disgraced movie mogul Leo Russell's business, the actress used insider knowledge from her friend Sally Miller, who had worked for the tycoon for twenty years, to help seal the deal. Her uncle, London-based entrepreneur Derek Stone, provided the capital. 'I'm delighted to have acquired this company, and I intend to build it up from its parlous state into one of the best independents in LA,' Chelsea Stone told *Stars!* last week. 'The last few months have been extremely hard for all of us and, now that the trial is over, it's time for me to move on.'

Leo could hear the guard laughing, watching him through the metal grille.

Slowly, carefully, he tore the magazine into tiny little pieces. Bit by bit, till it lay scattered all over the floor. He slumped to the ground, gazing at the blank wall. Bitch. *Bitch.*

Chelsea couldn't sleep.

It was the middle of the night. She was alone. She woke up as she did more and more often now, sweating. The nightmares were back. George's death . . . Maya's death . . . Maria's rape . . . all the bad things, melded and mixed, swirling round in her head so that she couldn't make out what was real and what wasn't.

It happened nearly every night now, and she didn't know what to do about it.

She couldn't tell anyone – there was no one who'd understand what she'd been through, what she'd done . . . No one to confide in. She'd accepted long ago it was just her. Would it be nice, to have someone to talk to? No. Better to be alone.

She got out of bed and pulled on her jeans, a baggy sweatshirt and a thick cashmere wrap. She picked up her car keys, pulling her long, thick dark hair out of the neck of her top, and eased on her knee-high Christian Louboutin boots. Then she strode out to the car, a brand new Aston Martin, sleek and silver. She got in and drove towards West Hollywood with the top down, wind in her hair. No one was around; it was three in the morning.

Yeah, no one was around. She got out of the car and walked towards the sleek black building. Home of her new offices. The security guard nodded as she flashed her pass; it said simply *Roxy Enterprises, Inc.* Her company. Her building. Her business.

She walked into her office, unfurnished except for a big shiny black desk and a huge black leather chair, and she sat down in the chair, swivelling round and round.

She stared out of the window. She thought about her plans.

Forget about the bad dreams, she told herself. She was going to be massive. Bigger than Oprah. Everything was under control, everything . . .

The dreams had been very vivid that night, and a single image, Maya, rigid and blue, dead on the floor, had stuck in her mind.

And Chelsea had remembered that she had one last thing to deal with – that Oksana girl. It had all gone quiet, and she wondered why. She knew she was probably going to have to get her sorted out. Rake up some of her old Soho contacts, get her silenced for ever. She didn't want her causing trouble, running to Amber like she'd promised to.

She had to be ruthless to stay on top. She couldn't trust anyone, had to operate on her own. Not even her mother, Derek, not even her sister. None of them.

But that was for tomorrow. Tonight – she pushed herself gently round on the chair again, smiling. Tonight she should just enjoy it all.

Chelsea sat alone in the darkened office. 'I'm happy,' she whispered. 'Yeah, I'm happy.' A sudden chill ran over her. She shivered, pulling her cashmere wrap round her shoulders, staring into space.

Yes, she nodded to herself. Success is the sweetest revenge.